REUNITED

Aramanda let out a soft sigh. "I recognize your face, your voice. I feel the same trust and love, and yet you are not the same. You cannot even remember my name. I am an intruder in a world that belongs only to you."

"I'm sorry," he said. "You . . . remember. I don't. To me, you're like a dream—too beautiful, too fragile to be real."

"Would you have me believe you feel nothing for me?" Deliberately, Aramanda breached the distance between them and stroked her fingers down his cheek.

"I don't know what I feel." He took her hand in his. "It's impossible."

"Is it truly impossible? Or do you only wish it to be?"

He said nothing for an eternity. At last, very slowly, as if he moved in a dream, he stretched out a hand and touched her face. The feathery kiss of his fingertips on her skin left her trembling. "Aramanda . . ." he murmured, saying her name as if it were a vow. . . .

A TIMELESS MOMENT

ANNETTE DANIELS

ZEBRA BOOKS
KENSINGTON PUBLISHING CORP.

To Ken, my love and my life are yours alone
and
To Jeff, thank you for your loving
support now and always

ZEBRA BOOKS are published by

Kensington Publishing Corp.
850 Third Avenue
New York, NY 10022

First Printing: June, 1996
10 9 8 7 6 5 4 3 2 1

Printed in the United States of America

There is a world
that exists outside the confines of the mind
and what it can accept and believe,
a world that exists only in the heart,
where all things are believed,
all things are possible,
and a love of ages always survives.

Prologue

Prestonville, Pennsylvania, 1874

"Your lover, my enemy, Aramanda." Gervase Montclair glared down at his niece, rigid with fury, the loathing clearly carved into the hardness of his face nearly causing her to flinch.

"I only ask that you listen—" Aramanda began, not giving way, but knowing now her pleas were futile. She had risked his rage . . . and lost more than she had ever dared imagine.

"Listen!"

Slamming a heavy fist into the desktop separating them, Gervase shoved back his chair and strode to stand inches from her. His height dominated her, his steel-gray eyes boring into the soft amber of hers. Gervase had no mercy in him, Aramanda knew. He could choose to break her spirit as easily as he could snap her delicate slenderness with his strength.

"You come to me with your tales of suffering among the cutthroats and thieves you have chosen to ally yourself with and expect me to sacrifice an empire for their sake. That will never happen. You are going to deliver Roarke Macnair to me or, by God, I will see you learn a new definition of suffering!"

"You cannot believe I would betray him! I have told you my feelings for him. They will not change and I will not simply *deliver* him to you. *That* is something that will never happen!" Aramanda stopped, horrified to feel the prick of tears burn her eyes.

She spun away, her straight spill of auburn hair masking the wetness that slid down her face, the silent evidence of her heart's weeping which she refused to let her uncle witness. "I should never have trusted you with the truth."

"The truth! The truth is you are a traitor to your own family. You have shamed us all. You have no right to call yourself a Montclair."

Without warning, Gervase's fingers dug into her shoulder, jerking her around to face him. "When he took you captive to force his demands on us, I shared your mother's worry. She wanted to surrender everything for you. I nearly agreed for her sake—and all the while, you were bedding the low-bred miner who is determined to destroy us! Did you truly imagine we would forgive that?"

"I had hoped you would understand. He is not my lover; he has become my life. I love him!"

The fury exploded on his face an instant before the back-handed blow caught Aramanda across the cheek. She stumbled, falling to her knees. Pain shot through her, and with it, her own anger flowered. "I had thought you a man of honor," she said slowly, looking up at him with the thought of murder in her heart. "Mother chose to believe so, and I accepted it because of her. I see now how deluded I was."

"Do not speak to me of honor," Gervase spat. "We are far beyond that. You will make your choice now. Either you tell me his plan or the rabble you profess to care so much for will suffer, to say nothing of your own family." He deliberately paused, a travesty of a smile curving his lips. "And your friend Liam Mac-nair will leave his prison cell by the end of a rope."

"Liam!" Aramanda struggled to her feet, anger pushed aside by fear. "What have you done?"

"What is necessary. One way or another I will break Roarke Macnair. He is vulnerable through his brother . . . and you."

"But Liam is innocent! He had nothing to do with the riots, the explosions at the mines! It was Roarke—" Her hand flew to her mouth the moment his name left her lips.

"Yes, it was Roarke, wasn't it? I have suspected for many weeks he led the Molly Maguires. But—" Gervase shrugged.

"One wretched Irish coal miner is very like another. If I cannot have the pleasure of seeing Roarke Macnair hang by the neck for his rebellion, then his brother will make just as good an example. Perhaps an even better one, since the wife and four children he will leave behind are quite likely to find themselves living on the street. Not a pleasant thought, considering they have no other family and winter is weeks away. The youngest son is your brother Oliver's age, I believe. And the daughter merely an infant—"

"Stop it! I do not need to be reminded of everything that is at stake. I know much better than you ever can."

Aramanda squeezed her eyes tightly shut, seeing too clearly a picture of Liam, beaten and alone in a dark prison cell, waiting to die for his brother's cause. Liam, the friend who trusted her, who believed she would fight for him and his family.

And side by side with the vision, she thought of Roarke, the man she loved, readying his rebels for an assault on the largest of the Montclair mines.

Only hours ago, she had dared to hope their love could transcend the bitter fight between her family and him, that they could find peace. Her dreams of love, of a family undivided by the demands of profit and cause, seemed possible with Roarke at her side. He had held her in his arms, vowing that love, trusting her with his secrets.

A trust and love she had betrayed by leaving him.

Soul of my soul, heart of my heart. You are all and everything to me, Aramanda. There is nothing else.

"Roarke . . ." She whispered his name, anguish a ceaseless ache, almost unbearable in its force.

"Do not imagine you can protect him." Gervase's thick voice dragged her back to the library at the Montclair estate. "And I cannot fathom why you should choose to. Surely you feel some loyalty to your family, to your mother if no one else."

"How can I betray him?" Aramanda cried. "How can you ask me to betray the other half of my soul? I cannot do it."

"Can you let Liam Macnair, an innocent man, die?"

"I . . ." She choked on her answer, feeling as if she were being ripped apart, slowly, without mercy.

"Tell me. You know his plan for attacking the mines. Where and when will it be?"

"Don't force me to choose."

"You should have known there would be a time when you would have to choose between him and your family. That time is now."

"No—I can't . . ."

"Then you will watch Liam Macnair die. I will make certain of that."

Aramanda felt a wash of sick fear and despair that left her mute.

"Tell me," Gervase demanded, ruthless in his insistence.

"Will you—" Swallowing hard, she tried to force the words out around the constriction in her throat. "Will you spare their lives—his life? Please . . ." She hated to hear herself plead, hated Gervase for bringing her to it. But she was willing to attempt anything to hear him promise, for Roarke's sake. "Please, for my sake. He released me. He is willing to compromise; I know it."

"I will make you no such promises. Someone will hang for these crimes, and you will choose who it will be. The decision is not mine."

"If I must beg you, I will."

"I'm afraid I must forgo that pleasure," Gervase said, taking her chin in his hand, his grip painful. "I will not let Roarke Macnair destroy an empire that took three generations to build. We are already near to ruin because of him and his ruffians. And you helped him to bring it about. It is your duty to make amends."

Aramanda wrenched away from him, stepping back but confronting him with her straight gaze of hatred and pain. "I made no mistake in choosing Roarke. I did nothing but love. That is not a sin."

"No, it is far worse. Enough of this! Make your choice. Tell me his plan, or Liam Macnair dies today."

"Today! You cannot—"

"I can and will. You have my word," he mocked, his smile taunting.

"I have nothing. You have made certain of that." *Forgive me, Roarke. There is no choice.* Aramanda looked at him, no longer hiding the tears. "The south mine, at dusk," she whispered, knowing she sealed Roarke's fate with her betrayal.

"If you are lying to me—"

"You have what you wanted," Aramanda said, scarcely able to stop from screaming the words at him. "There is nothing else I can give you."

She turned away again, her hands clenched at her sides, praying he would go. One hope remained with her—that once Gervase left, she could somehow escape this house and return to the mine in time to warn Roarke. She had thought of lying about Roarke's plan in order to protect him. But once her uncle had discovered the truth, nothing she or Roarke could do would spare Liam's life.

Her only chance lay in getting to the south mine before Gervase and his men.

"It will soon be over," Gervase said, moving at last toward the door. "I trust you will use the time alone to repent your mistakes." The door shut hard behind him and Aramanda heard the slight scratch of a key in the lock.

"Damn him," she muttered, running up to uselessly twist the knob. In frustration, Aramanda slapped the unyielding wood with both her palms. "And he will have told them all to leave me here, for my own welfare and protection, no doubt."

She gave a quick glance around the second-story room, her thoughts racing. Her gaze slid by the windows, slewed back, stopped.

Nicholas, even Oliver, had done it with unbecoming regularity. She'd repeatedly chided both her brothers for the stunt. Now, she felt like hugging them for showing her the only avenue of escape.

Rushing to the windows, yanking up the sash, Aramanda reached a hand out to the sturdy wooden arbor staked to the north side of the house. If Nicholas, taller and heavier than she, could accomplish it . . . Aramanda glanced at the lawn below, momentarily dizzied by what seemed a momentous height.

She snapped her eyes up. At the edge of the tree line, she could see the stables. Already Gervase had gathered his men.

Aramanda made her decision.

Knotting up her skirts, she sat down on the sill, edging a hand, then a foot to the rose arbor. When the slender strips of wood completely supported her slight weight, she started the interminable climb down, her eyes tightly closed. The moment her foot touched the ground, she clutched tight to the rough wood to keep from collapsing in relief.

The reprieve was brief. Taking a steadying breath, she dashed to the stables, commanded the startled stable boy to saddle her mare, mounted, and kicked the horse into a wild gallop before he found the wits to protest.

Daylight was fast fading in the distance, the last rays of spring sunlight disappearing behind the roofs of the Pennsylvania Dutch country farms. She flew through the timbered hills and laurel swamps of the northeastern Pennsylvania valley toward the Susqehanna River, the Blue Mountain stretching across the horizon at her back.

Anthracite coal beds ran for miles below the valley far beneath her horse's pounding hooves. Coal meant life—and death—to her, unyielding and hard as the lives it sustained, black as the midnight darkness men toiled in endlessly to turn it into profits for her uncle's empire. Her uncle lived for coal; today her lover could die for it.

The path to the mine wound down narrow ravines and across rushing streams, fingering around heaps of fallen rock. When she arrived breathless at the mine, she nearly rode over a gaunt, bedraggled figure as she fought to jerk the mare to a stop. "Scully!" she cried, recognizing the soot-smudged scholar's face. "Where is Roarke?"

"Are you mad, woman?" He grabbed her arm the moment she slid off the horse, shouting to be heard over the mayhem already started. Behind them, an explosion burst in a thunderous wave from the mouth of the coal mine, shuddering the earth. "What are you doin' here? It's too late for you to make any difference."

"I must find Roarke!"

"In this chaos? It won't do you or him any good now, lass."

Aramanda flinched as a second explosion, then another, roared out of the mine. Through the thickening acrid haze she saw the hand-to-hand fighting between Roarke's rebels and her uncle's forces surge and ebb with the violence spewing out of the mine.

"I must find him," she repeated, her eyes riveted to the scene. "I must."

Wrenching her arm from Scully's grip, she strode toward the heart of the conflagration of blood and flame.

"I saw him last at the mine entrance," Scully called after her. "It'll be too late by now—"

It cannot be too late. Please God, I cannot be too late. . . .

She found him lying less than a dozen feet from the mine entrance, half covered by wooden rubble, black rock, and soot. Looking down at him, at the dark, red stain spreading over his chest and shoulder, Aramanda could only stare as grief swept over her, sudden and merciless.

Dropping to her knees beside him, she stretched out trembling fingers and gently smoothed back a lock of dark hair that had fallen over his forehead, then touched the blue neckcloth twisted at his throat, the symbol of his precious rebellion.

As she did, a hand suddenly snared hers in a painful grip.

"Aramanda . . ."

"My God . . . Roarke. I thought you were—"

"Dead?" Roarke's eyes mocked her with a glint of familiar ironic humor, their twilight blue darkened to a midnight shadow. "Ah, love, wait a little longer and I'll oblige you. I won't flatter myself to think you sought me out for any other reason."

"I came to find you, to warn you—"

"—that you had betrayed me to your uncle? Did you intend to give me a sporting chance?"

"I intended to stop this from happening!"

"Then you never should have left me."

The pain and anger in his words sliced through her as sharply and swiftly as a double-edged sabre. "What choice did I have? There was no compromise for you. No other way than this—" She swept a hand at the chaos around them. "Never."

He shook his head—whether to deny or defend, she didn't know. "You could have chosen to trust me. To love me."

"I do love you! Oh, Roarke . . ." Aramanda laid her free hand against his cheek, her vision of him blurred by bitter tears. "We are the best half of each other, and I would defy eternity to make you believe it. We are on different sides of your cause, but I know now this feeling is the only destiny that can matter."

"My destiny now is in heaven or hell. It doesn't matter which. With you, I've lived in both." He closed his eyes for a moment, his hand loosening a little on hers. When he looked at her again, the clarity she remembered so well had clouded, dulled by pain and defeat. "Why?"

She didn't pretend not to understand. "Gervase gave me no choice. He would have seen Liam hang for your crimes." Her voice caught on a sob. "I could not let him die. Please, Roarke . . . forgive me; there was no other way. I tried to reach you in time, to tell you . . ."

"Promise me," he rasped.

"Anything."

"Promise me you will make certain Liam is set free. He never fought with me. I know, at least, you care enough to fight for his life."

"And yours."

"If you had stayed . . . it doesn't matter. You are here. That's enough." With a faint smile, he closed his eyes, leaning his face into her palm. "You always accuse me of attempting to change reality to suit me. Perhaps it's true, because I choose to believe you do love me. Because even now, I cannot stop loving you. If I could fight for any cause beyond this life, it would be you, my love."

His last words escaped on a sigh of breath. Aramanda felt a shudder course through his body, and then the hand on hers slowly slipped away.

She stayed by his side long after there was no reason to stay. He was dead. And she had lost everything.

Smoke curled around her, long fingers of gray and flat hands of black. Smoke . . . the sign of a soul leaving the body. His or her own?

Grief overwhelmed her once again, and she let it come, her body shaking with it. She slipped down and laid her head against his still heart, weeping for him, for herself, and for what could never be, beyond feeling anything but the engulfing black misery. An unending misery she had to bear, now and forever.

Finally, spent and trembling, she lifted away from him and, after a moment's hesitation, untied his neckcloth, crumpling it between her palms.

"Oh, Roarke, I would give my life to change all that has happened," she told him, pressing the cloth to her heart. "How could I have done this, let you die thinking I had betrayed you? There is nothing in this life or beyond for me. You were my life. If I had not sacrificed my soul, I would give it now to hear you say you forgive me, because I can never forgive myself."

Her tears started again as she slowly stood, unable to take her eyes from his face. She took a step backward. The motion felt clumsy and sluggish, as if her legs had forgotten how to move. She tried to turn, but a silvery haze seemed to close around her, making her light-headed and oddly numb.

In that moment, she felt suspended in a place between time, unable to go forward or back. Trying to cry out, she had the sensation of her body's collapsing into itself as she sank into a dizzying swirl of brilliant light and unending darkness, still clutching the scrap of blue cloth like a last salvation.

One

Sayer Macnair glanced out over the packed auditorium and spoke the closing words of a speech that would either begin or end his future.

He bent toward the microphone, delivering his summary in a rich, resonant voice, with a precisely balanced combination of persuasive force and emotion.

"It's up to you. Each one of you can make a difference if you're willing to take the risks, make the sacrifices. You can't change the past, but the tomorrow, if there's to be one on this planet, depends on what you do today."

Sayer paused, taking one last sweeping gaze over the nameless faces of his audience. He sensed them weighing his words against their impression of him.

They'd seen enough of him lately, he reflected with an inward grimace, flashed on their television screens and on the front page of the daily papers. The same picture: a tall man who looked more like an adventurer than a university professor, dark hair perpetually tousled, emanating strength and command, but his midnight-blue eyes expressing none of the passion he turned loose in his voice.

Sayer's eyes roved restlessly over the crowd and, for a moment, caught and held on one person, a young woman seated in the balcony closest to the stage.

She looked so pale, ethereal, an unearthly beauty come into

this realm for a breath of time. Sayer chided himself at the fanciful notion. Of course it was just that the lighting in the balcony was poor and the balcony itself a good fifty feet from where he stood.

He blinked, then stared up at her again, hoping to see her more clearly. He found her still seated, hovering on the edge of the seat, gazing back at him through a strange pale haze that surrounded her.

He'd heard of the New Age penchant for auras, but had never given it a second thought. Until now.

She seemed as insubstantial as a wraith. Yet through the eerie, otherworldly air that separated them, she looked at him with disconcertingly direct eyes. Eyes that seemed to reflect fire. Eyes that bored a hole straight through to his soul. Without a word, she drew him to her, held him, mesmerizing him with her silent captivation.

Sayer felt as if he had suddenly stepped outside himself. Part of him stayed on the stage, waiting for the response of the audience. The other side of him moved away, closer to her, and, for a heartbeat of time, saw her clearly. Straight auburn hair swept over one slender shoulder, delicate fine-boned features, a vision of elegance and grace; she was a beauty, an ideal too perfect to be real.

As suddenly as it happened, the odd sensation vanished. Still powerless to focus on any other face, he murmured a brief "thank you" into the microphone, clasped his hands behind his back, and stepped quietly away from the podium. She smiled, her lips full, inviting. A simple gesture, yet so poignant and unexpectedly intimate, Sayer felt an odd, unnerving twist inside.

Disturbed by the impact of his reaction to her, and doubting his own tired eyes, he briefly closed them. When his gaze slipped back to the balcony where the girl had been sitting, he found only an empty chair. She'd vanished.

Sayer stared at the red-velvet seat, the emptiness there swelling and spreading out across an invisible chasm of time and space to where he stood. He willed her to return as an irrational sense of loss welled inside him, leaving behind an inexplicable void.

He stood alone, silent, filled with longing and regret, confused and left with only the lingering notion that he'd lost the only person in the audience he was meant to speak to.

Uncharacteristically shaken, Sayer suddenly wanted only to rid himself of the strange feeling. Something deep inside him fighting him all the way, he finally managed to pry his eyes from the empty chair and, at least in appearance, return his attention to the whole of the audience.

The length of silence before the applause that would measure his success or failure might as well have been a lifetime. At times like this, it seemed he'd spent more than one lifetime working, planning, struggling to reach this point. Now, finally, he'd been invited to speak in one of the largest and oldest cities in the country, his hometown, Philadelphia. And he'd stood in front of the audience of thousands and told them all their tomorrows might not even exist.

He'd walked a dangerous tightrope today, said things that sounded extreme, radical—offensive. People never liked to hear the truth.

This topic had been especially volatile, though, because the mining industry in Pennsylvania already suffered from production drops and layoffs. And he had methodically and ruthlessly attacked it as environmental suicide.

Dead quiet draped the audience in mute paralysis for seemingly endless minutes after the last word had left Sayer's lips. Row after row of wide eyes and shocked faces answered his searching eyes.

He'd seen that same look thousands of times before on other faces in other cities, other auditoriums, in his own college classrooms. And as disturbing as it was to watch, it was a good sign. He'd reached them. It was a start, enough to wake them up from their self-absorbed daily lives to look at what they were doing to the world around them.

Nodding a final thank-you to the crowd, he moved to step down from the stage. His movement stirred the audience from its transfixed state and somewhere toward the back of the room a round of applause started. It caught on like fire to a dry forest, spreading and escalating to an impassioned display of support. They rose from their seats in a continuous human wave across every level of the auditorium, praising him with a lengthy standing ovation.

Sayer turned and raised a grateful hand to the crowd before leaving the stage. A dozen or more photographers and television cameramen flashed lights in his eyes, and a tangle of microphones and recorders were thrust his direction. Excited supporters rushed to thank and question him. Enraged opponents shouted challenges and curses over the noise, openly condemning his opinions.

One burly, bearded man pushed his way to the foreground of the crowd. "Damned radical! The mine I work in closed down 'cause of you and your notions! Why don't you just butt out of our business? We don't need you tellin' us how to run our union!"

Sayer knew at once the man was one of hundreds of miners put out of work by environmentalists' efforts to protect a tract of land that had been a habitat for several endangered species from the ravages of strip-mining. It was a cause he'd spent little time on, but the few quotes he'd given the media had been used over and over in papers nationwide.

The angry miner pressed in closer, rage flaring in his eyes. Reporters descended like vultures for the kill. They weren't about to miss a story like this. *Unemployed Miner Attacks Radical Environmentalist, Starts Public Brawl*—the headline flashed through Sayer's mind.

Sayer looked more closely at the man. Puffy, deep-set eyes, nose slightly twisted, aggressive chin, and a hard line for a mouth—it wasn't a face he would easily forget.

"Dr. Macnair, the car is waiting." Sayer's host for the event latched onto his shoulder from behind.

"It's all right, Jim. Just give me a minute," Sayer told him, shrugging off his friend's hand.

The media hounds stepped far enough aside to let the bear of a man push to the foreground and press his face inches from Sayer's. "So? How are my kids supposed to eat now that I can't work because you and your kind got the mine shut down? You stand there and talk about saving the earth! What about paying the rent? What about my family?"

Sayer faced the man's fury squarely. "I wish I had an easy answer for you. I really do. But problems that have taken centuries to develop can't be solved overnight. Until a final decision is reached concerning the strip-mining site, I can't promise you anything. I'm here to meet with representatives of the Department of the Interior to expedite a solution, hopefully a compromise. What I can do for you now is to direct you to the office in charge of relief aid in your area." He handed the man a card with the name and number of a coworker.

"I don't want no charity," the miner growled, knocking Sayer's hand aside. "I want a job!"

Sayer reached out and gripped the man's hand and placed the card in it. The man wrestled against Sayer and when he found he couldn't shake the grip he grimaced. Sayer lifted a brow at him, silently asking him if he wanted to risk embarrassing himself on national television. The man's hand relaxed in submission.

"I'm sorry about your job. Please, at least take the help that's being offered you and your family until this is resolved." With that, he turned and pressed through the crowd.

As he maneuvered his way through the throng, the confusion of voices blurred into an earsplitting clamor. He felt hand after hand grip his shoulders, slap the back of his Harris-tweed jacket. Strangers thrust their palms into his, one after another, fighting to grab his hand and shake it. Reporters crawled over each other like greedy ants to cajole or demand a quote.

As he thanked sponsors, shook supporters' hands, and made his way toward Jim's waiting Mercedes, frustration gnawed at his insides. He ought to be glad, delighted. This kind of response was all he'd ever dreamed of, wasn't it?

He needed public support as well as controversy to push people out of lethargy into action. The more people knew and respected his name, the better for the causes he fought for. He agreed with himself on all counts. And yet, what he couldn't answer was the *why* of it. Why didn't success, accomplishment give him the satisfaction and fulfillment he craved?

"Over there." Jim, a short, gnome-faced man with a full head of graying hair, beetle-black eyes never still, and a ready, broad smile, waved a thick hand toward the black car, signaling the driver to pull up to the curb.

Distracted, Sayer followed him out into the brisk spring afternoon. The scent of cherry blossoms wafted past his nose, reminding him of his Pennsylvania childhood. Colorado was home to him now; the breathtaking drama of the Rockies his sanctuary. But Philadelphia still held a part of his soul. It was a city where the past, history, merged with the present at every turn. Liberty Bell Pavilion, the Old Court House, the first U.S. Mint, Independence Hall, any direction he turned, he could see the past; yet time, progress, and necessity would carry it into the future.

He inhaled a deep breath of the fragrant aroma and climbed into the back seat and locked the door against the mixed mob of waving hands and pounding fists. "Philadelphia sure knows how to throw a homecoming party," he said as the crowd reluctantly cleared a path for the car.

Jim Hatcher eased back against the buff leather seat and pulled out a pack of Camels. "Take Doctor Macnair back to Thomas Bond House over on South Second, Rosen." He turned to Sayer with a grin. "Can't say you didn't ask for it in there today, my boy. You don't mince words."

"That's why they pay me the big bucks."

Jim laughed, his over-forty belly straining at the buttons of his Brooks Brothers suit. "We both know you're on the wrong side of the fight if money's your aim."

Sayer unbuttoned his casual jacket and adjusted his long legs to fit as comfortably as possible in the too-small space. He glanced out the window at the melange of architecture, past and present. Aged, some to the point of crumbling, weathered brick Federal buildings still looked as proud and determined to survive as the country's founders who had built them had been. Towering above them, starkly modern by contrast, glass and concrete offices and banks linked yesterday and today.

"Who says you can't have it all?" he asked, turning his attention back to Jim.

"Certainly no one watching your charmed life. Look at you, barely past thirty and you've made it to the big time. You're right on track to go straight to the top. You've managed, somehow, to keep everyone and everything from veering you off course; and if today is any indication of what your future holds, and we both know it is, your stubborn single-mindedness is about to pay off. No one can stand in your way."

Sayer stared back at Jim, the words echoing his own thoughts. "You're right, you know. This speech ought to have been the most satisfying moment of my entire existence. I decided on the flight here this morning that if I won the majority over today, I'd have reached every goal I've set to date."

"Not many people can say that."

"Well, maybe they're better off for it. I—I just thought today, finally, if all went well, I'd find some measure of satisfaction with my life, you know?" He turned to gaze out the window.

"I can't believe my ears. If I weren't sitting right here looking at you, I'd think my mind was going. This is all you've ever wanted, a chance to change the world. An audience, a following, a way to bring your ideals into reality. And after today, you'll have the support to start making that happen. I've never heard you talk like this before."

"I've never felt like this before." Sayer stopped short of trying to explain the dark, secret force that motivated him, an inexplicable need that drove him to keep stretching and reaching higher, outward for something—to stop the pain. For somewhere deep inside, today of all days, in the midst of a crowd of thousands gathered because of him, he'd never felt more alone.

"Maybe it's just that you realize you're going to have to make some tough decisions now. You're a college professor, Sayer, with an uncanny charisma that makes people want to believe every word you say, whether it's bull or not. You're a natural leader. I think you might find your life a great deal more comfortable if you moved into politics. And frankly, I couldn't suggest a better time to do it."

"We've had this discussion before," Sayer answered dryly. "I like teaching, and the university gives me absolute freedom as far as my speaking engagements are concerned. As for the money . . . I have more than enough for myself. Besides, the idea of politics leaves a bad taste in my mouth."

"You're an ambitious man. And you're a hopeless idealist. Sometimes the two just can't coexist."

"Ambition . . . is that what it's about? So tell me why do I find myself asking why *now* doesn't it mean a damn thing? Why do I feel as if I'm always pushing, working toward some goal, some ideal I'll never reach? Maybe what I want doesn't exist."

Jim grimaced and shook his head. "You're beginning to concern me, my boy. You've been working too hard. After this, you need to take some time off."

Sayer ran his fingers through the wave of hair dipping over his forehead, shoving it back. "It's all gotten so complicated. I spend most of my time pushing paper these days when what I want is to be back out there with my groups. I'm so removed now. I miss the days in grad school, working with them at the toxic cleanup sites, in the rain forests, on the shores after oil spills. Hell. I am going to take a firsthand look at the mining problems at least while I'm here."

"Not exactly my idea of a good time. But then you always were the man of action. But you know those do-gooders would fail without your guidance," Jim said, taking a long draw on his cigarette. "You're the one who makes things happen. You just can't do it hands-on anymore. You're their link to reform. You have all the contacts in Washington. Without you, your grassroots radicals wouldn't have enough funding or political clout to print flyers for a Boy Scout meeting."

Sayer shrugged. "I just feel—detached."

"It's better that way, Sayer. Trust me."

Jim lit another cigarette.

Sayer opened his window. "I don't get it, Jim. A branch chief for the Environmental Protection Agency and you still pump that stuff into your lungs. You get the facts firsthand."

"Oh hell, Sayer, don't start with me. Old habits die hard. Besides, unlike some of us," he stared at Sayer pointedly, "I feel no compunction to practice what I preach. I'm doing a job, that's all. I'm not some damned missionary."

"I wasn't asking you to be. I just wish you'd think about what you're doing to yourself, that's all."

"Why should I? I have you for that. You worry about the whole damn planet enough for both of us!"

"You sound as if you wish I would quit my 'crusade' as you call it."

"I'm not saying that." Jim took a deep draw and blew the smoke away from Sayer. "I just think you might be wise to temper your speeches, that's all. Today you spoke to your largest audience ever. Some of Pennsylvania's most prominent families, even the mining families, and certainly the unions, sent representatives to listen to you. You have a strong following, but your pet grass-roots environmental groups need funding. You can't afford to scare them away."

"I didn't get this far by backing down on issues. Besides, since when do you cower to industrial pressure? You're the only EPA agent I know who hasn't sold out. Isn't that why you decided to turn down that position in Washington and stay here in the Philly office? So you could run things your way without the kind of pressures your Washington counterparts are under?"

Jim covered a raspy cough with his palm. "That's part of it," he said, clearing his throat. "This is enough of a rat race for me. And my roots are generations deep here, as you well know. Which is precisely why there are certain important families here I have no intention of offending. You can escape back to your Rocky Mountain hideaway when this week is over, but I have to live here."

"Which families are you talking about? My dad was a miner, you know, and my brother Will still is." He glanced away. "Unfortunately, I've been so busy we've lost touch. I can't even remember which mine he's working in now, he's moved so often, but I wonder if the owner of his mine was represented today."

"Well, I was thinking specifically of the Montclairs. I saw the old man's son and one of their lawyers up on the balcony to the left looking more than a little ticked off. But I don't know whether they own the mine your brother works in or not. They've been buying some of the smaller companies out lately."

"The balcony two rows from the stage. That's where—" Sayer broke off not wanting to admit to his fantasy of the haunting beauty, the figment of his exhausted imagination. At the same time, he wondered why she'd made such an impression in so brief an encounter. It wasn't like him to be this disturbed over such an insignificant incident, no matter how lovely the lady.

"Was there a woman, a relative of the Montclairs, perhaps?" he asked, prompted by the lingering image of her wide, beseeching eyes. The sadness he'd seen there seemed at odds with the rest of her proud, almost regal countenance. She'd intrigued him. Somehow, she'd reached out, and even now, held him in a strange thrall.

Jim tipped his ashes out the window. "Not that I recall. But it's a large-enough family. There's a female lawyer somewhere among them, but you wouldn't see her sitting with them. She's a bleeding-heart liberal."

"She must be a thorn in their side," Sayer said distractedly. He was sure he'd seen someone in that chair. Either that or he was losing his mind. Which was a definite possibility, considering the schedule he was keeping: teaching back at the University of Colorado in Boulder, consulting, leading activist groups, speaking engagements all over the country and abroad.

"Stay away from those Montclair women or you'll end up with scars from the claw marks.

The car slowed in front of a three- and four-story, Federal-style building that housed the Thomas Bond House bed-and-breakfast. Jim slapped Sayer's knee. "I'll be calling soon."

"Thanks for the lift." Sayer climbed out of the car and paused for a moment at the edge of the drive, his mind on the mysterious beauty who'd appeared then vanished before him as he'd spoken today. She'd come and gone in the whisper of a moment; yet since their eyes had met, she hadn't left his thoughts. Something besides her beauty struck him. Something inexplicably familiar as though he'd met her before. *I know her. But from where?*

He struggled to place her and failed. So many people crossed his path, he thought, shrugging away the frustrating questions.

"Another time, another place," he muttered to himself as he turned toward the hotel.

What did it matter now? He'd never see her again.

The next morning Sayer rose early to take a few miles' run through the tree-lined walkways of Independence Park past Congress Hall, Old City Hall, Library Hall, the Liberty Bell Pavilion, red-brick monuments bringing history forward through time. He needed this hour to himself before he tackled the day's schedule of interviews and a luncheon speech before a local activist group. It was late in the afternoon when he finally drove his rented Range Rover back into old town Philadelphia to see about travel arrangements for a speaking tour in England.

He'd been invited to talk to students at Oxford, Cambridge, and two or three lesser-known English universities. It meant cramming even more work into his already-impossible schedule, but the opportunity was too good to pass up.

Besides, he found the busier he stayed, the less he felt the emptiness gnawing at the core of his being.

Sayer parked the truck at the curb of a narrow, cobbled side lane off Chestnut Street. A tugboat horn moaned in the distance, chugging its way down the Delaware River. He stepped out of the rover and had to reach around the girth of a Victorian wrought-iron gas lamp to plug the meter.

Starting down the sidewalk with long-legged strides, he glanced quickly from window to window. Little brick shops, cafes with French-lace curtains, and restaurants with welcome awnings in patterns from quaint to regal lined the walk. The travel agency he'd found in the phone book ought to be only a block or two farther toward Penn's Landing.

It was the only agency in the area near his hotel. He hoped it was open because he couldn't spare the time to drive the thirty minutes—forty-five, if he hit it at rush hour—it would take to get to the next closest.

Fighting traffic was the last thing he wanted to do after his hectic morning and nearly sleepless night. He'd spent the night wrestling the sheets, tormented by her . . .

Her, the auburn-haired angel—or witch—of his imagination that seemed to have taken up permanent residence in his thoughts since the day before.

Absently, he kicked an empty Pepsi can. It was a damned good thing she wasn't real, or he'd . . .

"What? I'd what?!" He caught himself talking aloud when a boy walking a fuzzy red chow puppy nearby turned to stare over his shoulder. He called the dog and crossed to the opposite side of the street hastily.

"I'd lose my mind, that's what," Sayer muttered, returning his attention to reading the polished metallic numbers on shop doors.

Wrought-iron numbers recalled the century before, seven-seventy-five, seven-seventy-six, seven-seventy-seven . . . *That was it.* He cupped his hands against the glass to peer inside and found the place looked more like a curiosity shop than a travel agency.

Shelf after disorganized shelf packed with oddities that appeared to be from all corners of the earth and as many eras in time crowded the room. Yet there in front of him, in the lower corner of the window, sat a neat little sign lettered in an elaborate calligraphy that spoke the language of a hundred years past: *Travel Agency.* Nothing else.

"Hell." Sayer shoved his fingers through his already wind-mussed hair, shoving back the one errant wave that stubbornly and perpetually fell over his right eye. Aggravated at the prospective loss of time if the shop didn't turn out to be a legitimate travel agency, something nevertheless compelled him to clasp the brass knob.

He shoved the heavy door open to the tinkle of tiny bells. One step inside the dark, almost cloudy, cramped room, an incongruous mixture of smells—dust, foreign spices, incense—assailed his senses.

Before his eyes fully adjusted, a woman appeared like a flood-light through fog. She plunged toward him headlong, arms out-stretched, hands reaching straight for his neck!

Instinctively, Sayer thrust out his palms to stop her from smashing right into him. Grasping her slender shoulders, he stopped her and opened his mouth to make a wry comment.

Then he saw her eyes.

Two

Joy struck Aramanda, momentarily flooding away every other feeling. "Roarke . . . you are alive," she whispered, breathing in the wonder of it. "You are alive! I thought—at the mine, you were . . ."

"I'm sorry," he said, the husky, rough-edged voice familiar, but oddly accented. A troubled shadow crossed his face. "I don't know you. You must have me confused with someone else."

"Someone else? How could I not know you? Roarke, we were there, together. It was minutes ago, we—" Aramanda stopped.

Minutes ago . . .

"I was at the mine, with you," she said, seeing those past minutes as she looked up at his face. "I felt—faint, and then I . . . It is impossible. We were at the mine, and now we are here." Bewilderment began to give way to the first stirrings of fear. The bruise on her cheek began to throb. Her gaze skittered around the cluttered little shop, seeing nothing she recognized.

Nothing but Roarke. "Where are we? Why have you brought me here?"

"I haven't brought you anywhere. I just got here myself." He looked her up and down, then raised a brow. "Your eyes, though . . . I did see you, earlier today, at the auditorium but—no, I'm mistaken. It couldn't have been you. The woman I saw didn't have a bruise on her cheek."

Aramanda touched the tender spot gingerly. "It happened only hours ago," she said, painfully recalling the slap of her uncle's hand.

"I'm sorry, really I am. Listen, I can understand if you've gotten lost," he said gently. "It's easy to get turned around in Philadelphia if you aren't used to the maze of side streets."

"Philadelphia!"

"Yes. If you need help getting back—"

"It cannot be!" Before he could finish, Aramanda broke away and ran to the window, peering outside. Nothing was as she recalled it. Not only were the shops and signposts unfamiliar, but the very substance and shape of the richly textured scenes outside the dusty glass panes were completely alien. She stared, stunned, until some sort of vehicle appeared to fly by the shop window, growling as it passed.

Aramanda jumped backward in fear, stumbling against him.

"Hey, easy does it. Are you all right?"

"No, I am not!" Pummeled by a confusion of wildly flailing feelings, she turned on him, catching her emotions on a ragged breath. Fear spilled over into anger and ignited. "You brought me here! You must have brought me here!"

"I don't even know you!"

"You know very well who I am, Roarke Macnair!"

"Roarke . . . I'm not Roarke—"

"You are! I know you better than I know myself!" Realizing she still clutched the blue neckcloth in her hand, Aramanda flung it at him, hitting him in the chest. "If you have conveniently forgotten me, surely you cannot have forgotten this, the symbol of your precious rebellion!"

"Look, lady," he began, annoyance dominating his expression. "I haven't forgotten you because I don't know you. And I certainly don't remember this—" He held up the blue cloth. As he did, a slight frown creased his face. His gaze abstracted as he stared at it; fingering the material, he found it disturbing.

"You do remember." When he said nothing, she prompted softly. "Your fight is ended. You have nothing left to gain by keeping us here." *Wherever here may be,* she thought, afraid to learn the answer, only wanting to return to the world she knew as her own. "Take me home. Come with me. We do not belong here."

He looked from the blue cloth to her, his frown deepening.

"Please, Roarke, take me home."

"Home?" His gaze narrowed, jaw tightening as a glint of ire flashed in his eyes. "I'm not taking you anywhere. At least not until you tell me who you are and why you keep insisting you know me."

"I do know you, Roarke Macnair! Why do you deny it?"

"I'm not Roarke Macnair! I'm Sayer Macnair, and I deny it because I don't know who the hell you are!"

"If nothing else, I would recognize you by your foul temper. No circumstance can change that. And I do not care what you choose to call yourself. We know each other. But . . . not here—"

Aramanda glanced around again, and the eerie coldness gripping her intensified. She did not belong here. She felt it keenly, as if her body and spirit had been forced into a void, a place she was never meant to be and could never truly be a part of.

She had been banished to a world of strangers and strangeness—her penalty for sending him to his death?

Yet here he was alive. Different in ways she could not yet define, but Roarke. Living, but lost to her—her love, who remembered nothing of all they had shared.

Fighting back tears, the confusing complex of apprehension and disorientation, Aramanda tried to force away the weakness inside that wanted to beg Roarke to help, to send her back to her familiar, safe world.

"Please, Roarke . . . I do not know this—" She lifted a hand to indicate the confines of the tiny shop. "I am lost here. I was at the mine, with you. . . ."

She reached out a hand, wanting to touch him, to reassure herself he was real and not some vision conjured by grief and guilt.

The combination of the vulnerability betrayed in her appeal and the strength she showed in not succumbing to her obvious fears found a softness in Sayer he hadn't expected. Dressed in clothing that made her look like an exquisitely detailed museum portrait, she could have been an aristocrat, a fine lady of a century past.

But with her coppery hair in disarray, the terror in her wide, searching eyes, and the bruise darkening her porcelain cheek, she seemed a princess lost in a world outside her castle sanctuary; she begged rescuing—obviously crazy, and definitely trouble. He should have walked away the moment he saw her.

Except he did remember.

She was the woman from his dreams, when he'd had that strange flash of vision after his speech yesterday. She couldn't be real—yet, despite his best rationalizations, she was here.

"I remember you . . ." he began, intending to prove to himself she was no dream.

But when her fingers brushed his shoulder, reality ceased and the whispers of a memory suddenly came rumbling through him like thunder. Not soft-edged, worn recollections of bygone dreams, but vivid images recalling the same feel of delicate flesh and bone sculpted under his hands, the haunting scent of the secret forest in her hair, the mirrored flame in her eyes.

And, stronger than any sensual memories, came the feelings, true and clear, remembrances of a love he could not forsake, for any cause or reason.

For one startling moment, he felt whole, the vague, disturbing wanderlust in him at rest, as if everything he had searched a lifetime for, longed for, dreamed of, had come together, beginning and ending here, with her.

Her lips parted to say his name and, in the vision in his mind, he kissed her, tasting the sweet echo of desire lingering on her mouth. The earthy, woody smell of the pine and oak married the wild roses of her perfume in the heat of the fire, embracing them both . . .

"We should not be here, Roarke," she murmured, glancing her fingertips against his face. The leaves beneath her rustled with a sibilant sigh at her slight motion, a bare sound mixed with the snap and hiss of the fire he had built.

He propped up on one elbow beside her and captured her hand, pressing a lingering kiss in her palm. "And where should we be, my lady?"

His mouth slid to her wrist, feeling the tiny pulse there quicken at his caress. Her answer didn't interest him; the silent language of her body told him all he wanted to know.

Looking down at her, fitted next to his side under the sheltered canopy of trees, he marveled at how the night and his touch had transformed her from the proud, defiant Montclair heiress to his Aramanda, his woman, his love.

With the scarlet-and-golden gleam of the fire poured over her skin, the flames lighting the unusual amber of her eyes, her hair spilling like a copper stream, she seemed to him a medieval enchantress, a hero's lady, destined to be the inspiration of myth and legend.

"We should be back at the camp," she said, tracing warm patterns on his jaw with her fingertip. "With your men. You have spent the entire day fretting over your schemes and most of the night here . . ." She stopped, averting her eyes, then slanting a glance up at him, a small knowing smile lifting the corner of her mouth. "You should rest. All those plans of yours— "

"Ah, Aramanda, always worrying everyone else, neglecting your own pleasures. I see I'm going to have to double my efforts at teaching you to be selfish. But I do have plans."

He nibbled at the tender skin of her forearm, then took his exploration higher, his lips teasing along the line of her shoulder and into the hollow of her neck. "I have plans for this night . . ."

Curving his free hand around her face in intimate possession, he tasted the delicate line of her throat. "And tomorrow . . ." He spoke the words against her mouth, his breath shared with hers. "And every tomorrow after this one, my Aramanda."

"Nothing is forever," she said, the slight breathlessness in her voice a telling betrayal of how he moved her, but still edged with a gentle resistance that could not be crumbled with either passion or power.

"Love. Love is forever."

"I wish that it could be, for us." Aramanda laid her fingertips on his mouth, stopping his reply. Her eyes clouded with emotion, deep gold hazed with a sadness that seemed beyond the moment, older than time. "It cannot be. I cannot love you. Not forever. Only now."

"But I can love you. Now and always."

Sliding a hand behind her neck, he brought her against him, letting her feel the strength in him that found its mate in her. "I love you so much I don't know whether your love will save or destroy me. Perhaps both. But it doesn't matter, for it will always be, despite anything that divides us."

"Your causes divide us. They always will, I fear. You cannot deny it, Roarke. You are always searching for an ideal, seeking to shape perfection from what can never be perfect."

"It can be," he insisted, determined to make her believe. "I—we can make it perfection. I refuse to accept anything less. One day you will believe it."

"You could make me believe, Roarke," she whispered, and as she wrapped her arms around his shoulders, pulling him into her embrace, her image blurred . . .

. . . became a shadow in the dancing flame and the unending darkness.

"You could make me believe." Aramanda heard herself say the words again in the confines of the strange shop, words she had told him a thousand lifetimes ago in a place to which she could never return. It hurt, more than she had believed it could, because it cruelly reminded her of all she had lost. "Oh, Roarke, I betrayed you. How can you still believe?"

"Believe?" His hands tightened on her shoulders.

Aramanda blinked as the note of confusion and astonishment in his voice swept aside the last remnants of the dream he had drawn her into. Roarke was dead. She had seen him die.

And yet he was here. The same Roarke Macnair of her heart. The same face—clean, strong lines and angles, with a mouth that could break a dozen hearts with one devil's smile or steal her own with a single kiss; the voice that could rouse a thousand men to fight or whisper words of love so tenderly it brought her to tears; the rebellious lock of hair falling over his brow that always tempted her to smooth it back. She met his eyes, the same exact shade of midnight blue, deep and penetrating. The same, yet different somehow.

She expected he would know her, even—here. But though he

searched her face, seemingly on the verge of remembering, he had forgotten. How could he? Why didn't he know her? For that matter, how could it be that he lived? It was impossible!

She was certain she must be mad, praying she was only caught in a nightmare from which she would suddenly awaken.

"Believe what?" he repeated. He looked at her, through her, as if he examined the deepest parts of her soul, searching for a clue to her, to himself. "And how could you betray me?"

"Please, Roarke." Aramanda closed her eyes, vainly trying to force away memories and visions too recent to have lost their cutting edge of anguish and despair. She looked at him again, unable to stop the tears this time. "I would have given my soul for a chance to change all that has happened. But not like this, not in a place where I am a stranger to you. I wanted to know love, to choose to trust my heart. Here—I am so afraid. Nothing is familiar. Nothing, except you."

Sayer stared at her, uncharacteristically silent. For a moment— *or was it hours?*—he'd been caught up in a vision so real he could still smell the roses of her perfume, feel the heat of the fire. *Aramanda.* Her name. Nothing he had ever heard before and yet so disquietingly familiar.

As if he had whispered it, over and over again, holding her in a lover's embrace.

The lingering strangeness of the vision left him feeling oddly detached, on uncertain footing.

"Look," Sayer said finally. "I—" He stopped, pushing back the errant lock of hair that fell over one brow with an impatient hand. "I don't know what to say. I don't know what you're talking about, and I don't know you. You've made a mistake—"

"A mistake? My mistake was in wishing for a miracle. Or perhaps this is my punishment for my sins, to lose even more than my soul. But I will not beg you to help me, no matter if I am condemned to this place or not. If I have lost all else, I will at least keep my dignity."

Spinning about quickly, wanting to leave him before she did resort to begging him, Aramanda stopped in mid-stride, awash in sudden dizziness. She put a hand to her forehead, the other groping blindly for some support.

His hands caught her waist from behind. He turned her to face him, steadying her until she could stand without swaying. Even after the vertigo had passed, she stood still in the shelter of his hold, looking up at him, not knowing what to say, to do, to make him believe.

Tension, born of yesterday's memories and the strange, compelling emotions of now, breathed in the silence between them.

"You should take her from here."

The soft voice, cracked at the edges with age, jerked both their attentions to a point behind. An elderly couple stood a few feet from them, the man leaning easily against an elderly armoire, the woman adjusting the slanted shade of a lamp to a more rakish angle.

"You should take her," the man repeated, indicating Aramanda with a withered hand. "She's had a long journey. She needs rest. Things will be much clearer tomorrow, I assure you."

Sayer slipped his hands from Aramanda's waist. "Take her where?"

The couple exchanged an odd glance. The man shrugged. "Wherever you are going. You are going somewhere, aren't you? You have some destination in mind? Why else would you come here?"

"Some destination——" For some reason, the gentle question irritated Sayer. "That's not the point. I thought she belonged here."

"I am not going with you no matter where it is that I belong," Aramanda snapped, tired of being talked about as if she were an unwanted horse at auction. She turned appealing eyes to the couple. "Please, if you would only let me stay for one night, just until . . . until——"

Until what? She was completely alone in a place she did not know, without money or family or even acquaintances. What could she do?

There seemed to be no answers; still, she would not surrender to the fate dealt her without a fight. Somehow, she would find a way to leave this place and return to her family and home. She looked quickly at Roarke. She would return, but with him? For a dizzying instant, she wondered if it were possible.

Had heaven answered her cry for a chance at redemption? Was she being given an opportunity to change both their fates?

"No, no, no," the old woman said, vigorously shaking her head. "I am sorry, my dear, but you cannot stay here. It is entirely out of the question. There is so little time, so very little time for you in this place. And you do not belong here." She looked hard at Sayer. "She does not belong here."

"Then where does she belong?" he asked. "You obviously know her."

The couple looked at each other again, then the man said, "If you like, I'll call the police and have her taken—somewhere."

"Somewhere. Wonderful." Frustrated at their attitude, bewildered by his own disturbing memories and feelings, by the woman's insistence on knowing him, Sayer tried to come up with a more acceptable solution.

"I will go."

His gaze snapped to her at the quiet assertion. She was afraid; he could see the fear clearly in her unusual amber eyes. But she held fast to her dignity even in this impossible situation.

"There must be a place I could rest for the night," she said. She flitted a glance to the windows. "If you could direct me . . ." She looked to the couple again, her plea for at least this small aid apparent on her face.

Sayer took one look at her and made his decision.

"Hell—let's go." Without preamble or an explanation to the elderly couple, he took Aramanda's arm and, ignoring her indignant look at his blunt command, propelled her outside the shop and onto the sidewalk, stuffing the blue cloth into his pocket as they went.

A light fog had crept up from the river, a quiet argent mist that gave the narrow street the same feeling as the shop interior of being divorced from reality's time and space.

"Where—?"

"You're going with me. I don't know if you're crazy or I am, but there doesn't seem to be a better alternative right now," he said brusquely, not looking at her. "We'll go somewhere—back to my hotel—and get this straightened out."

Ignoring the sideways glances and open stares of passersby, Sayer propelled her toward his car. As he reached to open the door, she stopped abruptly. He glanced at her. "What now?"

"No."

"No? No what?" Sayer saw she'd turned a deadly white. He felt a tremor shudder up her body, trembling through his hand. "What is it?"

"I—" Aramanda was staring at the Range Rover with something fast approaching horror. "What manner of carriage is this? I . . . I cannot . . . I—"

"Carriage?"

"Yes! If that is what it is. Where are the horses?"

"Well, in a manner of speaking, they're under here," he said dryly, motioning to the front of the vehicle.

"That is not an answer. You are patronizing me."

His voice softened. "It isn't life-threatening, honestly. Although I can't promise the same for my driving," Sayer said. Opening the door, he shoved aside a haphazard stack of letters and file folders and gently prodded her toward the passenger seat.

She balked, holding herself stiffly. "No, Roarke. I—I will go back to the shop or . . . anywhere. But not in there." Her eyes— wide, the pupils dilated—slewed from side to side as if seeking escape.

"No arguments." Sayer guided her to the seat with a firm hand. When she was safely inside, he strode around to his own door, noting as he slid inside how she had huddled up in the seat, sitting frozen in place, as if not daring to move or make a sound.

"It's only a short distance. Bond House. I think you'll like it. It's very old-world," he said, glancing from the high-buttoned neck of her dress to the swathe of cinnamon-brown skirts crumpled around dainty black boots.

Aramanda said nothing, unable to put her fears or emotions into words. She had no words for anything happening to her, no past experience with which to compare it. She was truly and completely lost.

His attempt at reassurance did nothing to ease the mayhem of feelings coursing through her. When the carriage he had thrust her into seemed to rumble to life with a muffled roar, she sucked in a hard breath, her fingers digging into the leather seat.

"My driving isn't that bad," Sayer said lightly, trying to ease her out of her fright.

What was the matter with the woman? From the look of her, he was convinced she'd never seen the inside of a car before, let alone sat in one. Except he'd found her in the middle of one of the busiest sections of Philadelphia, and unless the weird pair from the oddity shop kept her locked in an armoire, she had to have seen her share of traffic. There seemed to be no rational explanation for her behavior.

It would be easy enough, Sayer mused, as he guided the Range Rover away from the curb, to assume she was crazy and leave it at that. Yet, despite all logic and evidence, he couldn't bring himself to believe it.

Distracted by his thoughts, Sayer leaned over and flicked on the stereo, idly surfing the dial before settling on a classical station that poured the first striking crescendos of a familiar overture into the confines of the cab.

"Bach . . ."

The wondering voice turned his attention from the intermittent traffic to the woman beside him. "What?"

Aramanda was staring at the radio with wide, fascinated eyes. She made a motion to touch it but quickly snatched her hand back. "One of the Brandenburg Concertos. I first heard all six of them performed by the Philadelphia Orchestra in their premiere concert at the Academy of Music. I do so adore baroque music, and now it is here, with us—like a melody from heaven . . ."

The bittersweet lilt of the melding notes indefinably eased a little of the disorientation Aramanda felt at being suddenly separated from all she knew as reality. The beloved music gave her mind something familiar and cherished to grasp onto, to hug to her like a warm comfort.

"Their first concert . . ." Sayer muttered. "That was—"

"—1857. I remember every moment of it."

Sayer cocked a brow. "Do you? It must have been quite a concert. Considering it was well over a century ago."

"A—" Her eyes widened. She stared at him blankly. "I do not think this is the time to be amusing," she said, her voice flat.

"It's not a joke. It's 1996." When she said nothing, only looked at him with the same blank stare, he added, "Look around. Do you recognize anything as Philadelphia in 1857?"

She didn't move, and Sayer reached over a hand and nudged her arm. "Look around," he said softly. "Go ahead. I won't let anything inside to hurt you."

Very slowly, she let her eyes move to the window. Her gaze snapped back quickly. "I was only a girl then. . . ."

"You took a long time growing up."

"But—no. It is impossible. It cannot be! The year you told to me . . . it cannot be true."

"It is. You can't change that no matter what's happened to you."

"You have never lied to me. To anyone."

"And I'm not lying now. Why would I?"

"But I . . ." The color fled from her face with alarming speed. She went completely still, swaying slightly in her seat.

"Hold on," Sayer muttered. Cutting in and out of traffic, he swiftly pulled the rover onto a side street, then into a parking lot, braking to a jerking halt. He turned to her as she turned to him, her expression a clear reflection of horror and disbelief.

Without hesitation, Sayer pulled her into his arms, cradling her against his chest. She felt small and cold next to him, her slight body shaking with seemingly uncontrollable tremors. Around them, the music spun and swelled and soared in a tragic voice.

"It cannot be," she whispered, her voice expressionless, the emotion shocked from it. "It cannot be. I was there, at the mine, hours, *hours* ago. Not . . . not—" Her words broke on a sob.

"Tell me it is a dream. Tell me I will awaken and it will all have been a dream, a terrible nightmare. We will be together and none of it, *none of it,* will ever have happened. Tell me, Roarke. I cannot believe in anything but you."

"I can't tell you any of that," he said softly. Very gently, he eased her back and lifted her chin with his fingertips. "I won't lie to you."

"I know you would not. But I confess at this moment, I can almost wish you were not quite so honorable." She attempted a small smile, but it dissolved under a warm rain of tears. "You always wished for me to believe in the impossible. Now this—this is impossible and I want nothing more than to pretend it is all a lie."

Sayer stopped short of wincing when she looked at him, obviously hoping he would be able to produce a miracle. "I wish I had an answer for you," he said honestly.

Aramanda looked at him a moment, then said, "You do not believe me."

"I believe you're lost and frightened and you need someone to help you sort it all out. But—" Sayer hesitated, trying to phrase it as gently as he could. "You have to admit, your story is a little difficult to accept."

"Perhaps." Aramanda disengaged herself from his hold and turned facing forward in her seat again. Her hands folded tightly in her lap, twisting over one another. "I do not know what to say or do to make you believe. I do not know what to believe myself. You have never lied to me; yet how can what you say be the truth?"

"I don't think either of us is going to think of a solution sitting in a parking lot," Sayer said. Shifting the rover into gear again, he began maneuvering toward the street. "We'll go back to the hotel. It's quieter. We'll just talk," he added, as she hesitated, darting a look around her like a trapped animal seeking escape. "I promise."

"I—it is not that. I am afraid."

"Of me?"

"Of discovering we are both telling the truth."

"That would make life interesting," he muttered, half to himself. "But we aren't going to find that out sitting here. If you have another place you'd like to go, I'll be happy to take you there."

"I wish you could. For now, though, it appears I have little choice. I do not know how to return to yesterday."

"That makes two of us." As he guided the car back into traffic, Sayer slanted her a glance, seeing her tense again, her hands clench tightly together. "You said you had been to Philadelphia," he said quickly, trying to distract her from the ride she obviously found terrifying. "Is any of this familiar?"

"No—yes, that building over there—I recognize it; but the shops, even the streets, are like nothing I have ever seen. I do not know it like this. It is so different, so crowded. The carriages move with such haste. They look most dangerous."

"Different from what?" Sayer asked, hoping to elicit some practical information from her with the easy question. "From where you're from?"

"I am from here. From Philadelphia. You know that," she said, a touch of irritation coloring her voice.

"Yeah, okay. So you must know someone here, that couple in the shop for instance."

"I do not know them. I have never been there before today."

"They knew you."

Aramanda's shoulders lifted in a tiny shrug. "I cannot explain it. But if they did know me, they did not seem anxious to share my company. Perhaps, like you, they are not accustomed to people simply appearing without reasonable explanation."

A flicker of wry humor colored her words, and Sayer admired her ability to find any lightness in the circumstances. "Then how did you get to the shop in the first place?" he asked. "I'm pretty sure you didn't get there by car."

"No . . ." She rubbed at her temple, her forehead creased in concentration. "I was with you, at the mine, and there was chaos everywhere. Smoke and fire from the explosions, and fighting among your men and my uncle's. You were . . . I had come too late. I stayed with you—for how long, I do not know. Then, the smoke became too thick, and I turned to walk away."

"And?"

"And—I do not know. I only remember waking, as if from a dream, and finding myself in that shop. I felt afraid and I started to run from it. . . ." Aramanda turned to look at him. "And you were there."

"So I was."

Aramanda waited for him to say more, to offer some explanation of his own. When he said nothing, she let go a long breath, the ache in her heart a physical hurt.

Unable to bear the silence, she flashed a glance at the passing scenery, then swiftly dropped her eyes back to her hands. "You must love it here, like this. You always lived in the darkness, in the mines during the day, only coming out once it was already night. Do you stay here now because of the light?"

"I was born here," Sayer said, amused at her obstinacy in sticking to her story. "And I've never spent much time in a mine. I leave that to my father and brother."

"Liam?" Her head snapped up and hope flared in her eyes. "He is here with you then, too?"

"Liam?"

"Your brother. Or have you forgotten him also?"

"My brother's name is Will." Deftly, Sayer pulled the rover into the Bond House parking lot, switching off the ignition. Shifting sideways, he searched her face. "Maybe you've confused us with something or someone else," he said gently.

"No." Aramanda stared straight at him. "I could never do that, Roarke."

"My name is Sayer."

Aramanda shook her head. "I know you are Roarke. Even if you are not the same as yesterday, it is your soul, the match to my own. There is no beginning or end to the feelings we shared. If you have forgotten, I will always remember. I still hear your voice, feel your hand on mine." Reaching out, she brushed her fingers over his, closing her eyes as the vision of their last moments at the mine came rushing through her mind. When she looked at him again, tears misted her vision. "Perhaps it was a thousand lifetimes ago for you. But for me, it has only been a breath of time."

The feel of her stirred up the same incomprehensible feelings in Sayer of possession, protectiveness, and deep-burning anger he'd felt before when he'd first touched her in the shop. He wanted to dismiss her story as insane, to drop her off at the closest police station or hospital and leave it at that. Wanted to, but couldn't.

"I don't even know your name," he said at last, in the same instant knowing that he did.

Aramanda. Aramanda of his dreams.

"You know it. Aramanda. I am Aramanda and you are Roarke. Nothing can change that. Not even this." She swept a hand to indicate the scenery around them.

He was silent for so long Aramanda felt herself succumbing to despair once again. It always ended like this between them, a barrier between them keeping them from trusting, from belonging to each other, from sharing the love she so desired for her own. First his cause, then the threat to her family's future, her betrayal, her uncle's treachery, and now, it seemed, heaven itself had intervened with this strange fate to divide them once again.

Overwhelmed by hopelessness and fear, she fumbled at the side door of the carriage, wanting only to get as far away from him as possible.

"Where do you think you're going?" Sayer reached over and took her hand from the door handle. "Running away isn't going to resolve this. Look—I'm sorry," he said, "but you were right. It does seem impossible."

"Then you *do* believe me?"

"I don't know," he said bluntly. With an attempt at a smile he added, "And I'm not sure I want to know."

Aramanda wanted to be angry with him, but she couldn't find it in herself to add to his struggle to come to terms with the truth she so desperately wanted him to acknowledge.

She tried a tentative smile in return. "I do not know that I would believe my own story if it were you telling it to me. Even now, it sounds mad to my own ears—at best one of the fairy stories my brothers and sister so love to hear. But if you could remember anything. If you could recall the last minutes we spent together . . ."

"Last?" He shifted in the seat as if touched by an uneasiness. "I suppose to you I'm dead and gone." His voice held an attempt at flippancy, but she could tell the idea disturbed him.

"Dead . . . yes. In my world, at least." The tears started in her eyes again.

For her, it had been too recent, too soon to relive all over again. She didn't want to recall the images of the past, the violence he fomented that had been the first link in a chain of tragedies ending with her own treachery and his death.

The painful emotion shadowing her face moved Sayer to reach out to her. He didn't understand her reaction, or Aramanda herself, or women in general. But something about this woman turned every protective instinct in him on high.

"Aramanda . . ." he said softly, laying a hand on her shoulder. Her name tasted gentle and sweet on his lips, a savor of something both evocative and strange. "I don't know what's true, but obviously it's going to take more than a few minutes to sort out and it'll be much pleasanter to do in the room than sitting in a very public parking lot. And besides—" His mouth twisted up with in a wry smile. "—you've obviously had a long journey. No doubt you could use a rest."

"Yes," she said, her eyes haunted as she gazed out at the daunting scene surrounding them. "Perhaps it has been much longer than I knew."

"Yes, well—" Not knowing what else to say, Sayer moved out from behind the wheel and strode around the car to open her door. As she slid out, Aramanda accidently brushed several of the letters and papers on the seat beside her out onto the pavement.

Automatically bending with him to pick them up, she noticed the name neatly printed on the face of one of the envelopes: S. R. Macnair.

"S, for Sayer," she murmured. Slowly lifting her face to his, she gazed directly in his eyes. And R for—?"

Sayer looked straight back. "I think you already know."

Taking the letters from her, he tossed them back inside the Range Rover and closed the door behind. He made no attempt to move away; she couldn't have left him at the cost of her life. In a stroke of sunlight, alone together, they stood staring at each other for long minutes.

"R is for Roarke," Sayer said finally. "Sayer Roarke Macnair." His eyes never leaving hers, he took her hand in his and started leading her toward the inn. "And maybe that's why part of me believes every word you've said is true."

Three

Inside the suite at the hotel, Aramanda stood in the center of the sitting room, feeling distinctly ill-at-ease and out of place. "Do you think this is wise?" she ventured, watching Roarke shrug off his jacket and toss it over a chair back. "It is most improper."

In the midst of rolling up his shirtsleeves, he glanced at her, frowning. "Improper?"

"Being alone together in your rooms," she said, flushing when he started to smile. "I suppose it is more private, but it seems bold, even for you, to simply walk in without any explanation. Surely, anyone seeing us will think . . . they will assume that—"

The smile had widened into a rakish grin. "Yes?"

"Well, I suppose that it hardly matters. You always took an ill-mannered pleasure in being disreputable and it seems, in this place at least, I have no reputation to protect."

"Don't you?"

"Not here, not now, if what you say is the truth." Then, refusing to let Roarke unnerve her with his devil's humor, she braved his gaze with a straightforward look of her own. "And I should be accustomed to abandoning all propriety. After all, many of the things we did together were most improper."

Instead of the suggestive banter she expected in response to her blatant provocation, Roarke turned serious. He studied her, his expression intent. "Back at the shop . . ."

"Yes?"

"I can't explain it. I had a—" He hesitated, rubbing a hand over his jaw.

"What did you have? You might as well confess it to me. Your explanation certainly cannot be more difficult to fathom than mine."

"I wouldn't be too sure."

Aramanda took a breath, starting to prod him into telling her. "You do not have to tell me," she said, letting it out in a soft sigh. "If this is all vexing for me, it must be as vexing for you. I recognize your face, your voice. I feel the same trust and love, and yet you are not the same. You feel nothing for me. You cannot even remember my name. I am an intruder in a world that belongs only to you."

"Except that I . . ."

She waited, neither encouraging nor dissuading.

Sayer paused a few seconds. "At the shop, I had a—vision, a dream or something. Of you. I don't know what it was, all I know is it wasn't like anything I've ever experienced." The words came slowly, as if he forced them out around his unwillingness to believe. "We were . . . together, in a forest—"

"—close to the fire, under an infinity of stars. It is no dream to me. I remember every moment."

"It seemed . . . we were lovers."

"Yes. That and more. So much more. You must remember. Roarke . . ."

She took a step toward him and he tensed. Aramanda stopped, feeling a stab of hurt at his subtle rejection.

Her emotions must have shown plainly in her expression, for he immediately strode to her side. He stayed near enough for her to feel the heat of him, far enough to avoid a casual touch.

"I'm sorry," he said. "You . . . remember. I don't. To me, you're like a dream—too beautiful, too fragile to be real. I'm not entirely sure I didn't invent the whole thing."

"Perhaps you did, but for me it was yesterday. Yesterday when you held me, yesterday when we loved each other."

"I can't believe that."

"Cannot or will not? Would you have me believe you feel

nothing for me? Nothing when you lay your hand upon my breast?" Deliberately, Aramanda breached the distance between them and stroked her fingers down his cheek. "Nothing when I lay my hand upon your cheek?"

"I don't know what I feel." Sayer took her hand in his, his fingers tightening on hers for an instant. "It's impossible."

"Is it? Is it truly impossible? Or do you only wish it to be?"

He said nothing for an eternity. She waited, although the stretch of time seemed unbearable.

At last, very slowly, as if he moved in a dream, he stretched out a hand and touched her face. The feathery kiss of his fingertips on her skin left her trembling. "Aramanda . . ." he murmured, saying her name as if it were a vow.

In the next instant, he drew back, shaking his head as if to throw off the disturbing emotions that inextricably linked them to each other.

"This is insane." He paced away from her, shoving the wayward lock of hair from his forehead. "I don't know who's crazier, you for telling this wildly improbable story or me for wanting to believe it."

"Does it matter?" Aramanda drew in a deep breath and let it out gradually, trying to still the ragged pace of her heart. "Neither of us can change the truth," she said, hearing the weariness in her voice.

"Whatever that may be. And no, right now, it doesn't matter, because you look as if you're ready to collapse. Here—" Walking to her again, he took her arm and led her to one of the settees positioned near the room's windows, gently guiding her to sit. "I'll order you some tea. You can catch your breath while I check my messages."

With Roarke so near, alive and real, Aramanda thought that no matter where destiny had reunited them, no matter if time had changed him, he still possessed the power to affect her as no other man could. A fine, racing excitement ran under her skin as she watched the supple motion of his body when he walked to a low table next to the settee and picked up the curved piece of an oddly shaped box. Pressing one of the small squares on its surface, he waited a moment, then gave an order for tea to be sent to the room. She stared in wonder as he pressed a second, then a third square.

"Messages, please," he said, then stood with the thing to his ear for several moments, saying nothing. "Hold on . . ." Picking up a pen, he scrawled several notes on a sheet of paper. "I've got it, thanks. Dammit," he muttered, dropping the earpiece back into its cradle as he scribbled several more notes on the paper. "He's going to get himself into more trouble than he can handle."

"I see your temper and your language have not improved with time," Aramanda murmured. While he was distracted, she touched a finger to the box Roarke had used, then picked up another of the pens, studying it closely. "Who?"

"What?" Sayer's attention snapped back to her.

"Who is in trouble? One of your men?"

"Not exactly. A friend. Someone who should know better than to stick his nose where it doesn't belong. He's begging to get it broken."

"Then you and he share a common trait."

He looked at her a moment, startled, before his expression relaxed into a smile. "Touché. What are you doing?"

Aramanda was moving the tip of the pen over a clean sheet of paper, perplexed by its refusal to work. "It must be empty of ink. Or it has faltered. I do not know. But I cannot make it write."

"It works just fine. You haven't learned the trick of it," he said. Bending over her, he placed her hand beneath his on the slender rod. "Just press here, and—*voilà!*"

Her fingers followed his instruction, but her thoughts and senses abandoned their interest in the pen's instant ability to write, focusing on him. His palm on her hand, his familiar musky smell, the strength she felt in his slightest motion combined to battle and undo her resolve to hold fast to her dignity at all costs.

"Thank you," she managed, not trusting herself to look up.

Sayer left his hand on hers a fraction longer than the demonstration called for. Then, straightening, he moved to sit next to her on the settee, casually draping his arm over the seat back.

"You're welcome. Aramanda—" Hesitating, he searched her

face. His hand, inches from her shoulder, flexed and unflexed in response to the conflict she saw in his expression. "We need to talk," he said at last. "Despite what you say, I don't remember you or anything about you. I don't even know your whole name."

"Aramanda Cordelia Montclair," she said, carefully pronouncing each syllable. "My middle name is taken from my mother, whom you know well. Perhaps you will remember it now."

"Montclair—" Sayer stared at her openly. "Your family—"

"Yes? Do you know something of my family?" she asked, allowing a little hope into her voice. "It has been so long, they will be frantic by now, especially when my uncle discovers I was able to escape his locked room. He will be—"

Aramanda stopped, suddenly stricken by a dawning dread. "But, if you are dead, yet here, and I am here with you, then have they, too, vanished with my past? Am I truly so alone?"

Her last words ended on a note of grief so keen Sayer felt it like a knife's thrust to the heart. "You're not alone," he said gently, giving her shoulder a soft squeeze. "And I want to help you find your family again. They own one of the biggest mining conglomerates in northeastern Pennsylvania, don't they?"

"Our fortunes have survived to this time? My Uncle Gervase would be pleased to know you did not succeed in completely destroying his empire."

"I haven't given it much of a try. Yet."

Aramanda raised a brow. "So, the conditions in the mines are still your cause?"

"Mines?" His face hardened. "You don't know me as well as you imagine. I wouldn't fight in this lifetime or any other for that cause. If I could promise an alternate energy source, I'd close every damn one of them down tonight. And right now, the Montclair mines in particular."

"Close them all down?" Aramanda didn't bother to hide her astonishment. "You always fought for improvements. But I never would have believed you'd want to close the mines completely."

"Why does it surprise you?"

"Your brother works there. He and so many depend on them for their livelihood. That, we always agreed upon."

"Yes, but coal is an antiquated and environmentally destructive energy source, and—"

"I was right."

"Right?"

Aramanda felt the passion of her own convictions surge within her. This was the Roarke Macnair she knew—knew well and could both love and despise. "You have not changed. Your words are different, strange, but their meaning is still clear to me. Now or then, you have never considered how your fights will affect the people caught up in them."

"I am thinking of the entire planet full of people, now and for the future," Sayer said sharply, the first signs of ill temper beginning to show.

"You never see everyone. You never see the faces at all. To you, they are either those who fight with you or against you. You never see them as families, as individuals who laugh and cry and can be hurt by your zeal to make life better for them."

"We all have to make sacrifices if we want change. And how do you know so damned much about—" He broke off, shoving the hair off his forehead. "Hell. I'm sorry." His mouth quirked up in a rueful twist. "Why do I get the feeling you've had this same argument before?"

Smoothing her palms over her skirts, trying to damp down her own ire, Aramanda said tartly, "I have. With you, and many times." She speared his gaze with hers. "And you are just as single-minded and immovable as you have ever been."

"And you must be just as passionate and stubborn as you ever were," he said softly, his fingertips just grazing her shoulder.

"We are still on different sides of the same cause, it seems." A shadow of sadness passed over her, reminding her of the love and betrayals of the past. She looked down, her vision veiled by bittersweet memories.

"Are we? If I wanted change, a better life for the miners, what did you want Aramanda?"

Aramanda looked up, gazing fully into his eyes. "Your love, a home, a family undivided by causes and bitter fighting. My uncle's war with you caused a breach in my family; my own concerns for the mining families only widened it. We had no peace, you and I, and there seemed to be no way to find it. And it is no different now. You are still at war with the Montclairs."

"No . . . not exactly."

The uncharacteristic evasion in his voice instantly commanded Aramanda's attention. She glanced at him, questions in her eyes.

"There's been some trouble reported at their mines, but it's all a lot of rumors right now," he said carefully. "I have to do a lot more checking before I decide whether or not to wage war."

"It is obviously more than that. But you are just as obviously not willing to tell me." Aramanda held up a hand, stilling his protest. "You do not trust me," she said bluntly, "because my name is Montclair."

"They could be—hell they probably are your family," Sayer returned with the same straightforwardness. "Maybe that's where you belong. You've only—forgotten."

"Forgotten! It would certainly be convenient for you if I had. But I have not forgotten. I know my family well—my mother, my brother Nicholas, the eldest, and my sisters, Jessalyn and Penelope, and Oliver, the youngest. I can imagine what they are doing now, how worried they must be. Mama fusses if I even go out riding alone. She must be beside herself now, no one knowing how to comfort her . . ."

"What about your Uncle Gervase?"

The name sent a ripple of fear and loathing through her, stiffening every muscle. "Yes. My uncle. What do you wish me to say about him? He will not mourn my vanishing, I assure you."

"Not your favorite relative, I assume," Sayer said, the lightness of his tone belied by his slight frown. "And apparently not mine, either. You painted us as adversaries."

"You are—were. Is it were, then, Roarke? Is it all, all we shared, truly so long past?"

My destiny now is in heaven or hell. It doesn't matter which. With you I've lived in both.

She heard his words echo inside her as clearly as the moment he had spoken them. Feelings of grief and pain trembled through her and she gave a shiver, feeling haunted, cold. Alone.

Sayer's frown deepened. He shifted as if to touch her, and Aramanda quickly rose to her feet, unable to bear the feel of his hand on her . . . not when she knew that now she must tell him again how she had betrayed him.

"What is it?" He came up to her, and she felt his gaze intent on her.

"Gervase forced me to betray you." She took a deep breath and looked at him fully, hating the words, knowing she had to say them. "You destroyed his mines, disrupted his workers, created chaos with your rebellion. We disagreed over the violence you were not afraid to use to further your cause. I could not bear to see people—my family—caught up in it, not knowing if they would be hurt, or worse, hating the division among us. I had to try to protect them, at any cost. You thought that to achieve your vision of ideal conditions you had to win all. I thought there could be a compromise. I went to him . . ." Her hand strayed to the tender bruise on her cheekbone.

Sayer tensed, his hand clenching into a tight fist. He slowly opened and closed it several times, the murderous look on his face telling her more than words. Finally, he seemed to gain a measure of control and, with a surprisingly gentle touch, put his hands on her shoulders. "You don't have to tell me."

"Yes, I must." Aramanda let herself draw strength from his touch, courage from the protective sense she felt in it. "He threatened to hang Liam—your brother—for your crimes. I could not let Liam die, though he would have gone to the gallows for you. I cared for him, and for Bridget and the children. They loved him and depended on him. And he was innocent."

"And I wasn't." His flash of anger communicated itself to her through the quicksilver tensing of his fingers.

"I tried to warn you. It was too late. You . . . Gervase's men caught you by surprise. There was an explosion at the largest mine." She briefly closed her eyes against the vision, then looked fully at him. "Is it still too late?"

"I don't know. I don't know what to think. I shouldn't believe it. It's a crazy story."

"Only to you, because you do not remember. Roarke—"

Aramanda laid her hands on his, holding him tightly. "We must return. You must return with me. I feel . . ." She put a hand to her temple, and for a moment her gaze abstracted.

She swayed, and Sayer's grip tightened. "Aramanda?"

"It is nothing. Only I do not understand why I am here, unchanged as if my yesterday is only hours ago, and you are changed, with the past only a dream you do not want to remember. I feel . . . I feel it is wrong for me to be here. This is not where I belong. This—" She indicated the room with a glance. "—these things, mean nothing to me. The look, the feel of them, the sounds, the scents—I might as well be blind and deaf for all they are familiar to me."

Aramanda shook her head impatiently. "It is madness, madness. But I know in my heart I must return. Please, Roarke." She appealed to him with her eyes, her voice, her soul. "If I return, perhaps I can change all that has happened."

"You don't know that."

"Nor do you!"

"Then I'll find out!"

"And how do you expect to do such a thing?" Aramanda asked. "It seems impossible."

"You said I believed in impossibilities," Sayer said, flashing her a half smile. "But this won't be too much of a miracle. I'll try the library, ask a few friends at the university. There should be some historical record of the rebellion, the Montclair mines, and your family, if—"

He cut off his sentence, but Aramanda heard the words he left unsaid. "If I am telling the truth. That is what you meant to say, is it not?"

Something in him responded to the unspoken plea in her voice. Aramanda could see it in his eyes, sense it in the quickening of his heart, his pause in answering. She held her breath, waiting, knowing he was on the edge of believing or dismissing her forever.

"I want to believe you, although God knows why—"

"But you do not." Defeat weighing heavy on her heart, Aramanda pulled from his hold and sat down on the settee again.

"I still must try to return," she said, more to herself than him. "I will not surrender this chance without trying. There must be a way to return."

"The shop."

Aramanda raised her head. "The shop?"

"The travel agency," Sayer said, nodding as she began to see his plan. "They must know something about how you got here. We'll go back and talk to that old couple who own the place."

"We?"

"Yes, Aramanda Cordelia Montclair," he said softly. "We."

"Why are you willing to help me if you do not believe I am telling the truth?"

Sayer grinned. "Hell if I know. Let's just say I've adopted you as one of my causes and leave it at that for now. And since you're an official cause . . ." He eyed her up and down, bringing a flush of self-conscious heat to Aramanda's face. "I'm going to have to get you some clothes. You can't wander around Philadelphia looking like that."

"What is wrong with looking as I do?" Aramanda shot back, indignant. She indicated the fine cinnamon-colored cotton, long sleeves, and demure neckline of her frock. "This is quite respectable!"

"Respectable for 1867, maybe. Weird in 1996. You look like a character in an historical reenactment. We'll work on it after—" A deferential knock sounded at the door. "After tea," Sayer said, indicating the door with a smile. Striding to the door, he accepted a laden tray which he brought to where she sat, setting it on the low table in front of the settee.

Without thinking, thankful that at least tea trays had not changed dramatically with the rest of reality, Aramanda poured out two cups, automatically adding a large dollop of cream to one and handing it to him.

"Is something wrong?" she asked when he stared at the cup, then at her. "I put in nearly a third of cream. If you take any more, you might as well drink hot cream."

"How did you know?"

"How did I—" The question momentarily perplexed her until

she realized again that Roarke considered her a stranger, not an intimate who knew his tastes as well as her own.

"How did I know? I know you." Aramanda touched him with her eyes, her voice. "I know how you keep pushing your hair from your forehead when you are irritated, how your mouth twists at the corner when you smile. I know that you hate coffee and have a passion for raspberry jam and scones. I have seen you angry enough to murder a man and charming enough to persuade a queen to forsake a kingdom. I have heard you give such impassioned speeches that men were ready to die for your cause, and . . ." She paused, her voice falling to a soft breath of sound. "I have heard you whisper such words of love that I was willing to die in your arms."

She had shaken him; she could see it in his eyes. Whatever the cause, they had another chance to love, to live. Perhaps if she could convince Roarke of it, if they could return together to their true past, she could save him instead of destroy him and all that they were. If she could only breach the divide that eternally kept them apart, each with only half a soul.

"You walked into my life like a dream," Sayer said, his voice low and strained. "I've never been overwhelmed by anything or anyone, but now—" He stood quickly, pacing to the windows and back. "Now, I can't just abandon you. We're going back to that shop and get this straightened out. At the rate my schedule's going to hell, though, it might very well be the only thing I get done while I'm here."

Before Aramanda could think of a reply, something like the sound of a shopkeeper's bell made a burst of sound, shortly followed by another. Startled, she swept the room in a glance, searching for the source.

"Relax," Sayer said, brushing his fingertips against her cheek. His hand lingered there, then slipped away. "It's only the phone. I'll get it."

Picking up the earpiece to the odd box again, he rapped out his name. His voice relaxed a moment later. "I know. I should have been there. I'm sorry, Jim; something came up." There was a pause. "I know, I know, I missed the meeting with you and the boys from the Department of the Interior. . . . No, it's not like me. I got tied up at the travel agency. . . . Well, it's the best explanation you're going to get."

Aramanda couldn't help smiling to herself. If Roarke were somehow speaking to a man through that instrument, he must be very important indeed to command an explanation from Roarke Macnair! Not once did she recall Roarke ever explaining or defending his actions to anyone.

"I'm glad you were able to reschedule it," Roarke was saying. "Okay, okay, I know it's critical if we're going to push to resolve the battle between the miners and the Soil Conservation Society over that site. When are they going back to Washington? That soon? Can't you keep them here another day or so?"

Listening to Roarke, to the familiar voice speaking unfamiliar phrases—almost another language to her—Aramanda keenly felt the breach of time between them. Until now, her mind had shied away from confronting the date Roarke had told to her. It seemed an impossibility that defied reason and reality.

Now . . . what else could the truth be?

Aramanda had no answer; but half-hearing Roarke as he spoke to the man who was not there, she allowed herself to wonder what kind of life he had here. She knew virtually nothing about him or what he did, what causes he fought for or who his family was in this new reality—or what lovers he might have.

And she knew nothing about her own family. What had become of them? How had they explained her disappearance? Had Roarke's rebellion failed so completely then? Had Gervase made her mother, her siblings suffer for her betrayal? And had they despised her for it?

Questions, and only Roarke could help her find the answers.

"This afternoon? No, I can't. I have to finish settling my schedule for Europe. Things have gotten complicated." He flicked a sideways glance at Aramanda. "I have to make sure they don't get any more screwed up than they already are . . . when? Well, if it's just drinks . . . no, don't worry, I'll be there. Thanks for smoothing things over. Umm . . . Jim, one more thing." His gaze moved to Aramanda again and she could almost hear him carrying on an internal debate over how to figure her into his plans. "Would you mind if I brought a—a date?"

Aramanda wondered why for the next several moments Roarke held the instrument several inches from his ear.

"I'll take that as a *yes*," he said dryly when he finally brought it close again. "Trisha? I'm sure she won't mind. Five-thirty? I'll see you then. Damn," he said, as he laid down the earpiece and ran his hands through his hair. "This is going to be sticky."

"Is it?" Aramanda murmured, for the moment fascinated by the mystery of the box. She ran her finger over the smooth surface of the box. "It does not feel sticky. How did you speak to him?"

Picking up the earpiece, she held it near her own ear, feeling his residual warmth. "There is no voice. Only a buzzing sort of sound." She held the earpiece away, eyeing it suspiciously. "Is this another instance where there is a trick to it?"

"I'm afraid so. But I don't have time to explain it now. We've got to get you some clothes before we meet Jim."

Aramanda looked up quickly, briefly diverted from the dilemma of her wardrobe. "Jim?"

"A friend. He's helping me with a few problems. I promised we'd meet him for drinks."

"Drinks?"

"Get together—meet a few friends."

"A social event? Roarke, I—I cannot do that."

"Why not? I'm not just going to leave you here alone." Pushing his hair back from his forehead, Sayer tried to find words to persuade her without offending or frightening her. "We'll compromise. We'll do this tonight, then tomorrow we'll go back to the shop, do a little research. We'll keep looking until we track down your family and your past. What do you say?"

"I—How can I be expected to converse?" Aramanda told him, both exasperated and intimidated by the prospect of having to deal with anyone other than Roarke, frightened at leaving the comparative security of his rooms. "I do not know anything of current fashion or gossip or social events. I am no one here, without a reputation or family name. My family . . ."

A sudden image of her brothers and sisters, her mother, together in the sitting room, her favorite place in the house with its large windows overlooking the gardens and the dim, old colors of the rugs and chairs. All the dear, familiar people and things she longed to return to.

Her throat hurt with the effort to stay her tears, and she rose swiftly and went to the window, looking into the quiet purple softness of the encroaching evening. "I have nothing but my dignity, and precious little of that. At least allow me to keep that small comfort."

"You have much more." Roarke's large hands turned her to face him. "You're definitely intriguing, obviously intelligent, and you have enough stubborn resolve to make me want to believe in everything impossible." His hand lifted from her shoulder, and his fingers swanned her face with an almost reverent touch. "And you're beautiful enough to make me realize perfection is more than a dream."

"Only an Irishman with a golden tongue could woo me to do his will with pretty words and nothing more," Aramanda said softly, not willing to let him see how much his touch affected her, knowing the quiver in her voice belied her most determined attempt.

Sayer smiled. "Does that mean you'll go?"

"I suppose I have no choice but to attend your 'get-together.' But only if you allow me to first learn something about your Philadelphia society and its tastes and amusements. At least then I will have less chance of betraying myself as someone completely ignorant of society. Perhaps a newspaper . . ."

"I think it's better to remain as ignorant of society as possible, but I'll be glad to dig you up an *Enquirer* on the way out if it makes you feel better. Somehow, though," he added with an infectious, lopsided grin, "I think a woman like you could be socially at ease in any time or any place."

"I suppose it might even be amusing," Aramanda said, catching his smile and answering with one of her own. "Having no family name to protect, no reputation, I could behave in the most outrageous manner without consequence."

The glint of mischief in her eyes made Sayer raise a brow.

"This could get interesting. We are going to have to do something about your clothes, though."

"That again!"

"Yes, that again."

Plagued by uncertainty, a persistent sensation of being displaced, Aramanda still balked. "Roarke . . . leaving here, meeting other people—"

"Come on," he said, taking her hand. "Aren't you at least curious? I won't let anything out there hurt you, I promise. Even my own driving. And we can stop by the travel agency on the way. Maybe we can find some answers today, and then we'll have something to celebrate."

Aramanda nodded, saying nothing as she followed him out of his rooms. Roarke might find his answers at the odd little shop. But she felt sure he wouldn't like them.

Four

Sayer maneuvered down the busy afternoon streets in the direction of the travel agency, trying to keep his attention fixed on the road ahead but finding his eyes wandering to the woman beside him.

Engrossed in the latest edition of the *Philadelphia Enquirer,* Aramanda had been silent the past ten minutes except for an occasional amazed murmur. He'd noticed her expressions, though, from astonished to perplexed to dismayed, and it had taken all his willpower to refrain from comment.

Finally, she let the paper drop to her lap and, to his surprise, started to laugh.

"Are you going to share the joke?" he asked.

Aramanda turned to him, amusement shaking her shoulders as she pointed to the newspaper. "It is all so ridiculous! So many years and yet people have changed so little. Those in power still make fools of themselves over their vices and accuse each other of scandals, and very little real good is accomplished." She put a hand to her mouth, vainly trying to stifle her laughter. "I suppose it is not funny, yet it is! I am in a world of strangers who are all familiar!"

Her infectious laughter made Sayer smile in return. "I suppose it's true that history repeats itself."

"Perhaps." Aramanda slanted him an odd glance. She returned her attention to the newspaper, flicking the pages aside until she reached the food section. "This I find most amazing. You see—$1.26 for a dozen eggs? Why, a man would have to load more than three cars of coal, a half day's work, just to purchase breakfast for his family! Liam tells me he is fortunate to make $25 in a month during the busy season. How can laborers afford such costs?"

"Laborers are paid a little more than $25 a month," Sayer said dryly. "Some of them make that in an hour."

"An hour!" Aramanda looked shocked. She eyed him suspiciously. "Are you teasing me?"

This time Sayer laughed. "If I were, I could do a better job of it." He hesitated, then added, "So, did you find anything that sounded familiar?"

"Familiar? How could I know any of this? Ah—you still believe I have forgotten. No." Her expression shuttered, and she quickly glanced away from him to stare out the passenger window. "I have not forgotten. It is impossible for me to remember anything of this—this date."

The last word came out hard. Sayer winced, wanting to make her forget the absurd notion she came from the past. Yet at the same time, Aramanda herself made it hard to believe she belonged anywhere else. There was something otherworldly about her, and the reflective depths of her unusual eyes held an aura that clashed with reality.

"This world of yours, it is frightening in many ways," she said suddenly.

"Frightening? More so than a world of bloody rebellion, abject poverty, and families divided by a mining war?"

"There is that here, too, though it wears different faces," Aramanda pointed out. "No, it is frightening because it seems there are so few people with causes. There is violence with no meaning, no purpose other than greed or the desire to harm. And it is all so fast, so hurried, as if time were ebbing away and one must run to stay ahead of it. . . ." Her words trailed off and she shivered, rubbing her hands over her arms.

She had paled and for a moment Sayer was reminded of his first image of her, in the balcony at the auditorium. A fragile, ethereal figure, looking as if at a touch, she would vanish like a dream.

The impression struck him so strongly that his hand reached out to brush hers. Her skin warmed at his touch. The sensation vanished and Aramanda became very real.

She smiled, the gesture both sad and longing. Carefully, not looking at him, she began refolding the newspaper. "This was not especially helpful. I still know nothing about your work and the people you now associate with. What do you converse about at your get-togethers?"

"Oh, I don't know," Sayer said. "The weather, how bad the traffic is, whether the Phillies are going to win the World Series—nothing too strenuous. Except, in this case, it's more business than idle chitchat."

"Business? Is it business about the mines?"

"Yes." Sayer deliberately kept his tone dismissive to discourage her from asking questions he didn't want to answer right now. Not until he had some more answers about her. Turning a corner onto a narrow street, he indicated a row of shops with a wave of his hand. "Here we are."

He parked the Range Rover in front of a small, exclusive-looking boutique he'd noticed the other day when he'd been reading addresses on the way to the travel agency. There was no question in his mind that Aramanda must have only the best. She wouldn't be comfortable in anything less. And poorly made or ill-fitting clothes would be an insult to her. Her beauty, as near perfection as he'd ever seen in a woman, demanded nothing short of perfection to adorn it.

Glancing into the shop window before he plugged the parking meter, he smiled, confident the store could accommodate Aramanda's elegance.

Handing her out of the rover, he walked over to the parking meter, digging in his pocket for some change.

"What is that?" Aramanda came up behind him. "It takes your coins?" She bent over the meter, tapped it with her fingers, peered at its face. "How odd."

"We have to pay to park."

"Pay whom?"

"The city. Space is limited. And it's an easy revenue-maker."

Aramanda looked at him, her expression between astonishment and disbelief. "A few feet of ground are so in demand, the city makes money by renting them?"

"Overpopulation. One of my major concerns."

"Has the population grown so much?"

"Five billion—and a new baby born every three seconds."

"That seems impossible," she said, shaking her head. "I cannot fathom such numbers."

"No one can, so most people choose to ignore them."

"In this instance, I would certainly find it more gratifying to focus on individuals. I cannot see how you get any satisfaction contemplating the fate of five billion people. It would give me a headache."

"Dealing with individual people sometimes gives me a headache. Come on." Sayer noticed people were slowing as they passed, pausing to gape at Aramanda. Gently, he coaxed her away from the meter. "Let's go see what this place has to offer."

They started toward the boutique, but Aramanda stopped halfway to the door, sucking in a breath, her eyes alight with sudden wonder. "Oh, Roarke . . ."

She pulled away from him and ran a few steps to peer into the window of the shop next to the boutique. "It is a toy store!" she said delightedly when Sayer joined her there. "I have never seen such amazing things!"

Before he could object, Aramanda flung open the shop door and hurried inside, ignoring the startled glances from the plump, elderly man behind the counter and the few customers inside. Shrugging off any irritation he might have felt at her impulsive action, Sayer followed.

He found her kneeling beside a miniature train model, intently watching the lilliputian engine pull its cars through a maze of tiny trees, tunnels, and rock passes.

"It is wonderful!" she said, lifting her face to his. "My brother Oliver would love such a thing! How I wish I could return with it."

She gently fingered the miniscule trees and bushes, picked up a miniature cow and sheep for a closer look, then wonderingly touched the moving engine, smiling in delight as it slid under her fingertips.

Unable to resist her innocent pleasure, Sayer encouraged her to explore the entire store, pointedly ignoring the curious stares of the customers and clerk. She approached each new thing with a child's awe, fascinated most by the hand-held video game he demonstrated for her and a remote-controlled fire engine.

"Please, let me try it," she asked, taking the remote control unit he offered. Eyes shining, her lower lip caught between her teeth, Aramanda pointed it in the direction of the fire truck and wiggled the joystick.

The fire engine whirled in a complete circle, and she laughed. "What mayhem Oliver and Penelope could cause with this!"

"You're not doing too badly yourself," Sayer said, shaking his head and smiling as she abruptly shoved the joystick upward and sent the fire engine racing headlong into a precariously stacked display of boxed baby dolls.

The boxes toppled in a heap. Aramanda gave a guilty sideways glance and bit her lip.

The clerk behind the counter raised his brows, then shook his head and waved off Aramanda's mess with a look that clearly said he'd given up expecting adult behavior from the pair of them.

Sayer tried to look annoyed, failed miserably, and Aramanda began to giggle.

"I believe I need more practice," she said, as she helped him pick up and restack the boxes.

"Well, I was thinking of introducing you to roller blades, but after this demonstration—what's wrong?"

In the act of picking up one of the dolls that had half slid out of its box, Aramanda had stopped suddenly. She gently coaxed the doll out the rest of the way and held it in her hands, stroking its tight red curls with a reverence due a living child.

Tears came to her eyes. She blinked them away though she could not quite keep the tremble from her voice. "It is nothing. Only . . ." She stroked the doll's rosy cheek. "She reminded me of someone, someone who is no longer with me."

Sayer covered her hand with his, squeezing lightly. "We'll find your family and you'll see her again."

"No, no I will not." Aramanda brushed an errant dampness from her face with the back of her hand. "I will not because she is no longer with us, in my reality or yours."

Very carefully, she returned the doll to its box and put it atop the others.

Not knowing what to say to comfort the grief he sensed in her, Sayer simply took her hand in his and began to lead her out of the shop.

They'd nearly reached the door when Aramanda spied a basket of woolly stuffed koala bears. Sayer saw the child's delight flash in her eyes and wanted to keep it there.

"You know, you should always have a souvenir from your journeys," he said. Giving the bears a serious consideration that elicited a small smile from Aramanda, he finally selected the largest and fattest of the bunch, a plush, gray-and-white with a large, bright gold ribbon around its neck.

"This is definitely the one," Sayer said. Handing it to Aramanda with an exaggerated bow, he added solemnly, "A gift for you, milady."

"Thank you, kind sir," she said, and held the bear close as Sayer paid the clerk for the indulgence, glad he had succumbed to a moment's impulse when he saw the shadow of sadness lift from Aramanda's face.

"And now," he said, guiding her outside once again, "I think Mr. Bear is going to have to wait in the car while we do something about your clothes."

"Ah, I had hoped you had forgotten," Aramanda said, watching Sayer place the bear in the back seat of the rover. "Perhaps we could attend to this in your rooms, have a seamstress come there."

"Even if I could find a seamstress, and even if she'd be willing to come to my hotel room, which I seriously doubt, we don't have time. You need clothes now. Trust me on this one." Not giving her time to protest further, Sayer led Aramanda into the boutique.

They stepped inside and a matronly woman, her face caked

with makeup, walked up to them. Her drawn-on brows raised, she swept an astonished head-to-foot gaze over Aramanda.

"She needs a new dress," Sayer said flatly.

The woman repeated her evaluation on him. "I can see that."

Feeling a hot flush of discomfort under the woman's unwavering stare, Aramanda stepped over to a dress rack and fingered the cloth of several dresses. "The material is fine, but . . . there is little of it here." She turned to Sayer, confused. "I do not understand. I thought you said we were going to purchase clothing, not undergarments," she said, blushing as the last word came from her lips, and Sayer grinned.

"I—surely a seamstress could adjust this," she said quickly, indicating her dress.

"I don't think so," Sayer said, putting away his smile with difficulty. "We'll have to make do with what's here."

"But—" Aramanda stopped, self-consciously fidgeting with the skirt of her dress. "If you insist. It appears I do not have much choice."

Sayer stepped close to her and murmured in her ear. "It's something here, or nothing at all."

Aramanda blushed even more hotly, shooting him a vexed glance, but Sayer saw that his remark had succeeded in easing a little of her uneasiness and he grinned back at her, then turned to the clerk. "She needs something for evening cocktails. And a few things for everyday. Her luggage was lost in transit," he added with a weak attempt at an explanation.

"I see." The clerk walked to a rack of dressy clothing, flicking apart several hangers. She eyed Aramanda with professional appraisal. "You're a six, aren't you?"

"You must excuse me—a six?" Aramanda looked to Sayer for a translation.

"What size do you wear?"

"Size? I . . ." Glancing at Sayer again, seeing his teasing smile, she turned back to the clerk, lifting her chin and meeting the woman's eyes with a straightforward look. "I measure twenty-four inches at my waist, thirty-three here—" She pointed to her hips. "—and here—above, I am thirty-four inches. Is that what you wish to know?"

The woman shot Sayer a questioning look. He shrugged and she turned back to Aramanda, forcing a smile. "A six. As long as the bust is roomy, that is." She pulled several dresses from the rack and draped them over her arm. "This way, dear. You can wait outside the dressing room," she told Sayer over her shoulder.

He took a plush pink chair directly in front of the three-way mirror. "I want to see them on you, okay?"

"You have never before been interested in fashion," Aramanda said, giving him a suspicious glance.

"I'm trying to expand my horizons."

"I suppose that means you do not trust me to choose something proper for your get-together. I will show them to you, but only if they flatter me."

It seemed like an hour to Sayer before the clerk emerged from the dressing room laden with petticoats, corset, and the heavy gown Aramanda had shed. Her face, except for the bright lips and cheeks, had paled to paste. She held out Aramanda's clothing, handling it gingerly. "These fabrics, these seams, the hand-stitching, her underclothes—they're museum-quality garments. Priceless. Who is she?"

Sayer smiled confidently, standing up and moving closer to the woman in a suggestion of intimacy. "Old money," he said in hushed tones, as if parting with a well-kept secret. "Very eccentric."

"Local family?"

"Does the name Montclair ring a bell?"

"She's a Montclair? Good heavens, I had no idea one of them was—well, different."

"I can count on your discretion, can't I? Her mental condition is so fragile, any publicity might push her over the edge. The family is very protective of her."

"Of course. Certainly. I understand perfectly. Poor dear."

Aramanda's voice suddenly came from the dressing room, scandalized, with a touch of anger. "I will not wear this! I do not know what you intended me to look like, Roarke Macnair, but these garments are not even suitable to sleep in!"

"Just let me take a look."

"No!"

"Come on, Aramanda," he coaxed. Glancing back at the clerk, he stepped up to the dressing room door and whispered, "I've seen you in less."

"I thought you did not remember," she retorted.

"I have a good imagination."

"You do not need a good imagination for these garments." Her head held high, cheeks aflame, she stepped out of the dressing room, staring defiantly at him as if daring him to make a suggestive comment.

Sayer found himself gaping at her in awestruck wonder. "It's— you are perfect. You're beautiful."

He stared, mesmerized, as Aramanda turned in front of the three-way mirror, frowning as she tried to analyze his reaction to the simple, elegant lines of the sleeveless, black-crepe sheath.

The material fit her like an embrace, from the slightly revealing scoop of the neckline to the fitted waist and the hem that clung just above her knees. Aramanda frowned at the long expanse of bare leg, twisting to look at the dress's back that scooped even lower than in front. The dark, coppery red of her hair glinted with fiery highlights under the shifting lights, and the ivory of her skin became rich cream against the contrast of velvety dark fabric.

"You are staring," she said, noticing Sayer's intent gaze.

"I don't think I could ever get enough of simply looking at you," Sayer said softly, his eyes caressing.

The intimate look felt as if he stroked her skin with his hands, and Aramanda smiled, filled with a warm, liquid pleasure as she forgot her discomfiture, forgot everything but Roarke.

Her expression made something twist inside Sayer. It scared him that the feeling she elicited came close to worship. Who she was, where she had come from didn't matter. It mattered only that, for now at least, this strange, beautiful woman was here with him, looking at him as if he were the only man she ever wanted to be with.

"I didn't think one dress could bring about such a transformation," Sayer finally said.

"You are lovely," the clerk told Aramanda, fussing with the shoulder of the dress so it lay straighter against her skin. "Such beautiful hair, and with skin like that, you don't even need foundation."

"It is still indecent!" Aramanda said. She tugged at the hem, and her uneasiness returned. She had never felt so . . . so *bare.* "I cannot possibly wear this in front of anyone but you, Roarke. I would be mortified to be seen in a garment this short and . . . and revealing. I might as well attend your get-together in my shift!"

"This is actually rather modest compared with what some are wearing now," the clerk told her. "Why this is nearly knee-length. The current style is several inches shorter."

"Shorter! Why, such a frock would reveal . . . it would reveal all one's flaws."

"If yours are revealed, I certainly don't see them," Sayer said, the feeling in his voice betraying his attempt to stay matter-of-fact.

"It's the fashion, dear," the clerk said. "Short skirts are here to stay, they say. At least for another season. You look wonderful in it, I must say, just as though it were made for you."

Aramanda fingered the delicate fabric, fussed with the shoulders and waist, turned, and turned again in front of the mirrors. "I cannot wear this. I feel as if I am wearing my undergarments before strangers."

"Well, of course you do," the saleswoman clucked. "You need lingerie. A strapless bra would work best with that. I'm sorry but we don't sell them here. There's a shop just down the block, though, that does. I'll give them a call if you'd like and let them know you're coming." She started for the telephone behind the counter.

Sayer nodded absently, his eyes fixed on Aramanda. "You look breathtaking. But I want you to feel as comfortable as possible tonight, so if you don't like this, try on another one."

"I have looked at several of them and this is the most modest I can find that the seamstress says is suitable for get-togethers." She looked at him, lightly catching her lower lip between her teeth. "Do you like it so much?"

"I like you in it," he confessed. The husky note in his deep voice made her skin shiver. "But then I'd find you beautiful even in rags. Whatever you choose is fine with me."

"Do you promise me other women wear so little to such affairs?"

Sayer stifled a laugh. "Much, much less in many cases."

"I cannot understand it." Aramanda shook her head. "What has happened to women that they are willing to be seen dressed like—like this? Even women with no reputation to protect would not be seen in such things in a public place. My mother would have locked me in the attic for a year if I'd dared don a dress of this sort, even if I'd never left my bedroom."

"They got liberated."

"Liberated? Freed? To wear frocks that are next to undergarments on the street? Surely that is not one of your causes?"

"I'll try to explain that one in the car."

The saleswoman returned from making the phone call, a pair of mid-heel black pumps in her hands. "If you've decided on that one, I think these will match it perfectly."

Aramanda slipped the shoes on her bare feet. Though they fit, she wobbled around the store in them for several minutes while Sayer watched, amused at the way she scrunched her nose at the offending footwear.

They spent another hour choosing a few dresses for daywear, Aramanda firmly resisting slacks or shorter skirts after one appalled glance at them. She insisted instead on ankle-length dresses, light floating colors and florals with a touch of Victorian style. Finally, dressed in the black crepe again, she practiced walking about the shop in the unfamiliar heels while Sayer settled the bill.

"The lingerie shop is three doors down, then take a left at the crosswalk. You'll see it on the corner. It's called Marie's. Sandy is expecting you."

"Thanks. You have my credit card number. Could you send this along to my hotel? Oh, and I'll take her old clothes along with us."

"Certainly, sir, I'll take excellent care of her. And don't worry, I won't breathe a word of this to anyone," she said, stuffing the discarded pile of Victorian clothing into a plastic shopping bag.

"I'll mention your kindness to the Montclairs."

"Oh! Thank you. And do come again."

The clerk watched them leave the shop, Sayer's hand possessively curved against Aramanda's back, and sighed. "Such an attractive couple," she murmured. "Her so beautiful and him so dark and handsome. And so obviously in love with her."

Her face crinkled. *It's strange, though, about her clothing.* Museum-quality, she was sure of it, and looking as if it had been made only a few weeks past, although it smelled faintly of smoke and dust. The girl had a way about her, too, as though she belonged in a museum as well.

Ah, well, she thought as she packaged up the clothing to send to the hotel, it was all very romantic. Even if the poor girl was a little crazy.

After watching Aramanda struggle with the high heels, Sayer decided they had better use the time to walk instead of drive to the lingerie shop and the travel agency. He tossed Aramanda's discarded clothing into the back seat of the Range Rover beside the koala, plugged the meter again, and turned to find Aramanda, her eyes full of a mix of wonder and uncertainty, drinking in the people, cars, and buildings around them.

"It has changed so much," she said, catching his gaze. "I recognize a building here and there, but the whole picture of it is like seeing this city for the first time. Are people always so rushed, so rude to one another?"

"It seems that way," Sayer told her with a rueful smile. "People don't have much time for gracious greetings on street corners anymore. I feel like I spend most of my time dashing back and forth between cities and speeches and the rest of it buried in paperwork."

"It never used to be that way," Aramanda said, taking his arm as they headed down the sidewalk toward the travel agency. "I cannot imagine you fretting over papers, or even having a place to keep them. You preferred to be in the middle of the fight. I remember how you hated the times when you were away from it."

"I still do. I just don't have time anymore."

"I see," she said, sounding as if she didn't. "I hope it is not far. These shoes are a punishment to the feet. Why have women not been liberated from them as well?"

"Another societal contradiction, I guess. Just wait until I introduce you to Reeboks—liberated shoes."

"Those I would like to see now," she said with a grimace.

"I'm afraid you can only wear them with dresses like that in New York City."

"Different fashions for different cities?" Aramanda frowned slightly, glancing at a few passersby. "That, too, is odd."

"Odd is exactly what you see in New York. Look, the next door is the travel agency. How are your feet holding up?"

"I believe at least I have found how to balance in these shoes. But I prefer my soft boots."

"You're already walking and looking like a runway model."

"Oh." Aramanda flushed, darting a look around them. "I hope that is not an embarrassment to you."

Sayer grinned. "It means you are the envy of every woman we pass and I'm the envy of every man. Haven't you noticed the jealous stares?"

"I thought they were staring because of this dress," she said in a low, fast voice.

"They are, but not for the reason you think. Here it is." They stopped in front of the travel agency, and Sayer grabbed the handle, rattling it a few times. "What?" he muttered when it scarcely budged.

"It is closed. Look," Aramanda said, her voice sinking. She pointed to a tiny, neatly lettered *closed* sign that hung askew in the corner of the shop window.

"Hell." Sayer pounded on the window, ignoring Aramanda's raised brow at his curse. "I'll bet they're in there."

Aramanda cupped her hands around her face and pressed her nose to the window. "It is dark. I do not see anyone. Perhaps they truly are closed."

Sayer rattled the knob and pounded on the door again. Nothing. "It's useless. If they are in there, they're not about to open this door. I'm half tempted to break it down."

"Only half tempted? You surprise me. You never had any fear of the law. Even when you should have."

"I don't know what would have happened to me in your day for breaking and entering, but I don't have the time for a stint in the city jail right now."

"I should think that would be the least of your worries. Before, you would not have had to worry about prison. You would simply have been hanged."

"Nice," Sayer said with a grimace. "And efficient, I suppose. Not justice at its best maybe, but it would make me think twice about breaking down a door."

"It never has before." Aramanda stared at the dark store window, her eyes wistful. "Those two are my only hope of returning to my reality. They must help me. Oh, Roarke . . ." She turned to him, a plea in her gaze and voice. "If I could believe that my coming to your reality is the answer to my prayers, then I would leave my past behind to stay with you."

"You loved me—Roarke Macnair—that much?" Sayer felt a surge of unfamiliar emotion. Like longing and possession and a desire to regain something dear he had lost. "To leave your family? Your whole world?"

"I loved you that much. I do still."

"I hope he deserved you," Sayer said, lifting a hand to touch an errant auburn curl. "Though from what you've told me, I can't see how he could have."

"Not he. You, Roarke. You are my love, no other. And we

deserved each other. Because there was never another choice for either of us, despite all that divided us. You must know that."

She made no move to touch him, but Sayer inexplicably felt her hands on his body, stroking, caressing. The sensation was intimate and deep-reaching and real enough to make him feel exposed to the people who walked by them.

"No, I don't. You're asking me to believe that all my hopes, all my fears, all my—desires, belong to someone else. That's quite a leap of faith."

"You had that faith. Once. And you gave it to me. You showed me how to believe in myself, in us. I only wish now I had enough of it to find peace in my heart about my family. I know they are . . . gone." She stumbled over the last word, and Sayer knew she refused to say the word dead. "But Mama needed me to protect her from Gervase. He was pushing her to marry him to secure the family fortune, and she was weakening. Without me, she would have succumbed. The thought of my sisters and brothers living all those years with his cruelty . . . I cannot bear it."

Compelled by her pain to reach out, Sayer took her hand in his. "I wish you didn't have to."

Aramanda gazed up at him, anguish clear in her eyes. "I must find a way to return. If I could believe our destiny is here, I would stay. But I cannot. Time is so short. I feel I must return or we will never be together."

"How do you know that? What makes you so certain you don't belong here?"

"I—I cannot explain it," Aramanda said. She looked at the travel agency window again, and a slight frown creased her forehead. "I only know it is the truth. And yet . . ." She turned and looked fully into his eyes again. "Here, I have been given my heart's desire, to touch you, to be with you again. How is it possible to gain everything and nothing in the same moment of time?"

"I don't know." Without hesitation, Sayer pulled her close, holding her against him. Her emotion trembled through him, reaching his heart as a long ache. "Try not to worry now. We'll work this out somehow. We'll track down your family, and tomorrow we'll camp on this doorstep until those little moles crawl out. They have to go through this door sometime."

"Do you think so?" As if sensing his conflicting feelings at having her in his arms, she gently disengaged herself from his embrace. "I have the strangest notion those people knew we were coming and closed the shop rather than speak with us," she said, meeting his brisk stride easily now as they started up the sidewalk again.

"I was just thinking the same thing. They know a lot more than they're telling us. I hate to be a bully; but next time we see them, either they'll answer our questions or we'll stay put until they do."

When they rounded the corner and Marie's lacy, wrought-iron sign came into view, he slipped his arm around her waist, liking the way she felt against him. She made no protest, but leaned into him, fitting against his side as if heaven had created that place for her.

They stopped outside the lingerie shop. "No need to talk about this now," Sayer murmured soothingly. "It's not as though you can go back right now. Right? So, let's just deal with the present. With tonight. Tomorrow, we'll think about tomorrow."

"I have no other choice at the moment, do I?"

"No, but we can make your life a little easier. I suppose you'd rather do this on your own; so, buy anything you like or need in there, okay?" he said, handing her his credit card.

"Thank you," Aramanda murmured, barely glancing at the little square of plastic. "No matter where I belong, with you here, I feel safe. You always make me feel protected, no matter the danger."

"Let's hope I can live up to your expectations," Sayer said, letting her go and stepping back. She'd thrown him off balance again, one moment making him comfortable with their strange familiarity, the next disconcerting him with her intimate insights into him, the expectations of his character she took for granted.

He watched her as she went into the shop, beautiful and graceful in the clothes he'd dressed her in. Even so, it was as though she were only playing out a part for his benefit, the true woman disguised as she struggled to adapt to a reality alien to her and everything she was. She looked the part, but he knew somehow Aramanda was right.

She was in a place she did not belong. And he didn't have the faintest idea where she did belong or how to return her there.

Aramanda walked tentatively inside, grateful Roarke knew she would be embarrassed at shopping for such personal items with him at her side, but almost wishing he had come.

Accustomed to playing the role of aristocratic daughter of the Montclairs to shopkeepers who knew her, she now felt completely asea in this strange atmosphere where clerks spoke to her with familiarity about such personal matters.

A clerk who knew her name greeted her with a broad smile and a tape measure, and she found herself trying on an array of shocking underclothes. It appeared that in Roarke's new reality, all women were expected to dress like women of easy morals from the skin out.

On the other hand, after the initial discomfort wore off, Aramanda found herself rather enjoying the illicit indulgence. The colors and satins and laces dazzled her with their variety. She hesitated giving Roarke's little card to the clerk in lieu of actual money, expecting at the very least to have the purchases billed to an account.

But the clerk had the notion she was Mrs. Macnair and Aramanda found it easy to use the card to purchase dozens of satin and lace panties and brassieres, silk chemises and stockings, ruffled garters and a light cotton night shift, allowing herself to feel a wicked pleasure in doing so.

All the way to the place they were to gather for "cocktails," she tingled with the light, wickedly pleasurable feeling of thick champagne-colored silk against bare skin. Roarke's frequent glances her way heightened the sensation and made her wish they were returning to the privacy of his rooms.

Perhaps she would then show him the indecent things she had chosen. Perhaps *that* would recall his errant memory.

Her fantasies evaporated into a sudden shot of fear, though, as soon as the carriage stopped and Roarke came around to her door, holding out his hand.

"I do not think this is a good idea," she said, stepping down.

"It'll be all right."

Aramanda nervously ran the tip of her tongue over her lips. His eyes followed the motion, adding to her unsettled feelings. "I am certain I will say the wrong things. What if I do something that humiliates us both? If this is an important evening for you, I do not want to ruin it."

"Relax. It's not that damned important. And it won't last too long. Besides," he added, "you said yourself, you can say and do whatever you want. You've no reputation to protect, only one to make."

"I do not know that I find that comforting." She ran her fingers through her long hair one last time. "Oh, it is hopeless! I can do nothing without pins."

"I wouldn't say that," Roarke said with a grin, sliding an admiring glance over her body. "Just be yourself. They'll be captivated. Trust me. We went over your history in the car already. You've got the story down, right?"

Giving up, Aramanda let her hair fall over her shoulders in a silken rain of fire. "Yes, I suppose."

"Good. But don't worry, if you forget, the way you look tonight, I doubt anyone will care what you say."

"Shall I consider that a compliment?" she asked tartly, grasping his outstretched palm. "For all your pretty speeches encouraging me to speak my mind, I suppose in this time a lady is still required to look becoming but never have opinions on any matter of importance."

"That's not quite what I meant. I think I'm digging a hole for myself."

"If that means you cannot make up your mind whether you want a companion or an attractive possession with you, then I agree."

Sayer helped her down and handed the keys to a waiting valet. Before they walked inside, he bent to brush a feathery kiss across her lips. "It means I want you with me. You are a lady, Aramanda. A real lady. It shows in every move you make. I'm proud to be with you."

"I hope you will remember that when someone tempts you to leave my side."

"And leave you to the wolves? Not on your life."

"Wolves!"

"Men. Just an expression for men."

"Ah, appropriate. That one I will remember."

Taking her arm, he wrapped her hand through the crook of his elbow. "Ready?"

"Do I have a choice?"

She let him lead her to a table in a plush, ornately decorated lounge where three men and one woman sat talking. As they approached, all three men stood. Aramanda breathed a sigh of relief that the company they were to share were apparently gentlemen at least. Roarke's past companions had all been ruffians and miners. With the exception of his brother Liam and a few others, she'd always felt out of place in their presence, knowing she was not one of them no matter how much they accepted her.

The "wolves" did indeed stare openly at her from head to toe. But then, she could scarcely bring them to blame, considering how little she wore. The woman also stared, first at her, then at Roarke, and back to her. If the men were wolves, the lady was a tigress. Aramanda noticed she was dressed even more scantily than herself, in flaming red, her dark hair elaborately dressed, her lips as scarlet as the brief frock.

Aramanda smiled at her, the way she always smiled at women who looked at her that way. Often their expression softened at once; sometimes it grew harder, depending on their motive. This woman obviously resented her for being the woman on Roarke's arm. There was nothing soft about the glint in her dark eyes.

Such was the case with her cousin, Patricia. She had set her hopes on Roarke from the day she laid eyes on him, expecting seduction would work where Gervase's threats and iron hand failed. The way this woman looked at them now, Aramanda wondered if the circumstances were not similar.

"Good evening," one of the men said, ignoring Sayer. He extended a hand to Aramanda.

Surely he didn't expect her to take it in the way men greeted each other. What should she do?

As though sensing her uncertainty, Sayer reached out and shook the man's hand. "Jim, Trisha, hello. Allow me to introduce you to my friend, Aramanda Montclair."

Trisha arched a delicate brow. "Montclair?"

"A very distant relative," Roarke explained.

"How do you do?" Aramanda said, forcing herself to appear confident. Thank heavens Mother had taught her well how to hide her emotions in social situations. She managed even to hide her surprise at the similarity of the woman's name to her cousin's. Another coincidence of Roarke's reality?

"My daughter and I are delighted to meet you," Jim returned.

The agitated look on Trisha's face contradicted her father's graciousness. "What sort of a welcome is this, Sayer?" she asked, moving toward him. She slid a slender hand against his face, leaned close, and kissed him firmly on the mouth. "It's been nearly three years, you know. I thought you'd forgotten me."

Aramanda held her irritation in check. What did this woman mean to Roarke? What did he mean to her? she wondered.

As though he could read her thoughts, he drew back, shooting Aramanda an uncomfortable glance. "Has it been that long?"

"Yes. I was beginning to consider putting my name on the endangered species list to catch your attention."

"I've been very busy," Sayer said, slipping a reassuring hand across the small of Aramanda's back and urging her to take a seat.

Aramanda breathed a sigh of relief. Apparently he did not share Trisha's remorse over the long separation.

"You two can catch up later," Jim put in. "At the moment, I'm afraid my associates are pressed for time. This is Harvey Irons and Chuck Wallington, my guests from Washington."

"A pleasure to meet you," the red-headed man called Harvey

said. The other one—shorter, dark, and balding—nodded in agreement.

Sayer led Aramanda to sit down next to Trisha. She noticed the irritated flash in Trisha's eyes that must have meant the empty chair had been designated for him.

"Well, well, now I understand why you missed our first meeting," Jim said, smiling broadly at Aramanda.

"I had a feeling you would excuse my behavior if you met the cause."

Trisha gave Aramanda a brittle smile. "Sayer has certainly been keeping you a secret. How long have you known each other?"

Aramanda breathed one deep, slow breath to soothe herself—a trick her mother had taught her. "Only a short while."

"You have an odd accent. Are you from Philadelphia?"

"Originally. Roarke and I unexpectedly discovered each other here a few days ago," some perverse sense of humor made her add. "Now I feel as if we have known each other forever."

"Roarke?"

"Aramanda prefers my middle name," Sayer put in quickly.

"I thought you hated it," Trisha said. "You told me you did."

Aramanda saw a spark of annoyance in Roarke's eyes intended for Trisha and smiled secretly to herself. Perhaps he was right. There were advantages to not having a reputation to ruin or a family name to protect. "I have called him Roarke since we were first acquainted."

"Aramanda is here on vacation. She lives abroad," Sayer interjected smoothly, "but we don't want to take up Harvey's and Chuck's time exchanging personal histories. I know you both have a plane to catch."

"Yes, unfortunately we have to be back in D.C. tonight," one of the men said.

In the first nervous moments of their greeting, Aramanda had already forgotten which one was which. They looked alike for the most part—middle-aged, dark suits, white shirts, clean shaven. Respectable despite their unfamiliar dress.

"Then I'll get right to the point," Sayer began. "As you know, the Soil Conservation Society picketed and demonstrated against Winokur Company's mine up in Fayette County. They're asking them to close in compliance with reclamation statutes. The mine is in violation, and the society is threatening to file a civil suit, demanding it be shut down until reparation is made."

"The activists did manage to get a temporary closure through sheer harassment of workers," Jim put in. "Finally, after months of battling their tactics, which went far beyond picket signs—" He glanced at Sayer. "—the workers refused to show up on the job site. The management was forced to shut down."

Sayer shrugged. "That's what it took to get management's attention. They're now gambling the society can't afford the cost of a lawsuit. They're planning to reopen the mine next week."

A servant girl wearing an even shorter skirt than herself appeared and asked for drink orders. Aramanda turned to Roarke and he ordered for her, a light white wine.

"Is the mine in violation of the law?" Trisha asked when the girl had rounded the table.

"Absolutely," Sayer said without hesitation.

"Well, now, hold on there Dr. Macnair, let's not jump to any conclusions," Harvey said. "My colleagues in the Bureau of Mines are investigating the situation. That's as far as it goes right now."

"We're aware of the problem, and we're looking into it," Chuck added. "I don't know what else we can do for you at this point, do you Harvey?"

The servant interrupted then, delivering refreshments all around.

"As I said," Chuck resumed when she'd gone, "we're investigating."

Sayer gripped the table's edge, his jaw tensing. Aramanda recognized the gesture, almost feeling the heat of his temper. *This* was the Roarke Macnair she knew well, no matter what he called himself in this reality.

She felt the passion in him, the fire of anger as a living thing. And as always, the intensity of the volatile combination both stirred and frightened her.

"You know damned well what I want you to do," he said. "What you should do. Slap a criminal suit on the mine. It's in violation, and you know it."

The two men from Washington exchanged a glance. "What's your opinion on this, Jim?" Harvey asked.

"Well, my staff does find the mine to be behind on its obligation to reclaim stripped land. But I don't think any lawsuits, civil or criminal, are necessary at this juncture. Maybe a little pressure from the right quarters will solve the problem without losses in time and legal fees all around." He smiled at Sayer. "No need to start a war when a little skirmishing will do the trick."

"The publicity will certainly be more positive," Trisha said, patting her father's arm. "Compromise is always the least damaging to a company's image in these cases."

"I don't give a damn about their image," Sayer snapped, his tone drawing another raised brow from Trisha. "The mine is breaking the law. I want it shut down until the land can be reclaimed. That's my compromise."

"I am not surprised," Aramanda said before she could think to stop herself.

Every one of the group turned to stare openly at her. Sayer was momentarily speechless.

Aramanda, with their attention on her, plunged ahead, feeling a rash courage in knowing that anything she said could make no possible difference in her reality.

"Your words are different, but their meaning is the same," she said to Sayer. "You argue your cause, consumed with your beliefs, unyielding in your beliefs. You never see the possible compromise."

"And what is your opinion, Miss Montclair?" Trisha asked, her tone almost purring, her smile satisfied as she glanced at Sayer's tight expression. "Your family owns most of the mines in the state. Surely you don't advocate closing them all down?"

Aramanda straightened in her chair, her aristocratic breeding, innate family pride, and dignity taking over where her courage failed. "Although my knowledge of this particular circumstance is incomplete at best, I believe the greatest concern should be for the miners and their families. If the mine is inoperative, they do not receive their wages. How are the families surviving? Perhaps, if the mine is indeed in violation of a law, some of the workers could be made to repair the problem while others return to the mines. That way, all interests would be served."

The group fell deathly silent. Aramanda feared she had said something unforgivable, but could not regret it.

"Perhaps I spoke too quickly," she said, guessing that men in this time, despite what Roarke had told her, did not care for a woman with ideas on politics. Still, she refused to be intimidated by them or Trisha, who was staring daggers at her.

Looking at Sayer, she met his gaze fully. "But I do believe compromise is best, no matter what others will make of it."

"It's a possibility, in the best of circumstances," Sayer said, his voice hard, "but the chances of its working out your way are slim. The company will lose too much money if their people are out planting trees instead of mining coal. The management isn't going to comply with the law unless they are forced to."

Aramanda held her ground. "In your opinion, Roarke," she countered. "You were never willing to consider that option, and I see you have not changed in the least. But I do understand the notion of profits outweighing justice. My own uncle—my family has been guilty of the same reasoning."

Jim eyed her suspiciously. "You're not a lawyer, by chance, are you? There is a young lady in your family who is."

Aramanda paused and sipped her white wine, giving herself a moment to think. "She is a cousin."

Sayer's hand found hers under the table. He gave it a hard squeeze and Aramanda sensed his reassurance, although she knew he was angry at her bold remarks.

"What Aramanda is talking about has to do with one of her family's mines," Sayer said.

"Yes," she nodded, without the slightest notion what he was referring to, guessing he'd concocted the idea just then to explain her too-personal accusations.

"Are you forewarning us of your next crusade, Dr. Macnair?" Chuck asked.

"I'm a long way from finishing this one."

Harvey looked at his watch and shoved away from the table. "I'm afraid we'll have to be leaving for the airport in a few minutes."

Sayer backed his chair up and stood with them. "If that mine reopens, there's going to be trouble. I won't drop this until that land is taken care of."

"It's a shame you environmentalists are so underfunded. If your society just had the money to file their suit, then this little mess could be resolved without involving us." Harvey cocked his chin slightly upward at Roarke and looked at him directly. "Couldn't it?"

Sayer's eyes went hard. "It's these 'little messes' that have nearly destroyed this planet. But this one is going to be cleaned up—even if I have to put a shovel in each of your hands to do it."

"You're pushing the limits of your rights," Jim hurriedly put in. "And our guests' patience, I think."

Chuck gave an uneasy laugh and slapped a hand on Sayer's shoulder. "Now, there's no need for all this. Just leave this in our hands. A man like you has bigger fish to fry. We'll take care of whatever cleanup the law requires."

Jim stood then and pressed into the tight, tense triangle. "That's the best suggestion for all concerned for the time being. Let them finish their investigation, Sayer. Call off your radicals for a little while."

"I'm sorry, gentlemen, but I can't do that. You see, that's the problem. We've already run out of time." He reached for Aramanda's hand. "If you'll excuse us, I know you two have a plane to catch and we have a dinner reservation. Good night Jim, Trisha."

Trisha jumped to her feet. "But when will I see you again?"

"I'll be in touch. Thanks for the drink."

Aramanda murmured a quick good-evening, unable to resist Sayer's tug on her hand without an embarrassing scene. She let him practically drag her out of the elegant hotel to avoid drawing attention to them.

But the evening's confrontation left a sick, sad feeling in the pit of her stomach. It was happening all over again. They were divided once more, forever divided. Nothing had changed and, at this moment, she saw no hope of making a difference.

If she returned, if she stayed, Roarke would remain the man she had both loved and despised.

She was destined to lose him to his ideals. Past, present, or future.

Five

The softly spoken notes of a harpsichord greeted Aramanda as she stepped out of the mist into the doorway of the restaurant, Sayer's hand resting lightly at her waist. Tiny dancing flames of hurricane lamps cast a muted amber glow in the entry foyer, a welcome contrast to the sharp blazes of white light flashing by them in the streets.

The delicate music, the gentle golden glimmer, the familiar feel of her lover's touch, all might have been a comfort. Except that the moment she entered the narrow room, she was engulfed by the now-familiar, keen awareness of being an outsider in a place she did not belong.

The feeling struck her with force this time, dizzying her, and she stumbled a pace, saved from grasping out for some support by the quick pressure of Sayer's hands. She managed to smile away the look of concern he gave her, hiding the faint, hollow sensation inside until it passed.

The restaurant itself distracted her from it, at least.

A tall, slender woman with oddly bobbed blond hair stood behind a podium tucked in a far corner of the foyer, idly tapping a sheet of paper in front of her with a long, scarlet nail. Her smile switched from perfunctorily polite to brilliant when she recognized Sayer.

"Good evening, Dr. Macnair. We weren't expecting you this evening. It's such a pleasant surprise." The smile went from brilliant to dazzling, managing to imply much more than the word pleasant would allow. "I've seen your name all over the newspapers lately. In fact, I'm surprised to see there isn't a reporter or a television camera following you around. With all the trouble you've gotten yourself into, I thought you might still be hiding away in the mountains."

In Roarke's reply, Aramanda saw a flash of the infectious charm she knew too well. "My hiding places are more genteel these days, and I take great care to avoid the press when I can. Tonight, I made an impulsive decision. I hope you'll reward me with a table by the fireplace."

"For two?" The woman scraped Aramanda with a glance, a clear mix of jealousy and dismissal in her expression.

"For two," Sayer said firmly, taking Aramanda's arm in a possessive grip.

As the woman walked around the podium, Aramanda's eyes widened. The woman's icy-white dress plunged low enough to expose most of her bosom; and as she turned from them, she revealed a completely bare back down to her waist.

"You're staring," Sayer murmured as the woman left them alone at a table tucked in an intimate corner near a large open fireplace.

"I-I am sorry. I . . ." Darting a look around them, she leaned toward him and whispered sharply, "Why did you bring me to a . . . a bordello? If this is your notion of a place I would enjoy, then you have forgotten much more than I ever imagined!"

To her consternation, he began to laugh. "A bordello?"

"A house of ill repute then," Aramanda said, hot color rushing to her face. She sat straight in her chair, holding herself stiffly. "I confess, I do not see what you find so amusing. Is this where you take all the women of your acquaintance?"

"Only the ones who have defied destiny to find me."

For a moment, Aramanda thought him serious—until she saw the laughter glinting in his eyes and the upward twitch of his mouth. Primly crossing her hands on the table in front of her, she looked him square in the eye. "I trust the fare is at least adequate."

"More than adequate." He paused and then, as if acting on an uncontrollable impulse, reached out and took her hand in his.

"And I wasn't kidding. You're the first woman I've brought here. It's a bit too dignified and old-fashioned for most of the women I know. But, somehow, it suits you. And not because it's a bordello," he said with a flash of his wicked grin. Sobering, he searched her face before adding, "Plunging necklines and backless dresses are as common and as acceptable as short skirts in 1996, you see." Reluctance tinged his voice, as if his own comment made him uncomfortable.

"Yes, well, I am glad I was able to find something a bit more modest to wear at least. Though it seems all of the women you know wear as little as possible."

"You make it sound as if I have a harem."

"Do you?"

"Not in this lifetime," he said. "How about in yours?"

Aramanda flushed. "You could have, easily. It seems I still have much to learn about your reality," she added quickly. "More than I had imagined. For example, everyone has been calling you doctor. I am impressed. You practice medicine now?"

He smiled again. "Not quite. I'm not a medical doctor. I have a doctorate in environmental science."

"Environmental—" Aramanda shook her head, confused by the term.

"I work to convince people to stop abuses of the environment—lobbying for alternative energy sources and tougher environmental legislation, ensuring protection for endangered species, cleaning up polluting industries, that sort of thing."

"Ah—your causes. You are still fighting to create perfection from all that is flawed. You have only found different ideals to wage war for. Although the Montclair mines seem to be one of your main battles yet again."

"It isn't as violent as you seem to think. Maybe your Roarke Macnair used fire and mayhem to make a point, but my weapons are generally words and political maneuvering. And you certainly wielded a few words of your own to put us both in the middle of it back at Jim's little party," Sayer said, his expression torn between amusement and exasperation.

"You always insisted that I cultivate my opinions and speak

my mind. And you did remind me I have no reputation to protect—only one to make, you said," Aramanda told him, smiling. "I am only following your advice."

Sayer pulled a quizzical face. "Why don't I believe that? And by the way, there's nothing wrong with having ideals. I don't happen to care for many of the realities I see."

"No, you never have. And you are courting trouble as usual, it seems. I am beginning to realize time alters only the outsides of things, not the hearts of them." She studied his face, seeing both the Roarke of the past and the Sayer Macnair of the present. Two men, one soul. Could she somehow change the future of either?

The arrival of a waiter interrupted conversation, leaving Aramanda to brood over her thoughts. Waving aside the offer of a menu, Sayer ordered for both of them with the easy assurance of a man accustomed to having his ideas and opinions listened to and accepted. When the waiter returned with a bottle of white Beaujolais, he poured each of them a glass, lifting his in a lightly mocking toast. "To your past."

"And yours. Or, shall I say, to ours?"

"You have said it, and with determined frequency. You seem to have strong views on the subject of civil rights," he put in quickly, redirecting the topic. "Are you an activist? Or do you do some other kind of human rights thing?"

"Do? Do you mean work?"

"That's the usual meaning."

Aramanda took a sip of her wine, feeling confused all over again. "I do not work. It would hardly be seemly. My mother does not even care for the charitable works I do, though I have refused to forsake them. My duty is at home, helping to care for my family, learning all the skills of a lady."

She fingered the fragile stem of her wineglass. "I know how to behave exactly as those around me expect me to behave. I am quite adept at making polite conversation, painting in water colors, playing the piano, and running a household; and I know all that is required of me for making a good match, although I confess I am quite hopeless at embroidery." Tasting the wine again, she avoided looking at him. "I suppose it all sounds quite insipid to you."

"And to you," he said, raising his own glass. "I'm interested, though, in this charity work. Why does your mother object?"

"Because I spend much of my time among the miners and their families, helping where I can. She—fears for me."

"Is it that dangerous?"

"Dangerous . . . perhaps." Aramanda ran the tip of her finger around the edge of her glass. "But I believe she fears less for my safety than that I become too much like my father. He was an excellent man of business, yet he believed it his Christian duty to protect the welfare of the men who worked in his mines and their families. From the time I was five years old, he would often take me with him when he visited the mining families. I learned much, about sorrow and hardship—and I learned the value of family and faith in facing them."

Something unspoken in her voice made Sayer add, "And love."

She smiled. "And love," she said softly, then sighed, her smile vanishing.

"What happened to him, your father?"

Aramanda looked at her half-filled wineglass, her eyes on the shifting pattern of light against the liquid. "He died of fever when I was ten. He generously left my mother the largest share of ownership of the mines, but my uncle became manager. And Gervase is nothing like his brother. I must now make endless excuses about how I spend my days because he would punish us all if he knew the extent to which I have befriended the miners and their families."

She glanced up at him, a gleam of mischief in her eyes. "Because of that, I am becoming quite adept at subterfuge. It is at least one useful skill I have learned."

Sayer shared her smile, then asked, "Why don't you leave? Make your own way?"

"And go where? Do what?" She made an impatient gesture. "You alone wanted me to abandon home and tradition for an uncertain future. But you never considered how difficult it would have been for me to leave my mother, and my brothers and sisters who depended on me, to give up my entire way of life."

"Was that the only reason you refused?"

"No," she said, looking at him fully. "I wanted so much more than a life of fighting and hiding. I wanted to love and be loved, to have a family undivided by your causes. You, though, wanted to win your war. You still do, it appears. And you still have a way of making the impossible sound so simply done. It is not that way. Not for me. Gentlewomen do not simply 'make their own way.' Not unless they choose to abandon their morals and family reputation."

"Such a cynic," he murmured.

"I am realistic, Roarke. Or . . ." She lifted her wineglass again, smiling at him over the rim. "Should I say Dr. Macnair?"

Sayer smiled back at her, the gesture warm and unaffected. "You seem to find that amusing."

"It sounds so—so odd." Her smile widened as the wine and his smile spread a hazy warmth through her blood. "I remember all the evenings you would return from the mines, wearing more soot and dust than anything, the evenings you would sit by the fire in the taverns, drinking poor lager and spinning the most outrageous tales . . . not like this. This was my world. Now it seems our situations are reversed. I am lost in a moment of the past, unable to go forward or back, and you are here alone in this new future."

The arrival of the waiter bearing their dinner spared Sayer from making a reply. He found himself intently watching Aramanda as she sampled a small bite of the sauteed duck with its raspberry glazing, forgetting his own meal when her face lit with sensual pleasure.

Hers was a face that would remain in the memory of any man who saw her once. Not mere beauty, but line and shape that would retain its ethereal loveliness through all the ages of her life. She had an air of the medieval about her, the proud dignity and spirit of a knight's lady. As he watched her, echoes of a past he remembered only as a dream rippled into the present and reshaped themselves into feelings of unsated longing, unquenched desire.

"As I stare on and on into the past, in the end you emerge . . ."

"What did you say?"

Sayer came to himself with Aramanda's questioning gaze lightly resting on him. "I was just . . . remembering. A line from a poem I once read," he amended quickly. "It reminded me of you."

She raised a brow, but made no comment. "This is delicious," she said instead. "Although—" She stared pointedly at his own untouched portion.

"I'm glad you like it," Sayer said, stabbing his fork into an end of the tender filet.

"I do. I confess, I—" Her sentence broke, her gaze caught and fixed on something over his shoulder.

"What is it?"

"A man. For a moment . . ." Aramanda shook her head. "I thought I recognized him."

"Who did you think it was?"

"Someone from our past," she said, laying slight emphasis on the word *our.* "Scully McGehan. He is a friend. He fought with you, although I always considered him more a scholar than a rebel miner. It is so strange. The woman at your get-together reminded me of someone as well. But it cannot be. He does, though, appear to have recognized you."

Sayer craned his neck to look behind and immediately spotted the scruffy, gaunt figure. The man came up to the table with an apologetic smile.

"Dr. Macnair?" he asked, nodding politely to Aramanda. "Excuse me, but my name is Malcolm Breyer. I've been wanting to meet you for some time. May I have a word with you?"

Sayer extended a hand. "Of course, please join us. I'm so glad to finally meet you in person, Dr. Breyer. I've read every one of your research papers, and I'm very impressed with your work."

"I-I don't mean to interrupt," Dr. Breyer said apologetically, "but it is a matter of some urgency."

"Not at all. Aramanda and I would be honored if you would sit down with us, wouldn't we?"

"Yes, please do sit down."

"Thank you," he said, taking a seat opposite them.

"Dr. Breyer was a professor of biological sciences at Penn State until last May. Now he is the head of a grass-roots environmental group here in Philly."

"You do keep abreast, don't you? I will get right to the point . . . only, may I speak frankly?" He glanced over his bifocals toward Aramanda.

Sayer wrapped an arm around Aramanda's shoulder and smiled. "I assure you, your confidences are safe with both of us."

A deep frown settled over Dr. Breyer's pale brow. "There is a mine up near Scranton, you may know of it. I heard some disturbing rumors about it so I sent a couple of my technicians over from Penn State to check on it."

"I know the mine. My brother and his family live in that area," Sayer said.

"We believe there's radiation leakage in the shaft, but we don't have conclusive enough evidence yet to demand that the EPA shut it down. We're still in the testing phase, you see. We can't get a consistent-enough reading to go public without being shot down; but in the meantime, men are inhaling toxic gas every day."

"Radon poisoning?"

"Precisely."

Sayer shoved his hand through his hair. "Who owns the mine?"

"That's the main problem. The family who owns it has one of the oldest and greatest mining fortunes in the state. They're powerful enough here both socially and politically to silence our little environmental group."

Aramanda's stomach turned over. She knew instinctively what he was about to say.

"The Montclairs own the mine. I'm sure you've heard of them."

Sayer gripped Aramanda's bare knee under the table. "Yes, everyone in Pennsylvania knows that name."

Aramanda took the gesture as a signal not to reveal her identity. Obviously, Dr. Breyer would not finish what he had begun to reveal if he thought he was telling all to the adversary.

"Then you know what we're up against."

"Yes and no. Your credentials are irrefutable. If you say the mine isn't safe, Jim Hatcher will listen to you."

Dr. Breyer paused, seeming to weigh his next words with careful deliberation. "You don't know why I really left Penn State, do you?"

"No—I must admit it seemed an extremely self-sacrificing decision."

"It wasn't my decision at all. Oh, I've always supported a variety of environmental causes, namely the Green Alliance. But I had no intention whatsoever of leaving my position at Penn State to join them. I've never had the courage to be a hero."

"What happened then, if I might ask?" Aramanda put in, drawn by curiosity and a strange empathy for the sadness she heard in his voice.

Dr. Breyer glanced away, his thin shoulders shifting in an uncomfortable gesture. "I was essentially fired. Several of my colleagues, and some students as well, came to the conclusion my extracurricular involvements in environmental causes were diluting the efficacy of my teaching and my research for the university. And, of course, there were the rumors that some of the alliance members were using terrorist tactics as a means to their end. Not the sort of reputation a university professor covets. When my last grant proposal was rejected, it was the final blow."

He looked away. "They didn't offer me tenure. You know what that means. I had no choice but to look elsewhere. Not surprisingly, no other universities I applied to had any openings."

"But you did find another position?" Aramanda asked, genuinely concerned for the older man's welfare.

"Well, yes, but I would rather be back at the university."

"In other words," Sayer said grimly, "someone powerful enough to have you fired didn't like your digging too deeply, so to speak."

"Perhaps." Dr. Breyer shrugged despondently. "Every institution must keep its benefactors happy."

"Meaning the Montclairs."

"I don't doubt it. I can see the matter interests you. I hoped it would. You have a reputation for striding in where angels dare to tread, if you'll pardon the literary liberties. But be careful, Dr. Macnair. These people go for the jugular."

Aramanda shifted uncomfortably in her seat, but she held her tongue.

"Thanks for the warning, but I may just have an ally in the enemy camp."

"That is good news! Well, I'll be excusing myself now. It was a pleasure to meet you, miss—I'm sorry, but I didn't catch your last name."

Aramanda looked to Sayer and found him smiling. "Montclair," she said without apology.

"Mont—what!" Breyer's eyes flashed wide with shock.

"Don't worry, Dr. Breyer. Aramanda lives abroad. In fact, she refuses to be involved with the questionable family business affairs here."

Aramanda frowned at Sayer. "My family and I have often parted ways where the safety of the men is concerned. And I certainly encourage you to complete your work. Why, this may inspire me to move back home. So that I may become *involved*."

"Well, that is a relief," Breyer said, the tentative note in his voice betraying his doubt. "I will continue on, and take you at your word."

Aramanda bristled. "I am an honorable woman, Doctor."

Malcolm Breyer stared hard at Aramanda for a long moment. "I believe you, Miss Montclair. It has been a sincere pleasure to meet you." With that, he shoved away from the table.

"Thank you for coming to me," Sayer said. "I'll be in touch. Oh, and watch your back."

Dr. Breyer shrugged and, with a brief bow to Aramanda, turned to leave.

He stopped a few feet away, though, and came back to the table. "You should know that I will go public with my findings," he said bluntly.

Sayer raised a brow. "Public? Now? You said your test findings were preliminary—"

"I plan to try to get back inside for one more reading. I hope it's strong enough to confirm what I already know."

Sayer looked squarely at Malcolm Breyer. "Before I could back you publicly, which amounts to declaring war on the Montclair empire, I would have to see the evidence myself."

"Caution has never been among your tactics before," Aramanda murmured.

"You're certainly welcome to check my findings," Malcolm said, flicking a curious glance at Aramanda. "In fact, I encourage it. But it's going to be next to impossible for you to gain entrance right now. The administrators have successfully shut down our investigations for the time being. You see, they've managed to slow permit procedures to a snail's pace. But if you could spare the time, we'll get in—one way or another."

"I'll rearrange my schedule. As soon as I've wrapped up my business here, I'll drive up there. I have some research to do, and I plan to pay a visit to Aramanda's family anyway," he said, catching her eye. She frowned at him, suddenly silent. "Are you staying near the mine now?"

"Yes. With friends. Here's my address and number. Just call when you arrive." He handed Sayer the card he'd scribbled on.

"Thanks. But you realize, even if I am able to get in with your technical crew to take readings, it may take some time to pull together a convincing-enough body of information to go public. I don't fight battles without ammunition. I hope you'll reconsider about going public before I'm ready to support you. Once I check the evidence, you'll have my backing and the support of more than a dozen activist groups and I'm sure I can persuade Jim Hatcher to get involved. It'll be worth the wait to have that kind of credibility. And safer for you in the long run, I might add."

"I have nothing left to lose."

"You can't believe that. You're the same man you were before your recent misfortunes, and anyone who knows you will vouch for that. Some of these industries play hardball when they're threatened with having to close or foot the bill for a costly cleanup and restitution. Malcolm, this isn't the time to let your guard down."

Dr. Breyer pondered his words a long silent moment. "Waiting might be the better part of discretion," he said at last. "And if it's only a matter of a few days . . . my concern is for the workers and the effect such a leak could have on the surrounding area. I can't believe the Montclairs are ignorant of the situation. It appears they're simply choosing to ignore it. Perhaps if Miss Mon—"

"Taking on the Montclair empire now, Dr. Macnair?"

The three of them looked up simultaneously at the intrusion of the brash voice, Sayer recognizing a reporter from the *Philadelphia Enquirer* he'd had a run-in with before his speech at the auditorium. He got to his feet, not bothering to hide his ire at the interruption.

"The polite response is *no comment*. How did you know I was here?"

"Your friend, the hostess. Since the last I heard, you were supposed to be on your way to preach the gospel of ecology in Europe, I was interested to see what was keeping you in Philadelphia. It seems it's more than the charming scenery," the man said, sliding a glance at Aramanda.

"Speculation will get you a libel suit."

"So, there is more to it. Are you going after the Montclairs?"

"If I do, you'll be the last to know." Aware of the curious looks they'd drawn from nearby diners, Sayer kept his voice level and flashed a tight smile. "You know where the front door is. If you want to cause a scene, I'll oblige you. But I happen to know the manager prefers paying customers to prying reporters. And I know your publisher's home telephone number. I'm sure he'd appreciate getting an irate midnight call."

For a moment, it looked as if the man intended to take him up on his offer of creating a public ruckus. The moment passed and he shrugged. "Have it your way. This time."

When he'd gone, Sayer sat back down and picked up his glass, finishing off the remains of the wine in a draught. "The perfect end to a perfect day," he said, forcing a smile for Malcolm.

The older man look worried. "I seem to have put you in a difficult position. As well as disrupted your schedule."

"It isn't the first time, and I promise you it won't be the last. Difficult positions are my specialty. And my schedule was already shot to hell," Sayer said, looking at Aramanda. She stayed silent, her unusual eyes studying him with a disconcerting intensity. Sayer jerked his attention back to Malcolm. "It doesn't matter. This is too critical to let slide right now. I'll run up to Schuylkill County as soon as I can. Then we'll decide how best to attack it."

"Very well, and now I really will say good-night."

Sayer expected Aramanda to barrage him with questions about the mine problems the second Malcolm left them alone. Instead, she pushed idly at the remains of the food on her plate, lost in her own thoughts. "I'm sorry about the interruption," he said at last, uncomfortable with her silence.

"I am the one who should be sorry," she said. She looked up at him, her expression plagued by concern. "You have built a life in this time, and I have intruded on it. I am only now realizing how much. You would not say it, but I know your causes are more important to you than anything else. Then and now."

Anything else? More important than family, friends? Love? Sayer wanted to dismiss her words. But he knew they were true.

"I understand," Aramanda said softly, reaching out to touch her fingertips to his hand. "You wish to deny it, but I know your causes are the only hope you have of realizing your ideals. I hate the thought I could cost you that chance once again."

"Do you always worry so much about everyone and everything else?"

Aramanda smiled slightly, drawing her hand away. "It is my enduring weakness, I fear."

"Not a weakness. An endearing strength."

"You never considered it so before."

"Maybe I've learned a few things in a hundred years."

"It would take more than a century to change you, Roarke Macnair," Aramanda said lightly, laughing when he raised a brow and shot her a look of mock annoyance.

The waiter came to clear their dishes, returning with coffee and a tray artfully arranged with an assortment of truffles and miniature pastries.

"I should not," Aramanda said, even as she took one of the rich chocolate delicacies from the tray Sayer proffered her.

"I knew I would discover your passion sooner or later," Sayer teased.

"I always feel wicked, indulging in something so sinfully pleasurable. You are a terrible influence, you know. With you, I can never deny myself. I cannot even find it in myself to have regrets later." The sweet intoxication of dark chocolate and orange liqueur melted against her tongue, but her own words resurrected the taste of sinful pleasures only Roarke could create. He devised a banquet of them for her alone, spreading them over her body, tempting her with a kiss or a touch to sample the same from his own.

"You've left me."

Aramanda gave a start. "I—" Their gazes collided, hers a flash of gold reflected in his blue night.

"Wherever you went, I'd like to visit." *Or revisit,* a rebellious voice whispered inside his head. "You looked lost in paradise."

"Perhaps I was."

Sayer waited for her to say something more, but she stayed quiet, looking at him with a strange mix of sadness and longing in her eyes. He'd seen the warmth of desire there only moments ago, and it gave him an odd sensation—not entirely unwelcome—to realize she was recalling the passion she'd shared with him. Or at least with the man she remembered him to be.

The silence between them lasted until he'd settled the bill and they were both seated in the rover again.

"Where are we going?" she asked as he started the vehicle and began to guide it out onto the street.

He stopped the rover, shifting in the seat to look at her. "Back to the hotel. Did you have something else in mind?"

"No. It is only . . ."

"Only what?"

Aramanda glanced down. When she looked up again, her direct gaze held his. "I would like to be able to refuse, to tell you that I do have elsewhere to go, that I can return to all I know and leave this behind."

"Why?" he asked bluntly, inexplicably stung. "Considering the situation you say you're in—"

"Yes, I know. But all I can think of is that I am being drawn once again into your world, a world of causes and endless battles, bravely defended for the well-being of all with such fervor that there is no time to nourish the good of two." She paused. "No time for love."

"I won't lie and say my career isn't first in my life right now," Sayer said. "And I won't turn my back on whatever problems there are at the Montclair mines. But there's no need for you to be involved. We'll go to the shop tomorrow and find out where you belong. Then you can go home and leave me to fight my battles alone." Aramanda shook her head, and he made an impatient gesture. "What other choice do you have?"

"No other choice. I do not want any other."

Aramanda leaned her cheek against the warm smoothness of the leather seat. On a whim, catching sight of the stuffed bear Roarke had given her, she reached back and retrieved it, hugging it to her. "I have found you again; I have a chance to return and right what is wrong. That is the only choice I want." Closing her eyes, tired of trying to fight the insidious weariness inside, she murmured, "I will be certain this time I do not make the same mistakes. I will find a way home. For both of us."

Mercifully, he did not deny her. Aramanda felt the carriage move forward and accelerate, and she let her thoughts drift along familiar paths of the past.

"What are you thinking about?" he asked quietly after a few minutes. "Or shouldn't I ask?"

"I have no secrets from you. My family," she said, not bothering to open her eyes. Their faces floated in front of her, images from her heart, and her throat constricted. She clutched the bear more tightly, drawing small comfort from its fuzzy warmth. "I cannot help worrying for them, wondering about their fate. And at the same time, I am not certain I want to know. If it is too terrible . . ."

She left the rest of the sentence unsaid. "Surely you can understand," she added, keeping her eyes closed against unshed tears. "You have a family as well."

"I haven't seem them in years. I've been wrapped up in my work. My parents live over a hundred miles from here, and my brother and I have never been close."

Aramanda looked at him, seeing the tense set of his jaw, the hard, forward stare. "No? If your brother still works in the mines, you at least must be concerned for his safety, the hardships the miners must endure. The mine Dr. Breyer spoke of—"

"If what he says is true, then something will get done," Sayer snapped. "And the hardships of miners aren't as bad as you paint them. Besides, Will chose his profession, despite my advice. He's too hardheaded to change his mind now."

"I see. Then you are concerned for him," Aramanda said, as if she had not heard his last words. "But you pretend you are not, just as before. You are just as stubborn as he."

"No one is as stubborn as Will."

"Mmmm . . . you are not close to your family, but is there not anyone whom you care for, who cares for you? Someone special to you who shares your causes?"

"Not really." Sayer didn't look at her, but shifted in his seat, clearly uncomfortable with the personal question. "My career is family enough."

"Is it? Truly?"

"I'm sorry you're worried about your family, that you can't remember where they are," he said, sidestepping the question. "They must miss you terribly."

"I wonder. The not knowing, it must be terrible, as it is for me. And I am worried. So many things have happened, so many things that threaten to divide us."

Aramanda leaned back against her seat again, giving in to the tiredness dogging her by closing her eyes. "My mother has been so burdened with tragedy since Papa died so soon after Oliver was born. She raised her children alone and now she has the added problems of the mines. I fear she will give in and marry Gervase, especially if I am not there to support her. I believe he will go to any lengths to gain complete control of the Montclair fortunes. Even though she does not approve of my support of the miners, Mama relies on me for support."

"So she didn't approve of your involvement in Roarke's rebellion?"

Weary, Aramanda did not even attempt to remind him that to her, he was Roarke. "She feared him, and it distressed her I should have become so involved with such a ruffian. It only gave Gervase a stronger position, yet I could not forsake either side."

"What about the rest of your family? Couldn't they help?"

"Nicholas is too young to assume his responsibilities as eldest son and Jessalyn too worried over the extra household duties to put a stop to it. She will let Gervase bully her. And Penelope and Oliver . . . I don't know who will make certain they get their shortbread and jam at tea." Her words and thoughts began to drift. She snuggled her cheek against the koala. "Oliver's favorite bear needs mending, and Penelope has the sniffles again. . . . Gervase will have them all under his thumb if I cannot return."

Aramanda moved uneasily in her seat. She felt Roarke's hand on her hair—now or in the past?—soothing, lulling her back into the comfort of dreams. She let herself be drawn into the solace of nothingness, her head pillowed against the softness of the stuffed bear.

Minutes—hours?—later, she didn't know which, the motion of the carriage waned, then stopped, and Aramanda felt the cool damp kiss of the night air and Roarke's arms lifting her, cradling her to his chest.

"I can walk." She made a halfhearted protest, her voice muffled by his shoulder, too exhausted to even open her eyes.

"I've no doubt you can," he said, making no attempt to release her, "but there doesn't seem much point in it."

He piloted her through several doorways, to a place that seemed to lift her upward toward the night sky, before finally setting her on her feet long enough to open a final door with a key he fished out of his jacket pocket. Scooping her up again, Sayer kicked the door shut behind them and carried her through the darkness, gently laying her on the soft firmness of a bed.

"Roarke . . ."

"It's all right," he murmured, drawing a thick quilt around her. "We'll talk in the morning."

Putting her trust in him, as she had so many times before, Aramanda curled up under the enveloping warmth with the koala in her arms, letting the present slip away in the misty grayness of her dreams.

Sayer stood at the bedside, looking down at her for a long time. Finally, he left her to sleep, quietly closing the bedroom door behind him.

Alone in the sitting room, he pulled open the heavy drapes covering the triple spread of windows and looked out over the midnight glitter of Philadelphia. He had to decide about her; obviously, she couldn't stay with him forever. His hand strayed to his jacket pocket and he pulled out the frayed blue cloth, rubbing it between his fingers as he stared out at the sleeping city.

Tomorrow. Tomorrow, he would go back to the travel agency and talk to the old couple, get them to tell him where Aramanda Montclair had come from and where she belonged, get the whole thing settled as soon as possible. He didn't have time for this kind of disruption. He was due in London in a week, then back to New York, and then Washington, before—

Sayer sighed. Before—before what? Another lecture, another session of lobbying, more weeks, months of fighting the bureaucrats, the industry heads . . . trying to find the missing part of himself that forever evaded his best efforts. Searching, striving for elusive perfection. For peace.

He looked at the crumpled cloth in his hand, the feel of the material dredging up alien and powerful emotions that seemed to belong to someone else, another person who lived by sword and fire. A man who loved Aramanda Montclair with all his heart and soul.

. . . *Even now, I cannot stop loving you. If I could fight for any cause beyond this life, it would be you, my love.*

Sayer clenched the cloth in his fist, hearing the echo of an explosion and the despair of a lover's tears somewhere in a dark part of his mind. He didn't want to believe it.

But deep inside, his heart and soul couldn't deny it.

Six

A bare touch whispering against her face wakened Aramanda from a light, uneasy doze. She recognized a gentleness and a strength in the warm slide of skin on hers and the musky masculine scent that made her think of hours spent long ago with him in the heat of a summer's night.

The sheets twisted around her as she moved with the memory, remembering the pleasure and the hunger as she watched him come to her, his eyes hot with desire for her, hard muscle flexing under his clothes.

He bent to her, grazing her body with his, his presence a power she could not resist. Murmuring words of love against her mouth, he kissed her, and she tasted the echo of smoke from the fire that always burned within him.

Without opening her eyes, she reached out for her lover. "Roarke . . ."

The warmth cooled; motion stilled. Abruptly drawn out of her dream, Aramanda forced herself to look. A thin gray gleam had penetrated the room, turning blackness into uncertain shadow. But she had no difficulty knowing the man standing over her bed.

"What is wrong?" she asked, pushing her hair aside as she struggled to sit up. "It is early . . ."

"Very early. And the only thing wrong is you're awake. I'm sorry for disturbing you." Sayer's gaze slipped downward from her face, quickly up again. "I'd hoped you would still be sleeping. I risked checking because I didn't want you to wake up alone.

When I get back, we'll go to the travel agency first, then head up to Schuylkill County and do a little research. It's going to be a long day. I'd hoped you could rest as long as possible."

"Where are you going?"

"I couldn't sleep. I thought a run might clear my head."

"And what are you running from?"

The dimness hid his expression, but Aramanda sensed a ripple of amusement. "Myself, I guess. My greatest pursuer. There's no need for you to become a victim of my obnoxious morning routine, though. Go back to sleep. I won't be long."

He made a motion as if to touch her, checking himself a hand's breadth from her shoulder. The woolly vestiges of sleep clearing, Aramanda suddenly remembered she had awakened sometime in the night and stripped off her dress to sleep in the silk chemise and panties she had bought yesterday.

Now, the chemise hung off one shoulder, the fragile material revealing more than it concealed. And she realized with a wanton, aching satisfaction that Roarke, willing or not, had memorized every drape of the material, every nuance of exposed flesh.

"It has been too long already," she murmured. Feeling a brazen need, she slowly lifted her hand and ran her fingertips over his chest, tracing the hard angles and planes under the pliant material of his shirt. "So long . . . the past is a hundred lifetimes ago, yet the feelings, the touch of you is only yesterday for me. You believe I should not remember. But I do not want to forget I loved you. Then, or now. Please—" She hurried on when she saw the denial start in his expression. "Do not tell me again it is impossible, that I have forgotten, or it is only my fantasy. I do not want to hear that you would prefer I vanish without a memory."

"That's not what I want."

"Is it not?"

"No. I want you."

Aramanda caught her breath. She saw the truth of desire in his eyes, yet dared not believe it. "And I, you," she whispered. "There is nothing I want more than to be held in your arms again, to love you once more . . ."

Capturing her hand where it lay trembling against him, Sayer turned her palm up and drew his thumb up and down the sensitive hollow, his eyes intent on hers. Slowly, his gaze never leaving her face, he bent and pressed a lingering kiss into her palm.

"I can't get you out of my head. All I do is think of you, when I should be thinking of a thousand other things. I've tried to stop, to forget you, even for a little while, but I can't." He rubbed his fingers over her wrist where her pulse quickened for him. "You're inside me, and I can't explain why."

"There is no why," Aramanda said, trembling with the need he roused in her with even so simple a caress. "Why should there be? Why should it matter, if that is what we feel?"

"Because it does." Sayer pushed hair off his forehead with a jerking motion.

"Only if that is how you choose it to be."

"If I have a choice, then I'm making it because of you, Aramanda," he said softly, stroking his thumb over her palm again in a hypnotic rhythm.

"Because of me? You know how I feel for you."

"Yes. And that's the reason I can't make love to you now, even if it is all I think about, all I dream about. I do want you. But it's not yesterday for me. I'm not the same man you loved even if, somehow, this crazy idea of yours is true. I can't pretend I am, no matter how tempting it might be. And I won't lie to you; you deserve much more than that. You deserve anything I can give you, and everything I can't." His hand tightened on hers a moment longer; then, carefully guiding her hand back to the sheets, he stepped away from the bed. "I'll be back soon."

Before she could protest or even think of any reply, he quickly turned and left her room. A moment later, she heard the sound of the front door of the suite opening and closing.

Quickly tossing aside the bedclothes, Aramanda hurried to the window and pulled aside the curtains. The misty silver quiet of the predawn painted the gardens and street in front of the inn in pale hazy hues of gray, from charcoal to nearly white. Streetlights made glowing pearls of light, hovering above the pavement. Nothing moved; nothing spoke to disturb the fragile silence.

Aramanda waited, watching, until she saw him. He emerged

from the front door of the inn, trotting down the stairs to the edge of the street, where he paused, glancing back and upward.

Their gazes met, and time paused for an eternity of seconds. In that span, Aramanda felt more strongly than ever before the love that existed between the boundaries imposed by minutes or days or centuries. A presence of feeling that had no beginning, no end.

It vanished as quickly as it had come when Sayer turned and started running up the street, his figure soon swallowed into the early-morning gloom.

Her eyes followed him until all she saw was the same still scene of minutes earlier.

More than an hour later, wrapped in a white silk robe, Aramanda was sitting on the window seat in the main room of the suite, watching the sun edge its way toward the horizon, when he returned.

His breathing fast and slightly hard, his loose shirt damp with sweat, Sayer didn't see her until he'd taken several steps into the room. Then he stopped, staring.

She stared back, not knowing what to say.

"You look like a dream," Sayer said at last, his voice low and wondering. "Right now, I believe you are from another world. There can't be a woman like you in this one."

"Perhaps it is all a dream." *A dream of love. Or a nightmare of betrayal.* "You have been gone a very long time."

"I had a lot of thinking to do. After all the excitement yesterday, I thought you would sleep the morning away."

"I could not sleep." She turned back toward the window. "When I close my eyes I feel . . . haunted. I see my family, and I hate the idea I am causing them worry and pain. I have nightmares of being trapped in a place where I can never belong, yet I can never escape from."

"If you could only remember how you got here, what you were doing in that shop—"

"I cannot remember!" Aramanda rose to her feet in one swift motion, staying faced to the window.

Her image in the glass reflected her fear and despair back to her; the morning's first light diffused it, making her look unreal, a spirit figure trapped in a moment of reality. Behind her, Sayer looked even less real, a shadow of the man she loved, as unreachable as the lover she had left dead at the mine.

She curled her hands into tight fists at her side, opening and closing them in a vain attempt to stem the tide of panic crashing in waves inside her. "I have told you I cannot remember. I was with you at the mine, and then I was there. I do not understand it. I only know that I must return, but I do not know how!"

"If you don't belong here," Sayer said carefully, "then why did you come in the first place?"

Aramanda whirled about. Tears started down her face and she did nothing to stop them. "I did not come of my own will. I prayed only for a chance of redemption, to have you love me again. You died in my arms because of my betrayal! I could not bear that. But I did not wish this, to be here! How could I?"

Sayer had no answers for her, yet it hurt to see her suffer, tortured by her fears and her regrets. He started to come to her, to offer some solace, but she stopped him with a raise of her hand.

"I do not want your pity. I want your love, and I cannot have it here. Perhaps that is why I am here, as punishment, to see that while your soul has survived without my love, mine cannot escape the past without yours. Perhaps I will never return; perhaps I will be tormented like this, through eternity, never belonging—"

"Aramanda, stop it!" Sayer spoke more sharply than he intended, hearing the note of near-hysteria in her voice. He took a few steps closer, gently taking her by the shoulders and holding on firmly. "It's all right. I don't know what happened to you either, but I don't think it's as dramatic as all that. I'm sorry for pressuring you to remember."

"You did not pressure me. I want to remember; I want to know why I am here. I just do not know where to begin." She glanced away, shielding him from her pain. Drawing a deep breath, she looked up at him again. "I waited for you."

There was so much meaning in her words, so much she

couldn't say—a blind trust, a poignant tristfulness, a note of near-despair. She could see in his face that Sayer had heard it all and more.

"Well, I'm back now," he said quietly. "And if you'll wait a little longer, I'll grab a shower and then buy you breakfast before we go to the travel agency. Afterward, we'll hit the road to go see your family. It's the best thing to do," he said when she said nothing in reply. "If you see your family—"

Aramanda pulled free from his hold. "I have told you," she said stiffly, "the Montclairs in this reality are not my family. This is your foolish idea. Mama, my brothers, Penelope, and Jessalyn—they are in another place."

The renewed pain in her heart drove bitter words out of her soul. "My family is in my world, but I know no way back to them or to you. Why can you not believe me?" she cried, trying to keep her dignity pulled around her like a shield, knowing it could not protect her here. "I know no one here but you. And even you are not the same."

"Am I better or worse?"

Sayer's tone was light, but Aramanda sensed an underlying desire to know.

She waited before answering, taking time to study him, letting her eyes rove over the body she knew too well, in dreams and in waking. Finally, gathering her courage, she moved a hand's length from him.

"There is no better or worse. And perhaps I was wrong. Perhaps you are the same." Unconsciously holding her breath, she swanned her fingers against his jaw. "The same face . . ." Her hand skimmed lower, touching his shoulder, his chest. "The same body . . . leaner, perhaps, but the same."

She rested her palm on his heart. "The same man here. You do not carry your responsibilities as lightly as you used to; it is less a game, and you find less to laugh about. Yet it is your soul as I remember, as I know. You are still as ardent about your causes, courageous, yet too brazen at times, always passionate . . ." Her voice refused to go further.

Old feelings, new emotions clashed inside, between them, like flint to steel, sparking fire. Sayer's eyes reflected her image, and she willed him to see her in a different place, a different time from this, when she had touched him in the heat of shared passion with only the night between them.

"What about you—are you the same?"

"Aramanda."

"What?"

"Aramanda. My name. You refuse to say it when you do not want to remember the past. You are afraid, Roarke, afraid you will feel something."

"That's crazy! I—"

"Is it? Then say it. The Roarke Macnair I know does not fear anything. And certainly not the power of a name."

She could see he was loath to refuse her dare, and she felt a trill of anticipation. "Aramanda . . ." he began, firmly at first, as if he intended to prove to her he felt nothing. Except it ended as a husky whisper, and Aramanda knew he felt far more than he cared to admit.

His reaction made her determined to make him remember. He was her only chance at cheating fate. In her heart she knew without reason that only with Roarke could she defy destiny, return to their past and reshape it as she wished. It made no sense, but none of it did. It was the only explanation she could believe.

Boldly seizing her advantage, as he had done so many times, Aramanda leaned into him, raising herself up to graze a kiss against his mouth.

She intended only to prove to him he could not forget all they shared. Surely his soul, the other half of her own, would remember if his heart did not. But the moment the kiss joined them, Aramanda realized she would not be able to master the half-buried emotions she had ruthlessly exposed.

The fire flared suddenly, out of control. Sayer pulled her fully into his arms, his hand threading in her hair, and deepened their kiss until Aramanda felt nothing but the scorch of desire, the searing need to be one with him, again and forever.

He was the same. Blind and deaf to the world around them, she knew him as her lover, the only man who could make her whole, make her feel nothing mattered but this fusion of bodies and souls. The feeling was singing and fire inside her, with voices of angels and flames of wicked, wanton desire.

When he dragged his mouth from hers to taste the arched curve of her throat, Aramanda breathed his name on a ragged sigh. "Roarke . . . please—"

The sound of his name seemed to rip him from the spell she had cast. Sayer stiffened, then abruptly broke away from her, taking a few unsteady steps backward. They stared at each other, breathless, both shaken.

Trembling, Aramanda summoned up a brief defiance. "Tell me now you do not remember and it will be a lie. No matter what you call yourself, no matter how time has changed you, you cannot change what we have been to each other."

Before he could reply, she whirled away, not wanting him to see how much their embrace, the words, had cost her. She shouldn't have challenged him, she knew it as surely as she breathed. All the emotions, the soaring heights of timeless love and the black depths of eternal despair, rushed back, a hundredfold in their intensity.

Roarke might not remember, but she could never forget.

He said nothing for long, aching moments. At last, Aramanda heard him shift behind her. "I need that shower now," he muttered, striding from the room. She heard a door slam. And found herself alone once again.

Lowering herself to the window seat again, Aramanda pressed her cheek to the cool glass, closing her eyes to the brilliance of the risen sun and waited. For him—and for what was to come.

"You aren't dressed." One hand arrested halfway up the row of shirt buttons he was finishing fastening, Sayer stared at Aramanda. Still sitting where he had left her, she shifted slightly to face him as he strode into the room and stopped midway.

"I would like to bathe first," she said, her expression carefully bland. "I need you to assist me."

Sayer's hand jerked. "In taking a bath?"

"Only if you prefer it." She smiled slightly. "I did mean I need you to assist me in drawing it. I have guessed that in this place I do not have to call for hot water to be brought to my room. You did not."

"Not quite," Sayer muttered, annoyed at himself for jumping to the wrong conclusion about her innocent request and even more annoyed for letting it throw him off balance. Except that seeing her secret smile, the warmth in her eyes, he wondered how innocent it actually had been. "Come on. I'll show you the amenities."

She rose slowly, with an unconscious grace. The silk of her robe moved in sinuous rhythm with each step she took, making illicit suggestions about her body. When she walked by him in the direction he indicated, the warmth of her brushed against him and he sucked in a breath.

"Is there something wrong?" she asked, slanting him a glance.

"No. Should there be?"

"I would not think so. I did not think my request was so disturbing. If it is—"

"I'm running you a bath, not offering to vanquish dragons for you," Sayer said shortly. Inside the small confines of the bathroom, he rubbed a hand over his jaw, feeling a trickle of sweat run down his spine. "This won't take long," he said, reaching down to turn on the taps.

"Would you rather it did?"

"You aren't making this easy."

"I thought you said it would not take long. Is it so difficult then?"

"It didn't used to be." With a not-quite-steady hand, he twisted the water on.

Aramanda made a delighted exclamation. "How clever! It comes so easily." She bent next to him and cupped her palm under the stream of water. Her arm brushed his. "This is perfect."

"I'm glad you think so."

"Do you not think so? Surely you prefer it to washing out of a basin."

"I haven't done much of that lately. There's usually a shower handy where I am."

"A shower? I do not . . . what is this?" Before Sayer could stop her, she reached out and twisted the knob that started the shower, drenching them both in a torrent of warm water.

"Hell!" Sayer jerked back, swiping water out of his eyes. Aramanda started to laugh.

"That is a very useful invention," she said, barely able to voice the words. She sat down on the thick bath rug, her face lighted with laughter, her eyes dancing as she looked at him. "I will remember that."

"I wish you wouldn't." Sayer yanked a towel off the rack and handed it to her. As he did, he noticed the water had dampened the thin silk, making it cling to her wet skin. Steam from the heat of the water made a moist mist in the room and invited damp tendrils of auburn to curl intimately against her neck and face. "Here." He thrust it at her. "You're wet."

"So are you. But I intend to take a bath, so it does not matter to me. Does it to you?"

"I'll dry."

"That is not what I asked. No matter." Twisting around, she moved to her knees and, mimicking his actions, turned off the flow of water in the nearly full tub. She drew her hand through the water, then spread the wetness over the side of her throat with a long, languorous motion. "I believe it is ready."

"More than ready," Sayer said, his eyes fixed of their own accord on her sensuous stroking. "I'll leave you to it."

His mind gave the command to back out of the room, but his body refused to listen. Aramanda rose to her feet, the robe dropping off one shoulder, and the voice in his head faded from command to whisper.

"Perhaps you should dry yourself first," she said softly. Taking the towel from his hand, she gently rubbed a corner of it over the side of his face, then down his neck. "You are quite wet." She moved the towel lower, stroking it between the open edges of his shirt. Her fingertips glanced against his bare skin and he started, surprised by the lightning shot of awareness that bolted through him.

"I can—"

"I am sure you can. But I have your towel. Is my touch that displeasing?"

The expression in her eyes, between passion and uncertainty, as if she were not sure of her own power to move him, reached his heart despite his attempt to stay aloof from her. He covered her fingers, intending to stop her action, and instead found his hand caressing hers, holding her palm flat against his skin.

"This isn't a good idea," he said huskily.

"Is it not? Then release me." Her fingertips slid back and forth in a light tantalizing motion.

"I—"

"Release me, Roarke." She stepped nearer to him, letting her body brush his. Her free hand slipped up his chest to curl around his neck, her fingers threading in the hair at his nape. "Release me and I will ask nothing else of you."

He wanted to. He wanted to let her go and walk away and convince himself she had never come into his life and flipped it completely upside down in little more than a day. He didn't want the emotions she dredged up inside him and he didn't want to understand why this woman, above all others, could affect him like no one else he'd ever known.

But he might as well have wanted the world to stop turning.

"You've already asked more of me than anyone ever has, and without saying a word," he told her, his voice little more than a husky breath of sound. "I don't know how to let you go."

"I do not want to let you go," she said. For a moment, they stood together, not moving, caught in a suspended space in time that was neither the present nor yesterday.

For the span of a heartbeat, Sayer felt strongly the strange force that linked them, a power he couldn't explain or deny.

Then, Aramanda let her hand fall, gently disengaging her fingers from his and stepping away. "I do not want to release you, but I do not want to hear you tell me to leave. I think I need to have my bath now."

Sayer hesitated a second longer. Still wrestling between two opposing desires, the one to possess her gaining strength, he nodded and strode from the room.

Shutting the door behind him, he leaned against the hard wood, closing his eyes, his hands flexing and unflexing at his side. He heard a whisper of silk being shed and then the plash of water as she stepped into it, and he didn't need to see to picture her in the bath, the steam wound around her like a lover's embrace, water sliding off her bare skin where he wanted his hands to be.

He'd told her he was making her one of his causes. Now, he was beginning to realize Aramanda Montclair could overshadow every cause that had ever mattered to him, if he let himself fall under her spell.

"They'd better be here today or I won't be above breaking in," Sayer muttered as he ushered Aramanda out of the rover and locked the door behind her.

As he spoke, Aramanda watched tension pull the strong line of his jaw taut. She sighed. His mood hadn't improved after leaving the hotel and, unfortunately, neither had hers. She dreaded coming back to this place, yet knew she must. He wanted answers. She feared them.

What if the old couple knew nothing of her, past or present? Roarke had no place for her in his life, and without his love or at least his faith in her, she had nothing to keep her here and, she feared, nothing to help her return.

Worse, what if he decided it best to simply leave her here with the odd couple? She had played a hundred roles in her past, attempting to fit in at home, with the miners, in society, all the while feeling she never belonged in any one place.

Here, she was no one, had no role to play. Her family name even belonged to strangers she would never know. She was simply Aramanda, a stranger in an alien world where Roarke told her to be herself. Except, how could she, when she did not know who or what that was?

"Come on." Sayer took her hand and led her across the sidewalk to the shop. "That door had better be unlocked or I swear I'll kick it in."

"I am surprised you do not consider blowing it up," Aramanda murmured. She read the small calligraphy sign in the window as they approached. "It says that they are ope—"

Before she had finished the word, the bells on the door jingled and the little man stood in the doorway. "Do come in; we've been expecting you. Tsk," he said glancing at the watch he fished from his pocket. "You are a bit late, but then I suppose that's understandable, considering."

"Considering?" Aramanda turned to glance at Sayer at the same time he looked down at her, the questioning expression on his face mirroring her own surprise. "You have been expecting us?" she asked, reluctantly following the man inside.

"Oh, indeed. Why wouldn't we? You've done nothing but talk about coming back here." He craned his neck to look up at them, a youthful sparkle in his forget-me-not-blue eyes. "My wife has just set the pot on for tea."

Sayer shook his head in disbelief. "Now this place is a tea shop, too? Is there anything you don't do?"

"I don't go in much for water skiing anymore. The wife won't allow it. Pity." The man closed the door behind them, turned the *open* sign over to *closed*, and tottered across the store to stand behind the counter. "Please, make yourselves comfortable while I go tell Lila you're here. Then we'll sit down and have a little chat."

"Wait a minute," Sayer called after him. "We've been trying to get in here to see you ever since I found Aramanda here. I don't have any time or any patience for games. I want answers. Now."

"We weren't going to play games anyway." The old man offered a jovial smile brimming with too-large white dentures. "But the tea is still brewing. Three to five minutes, that's the limit." With that, he hobbled back through a curtained doorway and disappeared.

"I don't get it." Sayer scoured the shop with his eyes. "What's their scam?" he muttered, beginning to pace in front of the counter.

"He is rather odd."

Aramanda wandered a little away from him toward a shelf that held a variety of kitchen utensils she might have found in her own kitchen in her own home. One by one, she turned them over in her palm, examining each and finding every one to be as real as if cook had just removed them from the shelf to make her favorite raspberry trifle.

"This place makes me feel so strange," she said, acutely aware of the sense of displacement that had haunted her since she arrived. "It is as if it stands apart from the outside in a time of its own."

A shiver ran up her spine, and she felt cold despite the close warmth of the shop. She looked up, catching sight of the brilliant sunshine outside the window. "Look, it is so bright outside, but in here it is so—so gray."

Sayer stopped and stood absolutely still, gazing around the shop. "You're right," he said with an odd, quiet reverence in his tone, the kind of voice people use in church. "It's, well, almost foggy in here." With a shrug of his shoulders, he appeared to shake off the disturbing notion and swiped a finger over the counter. "Probably dust."

Aramanda smiled at his obstinance. "That window is quite large enough to flood the room with light, and yet it seems as though it is neither night nor day in here. Time seems to be of little use here."

"You said that before." Sayer walked over to a curio case and fingered an Egyptian sculpture of a cat. "You're just letting your imagination get the best of you. This place is odd, but that's probably because it hasn't felt a breath of outside air in a hundred years."

Aramanda winced at his choice of words, and Sayer hurried on. "All of this stuff, though—" He waved a hand around the room. "—doesn't add up. Most antique stores specialize in one era or another, or at least one continent. But from the looks of the merchandise, those two have managed to collect artifacts and junk from just about every period in history from all over the world. That ivory carving is African; that pottery is Mayan; and over there, that marble is Greek. If this stuff is genuine, they've got a fortune amassed here. I'm not knowledgeable enough to vouch for a lot of it, but some is definitely the real thing."

Aramanda moved slowly down a crowded aisle, brushing her fingertips over items as she walked. "My knowledge is more limited than yours, but I can speak for these." She pointed to the dishes and utensils and an ornate oil lamp. "They are undoubtedly genuine." She touched the lamp. "We have one very much like this in our morning room."

"Where have those two gone? I swear they remind me of elves or gnomes or some of those semi-human Shakespearean characters." Sayer set the copper urn he was fidgeting with back on its stand and strode to the front of the store. "We've waited the required three to five minutes."

"I do not have anywhere else to go," Aramanda said quietly. She put the piece of Belgian lace collar she'd taken a fancy to back on the bust it had been draped over and went to Sayer. "Perhaps they are planning how to help me return." She glanced up at him from under her lashes and said, only half-seriously, "Perhaps they are magical."

Amusement warred with irritation on Sayer's face and won. He laughed, taking her hand and giving it a quick squeeze. "It's more likely that they can't afford a maintenance crew to clean out this rat hole. It's beginning to make my skin crawl. I'm starting to wonder how two senior citizens can manage to make me feel like I'm being manipulated into following some hidden agenda."

Aramanda peered across the counter, straining for a look beyond the curtained doorway behind it. "I feel that as well, though I could not begin to tell you why. I suppose it could be my imagination. But it is disconcerting."

"Annoying is the word. But I'm through feeding into it. I'm going back there."

"No need, Dr. Macnair. The pot's ready." The woman appeared, ruddy faced and as jolly as the wife of St. Nicholas. Beside her, a teenaged boy pulled back the curtain to make way for her to carry her silver tea tray out into the shop. "Do follow me, please," she urged. "This way, back to the corner of the shop. We have a table set for four."

Sayer glanced to Aramanda and shook his head. Aramanda shifted her shoulders, not knowing what else to do but follow the woman. As they walked behind her, Aramanda couldn't help but notice that the boy at her side carrying a basket of pastries had skin the color of mahogany. As he moved, the long, black braid that hung to his waist serpentined down his bare back like a live snake. He wore only a leather loincloth.

"Thank you, Little Fox," the woman said when she'd set the tray on the table. "Just set those rolls here." She patted a spot on the white linen covering the table, then spoke to him in a language Aramanda had never heard.

"You speak Navajo?" Sayer asked.

"Why yes, how clever of you to know it."

"I don't know it. But I recognize it." Sayer took a seat at the primly set round table. "Who is that boy?"

"He's a visitor." The old man took a seat opposite Roarke.

"Like me?" Aramanda asked.

"Like all of our guests." The woman reached across her husband's chest and tucked a napkin under his chin. "Tea stains so terribly, doesn't it, dear?" she half-whispered to Aramanda.

Aramanda nodded. Feeling overwhelmed, she turned to Sayer and saw the frustration in his eyes begin to smolder. "This is all so lovely, so—like home," she said quickly. "But we have come to speak to you about your—your guests. About me and how I came to be here."

"And we're not leaving until we get some straight answers."

The old woman smiled sweetly at Sayer, patently ignoring his determined tone. "What a shame. I always think the crooked ones are so much more interesting." She looked back at Aramanda. "I do hope you like the Victorian china, my dear. I did so want you to feel comfortable today. I am sure being hurried about in that horrid vehicle of Dr. Macnair's and having to answer all his quite impossible questions has been a trial."

"This is beginning to feel like an episode of 'The Twilight Zone,' " Sayer muttered to no one in particular.

Aramanda furrowed her brows and silently questioned him, recognizing his tone if not his meaning.

"I suppose you could say that," the man said, tapping a finger to his lips. "I confess, I've never thought of it that way." He smiled suddenly. "It is—without the commercials, of course."

"I could say a lot of things—"

"Roarke!" Aramanda said quickly, laying a hand on his arm. "We want only—"

"Of course, of course," the man said. "You only want to know how you came to this place. And what we have to do with it. Perfectly understandable. Yes, indeed."

Sayer nearly choked on his first sip of tea.

The woman passed a basket of breads the likes of which Aramanda's own cook couldn't have surpassed. Aramanda took a currant bun. "I thought I would never eat these again."

"Oh, you will again," the man said. "If you decide to return. You tell your cook, though, more cinnamon than nutmeg. Lila's little secret." He winked.

Aramanda stopped short of taking a bite, sucking in a sudden breath. "Return? Then you do know!"

"Oh, of course. We know everything, my dear," the woman said. "You see Weldon and I, we—why, how rude of me, we haven't introduced ourselves, have we? Oh my, age is an awful thing. I am Lila Pepper, and this is my husband, Weldon. I've already said that, haven't I? Well, no matter. We are your monitors."

Sayer set his cup down with a sharp clack. "Our *what?*"

"Now, now, Dr. Macnair." Lila shook a grandmotherly finger of reproof at Sayer. "We know you are a man of science and that spiritual matters are most difficult for men of your intellectual leanings to accept. But, if I may be blunt, I'm afraid in this instance you have no other option. You either accept what we are about to tell you in good faith alone, or you shut your mind and heart to us and lose the chance you have been allotted—most generously, I must say. Not many are given such an opportunity, although I find that to be a shame, also. But you, you have the chance to find lasting love with the woman destined for you. Rather like winning the best prize on a game show, don't you think?"

"I think one of us is crazy."

"That is not true." Aramanda spun around to face him. "This is all true! Everything I have told you—" She turned to Lila, filled with a strange, racing excitement. "I told him much the same story—it all happened, did it not? Please, tell me it happened. I have thought I truly was mad these past hours, that no one, not even Roarke, would ever believe me."

"Well, of course it's all true," Weldon piped in. "Why wouldn't it be? You don't think we would waste time making all of this up simply as amusement, do you, when there are so many more interesting things in the cosmos to do?"

Sayer's eyes darkened and narrowed. He turned to Weldon. "Who the hell are you?"

"Watch your language, son; there are ladies present. And that answer depends on whom you ask. Once, we were just like you. We lived out our lives and died peacefully in our old age. At least, as far as recorded history tells, that is. About '62, '64? Oh—when was it, Lila?"

"You died in 1763, and I died three years later, dear."

"Never was good with dates." He shrugged. "Anyhow, you might say we were selected, along with hundreds, perhaps thousands—I couldn't say; I'm bad with numbers, always have been—of other folks who apparently had the right qualifications, who moved on to the next level, so to speak. Try that scone, my dear," he urged Aramanda. "Lila's had a lot of practice making them. After nearly two centuries, she's near got it perfect."

Aramanda stared at the scone, then back at Weldon, her mind numb with trying to assimilate all that had happened. "I am not sure I understand."

"Big surprise," Sayer said under his breath.

"These things are difficult to grasp," Lila said. "Weldon is better at explaining than I am. I prefer to think of it as fate and leave it at that."

"You've always been so haphazard about details. They want to know *details*," Weldon said. "You see, sometime during our deaths, we found ourselves on the next level. The committee gave us our eternal mission, I suppose you could call it."

"Committee?" Aramanda asked.

"A committee," Sayer put in. "Nice to know even destiny is democratic about these things."

"Oh, very democratic, Dr. Macnair," Weldon said, his expression perfectly sincere. "Well, as I was saying, the committee taught us how to aid and alter misguided fates. We've been living in a realm beyond what you know as time ever since. It's a place where past, present, and future all exist simultaneously. People like us are sent by the committee to help those like you find the destiny intended for them which they somehow missed. Rather like a road map, we are."

"You might say our clients took a wrong turn and we're here to help get them back on the path they were supposed to take," Lila said, smiling as she poured more tea in Sayer's cup. She nudged the cream pitcher a little closer to his hand. "Oh, I nearly forgot—your documents for your European speaking tour are in order, Dr. Macnair. You depart next Sunday; don't forget to pick them up on your way out today. You might want to catch that plane, although I doubt it—well, that's certainly up to you."

After a few long, silent minutes, Sayer shoved away from the table, his body tense. "I never gave you my agenda."

Lila cocked her head. "No. You didn't, did you? I'm certain you will find the accommodations acceptable. Such a charming place, London. All of your transfers have been arranged in conjunction with the universities you will be speaking at. But if you should need to make any changes in your schedule—"

"Please don't hesitate to call," Weldon finished his wife's sentence.

Sayer stood up. "I'm ready to call—a psychiatrist."

"It must be true," Aramanda said, moving next to him. "I know it sounds mad, but it is the only thing that also makes sense. Yet—" She turned to Weldon and Lila. "—I do not understand.

You said I could return. Then why did I come here at all if this is not the place I belong."

"Ah, well, that is a bit tricky," Weldon said. He ignored Sayer's grimace. "Most people, you see, move on in soul from lifetime to lifetime, changing and growing, but carrying their experiences with them. The consequences of our every action are definite: positive actions bring us happiness; negative actions, suffering. An action, even done many, many lifetimes ago, never loses its effect, even through time. Because these actions are done in an infinite number of lives, there's infinite potential for an infinite number of outcomes. I said that rather nicely, didn't I, my dear?" he finished, beaming at Lila.

"Yes, dear, but of course you didn't explain to the poor girl what it all means to her," she said. Lila smiled at Aramanda. "You became trapped."

Startled, Aramanda glanced at Sayer then back to the couple. "Trapped?"

"Oh, yes. Because of the terrible wrong you felt you committed, and the loss of your love, you became trapped in one moment of the past, unable to move forward. If we hadn't intervened, well . . ."

"You might have come back as an ant, or something else quite lowly, just to punish yourself," Weldon said. "At the least, you never would have found the love and family you want so badly. That would have been the consequence of your action."

"And *you*—" Lila stared pointedly at Sayer.

"I've been waiting for this," Sayer muttered.

"So you should. You see what has happened to you. You're so *empty.*"

"I—"

"Don't interrupt. It's not polite. You lost her because you refused to change. Now the only way to resolve this tiresome situation is for you both to return."

"Both of us? Then that is why I am here, to convince Roarke to return to his past?" Aramanda asked.

"A Herculean task, I agree, especially since he is not Roarke," Lila said matter-of-factly.

"But I thought . . ." Shaken, Aramanda took a step from Sayer. She put a hand to her temple, feeling dizzy, a sick sense of loss and fear rippling through her.

Sayer moved to touch her, but the look on her face stopped him. It was a dawning dread, a confusion of what she had believed and what she must accept.

"Now, my dear, don't lose your courage," Lila said softly. "His soul is the same, but he can't be the same person. Roarke died, and he has had so many experiences since then. How could he be the same man? What matters is that he has Roarke's soul and you are destined for each other. And *that* you must believe because so much depends on it, so many people's lives."

"So many people?" The words came from Aramanda, barely a whisper.

"Oh, yes," Weldon put in. "We're all like actors in a play. You may think your part is small and unimportant, but if you don't give your cue at the proper time, perhaps by simply being in a certain place and time, the whole production crumbles. And even the smallest negative action can cause great suffering. You both missed your cues."

"That is why so many people are strangers, yet familiar," Aramanda murmured more to herself than anyone else.

Sayer, his whole attention fixed on her, felt a twinge of alarm at her dazed expression. She looked in shock. He couldn't blame her, but he didn't have the slightest idea how to help her.

"Recycling," Weldon said, beaming on them. "Dr. Macnair should appreciate that."

Sayer muttered something under his breath that sounded to Aramanda like a particularly vile curse. He held out a hand to Aramanda, not touching, offering only his solace. "You can't believe this," he said.

"I . . ." Aramanda hesitated. She drew a deep breath, seemed to find some inner strength to overcome the blow she had been dealt. "I do not know. I only know I wished for a second chance, to love and be loved again by . . . by Roarke. And they know—where I came from, what I want. They know. How could they know?"

"How the hell should I know? This goes against everything I have ever believed. Or not believed! Dammit, Aramanda, I have a hard time accepting the notion of a God or a heaven or a hell, much less the idea of dead people who live outside of time."

"But I am here. And no matter who you are, I cannot deny what I feel for you. Can you deny your feelings for me?"

Sayer started to lift a hand to touch her face, then jerked it away. "I don't know what to feel—or think."

"All they have said confirms what I have told you from the beginning."

"There could be a reason for that. You were here, after all, when I ran into you. The three of you could have worked this story out before I ever set foot through that door."

Aramanda drew back and squared her shoulders. "To what end? What have I asked of you? You took me in willingly."

"They left me little choice, if you recall. Not that I didn't want to help you," he added, his voice gentling. "But you have to admit, my explanation sounds a lot more rational than theirs."

"If you are accusing me of consorting with them to win your attentions, then by all means tell me why. What have I to gain by baring my heart to you? So far, my only reward has been for you to treat me as if I were, at best, slightly mad!"

"Aramanda—"

"No! Do not give me any more of your rational explanations. Only answer me this question. What brought you to this door? There surely must be other places in this city you could have gone to arrange your travel. Why did you come here? Did we plan that as well?"

Sayer stared at her, for once speechless. His eyes searched hers for a long moment, and she could see he searched inside himself for the answer as well. Finally, still looking directly at her, he said bluntly, "I can't answer that."

"But you will find a logical-enough reason to keep you from believing us," Lila spoke up. "If you choose to. That is up to you."

"Lila is right. We cannot make your choices for you. We can only present the options, such as they are."

Aramanda stepped back from Roarke, hugging her arms around her body, feeling cold inside. She had feared he would never believe her, would choose to leave her alone in this place. Now, even her worst nightmares seemed laughable compared with knowing he was not the same man she had loved in her past.

He had no reason to put his faith in her. No reason to want to return to recapture what had been lost.

"I wanted another chance for love," she said quietly, feeling the pain like a dull ache that threatened to overwhelm her heart. "Now, I want only to return to the place I belong and it is not here."

"I'm not saying I don't believe you," Sayer said, impatiently pushing the hair off his forehead. "I'm just trying to think logically. I do feel—something. I did the first time I had that vision of you and have every day since. I can't explain that, even though it happened. But what you ask, what you've described, a love that means more than anything else in my life—I've never even considered that possibility."

"And you will not consider it now." Aramanda turned away, not wanting him to see the tears stinging her eyes. "If I return, will it be before Roarke . . ." She could not say the word, appealing to Lila and Weldon with her gaze.

"I cannot tell you that, my dear," Lila said. "All I can tell you is that love and the actions you both take because of love will determine your future. As it did your past. And I can say that you have very little time left here to convince Sayer to return with you. You are right; you do not belong here. It is very bad for your body and soul; and the longer you stay, the worse it will become."

"Then how do I return?" Aramanda asked. "From here?" She glanced around the shop, half-expecting some miraculous portal to the past to appear.

"No, no, of course not," Weldon said. "You'll find the way, from a place you were before."

Aramanda frowned. "That is not very helpful."

Sayer threw up his hands. "Nothing they've said is helpful. But okay. Fine, say I buy this. What if Aramanda and I have been given a second chance to fix everything right the first time? Why didn't I know her at once? Why don't I have the same memory she does? My life is full, busy, established."

"Is it?" Weldon asked. "You have everything you want?"

"I—that doesn't matter," Sayer said quickly. "Why did she come now, to this place? Why not fifty, a hundred years ago, or tomorrow? Why here?"

"So many questions," Lila fussed, pouring herself another cup of tea. "Where is your faith, Sayer? Oh, don't bother to answer. As to your question, she is here now because the events of the past have cumulated to the point where now is crucial. If you don't redeem the past and find your way back to each other then . . . well, tragedies have a way of repeating themselves."

"That's not an answer. I don't understand why I have a life here and Aramanda doesn't. She came to me as a stranger. She has no life here, no family, nothing."

The words stabbed at Aramanda. "You are right. I have nothing here. That is why I must return."

Sayer's expression softened. "Aramanda . . ." He reached out for her.

She stepped back, shaking her head. "No. I must return. And you must decide if you will return as well."

"Is that what you want?" Sayer asked. "What if you stayed instead, here in my reality?" He turned to the couple. "Can she?"

Lila and Weldon exchanged a glance. Lila spoke up, her tone soft. "I—no. She cannot stay. She does not belong here. Her second chance comes only if you return together."

"And if she goes alone?"

Weldon shook his head, distressed. Lila gave Sayer a hard look. "If she returns alone, there will be no future for her," she said. She looked at Aramanda. "Remember that, my dear."

"I will." Aramanda met Sayer's gaze fully, unwavering. "In my heart I know I will always love Roarke and you are what he has become. Whatever choices I must make, whatever I am or become, that will never change. But you must choose whether to return. I cannot choose for you."

Sayer took a stride forward and lifted a hand, brushing his fingertips over her face, his eyes dark and unfathomable. "If ever a woman existed that I could love for an eternity, you're as close to that ideal as I've ever known." His hand fell away, taking his warmth from her. "I just don't know whether I could love anyone that much. I don't know if I can."

"You mean to say you don't know if you are willing to let love be first in your life," Lila said, nodding sagely.

"I didn't say that!"

"No, you didn't have to. Did he, Weldon?"

"No, of course not, my dear. But you won't have much choice in the matter if you do love someone so completely," Weldon said, frowning slightly. "It's not like deciding what brand of soap to buy, you know."

"Maybe that's what I'm afraid of."

Instead of his words increasing her apprehension as she might have expected, Aramanda felt a strange sense of calm settle over her. She held herself with dignity, letting her gaze touch Sayer. "I must return, I know that. Whatever happens from this time on, I know it is what I must do."

They looked at each other a long moment, lost in one another's gaze, searching each other's soul.

At last Sayer broke the spell, glancing away and running a hand through his hair, his expression uncertain. "I—we should go."

"Yes, you are a busy man, too busy," Lila said. "Take time to finish your tea once in a while. And you, my dear . . ." She rose and walked over to them, laying a hand on Aramanda's arm. "No matter how difficult things become, you must remember what I'm about to tell you; when the moment is right, the meaning will become clear. The past is the only path to the future; until one is laid straight, the other will always be blocked, sometimes forever."

"I do not think I understand," Aramanda said.

"You will. But keep in mind, your time in this world to find your path is short." Lila stepped back, exchanging a glance with Weldon, who nodded sadly in agreement. "The only forever is in your heart."

Seven

Morning's coolness gave way to a lazy afternoon heat, and midway through their trip to Schuylkill County, Sayer rolled down the windows of the Range Rover and let the spring warmth draft into the cab. The rush of air seemed to ease the oppressive quiet that had settled between him and Aramanda since they'd left the hotel.

She'd said nothing after their—confrontation, encounter, hell, what could he call it?—at the shop. And it was driving him crazy. What was she thinking? What did she feel? He shifted in his seat, uncomfortable with both the memories of the morning at the hotel and their meeting with the old couple.

He didn't even know what he thought. And he didn't want to admit what he felt. It was impossible.

"How come it is so easy for you to believe you can attain the perfection of your ideals, yet you are so unwilling to believe in the reality of my past?"

Sayer started, briefly snapping his attention from the road to Aramanda. "Are you a damned mind reader now?" he retorted, a little more sharply than he'd intended.

She gazed back at him, her expression remote and unreadable.

"You haven't said a single word for nearly three hours, and then you suddenly blurt out a question like that. Does it come naturally or are you doing your best to unnerve me?"

She didn't smile, but her unusual eyes softened with a brush of amusement. "You were thinking about it, I could tell. You do not mask your feelings well. When something is troubling you, you have that particular scowl."

"Do I now? You haven't known me that long."

She gave a slight shrug. "You have not answered my question."

"No, I haven't. Because I don't have an answer." Sayer kept his attention fixed on the road. "In a few short days, you've managed to turn my life upside down, throw me miles off course, and make me question every reasonable thought that comes into my head. No one has ever done that before. I don't like it."

"That is obvious." Aramanda turned and stared out the passenger window. Sayer slid a glance at her. Only the wind, tugging a few errant strands of hair from her waist-length braid, disturbed her stillness. "I understand now why it disturbed you to be called Roarke."

"Because it's not my name. My name is Sayer."

"I know that now. And I am sorry."

"Don't be." He glanced at her, giving her a lopsided smile. "Besides, I've kind of gotten used to it."

"Have you? I confess I cannot think of you by any other name, even though I know it does not belong to you."

"I suppose that means I'll have to get used to hearing my middle name more often."

Aramanda turned and looked at him fully. "No, Sayer, you will not."

Sayer's hand jerked on the wheel and the rover swerved a few feet toward the road shoulder. Cursing under his breath, he brought it back under control before snatching a glance at her again. "You look like an angel, but I'm beginning to think it's all a clever disguise."

"How charming of you to say so. At least I do not have a devil's temper."

"Maybe a few dozen extra lifetimes have mellowed it," he said, reaching for a measure of sardonic humor and just missing.

"I sincerely doubt it. You may appear more civilized, but I suspect that underneath that veneer you are still a hot-blooded Irishman spoiling for a fight, with never a thought of losing. I know that is part of the reason why you are so anxious we visit these Montclairs of yours."

She paused, studying him for a moment with disconcerting candor. "You cannot bear injustice, just as Roarke could not. Time could not change that. But what made you choose to fight the world's flaws? I would like to know."

"It's not nearly as dramatic as you envision," Sayer said lightly. "My dad has always been a miner, and growing up, I saw a lot of the hardships and dangers that went along with the job. I also saw the devastation the mining companies would inflict on the land and wildlife."

He glanced at Aramanda. She said nothing, only encouraged him with her eyes, so he went on. "When I was about seven, just beyond my backyard there was a section of forest I considered paradise on earth. In a few short months, a strip-mining operation came in and turned it into a version of hell. People and wildlife got pushed out, and nobody ever stopped to consider the fairness of it. I looked at that scene outside my window for nearly ten years, and I swore I'd never let anyone destroy another paradise. A childish vow, but I never forgot it."

He paused, then added, "I suppose Roarke's past is a little more exciting."

Aramanda shrugged. "Only different. It was the war that changed Roarke."

"The war?" Sayer felt foolish even asking what she meant. But curiosity overrode his reluctance to admit that hearing her talk about the past she avowed they shared felt like waking from a sleep of ages and having someone describe the life you had buried in your dreams.

"Yes, the war. Between the Union and the Confederacy." She sighed, her voice flat, as if she were weary of having to explain things she thought he should remember.

"During the war, so many more of the Irish and German immigrants were selected for service than those American born. Though you—Roarke—volunteered to fight, he told me terrible stories of how poor men were taken from their homes by the military, their wives and children left without support. And, in the things he did not tell me, I guessed in the two years he was in battle the stories were even more terrible. Returning to the mines, I do not think he could bear to see the suffering continue, and certainly not the injustices."

"If things are—were so terrible, how come he had to convince you of it?" Sayer asked. "Did you condone your family's practices, even though you knew how bad it was?"

"It was not as simple as that! I have family, *people* to consider, people you were willing to sacrifice for your cause." She had paled, and a faint trembling shook her body. "You thought me weak for sacrificing my own feelings, my own needs, for others, for leaving myself defenseless against the pain of caring without considering the cost. And you were considered strong because you could put your principles above all, dependent on no one, determined to settle for nothing beneath your ideals."

"That doesn't sound like the description of a man you would profess eternal love for," Sayer said mockingly, a streak of bitterness darkening any lightness in his tone.

"I loved . . ."

She stopped and Sayer heard Roarke's name on her lips. The sound of it was beginning to grate.

"I loved Roarke because of that, and more. He showed me how to dream, to dare to say and do the things I longed to do. I loved the gentleness he showed in loving me, the courage to fight, and his dedication and tenacity. But I could not abide his putting his dedication to his cause above others, above us."

With an impatient shake of her head and a sigh, she added, "And it is still the same now—the one thing that will divide us throughout eternity, it seems. You must see it, too, this time."

She looked at him, anguish clear in her eyes. Before he could think of a reply, she cried, "For God's sake, you forced me to betray you and you died for it!"

Her words shot electric emotion through Sayer.

You forced me to betray you . . .

He found himself strangling the steering wheel hard enough to imprint it with the shape of his palms. The words shouldn't

mean anything to him. But they hurt. Intensely, beyond understanding or forgiveness.

A sign, announcing a rest area, flashed by; and without explanation to her, Sayer wheeled the rover around off the highway,
stopping it with a jerk at the far end of an island of trees.

Aramanda, her face white, looked at him, but said nothing.

Sayer glanced at her once. Then, shoving his door open, he
strode off in the direction of the farthest outcropping of trees,
amazed and appalled by the violent, primal feelings possessing
him.

Even more disturbing was the familiarity of them, as if he had
lived with those same emotions much longer than this lifetime.
And for reasons he clearly understood.

Aramanda found him leaning against a tree, his hands shoved
deeply into his pockets, scowling at the wind-rippled surface of
a small pond. She hesitated, then walked up to him, stopping a
few feet away.

"You have been gone a long time. I thought I would see if you
needed . . . anything," she said softly, not apologizing to herself
or to him for caring.

He flicked one swift look at her before fixing his gaze on the
pond again.

"When you said—what you did . . . it hurt. I wanted to hurt
back. I had to get out of there before I said or did something
we'd both regret." Drawing in a deep breath, he let it out slowly.
"I don't understand it. It shouldn't have meant anything to me.
But it does."

"I wish with all my heart it meant nothing. I never wanted to
cause you pain. But it seems it is all I can do, in this life or the
last. Please, believe me, if I can change what happened, all of it,
I will do it. I will return."

"I was beginning to believe nothing was impossible. But there
are a few things."

"If I return, perhaps I can change this reality for you."

An almost panicked urgency rose inside her, and Aramanda moved close to him and gripped his hand in hers, desperate to convince him this time as she had never been before. "I must return. And you with me."

Sayer's face tightened. "I can't do that."

"Why not?" The word wrenched from her.

"Because I don't have the first damned idea of how to get you back! Like it or not, you're stuck here."

"I will not accept that. There must be a way. Weldon and Lila said there was."

"There isn't. They're crazy."

"There must be! There must be—" Choking on a sob, Aramanda lost her fight to hold back the tears burning her eyes.

Sayer took one look at her face and cursed softly, gathering her into his arms.

His hand made soothing patterns up and down her spine. "Dammit, woman, if you don't drive *me* crazy, it won't be for lack of trying. I'm sorry. If I could give you what you want, I would."

"Except you believe what I want is impossible." Aramanda lifted her head from his chest.

"Maybe it's not."

"What do you mean?"

"I mean that you said you wanted a second chance. You have one. From your point of view, it might not be under the best of circumstances, but it's more than most people get. You may not be able to do anything about your past, but you've got your shot at the future."

"I do not believe that."

"Why not?" Sayer asked, scowling. "Because of what that nutty couple told you about the past dictating the future?"

"It is true." Aramanda loosed herself from his hold and walked a few steps from him.

She looked out at the pond, the wind blowing her hair back, molding the light floral cotton to her slender body. "And if it were not, if I stayed, would you take the time to rediscover all we have? Would we be together?"

"I won't make you promises unless I intend to keep them," Sayer told her, unable to keep his eyes from her. "To be honest, right now this whole situation is too insane for me to tell you what I'll be willing to do in the next hour, let alone for the rest of my life. If that's what you want, then I know I can't promise it to you."

"It is."

"Aramanda—"

She turned to him, the sadness in her eyes stilling his protest.

"But not now, not here. Now, you can give me something I want." Looking far into his eyes, Aramanda willed him to remember. "You can believe me."

"Maybe part of me does. Because of this."

Sayer took two strides to her side and, bending to her, kissed her, a tender caress that blended swiftly into passion, powerful and consuming.

He touched her surely, possessively, telling her with silence and the warm, urgent pressure of his body that he remembered the feelings and the desire, if not the time they both shared.

When they finally pulled a little apart, Sayer gently smoothed a clinging streak of auburn from her cheek, his expression both troubled and wondering. "Don't ask me to explain it, because I can't."

"I would not dare," Aramanda murmured, content for the moment to trust and be trusted. "I cannot explain it either. I know you are not the Roarke of my past and yet I know your soul is the match to my own. It defies reason, and that should keep me from believing."

"Somehow, I think you would dare anyway." Sayer stepped back and took her hand, curling her fingers around his. "Come on, let's get this visit to my Montclairs over with. I may not find any answers for you, but something tells me they might be the answers to a few questions of my own."

"Nervous?"

Aramanda started at the staccato question. "Yes. A little." She looked out at the swift-moving gold-and-green vista, knowing without Sayer's telling her that they would reach the Montclair estate in a matter of minutes.

"I remember this countryside. I would ride through the fields every morning, long before anyone else was awake. If I close my eyes, I can smell the pine and wildflowers of the forest where—" She broke off, a warm flush rising in her face.

"Where?" Sayer prompted, flashing her a curious glance.

"Where we—Roarke and I met." Aramanda drew a deep breath, then flung caution and hesitancy to the wind. "Where we loved each other. Sometimes in the day, in the sunlight. But always at night, always in the darkness when I did not know where I left off and you began."

Sayer's hand slid up and down the curve of the steering wheel in a slow rhythm, flexing and unflexing against the smooth leather. He said nothing, his eyes fixed on the road ahead.

"What if these Montclairs of yours refuse to see us?" Aramanda asked quickly, wanting to ease the uneasy tension in him she had provoked.

"Nice recovery," he murmured, flashing her a half smile. "If that happens, I suppose I'll have to revert to being uncivilized and drive through the gate or scale the wall."

When Aramanda raised a brow, he laughed and reached out to give her hand a quick squeeze. "Don't worry, I'll think of something. It wouldn't be the first time I've had to resort to stepping over a line or two."

"I confess I cannot be surprised," Aramanda said, laughing with him. "I have no doubt you are wishing for the slightest opportunity to bully your way over the first line you are presented with, no matter how respectable you claim to have become."

"I've only claimed to be more civilized, sometimes," Sayer returned. "Look—we're here."

Aramanda caught her breath as they turned onto the long, curved drive and the stately Georgian manor swept into view. Time had been gentle with it, its years showing only in style and an air of stoic elegance. The woodwork had been repainted a deeper shade of white to contrast with the rich red of the brick, and a wrought-iron fence replaced the low stone wall that had once surrounded the estate.

"It is still—"

"Home?"

She shot Sayer a dark glance. "No. Not now. But . . . it once was."

Sayer stopped the vehicle just to the left of the front stairs. He paused before opening his door, taking both her hands in his. "Don't worry. This won't take long. I won't let anything happen to you. You don't have to stay if you don't want to. I promise."

The constriction in her throat leaving her mute, Aramanda only nodded, allowing him to lead her up the stairs to the front door. Glancing at her, Sayer thumbed the bell, and waited. After a few moments, she caught the faint sound of footsteps and then the click of the door handle being pressed.

Aramanda gripped Sayer's hand, feeling caught up in the center of a maelstrom, with memories of the past rushing to collide with the realities of the present.

"Yes? May I help you?"

The soft woman's voice coming out of the shadows of the half-open door made Aramanda start.

"Hello." Sayer stepped forward, giving the woman a smile guaranteed to beguile and disarm. "I'm Dr. Sayer Macnair. We're doing some survey work on the local mines for the University of Pennsylvania. I'm sorry, I know I should have called first, but as the Montclairs are such avid supporters of the university and I was already in the area, I thought I'd take the chance one of the family would be able to see me, perhaps Gerald Montclair? I left several messages for him, but was never able to reach him at his office."

"He's been quite busy this week." The woman, middle-aged and wearing a severe black dress, had opened the door a little further. Trying to keep her attention on Sayer, she slanted several curious glances at Aramanda.

Aramanda avoided looking directly at her, sure the woman would see her exasperation at Sayer's outrageous lies clearly marked on her face.

"And I'm sorry, but Mr. Montclair isn't here now. I don't expect him until later this evening. Perhaps you'd like to leave a message."

"Is there someone else in the family at home? Mrs. Montclair maybe?"

The woman's eyes widened slightly. "Mrs. Montclair?" She glanced in the direction of the gardens. "Mrs. Montclair doesn't receive visitors. I'll tell Mr. Montclair you were here. If there's nothing else . . ." She looked again at Aramanda.

"I'll leave you my card. We'll be staying in town for a while." Sayer fished in his jacket pocket for the card, leaving the woman to stare openly at Aramanda.

Determined to hold fast to her dignity, Aramanda this time met the other woman's eyes fully, causing her to give a quick, apologetic smile.

"I'm sorry," she said. "It's just, you look so much like . . . you remind me of someone."

"One of the Montclairs?" Sayer intervened smoothly, his smile guileless.

"Actually . . ." The woman glanced over her shoulder, then turned back to Sayer and Aramanda. "Mr. Montclair would have my job if he knew, but if it's only for a moment—there's something you should see." Gesturing to them to follow, she led them down a long, dim hallway.

Aramanda caught Sayer's swift sideways glance.

Yes, I know this house, she wanted to tell him. *But only as a shadow of the past. There is no one, nothing here that belongs to me anymore.*

At the end of the hallway, the woman opened a door to a room Aramanda knew as the library.

"They've hung some of the old family portraits in here—Mr. Montclair takes great pride in his family's heritage and he insisted on it—" she was saying. "It's really quite amazing—"

She stopped midway into the room and pointed to an oil painting hung over the fireplace mantel. Aramanda sucked in a breath, shocked at seeing so clear a proof of the past. Beside her, Sayer tensed, his hand clenching painfully on hers.

"If you put your hair up and wore that dress, no one could tell the difference between you," the woman said, glancing from Aramanda to the painting. "It's really remarkable."

"Yes, remarkable," Sayer murmured. He stared at the painting, looking as if he'd seen proof of the impossible.

Aramanda Montclair, dressed in an elegant pale-green satin Victorian gown and the family emeralds, looked back at him. She was magnificent: regal, proud, serene, determined. From the confident lift of her chin to the straight posture of her supple white shoulders, she exuded every ideal of grace and beauty.

Turning to the flesh-and-blood Aramanda, he locked gazes with her, and Aramanda felt everything he could not say. For an instant, all the time lost between them was suddenly regained in the memories of a single moment.

"I think she is the most beautiful of all of them," the woman prattled on, oblivious to the river of emotion between Sayer and Aramanda. "It's sad she died so young."

"Did she?" Aramanda whispered, still looking at Sayer, feeling light-headed.

"Yes, she was supposedly murdered by a vigilante miner who were trying to destroy the Montclairs. She had fallen in love with him, but he wouldn't give up his violence, his battle for the rights of the miners for her. He blew up one of her family's mines, and she died in the explosion."

"That is not—" Aramanda cut off her sentence, horrified at herself for nearly blurting out the truth. "That is not a very romantic story," she amended, forcing a smile for the woman.

"No, it isn't," the woman agreed. "Some of the others, though—"

"We should be going," Sayer said abruptly. "If you'll tell Mr. Montclair I was here . . ." Aramanda was compelled to follow when he turned and started striding toward the front door, his hand still locked around hers.

He left the woman at the door with a quick word of thanks, not pausing until they were down the stairs and nearly to the car.

There, Aramanda balked, forcing him to stop. "I am sorry you did not get the answers you wanted," she said stiffly. "But there is no need to drag me about like so much baggage."

Sayer looked down at her as if seeing her for the first time. "That painting in there—it was you."

"Yes."

"Yes? That's it? Just yes?"

"What would you wish me to say? That I know nothing about it? That it is just another part of the fantasy you think I have contrived? You know that it is not the truth. I will not give you a lie simply to make you comfortable with what you want to believe."

Without giving him time to reply, Aramanda tugged her hand from his. She walked away from the car in the direction of the neatly manicured gardens, stopping to stare blindly at the jewel tones of a phalanx of early silver and pale pink roses.

After a moment, she heard Sayer's footsteps behind her. The warmth of his body touched hers before his hand brushed her shoulder, turning her to face him.

"You're right," he said quietly. "For the first time in my life, I did want a lie. I don't even want to trust what I saw and heard in there. All this time you've been asking me to remember feelings I swore belonged to someone else. But in there . . . in there, looking at that painting, those feelings were suddenly mine."

He reached out and traced his fingertips over her face, like a blind man suddenly gifted with sight. "I remembered loving you." His hand slid away. "It doesn't make any sense."

"Must it?"

"It should."

Aramanda shook her head, smiling. "Why? Can you explain beauty or faith?"

Plucking off one of the roses nearest to her, she held it out to him. "Can you explain how perfection can be so simple? I once asked my mother how I would know if the love I felt for someone would be forever. She said I would know when love was the only answer to any question I had or would ever ask, when because of love, I was willing to believe what could not be believed. When nothing could ever be impossible again."

"With you, I can't think of anything that's impossible," Sayer said softly.

Taking the rose, he crumbled the blossom between his fingers until the silvery-violet petals came loose in his hand. Moving with infinite slowness, he caressed the curve of her throat and shoulder, spreading the fragile essence of the petals against her skin. "You make me believe in miracles."

Aramanda felt the power of a miracle when he gathered her into his arms and kissed her, deeply, withholding nothing. She held tightly to him, taking all he offered and more.

He was not the Roarke she had left behind so long ago in the past. But her soul hungered for him, a hunger never sated, a pure need without compassion or pity that drove out everyone and everything but her love for him.

Past, present, future, it did not matter. Only this feeling mattered.

Sayer's mouth followed the fragrant path left by the rose petals, tasting her skin, and she sensed an echo of her own need in him. Letting her head fall back at the urging of his touch, she twisted her fingers into the hair at his nape, telling him with the language of her body she wanted this and all he could give.

When his hand slid intimately against the curve of her breast, she sucked in a breath, pushing closer even as the words of yesterday slipped from her lips. "We should not. Not here."

"Yes, here," he whispered hotly in her ear. "Here, anywhere, love. What does it matter?"

"My family—" Aramanda stopped, awash in confusion. Her family wasn't here—were they? But she had been here in this garden with Roarke, yesterday.

And now with this man, with Sayer.

Yet where did she belong? To whom did her heart belong?

"What's wrong?"

She opened her eyes to find Sayer looking at her, concern coming together with the passion still in his eyes.

"I . . . I do not know. I—it feels strange to me, to be here with you like this. Roarke and I were here together in this garden once. He brought me here, secretly, to visit my family and we . . . It is just as before except—"

"—it isn't."

"No. It is as if I came here expecting to meet a friend and found a stranger. Only the feelings are the same."

"I know."

The admission startled her. "Do you?"

Sayer kissed her gently with more emotion than desire. "Yes, I do. I may not like them, or want them, but I can't get rid of these feelings, whatever they mean. My problem is deciding what to do about them."

"Yes, that is a difficulty, is it not?" She smiled. "It is not as easy as deciding right and wrong. Love is always a distraction."

"You're a distraction," he said lightly. "And you're right, we shouldn't be here. Neither of us belongs here."

"Do you believe that?"

"You haven't left me much choice."

"That is not an answer."

"It's the best I can do right now." He pushed the hair off his forehead, his expression serious. "I just need time to sort this out."

"Time is something I seem to have an endless supply of," Aramanda said. She intended the words as a light quip, yet as soon as she'd said them, she felt a coldness touch her inside. She shivered despite the warmth of the sun.

Sayer took her hand, frowning slightly. "What is it?"

"Nothing. It is just . . . I feel I do not have time. That soon . . ." She shook her head, unable to explain.

"It's this place. I shouldn't have brought you here. Let's go." He turned to lead her back toward the rover.

As he did, a slight motion in the garden behind them caught Aramanda's eye. She glanced back and, for a moment, saw the slight figure of a woman bend down to snip off a spray of lilac. When the woman straightened, laying the flowers in the basket she carried, the sunlight showed the silver and auburn of her hair.

Sudden tears misted Aramanda's vision and, in the next instant, the woman disappeared behind a row of shrubbery.

"It must have been Mrs. Montclair," Sayer said, still looking out over the gardens.

"Yes. Mrs. Montclair."

The sadness in her voice reached him, and Sayer squeezed her hand. "But not yours."

"No. In this place, my mother is . . . gone. They all are. Seeing her . . . I realized again how I do not belong, how truly alone I am."

"You aren't alone, Aramanda," Sayer said softly. Enfolding her in the sanctuary of his embrace, he held her against his heart. "Maybe we're both crazy, but we're in this together. No matter where we end up."

Eight

"There's not much here. Not much more than we already knew, anyway." Sayer closed the last of the books he and Aramanda had been pouring over for the past two hours, pushing the heavy volume aside. He leaned back in the uncomfortable library chair, trying to fit his tall frame into a more accommodating position, and looked at Aramanda for confirmation.

"Yes," she murmured, still engrossed in her own book. She'd found the thick, leather-bound tome detailing histories of the area's more prominent mining families in the old and rare book section of the city's main library and had spent nearly thirty minutes studying it.

She ran a fingertip over a passage, scanning the type for familiar names. "There are many references to the Molly Maguire rebellions, but here, at least, after Roarke's death, the movement seemed to have lost its momentum. If Roarke had lived long enough to help them unite and bring about true reform . . ." Her voice trailed off on a melancholy note.

Sayer couldn't help but notice how, since their visit to the travel agency, she had begun to divorce him from the love of her past. She hadn't called him Roarke for hours. In fact, she hadn't but once even said his name at all.

He ought to be relieved, he told himself. Instead, he felt only a strange ache of loss.

He'd spent the last two days trying to convince her they had no past together and now, perversely, he wanted that past back.

He wanted to be the hero she loved with all her heart and soul. He wanted to be Roarke Macnair.

Except both of them knew he wasn't.

"We might as well push on," he said for something to say that would distract him from his feelings. "I still want to run by Will's before we head back to town."

Aramanda seemed not to have heard him. She stared at the open pages of the book, her lower lip caught between her teeth.

"Aramanda?"

She looked up, and he saw tears blurring the clear amber of her eyes.

"What is it?"

"Nothing . . . everything. I should not have done this." She abruptly closed the book, shoving it away from her.

Sayer straightened in his seat, looking at her more closely. "What did you find? Something about your family?"

"Family, friends." Aramanda put her hands over her eyes for a few moments, taking in long breaths. When she looked up at Sayer again, the wetness had spilled onto her cheeks. "Roarke's rebellion failed, and they died with him—Scully, Liam, many of my friends. My mother married Gervase, and his hold on the Montclair interests endured. I cannot even find references to my brothers and sisters except that Nicholas left the estate and never returned and Jessalyn further divided the family by making a miserable match simply to escape. And I . . ."

She shook her head, dropping her gaze. Her teardrops fell on the polished surface of the table like soft rain.

"Yes," Sayer said very gently, "I know." He reached out and took her hands in his. She clung to him, her gaze raised to his as if he were her only chance of redemption.

"Aramanda Montclair died young, supposedly in the explosion Roarke triggered. She never had the chance to marry or have a family of her own. And no one in the Montclair family had the courage to continue her charitable work among the miners after her death. The suffering continued, worse than before."

"And so that is what I return to, a place with no future," she whispered, the pain in her voice so keen Sayer winced.

"It doesn't have to be that way." He raised a hand and lifted her chin to look into her eyes. "Stay."

"I cannot." She touched his face. "Return with me."

"I can't."

"Then we are lost."

The despair in her voice, drawn in the droop of her body, spurred Sayer to action. "No, I can't accept that either. Come on." Standing, he brought her to her feet and took her hand to lead her out of the library. "Let's get the hell out of here. It's too depressing and we aren't accomplishing anything."

Once inside the rover, Sayer left the keys dangling in the ignition and, without a word, turned to take Aramanda in his arms. He held her tenderly, as he would a child, stroking her hair and back, offering silent solace as she spent her grief in a storm of weeping.

"I am afraid I have no courage to lose," she said at last, swiping away the wetness on her face, still cradled against Sayer's chest.

"That's not true," Sayer said. He looked down at her and very gently brushed the damp tendrils of hair from her cheek. "You're the bravest woman I've ever known, the most compassionate, the most generous in spirit, and certainly the most beautiful. There's no one I know, woman or man, who could have survived the way you have these past days. Under the same circumstances, I don't think I could have done better."

His tribute moved her beyond words, and Aramanda clung to him for a moment longer, drawing from his strength, feeding on the encouragement he offered. "I could not have done it without you at my side," she said. "You have always inspired me to have the courage to do what must be done."

"Well, what must be done now is that you wipe your face and prepare for dinner with my brother," Sayer said lightly. "I need you at my side for that. Maybe you can inspire me to have the patience not to get into another verbal brawl with Will."

Aramanda couldn't help but smile at Sayer's attempt to divert her from her misery. "I do not think anyone has the courage for that task. But I will try."

"Good." Kissing her forehead, he slowly released her, smoothing back her hair and bestowing a final kiss on her hand before starting the rover. "Because I'm going to need all the help I can get."

A few final splashes of red and gold faded into darkness behind the treetops as Sayer maneuvered into the front drive of his brother's modest, brick rowhouse.

"Are you certain his wife has had time to prepare a meal? We gave her less than two hours' notice," Aramanda said. "It seems terribly inconsiderate not to allow her more time, especially when you tell me it has been years since your last visit."

"That's what microwaves are for." Sayer stopped the rover, pocketing the keys. Coming around to her side to hand her out, he said, "Don't worry, no matter how much notice I give Will, he's never comfortable when I'm around. We won't stay long. There're just a few things I want to ask him about concerning the mines."

"I am sorry."

"Why? You've been telling me the whole way over here how uncomfortable you are with the last minute's notice."

"I am not sorry for that. I am sorry you and your brother are no closer in this time than you were in the past. I have never been wholly at ease among my family, but I cannot imagine being estranged from them so that I chose not to see them for years at a time or anticipated battles the times I did."

"You don't know Will," Sayer said, taking her hand. He rubbed his fingers over hers in an almost unconscious caress. But while his touch was warm and gentle, his jaw tightened and his eyes were hard. "We don't see eye-to-eye on anything, and he's too stubborn to see any other point of view."

"Unlike you of course." She was saved his retort as they reached the door and Sayer pushed the bell.

In a few moments, the door swung open on a brightly lit room brimming with squealing children. A small, dark-headed boy about the same height as the door knob with eyes the color of

Sayer's poked his head around the door and craned his neck to look up at Aramanda and Sayer.

Aramanda smiled. "Hello."

"Hi! Are you Uncle Sayer's wife?"

"No." Aramanda laughed. "I am only a friend."

"Hey, Nat, is that really you?" Sayer swung the grinning child into his arms. "I think you've grown a foot taller. Let me see if you weigh more than a puppy yet."

"Nat, ask them inside." A harried-looking young woman with a tiny bundle in her arms bustled into the room. She shifted the baby to a one-handed grip and pushed strands of lank, pale red hair from her forehead. Large gray eyes swept Sayer and Aramanda in a quick, appraising glance.

"Hi, Sayer. I'm sorry, I had the TV on in the kitchen and I didn't hear the bell." Hurrying over, she held out her free hand to Aramanda. "I'm Liz. And this is Savannah. Sayer hasn't even met her yet." She beamed down at the infant in her arms, the anxious lines of her thin face softened by her love for her daughter.

A baby girl . . . a memory of a small, cold room and a red-haired woman in a rocking chair, her arms empty, visited Aramanda. Her heart constricted, and she swallowed hard, forcing a smile.

"She is beautiful," she said, reaching out to gently touch the baby's tuft of bright red hair. Savannah twisted to look at her, waving her fists in the air, and smiled her toothless smile. "How old is she?"

"Three months this week," Liz said. "It took me three boys to get my precious little girl. Now that we have Savannah, our family's complete."

"Such a precious child," Aramanda told her, blinking back sudden tears.

"Thank you—I'm sorry, I don't know your name. Sayer isn't usually this uncivilized," Liz said, flashing a teasing look at her brother-in-law.

"It's good to see you again, too, Liz," he said. He swung Nat to the ground, then bent and lightly hugged Liz. "This is Aramanda Montclair. She's a friend."

"Montclair?" Liz's voice went flat.

"A very distant relation," Aramanda put in quickly, feeling a familiar twinge of guilt. It seemed her family's reputation had not improved among the miners even after the passage of so much time.

"Oh. Well, come on in and have a seat. I got your message on the machine after work, Sayer. I heard you were in Philly, but I didn't think you'd be coming up this way. You don't usually." Her voice held both reproof and regret, and the tone told Aramanda more about Sayer's relationship with his brother than any of his explanations. "If I had thought you'd be by, I'd have put in a roast or a turkey. Afraid it's potluck tonight, though."

Aramanda slanted Sayer a glance, feeling more uncomfortable. It was difficult enough, being in yet another strange place where people spoke of things she had no knowledge of and never would. But to know they were intruders as well . . .

If he felt the same, he didn't show it. He only shrugged. "I'm sorry; it was a last minute decision. Listen, if you haven't started dinner, how about if I take us all out? If it's too late for the boys, you could grab a sitter and just make it the four of us."

"I wouldn't know how to act without the boys hanging from me," Liz said with a laugh. "Besides, I don't know when Will will get off tonight. He's been putting in long hours. So, you'll have to settle for microwave fare tonight."

"Anything will be fine," Aramanda put in. "Roarke did not give you much notice."

"Roarke?" Liz looked at Sayer, raising a brow. "I thought you hated your middle name."

He sighed. "It's a long story." At the same time, he felt a strange twinge, both pleasure and pain, at how easily the name had slipped from Aramanda's lips.

"I'll bet it is. And I'm dying to hear it. In the meantime, don't worry about dinner. This works out better. The boys have already eaten, and I'll be putting them to bed shortly."

"Not me, Mama. I'm the oldest!" Nat cried out. "I go to bed a half hour later!"

"That's right. You can stay up your extra half hour. That way, Uncle Sayer will have a chance to see your dinosaurs."

"Yeah! I have the whole Jurassic Park collection on my dresser, and all the ones from the museum."

Sayer mussed his nephew's hair. "Good going, Nat. I want a tour of the whole collection."

Savannah began to fuss, and Liz bounced her gently in a soothing motion. "Will is usually home by now, but there's been trouble up at the mine lately, so he's been putting in extra hours to make up for lost time. I hope he won't be long."

"What kind of trouble?" Sayer asked, and Aramanda saw the tension ripple over him, tightening his shoulders and jaw.

"Oh, something some environmentalists stirred up. Probably some damned radicals just like you!" She winked at Sayer and stooped to pick up a tattered blanket from the floor. "If it's not them, it's the union guys screaming about wages and lost workdays because of the picketing. We never have time to catch our breath around here, with one thing and another."

Aramanda turned to Liz. "Let me help you prepare the meal, please. I come from a large family and I am used to working with little ones underfoot. Roar—Sayer can stay here with the children. It will be good for him to be reacquainted with his nephews."

Liz looked doubtful, eyeing Aramanda's expensive clothing from head to foot. "Well, if you're sure you won't ruin that dress."

"You haven't been in a kitchen for a while," Sayer put in, giving her a knowing glance. "After the day we've had, maybe you'd rather take it easy for a while."

He was giving her a simple path out, but Aramanda wanted to do something, anything, to distract her from the odd feeling of being displaced that started to grip her the moment she'd walked into the house.

"I am quite certain I want to help. I have always loved cooking,

Annette Daniels

and I am certain the kitchen cannot be much changed from my own."

"Don't be too sure about that," Sayer said. He smiled, though, and gave her hand a quick squeeze.

Aramanda glanced back over her shoulder before turning into the kitchen behind Liz. Amid squeals and wriggling bodies, she spied Sayer, already being tugged down to the boys' level. He settled on his back on the rug and, completely at their mercy, began bouncing them two at a time on his long legs.

His laughter, rich and resonant, mingling with theirs reminded her of a time when he'd played as easily with his brother Liam's children and her own young brother, Oliver. With a slight shock, she realized this was the first time she had seen him this at ease, this lighthearted. In some ways, Sayer Macnair had, indeed, changed from the Roarke she had once known.

"You make a marvelous carnival ride," she called to him.

Toppling a squealing Nat to the floor, he grinned back at her. "There's always room for one more."

"Not this time," she said before disappearing into the kitchen. "But I will remember your offer."

A short while later, Will shoved open the front door, stopping cold in the entry when his eyes met Sayer's.

Will hadn't changed much and Sayer wondered, as he always did, how they could look so much alike but be so radically opposite in every other way. A little shorter and stockier, Will shared the same dark hair and deep blue eyes, except his features were more mobile, more likely to reflect quick changes of temper.

The children abandoned their new ride at once and ran to jump on their father. "Daddy, look! Uncle Sayer came to see us," Nat cried. "He's going to send me some new dinosaurs from the Carnegie collection! It'll be so cool!"

Will pulled off his sooty black boots and coat and tossed them on a square of linoleum beside the small, hardwood entry. "Is he now?"

Sayer pulled himself to his feet and straightened his clothes, running a hand through his ruffled hair. "I guess you didn't get my message."

"No. I don't have a secretary."

Sayer's fists knotted at his sides. No matter how many years went by, the same old tension reared its ugly head every time he was in the same room with his brother. That's why he'd practically stopped visiting altogether. It was no use to try to have a close relationship—hell, any kind of relationship—with someone who so obviously resented him. Even the barest communication in recent years seemed more than Will wanted to share.

But Sayer refused to let go completely. Whether he liked it or not, he was Will's only brother and he wasn't about to let him forget it.

"I'm sorry for the short notice. I left word with Liz, hoping she could call you before we got here. It was an impulsive decision or I would have let you know sooner. And I would have brought the kids something. I'll be sure to send some things along as soon as we get back to Boulder."

"We?" Will lifted and kissed each child in turn.

"I brought a friend."

"That's a first. I didn't know you had any." Will bent and pulled off socks that might have been white, but were now the color of the coal covering them. "What brings you up this way?"

"Business, mainly."

Will paused and shook his head slightly. "Figures. What else could it be? Give me ten minutes to shower, and I'll be ready for dinner. You are staying for dinner, aren't you?"

"If you aren't going to kick me out. Aramanda is in the kitchen helping Liz now."

"Aramanda?" Will gave a short laugh. "I can't wait to see what goes with a name like that." With that, he picked up his dirty socks and headed down the hallway.

"You might when you hear her last name," Sayer muttered to himself before resuming his role as horse to the excited boys, who were now dangling from either arm, cajoling him back to the game.

An hour later, helping Liz put the boys to bed, Sayer couldn't stop himself from wondering how his brother and Aramanda were managing alone in the kitchen. Will hadn't said anything when he'd introduced them, but he'd caught the flash of anger in his brother's eyes and he knew Aramanda had, too.

"You won't forget about the dinosaurs, will you?" Nat asked for the fifteenth time as Sayer started to leave the bedroom.

"Not a chance," Sayer assured him. "As long as you don't forget to send me a note so I know they're the right ones."

"I promise!"

Sayer flashed his nephew a grin before he flicked off the light, the smile vanishing the moment he closed the door behind him. He strode quickly to the kitchen, not knowing what to expect, guilty about leaving Aramanda to cope alone, especially in a place she would find completely unfamiliar, even frightening.

Anticipating a stony silence, it came as a shock to find them laughing and talking like old friends when he walked in.

"But I have never seen such a thing!" Aramanda was saying. Sayer saw her bent close to the microwave, running her fingertips over the digital display. "Why, cook would be able to prepare a meal for dozens in less time than it takes to prepare one trifle with such an oven."

"Even with a cook, I can't believe you've never seen a microwave before," Liz said, laughing, coming in before Sayer. "What do you have in your kitchen, a wood stove?"

"Why, yes," Aramanda said, looking surprised.

"And you complain when the electricity goes off," Will teased his wife.

Liz pulled a face and tossed a dish towel in Will's direction, laughing with Aramanda at his futile attempt to dodge it.

Sayer paused in the doorway, watching them. Will never relaxed and laughed or joked with him the way he was now with a woman he had only met a few minutes earlier. The realization pricked him with a mixture of sadness and envy, feelings that intensified when their light mood vanished as soon as they saw him.

"Well, I guess you aren't holding her last name against her," he said, taking the battered wooden captain's chair next to Aramanda in the cramped kitchen.

Will shrugged. "Not her fault she's tied to those money-grubbing snakes. Besides, that's the name that signs my pay-check."

A flicker of hurt crossed Aramanda's face, moving Sayer to brush his hand over hers. She held fast for a moment before her face composed itself into a smile.

Will caught the exchange between them and looked from one to the other, a slight frown creasing his features.

"What would you like to drink, Aramanda?" Liz asked, mov-ing the baby seat where Savannah slept peacefully over to a spot on the countertop close to her seat. She then set out a simple salad, tater tots and microwaved frozen lasagna. "I have beer, Koolaid, or diet Coke."

Aramanda glanced at Sayer in confusion, and he answered for her. "We'll both have diet Coke, thanks. So, tell me, Will, what's going on at the mine? Liz mentioned there's been trouble."

"Some of your damned environmentalists have been stirring up a ruckus out front, picketing and so forth. The union guys are real happy about it, I'll tell you." He took a helping of salad and shoved the bowl across the table to Sayer. "You'd know more than I do about it I'd guess. All I know is there was a crew of technicians from some group who set up camp for a few days outside the mine. They were doing some testing inside until the union men threatened to kick ass and the Montclair lawyers had them thrown out."

"Do you know what they were looking for?"

Will looked away.

"Well, do you?" Liz asked pointedly.

Will shoved a tater tot around his plate a minute. "I didn't want to say anything to you because I didn't want to go and get you all worked up over nothing."

"What's your idea of nothing? Come on, Will, I have a right to know."

"Oh, there's some rumor going around that there might be traces of radon in the mine, that's all."

"Radon! That's all! Why didn't you tell me? Why haven't I heard anything about this on the news?"

"I can answer that," Sayer said.

Will dropped his fork to his plate. "Sure you can. You've always got the answers. That's why you're here, isn't it? You're in with them, trying to get me put out of work."

"I'm here to look into the radon issue, but I don't want you to lose your job. Unless your life is in danger."

"And what makes you think my life won't be in danger, not to mention my wife's and my four kids', if I can't put meat on the table for them?"

Liz shifted uncomfortably in her seat. "Will, please—"

"I didn't come here to argue about this," Sayer said.

"Of course not. You never want to get into any discussion about the people's lives you screw up while you're out there trying to save the damned planet!"

Sayer shoved away from the table and turned to Aramanda. "He sounds just like you, you know that?" Raking his fingers through his hair, he took a few steps from them.

Aramanda recognized the grip of tension in his straight, stiff movements. She sensed his struggle against his rising temper, and she wanted to stand up and walk to him, place her hands on his tense shoulders, and calm him with her voice and touch. But she knew to do so would only have the reverse effect. Instead, frustrated, she held her tongue and waited with the others for the storm to either pass—or vent itself in full force.

After a long moment, he turned back to face them, his jaw set in a hard line, determination firing like lightning in his eyes. "Why the hell do you think I'm trying to stop the poison in that mine? Why do you think I do any of this? Why do you think I'm trying to save what's left of this planet? For the rats? The roaches? They're the only ones who will survive if we continue this systematic destruction of the earth. I'm trying to save it for the people. For you and your children and their children, Will. And I'm damned sorry if that means in the process people lose their jobs sometimes. But something has to be sacrificed. Something has to give for God's sake!"

"If the mine closes, is there other work for the men?" Aramanda asked Will.

"This is a mining town," Will told her. "If the mine closes, we have no life left here. Mining is all I've ever done. All I can do. Most of the others are in the same position."

Sayer gripped the edge of the table and leaned toward his brother. "Would you rather risk your life than find a new one?"

"So easy for you to say, mister college professor. You and your education and your easy life. You're only responsible for yourself. Always have been. But I chose to have a family, take responsibility for someone else, and I like it that way."

"That's not fair, Will. We both came from the same parents. We had the same upbringing. We went in different directions, that's all. I've earned everything I've gained with hard work, just like you."

"Yeah, show me your hands then. Show me those lily-white nails."

"What?"

"Come on. Show me. You're nothing but a paper-pusher who gives pretty speeches."

Aramanda saw the muscles along Sayer's jaw jerk. The argument stung her with the memories of so many just like it she'd heard Roarke have with Liam. And more than once their disagreements had flared, ending in blows and bruises.

"Look," Will held up his hands and turned them around, "see the scars, the calluses? These nails will never be lighter than that black pot on the stove. That's what real work does to you. You don't know what you're talking about, big *brother.*"

Sayer balled his hands into fists and flexed them. "I'm going to that mine tomorrow. If I can prove the reports I've been getting from my contacts there, I'm going to get that place shut down. One way or another. You might not care whether you live or die, but I do."

The tension, the harsh words, the flaring anger between Sayer and Will made Aramanda feel she had never left the past. It had always been this way when Roarke and Liam were together; she had always been caught between the battles of her lover and her friend.

She glanced to Liz and found her eyes red, brimming with tears. Reaching under the table, she impulsively grasped the woman's hand. Liz responded with warmth, desperation, and gratitude in her trembling grip.

Aramanda drew in a breath and lifted her chin. "I am certain you do care," she said, meeting Sayer's hot eyes squarely. She glanced at Will. "Both of you. But you are both too stubborn to admit there might be room for compromise between you. Perhaps you could try listening instead of shouting at each other."

Turning to Liz, she squeezed the other woman's hand. "I will help you clean up the kitchen. If they persist in arguing, they can just as easily do it in another room."

Sayer stared at her, his expression angry; and for a moment, Aramanda thought he would refuse her. Then, he let go an explosive breath and shook his head. "Fine. If that's what you want." He turned around and left the kitchen, not looking back; and after a moment, a stone-faced Will followed him out.

"Thank you," Liz said, letting go a sigh of relief. "They're both so hot tempered, I never know how to handle it when they start in on each other. Sometimes, I think it would be better if Sayer didn't visit; but he keeps coming back, although Lord knows why."

"He is single-minded about pursuing his ideals, even in relationships," Aramanda said. Standing up, she began to stack up the plates and carry them to the sink. "Roarke is always seeking perfection, and he is frustrated when others do not understand or share his zeal."

"You seem to know him very well," Liz said, getting to her feet and checking on Savannah before starting to scrape food scraps into the garbage can. "Have you known Sayer long?"

The casual question made Aramanda uncomfortable. She did not like to lie, but then she could hardly tell Liz the truth. "Long enough to know what he is like."

"And you care about him?"

"I—yes." Though the feelings behind her answer were complex and the situation bizarre at best, this she would not lie about. Roarke or Sayer, she did care. "I do."

"It shows, you know," Liz said. She gathered up the used glasses, emptying the dregs into the sink. "Even Will commented on it, and he doesn't usually notice things like that, especially where Sayer is concerned."

"Has it always been like this between them?" Aramanda asked, quickly shifting the subject.

"Pretty much so. Will and I have been married ten years, and it's never been any better since I've known the two of them. Will's always resented that his parents scrimped and saved to send Sayer to college while he drifted into following his father into the coal mines. And he obviously doesn't appreciate Sayer's crusades against the mine owners," Liz added, pulling a face. "I know the causes Sayer fights for are important, and I admire his courage and dedication in taking them on. But he doesn't always see how it hurts people like Will who don't know any other way to make a living."

"I know," Aramanda said softly, looking at the closed door separating her from Sayer. "He cannot tolerate injustices, and yet in fighting to right them, he detaches himself from the people he cares so much for."

In the process of wiping off the table, Liz paused and looked up at Aramanda. "You're in love with him, aren't you? It's all right," she said when Aramanda hesitated. "Just take care of yourself. You know so much about Sayer, you should also know he could hurt you. He might not be able to love you the same way you love him."

"That I do know," Aramanda said, turning to mask the pain she knew showed in her eyes from Liz. "I have known it since we first met."

They finished cleaning up the kitchen, and Aramanda followed Liz to the living room.

"We should be going," she said, looking at Sayer, who stood in front of the window, his back to the room, hands shoved in his pockets. Will sat slumped in a chair, staring at the floor, rousing himself at her words. "Thank you for a wonderful meal. I hope to see you both again."

"Me, too," Liz said, trying a smile. "I hope it's often. You're good for Sayer, I can tell. He actually listens to you, and that's an accomplishment for anyone."

"I tell him that, but it seems stubbornness is an inborn Macnair trait." Aramanda stole a glance at Sayer. He finally turned, walking to her side, putting his hand on her waist as he went with her to the door.

Will followed them to the front door. "Don't let him bully you. He's been known to do it before."

"Yes. I know."

Sayer shot his brother a hard glare. "Thanks." He paused, then added, "I'm sorry things worked out this way."

"Nothing new," Will said, forcing a laugh.

"Maybe I'll see you tomorrow. I'm planning to visit the mine." He turned to Liz. "Dinner was great. And I am sorry about the argument. I'll see you soon, though, okay?" He opened the door and ushered Aramanda out.

"Sayer!" Liz rushed after them when they had taken several steps down the walk, putting a hand on his arm. She glanced back at Will, still standing in the doorway. "I understand what you're trying to do. Please, try to understand Will. He's only thinking of us."

Sayer looked at her tear-wet face and impulsively bent down and hugged her. "I know, Liz; I do understand. I just can't accept things the way he does, that's all. I want to make life be the way it ought to be instead of the way it is."

She smiled up to him. "I know. Always the idealist. And I hope you find a way to accomplish your goals." She glanced at Aramanda. "Both of you."

Nine

Sayer threw a sheet on the couch in the living room of the suite of the old-fashioned inn they'd checked into and made a halfhearted effort to straighten it. "Toss me a blanket and pillow, would you?" he said, not looking at Aramanda.

"You do not have to sleep there." She handed him the extra blanket she had found folded at the foot of the bed, her fingers glancing his. She knew what she offered him and all the implications, yet she could not stop herself from saying the words.

He looked tired and angry, and she wanted to give him back some of the solace he had given to her in her grief and desperation. She had come to accept he was not the same lover of her yesterdays; yet, in spirit, he was the man she loved, and no amount of impossibilities or reasons could change that.

Nor could they change her desire for him.

Sayer's eyes slid over her, and Aramanda saw a look of hunger there before it was shuttered behind an unreadable wall. "I'm not very good company tonight. I'd rather be alone."

"Sayer . . ." She hesitated over the name. "Please, would you speak with me? I know how much tonight has upset you."

"No, you don't. *That's* one thing you couldn't know."

The harshness of his tone flicked at sensitive places in her heart. Aramanda hid her hurt though and faced him with a calm she did not feel. "Perhaps not. But I do know that this anger is doing neither you nor your brother any good."

"Maybe flattening him would knock some sense into his thick

skull." Sayer slammed the pillow down onto the couch. "Tonight, I was tempted as hell to do just that."

"I so admire your self-control," Aramanda said with a slight sardonic cant to her tone. "You are certainly more civilized in this time. Of course, you have lost your sense of humor."

"Thanks so much for the critique. I don't seem to find much to be amused about these days. I've about had it up to here with stubborn people who can't see a car coming until it runs them over!"

He strode over to the French doors that led to the balcony of their room and flung them open, standing spread-legged between them. His stance reminded Aramanda of the dozens of times he'd stood on tables at Tansie Caitlan's tavern, rousing the miners to action with his impassioned speeches.

"I'm sick of paper-pushing and negotiating and leading committees who never get their asses out of their chairs. Why is it so damned hard just to get things done? How difficult is it to grasp the notion that we're running out of time?"

"How difficult indeed . . . but I believe we are talking about two different things." Aramanda lowered herself to sit on the edge of the couch, reached down, and tossed off the sensible flats she had worn at Sayer's suggestion. "But it is strange you should say such things," she murmured softly. "That is how I feel. As if I am running out of time."

Straightening, she looked to Sayer for a response and realized he hadn't heard a word she'd said. She nearly repeated her comment, then caught back the words, knowing that at this moment, he was lost to her. Lost in his thoughts, he was concentrating only on his commitment to the whole of humanity, his beliefs, his goals, everyone and everything except her. Except the two of them.

She watched him for several minutes and let the memories, both of the past and of the last two days, come to her and blend until she could see both the Roarke of her yesterday and the Sayer of this time in one man. One man with the soul that was a match to her own.

One man lost to her. Yesterday, today.

At last, when he did not turn to her, Aramanda slipped quietly into the bedroom. She picked up the stuffed bear she'd insisted on bringing, and curled up on the bed with it hugged in her arms, not even bothering to undress, waiting long into the night for sleep to come.

She awoke the next morning to the deep resonance of Sayer's voice.

Rubbing her eyes open, she found he was speaking not to her but to the machine on the nightstand near her bed. She rolled over and listened to the one-sided conversation, partly closing her eyes again so he would not know she listened.

"I know, Jim. Yes, I've canceled them all."

Aramanda didn't need to watch him to recognize the rapid thump, thump, thump of his pacing back and forth next to the bed.

But she did watch him through half-closed eyes, her gaze following his long strides, the flex of muscle under his open shirt when he raised a hand to rake the hair off his forehead, the motion of his mouth as he talked into the curved handpiece.

"Those reporters will be up here today. I called them yesterday afternoon after we checked in to tell them I'd be at the mine today. A little publicity won't hurt, if we handle it right. It might put some pressure on the Montclairs. What? Yes, *we*. She's still with me."

Aramanda flinched at the sudden hard edge to his tone. With every passing hour, she felt more like an intruder in his life. It was a sadly familiar feeling, more hurtful than the sense she did not belong in this reality at all.

Her coming here had changed nothing. More and more, she began to feel destiny had been cruel in teasing her with a second chance for happiness. How could she believe Sayer would ever return with her to their yesterdays to right the wrongs that would forever divide them?

It was true, what the strange couple in the shop had said, she could not escape the consequences of her actions. Yet was she also forever being denied a chance at redemption for love's sake?

"Anything they wanted to ask me at the press conference I

Annette Daniels

missed they can ask me here. I'm not sure how it will turn out. It's my understanding that we can't get inside anymore. But I'll just have to go and see about that."

He sounded more and more like the Roarke of her past, single-minded, determined to reach his goal no matter the cost.

And she felt the same inside, longing to find a place she belonged, to find herself, to realize her dream of love, and yet not knowing if she could ever have it with the man she had given her heart to.

"No, I haven't changed my mind about Europe," Sayer was saying. "It's all set. I'll get back on schedule. This just came out of nowhere."

He fell silent, then lowered his voice. Feeling shameless, Aramanda strained to listen.

"That's not the same thing at all. I told you, she lives abroad. Come on, Jim, don't blow this into something it's not. The only other thing I have to change is that interview for the *Journal of Ecology*. I'll just give the editor a call. Sisk—yeah, that's his name; he'll reschedule the interview after my trip to Europe. Don't worry so damned much. It's just a minor setback."

A minor setback. Is that all I am to him in this place?

Aramanda turned her back to Sayer, feeling more alone than she ever had. She knew she did not belong here and had to return; but the longer she stayed, the more her faith that he would follow waned.

And if he refused to return with her, she would be alone not just for a lifetime, but for eternity.

As the rover climbed the rugged gravel road to the mine site, tension knotted in Sayer's stomach like a clenched fist. It wasn't only the confrontation with Will or all of the schedule changes he'd had to make or even the anticipation of any number of situations that might erupt at the mine today.

His worry centered above all of these on Aramanda.

Sayer glanced at her, seated next to him, his eyes drawn to the timeless beauty of her face. She'd scarcely spoken to him over breakfast or during the drive; her uncustomary silence and the paleness of her face disturbed him deeply.

She seemed so distant since they'd left Will's house—preoccupied, sad, holding herself aloof from him as if she feared revealing anything of her feelings or thoughts. He would have understood her mood better if she'd been angry with him for arguing with Will or for retreating into himself last night and shutting her out.

But that wasn't what was bothering her, he knew. He looked across the seat to her again, and this time she shifted and gave him a small, remote smile. But her beautiful eyes didn't reflect fire or pleasure, they reflected an inward pain and, strangely, a flicker of fear.

He hadn't realized until this morning how, unconsciously, he'd begun to feel connected to her. The emptiness that always dogged him had dissipated by measures since the hour she appeared in his life. He'd noticed, but attributed it to the hectic pace they'd been keeping and the strange circumstances surrounding her appearance in his life.

He hadn't had time to think any more about his secret loneliness, the aching lack of fulfillment in his life. Until now.

Time with her had made him see that his lonely life had taken its toll. He felt the emptiness keenly and realized he didn't want to live with it any longer.

But even as he'd watched her sleeping today, before dawn, holding tightly like a child to the ridiculous stuffed koala, Sayer had known somehow that during the night she'd shut some invisible door to him, leaving him suddenly, terribly alone. He'd sensed her withdrawal, had felt the distance settle between them.

He had never realized how much it hurt to be alone.

"Strange," Sayer murmured at length to dispel the uneasy silence, "you're here beside me, and yet I miss you. Aramanda . . . it's as though you've drifted far away from me."

As he swung the rover to a parallel stop beside the gated entrance to the mine, she turned to him and swanned her fingertips against his cheek. Her skin felt cold on his.

"As you did from me yesterday. But I am here. I am only a bit preoccupied, that is all. Look." She gestured out the front window to a group of men pointing back at them and gathering to walk toward them. "Your adoring followers have seen you. You must put all of your energies toward the problem at the mine now."

Sayer glanced at the crowd, then back at her. "I suppose. I tried to focus on the mine all during the drive here. But instead, all I can think about is you—you and me. I don't know what's wrong with me."

He reached out and took her hand, rubbing his thumb over the hollow of her palm. He felt a slight tremor ripple through her, and it heightened the tension in him. "I've never had this problem before. You've cast some sort of spell over me."

"You know what it is you wish to do here," Aramanda said, and the sadness and anxiety echoed in her voice as well. She glanced away from him again toward the gathering. "They are waiting for you."

"Come with me."

Aramanda looked at him, then at the crowd, and shook her head. "No, it is too . . . overwhelming. I am not comfortable in such crowds. I have never been. That is your talent, to inspire the masses. I—I will follow you in a moment."

"And afterward?"

Aramanda's fingers curled around his, and she clenched his hand before gently disengaging her own. "I will be here when this is ended."

"And how about when the rest of it is over?" Sayer asked. He waited for the answer, hands gripping the steering wheel.

"Then . . . I do not know. How can I?"

A man in a white moon-suit that resembled an astronaut's garb minus the helmet tapped on the window and pointed to the crowd.

Aramanda started, and Sayer slanted a concerned glance at her before waving and nodding to the man, indicating he needed a moment.

"Damn. I'm expected to give a statement." He took her hand again. "Aramanda—will you be waiting? If we get separated—"

He glanced around back. "There is quite a crowd gathering. Malcolm said he was going to keep this quiet, but obviously it's going to be anything but. I'm sorry. I thought there'd be a few people here, but I didn't expect this."

"They do seem rather agitated," Aramanda said. She frowned as she followed Sayer's gaze to the crowd. She drew in a long breath, but it came out unsteadily.

Something in her expression set off a warning bell in Sayer. "What's wrong? What are you afraid of?"

"I . . . nothing." The tip of her tongue wetted her lips. "I just did not anticipate there would be this manner of rebellion."

"It's not a rebellion, just a protest rally," Sayer said, trying to soothe her with the stroke of his voice. "Don't worry. I know most of them, and words are their biggest weapons. They just like to put on a good show to get their point across." His hand tightened on hers. "You'll meet me here, in the truck, won't you?"

"Of course," Aramanda said, looking faintly surprised at his insistence she wait for him. "I have promised you I would. I shall be here. Come now, you must not keep them waiting any longer. They look most anxious to speak to you."

Tempted to shove the key in the ignition and slam his foot to the floor to get them the hell away so they could talk in private, Sayer banished the fantasy and swung out of the truck, taking one last look at Aramanda before giving his attention to the waiting man.

"Hello, Dr. Macnair," the man in the moon-suit greeted him. "Dr. Breyer is waiting over there. If you'll follow me—"

Sayer shook his hand. "Lead the way," he said, glancing back over his shoulder into Aramanda's fathomless, amber eyes.

She gave him a ghost of a smile and, behind the curved glass with its golden wash of sunlight, she appeared faraway, a shadow-woman without substance threatening to vanish from his sight.

Sayer chided himself for his fantastical idea but more so for the gaping void he felt in the pit of his stomach at simply walking a few yards away from her. It was as though he were leaving a part of himself in the front seat of the rover.

Which is ridiculous. She'll be there when this is over. Where else would she go?

The man beside him was briefing him on the day's events so far, but Sayer unwittingly tuned him out.

Concentrate, dammit! You've got serious work to do and you can't afford to let your mind wander to her. She'll be there. She has to be.

He was needed here. His responsibility, his passion was for his beliefs. Everyone had to make sacrifices. And he'd always considered his price to be the relinquishing of a personal life. Of love. Now wasn't the time to question his priorities.

Except that the woman waiting for him in the truck made all those priorities seem small and insignificant.

The crowd outside the gate was growing in size and in restlessness. One by one, cars and vans marked with the local television and radio stations' call letters were pulling up and stopping to let the camera crews and reporters out to set up their equipment; the print reporters were working the crowd, notebooks poised, looking to pick up a few color quotes.

A few photographers, wearing necklaces of cameras and vests crammed with film canisters and lenses, jockeyed for the best positions, snatching shots here and there while waiting for the real action to begin.

Several sheriff's department cars and a half-dozen guards posted by the Montclairs stood in small groups, warily eyeing the crowd, talking amongst themselves.

The man in the white moon-suit led Sayer through a swarm of college-aged radicals toting picket signs decorated with slogans and skull-and-crossbones symbols to where Dr. Breyer stood talking to several other men and women, some in moonsuits, others in white t-shirts with red lettering like bloodstains that screamed "NO POISON!"

"Malcolm," Sayer called as he drew near, raising his voice to be heard above the call to protest one of the white-suited picketers shouted through a bullhorn. "What the hell is going on here?"

The men and women, predominantly young, in the white

moon-suits, some wearing gas masks—Sayer noticed upon closer inspection—had been turned into walking protest signs with bold red-and-black lettered banners draped over them demanding the Montclairs "SHUT DOWN THE MINE!" and "STOP THE POISON!" Another banner had been hung on the fence near the mine entrance, and two of the picketers struggled against an errant breeze to tie up another at the very top of the fence.

"Ah, Dr. Macnair, welcome!"

Sayer extended a hand, but didn't return Malcolm's smile. "I asked you a question."

The older man ducked his head slightly and shrugged his bony shoulders. "I told you I had nothing left to lose. I let the word out to a few friends in other environmental groups that you would be here today. And this—" He waved a hand at the line of cars heading up the road toward the gates. "—is the result. You are a famous man, indeed, Dr. Macnair."

Sayer's jaw went rigid. "I warned you about getting the press involved too soon." He shoved a hand through his hair. "Dammit, Malcolm, we don't even have conclusive evidence there is radon leakage. All we have are suspicions and rumors."

"I know. And that is enough. Whatever my failings, Doctor, I have always been a meticulous and accurate scientist. If we can raise public attention enough, something will be done to further the formal tests."

"Or we'll just make the six o'clock news and be laughed off the air as another bunch of crazies crying wolf about the big, bad industry guys. We need to establish credibility. And, while I appreciate your efforts and those of the groups you contacted, moon-suits and radical chants don't give environmentalists a good name."

Something dark crossed Dr. Breyer's face then. Anger, Sayer thought, anger that went well beyond his noble championing for the right to close down the mine. "It's done. It's too late. We're going public today, with or without your support."

"I didn't say I didn't support your cause, if—and it's still an if—you've got a cause to support. I always support rational or even radical action based on sound evidence. But I won't be made a pawn in a personal vendetta."

With that, Sayer turned on his heel and started striding back toward the rover. He didn't like the direction Malcolm was taking things, and all he could do now was try to contain it.

This whole thing had gone wrong from the beginning, and he had a bad feeling about how it was going to end.

Her nerves crawling like ants under her skin, Aramanda finally forced herself out of the truck. She had dreaded coming here today, to the very place she had last seen Roarke. To the place she had lost him so long ago in time, but so briefly in her memory . . .

The place she feared she would now lose Sayer and her chance to find love again.

Uncertain of his reaction, she had not confessed her fear or feelings of grief to Sayer. He might not believe or understand them, and at the least, it would distract him from his task here.

Aramanda nearly convinced herself it would be best to wait for him here, protected from the rebellion outside. But she could not bear to simply sit and wait. Not this time.

As she walked through the milling crowd, excitement and anger shot like fireworks between the rebels, evoking strong remembrances of the day Roarke had been killed.

She glanced over their faces and found in their eyes the same fierceness, the same hard determination to change what they found intolerable. They would have their say today, whatever the risk. She knew it as surely as she knew Roarke had been their voice yesterday and Sayer would be today, whatever the cost.

A young bearded man near her shouted a challenge to the guards posted at the fence gates, then tossed a cylinder that sent up a column of violet-colored smoke when it landed near the guards' feet. One of the guards kicked it aside, gesturing angrily to the police officers.

The protesters responded by throwing another cylinder, this one spurting out a yellow, acrid-smelling smoke.

With the guards and police officers distracted, two of the white-suited protesters made a dash for the fence and started scaling the thick wire.

Aramanda unconsciously shrank back as she watched several policemen yank them back down before they made it halfway up, shackling their hands behind them and ushering them to waiting vehicles with brightly flashing red and yellow lights.

A vision came to her, vivid in its intensity . . .

Roarke, lying less than a dozen feet from the mine entrance, half-covered by wooden rubble, black rock, and soot. A dark red stain spreading over his chest and shoulder, his blue neckcloth twisted at his throat—both the symbols of his precious rebellion.

Smoke and fire and the shouts of his rebels chorusing around them.

Her own grief as sharp as a sabre's thrust. "Roarke . . . I thought you were—"

"Dead? Ah, wait a little longer, love, and I'll oblige you."

"Did you get a pamphlet?" A woman with straggling blond hair and bits of metal piercing her ears and one side of her nose pushed a folded square of paper in Aramanda's hand.

Reality came to Aramanda in a dizzying flash. She blinked and put a trembling hand to her temple.

The woman eyed her curiously. "Are you all right? You look like you're about to pass out."

"I . . . thank you. I am—"

"Look!" the woman pointed to the right where the crowd, nudging and pushing forward, began to gather around one man. "Dr. Macnair is getting ready to speak. Now we're really going to get some action."

The woman hoisted the picket sign she'd leaned against her leg and trotted off toward the gathering. Aramanda took a deep breath and followed.

Fortunately, her height enabled her to peer over the shoulders of others to see Sayer standing in the center of the group, men and women nearby shoving small, rounded, black instruments with odd combinations of letters on them close to his mouth.

Aramanda saw the command and assurance Sayer projected. He immediately became the center of attention, and she felt anew the power he had to convince multitudes of the right of his cause, to persuade them to follow him, whether to paradise or into hell.

"So, Dr. Macnair," a thin man in spectacles asked him, "is there or is there not a radon leak in this mine?"

"I don't have sufficient evidence to answer that definitively yet. I can say I've long been concerned with the conditions in the Montclair mines and I'm convinced there's cause for an investigation."

"Then what are you doing here if you aren't here to start a riot?" another man called out.

A low rumble of laughter rolled through the crowd.

"I came to look into the matter and draw my own conclusions."

"Come on, Dr. Macnair, isn't that sort of like the President calling a meeting with the joint chiefs of staff and saying it's just to see how their day is going?"

"You know there's poison here or you wouldn't bother to come," one of the protesters, a tall man with a long ragged beard and a bandanna tied around his head, called out. "You've been trying to close down the Montclair mines for years, and we're ready to help you do it today!"

A loud cheer and a rousing round of applause went up among the protesters. Aramanda, jostled by the people next to her who began to thrust their signs and fists in the air, saw Sayer, his expression compounded of anger and resolve, raise his hands to regain their attention.

"I'm as ready as you are to close down *this* mine if we can prove there's radon here. I want the proof first."

"And you'll get it, even if you have to make it up, won't you?" a burly man with a hard face and twisted nose shouted up at Sayer. "You want to put us all out of work!"

Sayer stared hard at him for a moment, and from the look on his face, Aramanda guessed he recognized the man. "If it's there, I'll find it. If it's not, I'll be the first to admit it. Now, I think we've all done enough talking. I've got some tests to run, and we're going to find out who's right."

He shouldered his way through the crowd, halted every step by someone stopping him to ask a question, shake his hand, utter a word of support—or deliver a threat.

Aramanda saw him look over the faces nearest him, searching the crowd with a seeking, almost desperate expression. She lifted a hand to attract his attention, but a man shoving his way to the forefront blocked her from Sayer's view.

"Wait, Dr. Macnair," the man shouted over the noise of the crowd, "one more question. If you don't believe there's radon poisoning here, then why did you call out the troops? You have a reputation of storming the gates to prove your point. Is that what you have planned today?"

Behind them an uproar of shouts from the protesters drew the attention momentarily from Sayer.

"Hey!" A young man with hair halfway down his back jumped onto the wired gate and scaled it to the top, pumping a fist in the air, yelling to the crowd. "Why don't you media vultures do something to save lives once in a while instead of just capitalizing on death! Stop the poison! Stop the poison!"

Several of the other younger rebels followed the first one's example, lunging for the fence and scaling it rapidly. The cheers of the crowd picked up the chant and urged them on.

Police materialized on all sides. The crowd swarmed in around the youths, blocking their way. One of the guards shoved at a protester who tried to dart around a barricade. The protester threw a wild punch, hitting the guard squarely on the chin and knocking him back.

The scuffle sparked other pushing and shouting. A few fights broke out among the protesters and the police and guards struggling to keep them from the fence.

Aramanda tried to keep her balance in the surging chaos erupting around her. She caught a glimpse of Sayer, and her heart caught in her throat as she saw him push his way through the crowd to the heart of the fighting.

He shouted something she could not hear amid the commotion, but she knew the hard determination on his face as surely as she breathed. He would deliberately put himself in the midst of the turmoil and damn the risk.

Aramanda called his name, straining to get to him. Her heart pounded in a panicked rhythm. "Sayer!" she screamed until her voice failed her.

The crowd surged out of control, drowning her cries in mayhem. Sounds of the chained fence rattling crashed and clamored against the air like discordant percussion.

The crush of the crowd finally overcame Aramanda's attempts to reach Sayer. Whirling to run for the truck, the place he would look first for her, she glanced back one more time to try to at least see him.

As she did, from the corner of her eye, she caught sight of Malcolm Breyer slipping through a spot where the crowd forced the gate back enough for a person to squeak through.

In the next instant, Sayer's dark head, then his chest and long legs, materialized through the same opening.

"No! Roarke!" For an instant the present became the past and Aramanda saw him running from one of the mine shafts, the fire of his creation at his back.

Memories of yesterday's terrors flooded her with relentless force. Her vision blurred and she felt pulled between this reality and her own. She could see neither clearly, felt the furious tides of past and present clash and rage, conflicting lashes from a brutal storm.

Dizzy, her body numb, Aramanda threw back her head and covered her ears against the sound, the fury. Against the past. Against the moment.

The shots struck and vanished before she fell to the ground.

Ten

Very slowly, as if time had slowed to a near stop, Aramanda felt reality slipping around her again. Hours . . . an eternity? How long had she lain in this endless darkness?

Gradually, she became aware of her body again and realized her head throbbed with a steady pulse of pain. She moaned and tried to move.

A strong arm gripped her shoulders, gently lifting her until her face rested against a hard, warm surface. An erratic drumming sounded in her ear.

"Aramanda!"

A dream . . . that voice, both soft and rough, the scent of him like the forest at midnight, the warm stroke of his hands on her face. Surely a dream.

"My God, Aramanda—can you hear me?" Her name sounded like a prayer on his lips, and she felt a tremor in his strong hands. "Aramanda, come back to me."

Her heart lurched and she forced her eyes open. "Oh, Roarke . . ." Aramanda closed her eyes again, flooded with sweet relief he was not a dream. "You are alive. I heard a gunshot . . . I saw you running toward the mine and I thought—" She could not finish the sentence.

"I'm fine," Sayer said, his voice edged with concern. "But I'm getting you to a hospital—now. Where are you hurt? What happened?"

Aramanda struggled to focus on his face. She realized she was lying in the same place, near his vehicle, and the air around them was still. Only a few voices murmured in the background. "I am not hurt at all. It was nothing, only a moment of faintness."

"Nothing! It's been fifteen minutes since I found you, and God knows how long you were lying here senseless before that. I don't call that nothing! What happened to you?" Sayer brushed the hair from her face with his free hand. He watched her intently as if trying to read the truth in her eyes. "Did someone hurt you?"

"No, no, it was nothing like that," Aramanda said quickly, laying her hand atop his. "I—I only feared for you. Coming here, seeing your rebellion, it seemed all the madness was happening again. It felt as if the past were repeating itself and I were being forced in this reality to see you—to see . . ." She faltered to a stop and couldn't stay the tears welling in her eyes.

Sayer closed his arms around her, cradling her tightly against his chest. "Shhh. Everything's quiet now. I should never have brought you here. After what you've told me about your past, I should have realized it would be painful coming back here. But it's over now. It's over."

"Is it?" Aramanda kept her head against his chest simply to hear the sound of his breathing, the ragged racing of his heart. Her fingers brushed his arm, his shoulder, reassuring her he was alive, whole, with her. "I do not think I could bear to lose you again."

"You won't," Sayer said, his words a vow. He kissed her forehead, his hand stroking up and down her spine. "Unless, of course, you get fed up with my dirty socks and kick me out."

"No," she murmured, "I shall simply teach you to wash them."

He gave a light laugh. "Fair enough." But in the next instant he crushed her to him as though she might vanish into thin air if he didn't hold her closely enough.

She clung to him, taking pleasure in the security of his arms enfolding her.

"Are you sure you're not hurt?" Sayer repeated.

"I am not hurt. It was only the feelings of being trapped between two times and reliving the tragedy in both." She raised her head to look up at him with a rueful smile. "You must think me weak."

"No. Never. You feel deeply, that's all, and I consider that a strength. Are you sure you're all right?"

Aramanda glanced her fingertips over his mouth. "Yes, again."

"There are lots of rocks here. You might have hit your head."

"I did nothing but faint. Truly, I may have a bruise or two, but nothing else. Believe me. You may release me now, if you wish." She looked around them. "The crowd appears to have gone."

Sayer continued to hold to her as if he had no intention of ever letting her out of his arms again. "I don't want to release you. Not yet. Aramanda . . ." He buried his face in her hair, his hands tightening on her body. "I was afraid I'd lost you. I looked everywhere and couldn't find you. Nothing mattered more to me then finding you."

"You have found me, and we are together. That is all that matters."

"Yes . . ."

His hesitation made Aramanda look at him questioningly. "Has something happened? I remember seeing Dr. Breyer slip inside the gate and you following. I heard the gunshot and—"

Her expression turned to sudden dismay. The quality of Sayer's silence told her the answer before he gave it. "It cannot be. Not Dr. Breyer."

Sayer pulled back from her slightly, his eyes hot with regret and anger when they met hers. "He's dead."

Aramanda crossed herself, the tears now sliding down her cheeks. "May God preserve his soul. Who would do such a thing? Was it the guards, because he was attempting to get into the mine?"

"No," Sayer shook his head, "they don't shoot people for trespassing. Several of the protesters were charged and hauled off to jail, but they won't be there long. No one knows who fired the shots." His voice trailed off, his gaze abstracted as if he were replaying the past hours in his mind, searching for one face.

"What about the man with the twisted nose?"

"How did you know—"

"I saw him confront you during your speech. His was not a face I would easily forget. He reminded me of one of your rivals in our past, a man who used violence as a means to an end even more than you once did, and for no other reason than that he did not care for the company a man kept or the views he held."

Sayer nodded in understanding. "I've had a run-in with this guy before, after a speech I gave in Philly. He's hooked up with the union somehow. But I don't think he'd come here, start an argument with me that could get his face on the front of every newspaper, then murder Malcolm. That doesn't make much sense."

"But you do believe Dr. Breyer was murdered."

"I believe someone thought Malcolm's suspicions posed enough of a threat to make his death necessary," Sayer said, his eyes moving to the mine.

"Perhaps it was an accident?" Aramanda said doubtfully. "The crowd became so volatile; it all happened so quickly. Perhaps somebody meant only to warn Dr. Breyer from the gates."

Sayer shrugged. "It's possible, but not probable. My gut instinct tells me the pandemonium in the crowd only aided a plan to stop Malcolm and his radon testing."

Aramanda considered his idea for a long, silent minute. "Do you believe the Montclairs were responsible?" she asked quietly.

"I don't know." Sayer looked squarely at her. "The Montclairs have a lot to lose if the mine is closed."

"But surely now there will be an investigation, into both Malcolm's death and the conditions at the mine."

Sayer's mouth twisted in a derisive line. "Bought and paid for by the Montclairs, no doubt. If they wanted to keep things quiet, no one would ever know the truth, because someone in the family would pay or pressure the investigators to keep quiet. Oh, there's a chance a detective might rise above the temptation and probe into the case, but the Montclairs would do everything in their power to see that didn't happen."

"So much has changed and yet so much is the same," Aramanda said. She suddenly felt a deep-reaching weariness that was more than physical. Her very soul felt drained, exhausted. She leaned against Sayer again, letting him support her weight.

"I suppose that's true," he said, holding her close, stroking her hair. "The tragic irony in Malcolm's death is that right now I'll bet whoever is responsible is probably almost as upset about it as we are. But for entirely different reasons."

"I do not understand."

"If Malcolm were murdered, then it only makes sense that someone wanted to kill him before he went public with his information. The moment the other environmental groups and the media learned of his suspicions concerning the radon in the mine, there went any chance to silence the whole issue." Sayer's eyes went hard. "In fact, I'd like to tell the Montclairs and everyone else I know just how unnecessary Malcolm's death was."

Aramanda started to ask him his intentions, but at that moment, she heard someone call Sayer's name. She and Sayer turned to look as Will trotted up to them, breathing heavily.

"Sayer! Is she all right?" Will looked from his brother to Aramanda. "I saw you fall, but I couldn't get to you. Too many damned people running in every direction. It's taken me this long to get through all the mess and then to convince the cops I knew you."

"I am perfectly fine, Will. Thank you for caring."

"How about you?" Sayer asked, his words clipped. He looked his brother up and down, letting go a long breath. "I didn't expect you to be here. You didn't get caught in the middle of it, did you?"

"Me?" Will glanced at Sayer, his shoulders shifting uncomfortably. "I didn't plan to be here, but they shut down work today, so I thought I'd come by and see what you had to say. Me and a few of the other guys stayed on the sidelines, sitting on the hoods of our cars, watching and waiting it out. I didn't see any reason to get in the middle of it."

"A wise decision," Aramanda murmured. Will's eyes kept straying to her, and she realized how it must look to him, Sayer sitting next to her on the ground, clasping her so tightly.

Gently, she eased out of Sayer's arms and let him help her to stand. He kept his arm around her waist, and Aramanda felt a flush start up her face at Will's glance. "I am able to stand. I am not injured."

"Maybe. But we're going back to the hotel so you can rest," Sayer said, refusing to release her. He turned to his brother then, the only sign of emotion a muscle jerking along his jaw. "I'm still surprised to see you here at all."

Will shrugged, not quite meeting Sayer's eyes. "I told you, I wanted to check things out for myself."

"I thought you didn't like my speeches," Sayer said lightly. He hesitated, then added, "This wasn't the way I wanted it to turn out. You have to know that."

"No. I don't know that." Will kicked at the ground with the toe of his boot. "What I do know is that you'll have the whole country watching your face on the news tonight. Now there'll be so much controversy, the mine probably won't reopen for months, or not at all, since that crazy old coot got himself shot."

Sayer glanced off to the spot where Malcolm had fallen. "He wasn't always crazy," he muttered, running his fingers through the heavy dark wave of hair on his forehead to brush it back. He looked back at his brother, and for a moment, Aramanda saw his expression waver.

"Look—I wouldn't be here at all if I weren't worried about what radon poisoning could do to you and everyone else who works here. Why can't you get it through your head I didn't come to start a brawl or close it all down just to give myself something to do?"

"Because you have a reputation for starting trouble," Will said. "Because it never occurs to you to think about what happens to guys like me who don't have a choice when it comes to getting caught up in the middle of your fights."

"I didn't think it would be your choice to die of radon poisoning. Maybe I was wrong. Hell—" Flinging up a hand, Sayer looked away, then back again. "This is going nowhere. I think we'd better call it a day."

"Yeah, maybe we'd better. I should let Liz know what's been going on before she sees it on TV."

"Good idea. And by the way—" Sayer put a hand on his brother's shoulder, ignoring it when Will stiffened. "Thanks for that little talk you had with the sheriff. He told me he decided against arresting me because he knew you. You didn't have to do that."

"Arrest?" Aramanda's gaze slewed from Sayer to Will. "You did not tell me—"

"Because it wasn't important," Sayer said. "The sheriff figured if he were handing out charges of trespassing and assault, I should get a few, too. Will put in a good word for me."

"No problem," Will said, shrugging off Sayer's gratitude. "I know how tight your schedule is. I didn't want you to waste a night in jail—even if it wouldn't be the first time you've been there in the name of your good causes."

"It's never my first choice. I hate the food. Listen—" Sayer let his hand fall away, shifting his weight from one foot to the other, glancing away and back again. "I'd like to give you a call before I leave town, just to see how things are going. If you need anything—"

"I won't," Will said shortly, but his hard expression relented. "But call before you go. Liz and the boys would like to hear from you."

"Sure. No problem." Sayer looked down at Aramanda. "We should be going. You need rest, and I could use a break myself."

"Of course. Goodbye, Will," she said, smiling. "May God be with you and your family."

"Hey—" Will lifted a hand to touch her shoulder. "—don't make it sound so permanent. You can always come back up and visit us." A smirk touched the corner of his mouth, and he nodded to Sayer. "With or without him."

Aramanda swallowed hard. She forced her mouth to keep its smile. "I would like that very much." She felt Sayer's eyes hot on her, felt the tension in him in the corded grip on her waist. Sincerely, but without much confidence, she added, "I hope I will have the opportunity."

* * *

"Do you think this is wise?"

"No." Sayer shifted gears on the rover with unnecessary force and shot her a look that dared her to challenge his decision. "But it's necessary."

Aramanda stayed silent, realizing it was useless to argue with him in this state of mind. After they had left Will and the mine, Sayer had made it clear he intended to return to the Montclair estate immediately. He'd insisted she wait for him at the inn; but Aramanda, equally inflexible, had refused to let him leave her behind.

Not for the first time, she felt an apprehensive chill at the thought of Sayer confronting the Montclairs so soon after the tragedy at the mine. In hot blood, he might say or do anything; and if these Montclairs were anything like her uncle in temperament, the ensuing battle could end as badly as the rebellion at the mine.

Yet she could not retreat now, anymore than Sayer would willingly turn back. As the Montclair estate came into view ahead of them, Aramanda could only say a silent prayer for him, for herself, and hope destiny would not repeat itself.

Sliding the window to the gatehouse open, the guard at the gate to the Montclair estate raised a suspicious brow at Sayer as he eased the rover to a stop. "May I help you, sir?"

"I'm Sayer Macnair. Tell your boss up there in the house I know Dr. Breyer was murdered and, if they refuse to let me in now, I'll be back with a couple of friends from the FBI."

"Yeah, I'll do that." With a scowl, the guard shoved the window shut and picked up a phone.

Sayer tapped restless fingers on the steering wheel, fighting the frustration roiling inside him. "You can wait in the rover, you know," he told Aramanda, slanting her a glance. "If I get inside, it's not going to be pleasant."

She shook her head. "I am coming with you. I will not let you face this alone, not after all that has happened. And this is something, also, that I feel I must do."

"What are you talking about?"

"Before, in my time, every time my uncle committed some cruelty to another," she said, staring out the windshield at the estate house and seeing it as it was in another time, another reality, "I always felt reparations for the injustice were my responsibility because he acted in the Montclair name. Yet I never fully committed myself to the role of helping the miners and their families. I knew my uncle would use his anger at me for mingling with the miners as an excuse to punish and control the rest of the family. I was always divided, and ashamed because of it."

She turned her gaze to him, forcing herself to meet his eyes without flinching. "I lost my love, my soul, because I could not choose without betraying either the miners or my family."

Sayer stared at her, feeling he was looking at her for the first time. "Women like you don't exist anymore."

"Am I extinct then?" she asked lightly. "Like your precious animals?"

He flashed her a sharp glance that told her he was not amused. "Don't say that. You're here with me now; and as long as you want to be there, I want you at my side." Reaching over to grasp her hand, he rubbed his fingers over hers, needing simply to touch her.

"But you are a rare and precious breed, Aramanda," Sayer said softly. "That I will say. There aren't many people I know who are as willing as you to open themselves to the pain of caring so completely for everyone they meet."

The guard's window slammed open once more, the sharp sound coming between them, staying any reply Aramanda might have made. "Drive in," the guard snapped. "Mr. Montclair's secretary will meet you at the house."

"It's about damn time." Shoving his foot down on the accelerator, Sayer maneuvered up the long drive and swung the Range Rover around the circular area in front of the mansion, stepping on the brake only inches behind a black stretch limo.

The bumper of the rover just touched the back bumper of the limo when he jumped out and went around to help Aramanda down.

Before he made it to the passenger side of the rover, a tall, stiff-looking man with sparse blond hair and a starched blue suit was already at his door. Cold, gray eyes looked Sayer up and down. "At last I get to meet the infamous Dr. Macnair."

"That's right. Are you the secretary?"

The man ignored Sayer and walked around the rover to open the door for Aramanda. "And companion," he added, scanning her body with undisguised admiration.

He offered Aramanda a hand, but she shook her head, pushing the dark sunglasses Sayer had loaned her more firmly up. She lifted her chin, consciously assuming the aristocratic arrogance her uncle had cultivated. "Your business is with Sayer."

Sayer deliberately put himself between Aramanda and the man. "And you haven't answered my question. Who the hell are you?"

"Rudolph Quinn, Mr. Montclair's personal secretary. He asked me to speak with you."

"I want to talk to Mr. Montclair in person."

"That's not possible," the secretary told him. "In light of the recent circumstances at the mine, Mr. Montclair isn't accepting visitors today."

"How convenient," Sayer sneered. "I suppose you're here to give me all the prettied-up public relations bull about how concerned the Montclairs are about this tragic situation and how everything possible will be done, et cetera, et cetera."

"Dr. Macnair—"

"Don't bother. I've heard it all before."

"And precisely what did you come here expecting to be told?" Quinn asked coldly. "There was an unfortunate incident at the mine, but I've heard those of your radicals who caused the disturbance are in jail. Apart from that—"

Sayer felt hot blood begin to throb in his temples. Aramanda had told him he was civilized. Right now, he felt anything but.

She put a tempering hand on his arm. He shook her off, his hands flexing into fists at his side.

"You know damned well what went on at that mine today! Malcolm Breyer was murdered by someone who wanted to make sure he never got a chance to talk about radon poisoning. I came to tell you it's too late. He talked to me, and I'm going to tell anyone who'll listen."

"Feel free," the secretary said, giving Sayer a cool, appraising look. "You environmental terrorists break the law, someone gets hurt—or worse—and you blame your bad judgment on solid business people like the Montclairs. It's an old trick, Dr. Macnair. I'd say it's run its course."

"Listen to me." Sayer grabbed a fistful of suit at Quinn's shoulder, the temper he usually managed to keep in check taking command. "I know he was murdered. And I believe there's radon in that mine. You won't see the last of me until I prove both."

"Sayer, no!" Aramanda clutched his arm again, her face pale. "Do not do this!" She tried to pull his hand free, and her sharp motion dislodged her borrowed glasses. They fell to the ground with a clatter.

"Stay out of this, Aramanda," Sayer said through gritted teeth.

Quinn twisted in Sayer's iron grasp like a rat hanging by its tail. He shifted his glare to Aramanda.

Abruptly, his glare turned to a gape; the color in his face drained. "Aramanda—Montclair?" Confusion pinched his face into a grimace.

"It's none of your damn business who she is!" Sayer's grip tightened.

"Gary! Jeff!" Quinn shouted over his shoulder, forgetting Aramanda for the moment. "Get this dog off of me!"

Two burly men shot out of nowhere and descended on Sayer, prying his fingers from Quinn's shoulder. Sayer released Quinn with a shove and knocked the bodyguards' huge paws off him with the back of his fists.

Breathing hard, Quinn hurried to smooth down his white shirt, tie, and jacket, his hands not quite steady. Keeping a wary eye on Sayer, he turned suddenly on Aramanda. "Who are you?"

She faced him with a lift to her chin and fire in her eyes. "That, sir, is none of your concern."

Quinn's gaze narrowed at them both. "Get out of here. Both of you. And if you come back to accuse the Montclairs again, of anything, you'd better bring your lawyer with you!"

Sayer slammed the door to the rover after Aramanda got in. "I'll do better than that. I'll bring proof."

He shoved the rover into gear and sped up the drive, wanting nothing more at the moment than to get as far away from the Montclair estate as possible.

Aramanda stared at the heavy chains that bound and locked the gates to the mine. "Why did you bring us back to this place?"

Beside her, Sayer leaned into the wire fence, looping his fingers through the holes between the chain links. He stared at the cavernous mine several hundred feet away on the other side of the fence. "I can't explain why. I just had to come back here."

"Is it because of Dr. Breyer?"

"Partly."

Aramanda watched his grip tighten on the fence until his knuckles went white. "You cannot mean to take responsibility for Dr. Breyer's impulsive actions. It was not of your doing."

"It shouldn't have happened! Dammit!" Sayer slammed a fist into the fence, sending a clanking noise rippling down the metal links. It resounded into the silence around them, a harsh discord in the early evening stillness.

"Perhaps not. But there is nothing you can do for him here. You cannot change what is past." As the words slipped off her lips, Aramanda realized she was speaking as much in regard to herself as to him.

Returning to this place, the place where she had lost Roarke and her love, for the second time in one day was almost more than she could endure. When Sayer had turned toward the mine instead of the inn, she had been sorely tempted to beg him not to come back here.

This place intensified her feelings of being displaced; it seemed to sap the strength from her limbs. From her spirit, her very soul. She felt unsettled, afraid, beset by a thousand feelings she could not explain.

"I do not like this place," she whispered. She wasn't aware she'd spoken the words aloud until Sayer turned to look at her.

"This place . . . it's a key to your past, isn't it, Aramanda?"

"Yes—it is," she admitted softly. "I wish it were not so. There are so many memories here, so much I do not wish to recall. And yet . . ."

She broke off, not certain how to put into words an indefinable feeling that the mine was more to her than simply a reminder of yesterday.

Sayer glared at the gates again. "I need to get in there."

"Please, do not attempt it. Not now. I am certain there still must be guards here. You are risking your life needlessly."

"Aramanda . . ." Sayer came to her and, taking her shoulders, looked long into her eyes. "What's wrong?"

"I do not know. I do not know," Aramanda said, feeling a strange overwhelming mix of sorrow and trepidation. "When I am here, I feel as if there is so little time left to me. I feel the past most strongly here. I feel it drawing me away."

She caught her lower lip between her teeth and raised her eyes to his. Inexplicable tears blurred her vision. "Away from you."

"That can't happen." Sayer's eyes, midnight dark, held hard determination. "I won't let it. The answers, all of them, yours and mine, are in there."

"No, it cannot be." Yet even as she denied him, Aramanda knew he spoke the truth.

This was the place where she had first loved Roarke, where he had died. And it was here, she realized, that this man had come to care for her, too. But enough to return with her to a place where they could change all that had passed?

Or had she been right when she'd spoken to him of burying his ghosts? Could she believe that love alone had the power of redemption?

A cold rush of panic shot through Aramanda and she reached out to touch his face, suddenly needing to prove to herself he was still with her in flesh and blood. "I cannot lose you again. I cannot bear that."

Sayer's expression softened and he pulled her to him, closing the space between them. "Don't be afraid. You aren't going to lose me. Whether or not we stay together is up to us, not some cosmic destiny or anything that could happen here. Believe that, Aramanda."

"I believe, yet I also remember," she whispered, shuddering despite the warmth of him wrapped around her. "I remember everything that happened yesterday as though it were only a moment past. I remember loving and being loved and believing it could be forever. And now . . ."

She pulled away slightly and looked at Sayer. "Is it the same? Can it ever be the same? Do you remember those feelings, in your soul? Or am I lost to you as I fear you are to me?"

The muscles in Sayer's arms tensed beneath her fingers. He searched her eyes, his own troubled. In the past days, she had avoided directly asking him to tell her his feelings.

Now, she forced him to face everything inside him. How could he trust it? How could he believe in her forever?

"I don't know if I can feel that way," he said finally. "I only know I care deeply for you. I need you. When you're not near me, I feel . . . empty."

Sayer touched her face, tracing her features with a gentle hand, each soft line and plane infinitely precious to him. "No, it's much worse than that. When I couldn't find you in the crowd earlier today, each second seemed like eternity. Until I finally found you, I thought I was losing my mind, imagining everything that could have happened to you. Those minutes without you, wondering where you were, if you'd given up and taken the chance to leave—Aramanda, I've never felt more desperate, more lost. I don't want to lose you."

She smiled slightly, reaching up to stroke the wave of hair from his brow. "Is that love? Is it forever?"

"I don't know." Sayer glanced away. He didn't want to lie to her, but he wasn't sure of the truth.

When he looked back at her, he knew from her expression she saw the conflict on his face. Taking both her hands in his, he held to her tightly.

"Love is a word I have trouble using, especially to someone I've only known a few days."

Aramanda's lips parted—to protest, Sayer knew. Then she stopped, catching her lower lip between her teeth as if to still the words.

"But if love means I'm not a whole person without you, if it means you're my joy, my comfort, the reason I've wanted to wake up these past days, then I love you," Sayer said softly. "Nothing ever mattered this much before. I care for you in a way I never imagined myself capable of caring for anyone."

"Or anything?" Aramanda drew a steadying breath, almost fearful of saying the words, but determined to speak them. "What is still first in your heart? Your causes, your ideals? I never worried about another stealing your love from me, because your mistresses were always your causes. I fear they will divide us now as before."

"I'll admit, I never imagined anyone could challenge my devotion to my work," Sayer said, his voice taking on the same passionate timbre Aramanda had heard him use so many times in her past, the intensity of his expression a resolve to convince her. He traced his fingertips over her face, lingering on her lips. "I never wanted anyone badly enough to choose. But in a few crazy days, you've changed all of that."

"Have I?"

"It doesn't make any sense; I'll never understand it. You've turned my life upside down, Aramanda, and it'll never be the same again."

"And do you wish it to be?"

"I never thought I'd say this, but God no." His mouth twisted in a rueful smile, mocking his own inexplicable feelings. "I want to deny it, even now, because it's crazy to care about someone I've only known a few days under the strangest of circumstances. But I can't deny it. I can't say you don't matter to me, because you're all that does matter."

"Oh, Sayer . . ."

He bent to her and, cupping her face in his hands, lowered his mouth to cover hers.

Aramanda slid her arms up around his neck and wound her fingers in the soft curls at his nape. She drank in his kiss, meeting his passion, his need, with her own. "I never want to be without you again," she whispered against his mouth, "whatever reality destiny chooses for us."

"This is the only reality I want."

Sayer crushed her to his hard chest, his kiss delving to the depths of her demand. Sweeping his hands down her shoulders, he caressed his hand down her spine, bringing her fully against him so she felt coupled to him, body and soul.

Pleasure melted through her like the first warmth of spring after the cold bleakness of winter, leaving every sensation blossoming in its wake. Familiar whispers of longing began to stir and whisper suggestions both illicit and tantalizing.

His kiss tasted of temptation and where he touched her burned. Aramanda melded herself to him, wanting to capture each sweet nuance of him in her heart. Wanting to become desire's prisoner, needing him and only him.

For the first time since she had rushed headlong into his arms, Sayer held back nothing, telling her with the urgent press of his body to hers, the ardent embrace of his hands, that he wanted her. She felt both the flash and fire of a summer storm and the tenderness and sweet satisfaction of a soft spring rain inside her, a blending of emotion so heady and deep it made her reel from the intensity of it.

Yet at the same time, a dark urgency haunted her like a relentless nemesis, threatening to snatch back the fulfillment she had found with Sayer in this time.

You must return. The past is today and can never be forgotten.

"Let's get out of here," Sayer whispered hotly in her ear. "I want to be with you."

"Yes . . ." Aramanda shivered at the naked desire in his voice. "It is what I want, to be with you."

Something in the texture of her voice made Sayer pull back to look into her face. "You don't sound so certain of that. What is it?"

"It is . . . I do not know how to explain it." Her fingers twisted

4 FREE BOOKS

These books worth almost $20, are yours without cost or obligation when you fill out and mail this certificate.
(If the certificate is missing below, write to: Zebra Home Subscription Service, Inc., 120 Brighton Road, P.O. Box 5214, Clifton, New Jersey 07015-5214)

Complete and mail this card to receive 4 Free books!

YES! Please send me 4 Zebra Lovegram Historical Romances without cost or obligation. I understand that each month thereafter I will be able to preview 4 new Zebra Lovegram Historical Romances FREE for 10 days. Then if I decide to keep them, I will pay the money-saving preferred publisher's price of just $4.00 each...a total of $16. That's almost $4 less than the regular publisher's price, and there is never any additional charge for shipping and handling. I may return any shipment within 10 days and owe nothing, and I may cancel this subscription at any time. The 4 FREE books will be mine to keep in any case.

Name _____

Address_____ Apt._____

City_____ State_____ Zip_____

Telephone ( ) _____

Signature _____

(If under 18, parent or guardian must sign.)

LF0696

AFFIX
STAMP
HERE

ZEBRA HOME SUBSCRIPTION SERVICE, INC.

120 BRIGHTON ROAD

P.O. BOX 5214

CLIFTON, NEW JERSEY 07015-5214

against his shirtfront. "I remember too much. I remember being with Roarke—" Her eyes met his. "—with you, the last day we loved. It felt desperate, as though we knew it would be the last time. I feel that way now. As if it were the beginning, and yet it is only for a brief time."

Sayer gently rubbed the back of his hand against her cheek. He wanted to reassure her, but he caught some of her distress and it fed his own uneasiness. "I wish I could say I remember everything you want me to remember. I wish I could promise you it would make a difference."

"But you cannot."

"No."

"And I know you cannot," she admitted. "No more than I can believe our time together here is forever."

"Maybe it could be," Sayer said, lifting her chin so their eyes met, his hand caressing her face.

"You know I must return."

"Why? Why can't you just forget your past and go forward with me?"

Grief and regret welled up in her. She laid her cheek against his heart to hide her tears. "How can I, when I know I do not belong here? You are not the same man, yet I am unchanged. Perhaps . . . perhaps if you were then as you are now, perhaps yesterday would have ended differently and we would have had forever together."

Sayer smiled slightly. "Am I so different? You keep telling me I haven't learned a thing in a hundred years."

"You are still the idealist I love, and you still drive me to the brink of madness by rushing headfirst at danger. But you are more temperate, more reasoned in your tactics for reform."

"Me . . . temperate?" He laughed. "That's a first."

Aramanda lifted her head to smile at him. She stroked her fingertips down his cheek, the feel of him a strange blend of yesterday's memories and today's passions. "The Roarke I knew would have welcomed the violence today and not counted the cost in challenging the police or the Montclairs. Nothing your brother would have done would have kept you out of jail, or worse."

"I don't have much of a taste for jail these days, although I won't say I've never seen the inside of a cell," Sayer said, his mouth twisting. "But maybe time has mellowed me. I don't advocate your kind of violence unless there's nothing else left."

"You—Roarke once did. And it caused his death. And the death of our love."

"Aramanda . . ." Sayer didn't know how to respond. Part of him hurt to see the sorrow clouding her amber eyes and wanted to comfort her. And part of him, primitive and possessive, wanted to eradicate the memory of Roarke Macnair, the man to whom she had so completely given herself, body and soul.

"If I could change everything that's happened, I would," he said tightly.

"If you would return with me, I know we could change it together." Aramanda clung to him, desperate now to convince him, to make him believe. "If you would trust in our love, if you would believe it is your soul at stake, as well as mine—"

"If, if!" Sayer flung up a hand. Jerking away from her, he shoved the hair off his forehead with a sharp motion. "It's impossible. We have a chance here, now, not in some past life."

He turned on her quickly and grasped her shoulders. "Forget about him. I don't want to be alone anymore. I can make changes now, I can do anything if I have you by my side. Stay with me, Aramanda. Forget about Roarke Macnair, whoever he was. We love each other now. I can make you forget."

"How can I forget to breathe or cause my heart not to beat?" Aramanda cried. "You are the other half of my soul, yesterday and today. But we cannot ever be together unless the past is righted."

"It's over! Can't you accept that? Or did you love him that much?" Sayer heard his voice rise, felt himself losing control of his feelings, but couldn't stop. "Are you telling me you can never love me that way? Is that why you keep talking about returning?"

"I—"

"You can't return! There's nothing to go back to!"

"Sayer . . ."

Aramanda looked up at him, helpless to know what to say to him that would convince him she loved him and the Roarke in her past with equal fervor. How could she not, when they shared the same soul, the same spirit that matched her own and made her whole.

Yet how could she convince him their future lay in their past? *We repeat the past in the future,* Father Creeghan had once told her. *Those things left undone, sins left unforgiven, have echoes far beyond today.*

"You've left me again," Sayer said flatly. He released her and she saw the anger flare in his eyes. "Are you with him?"

"I am with you," she said gently, "then and now."

Reaching out, she took his hand, easing his clenched fist until his fingers curled around her own. "Take me away from this place. Please, Sayer."

He did nothing for so long Aramanda wanted to scream to break the silence. Finally, with a sudden, jerking motion, he pulled her against him and, threading his hand in her hair, kissed her deeply, passionately, almost roughly.

Just as abruptly, he released her and they stared at each other, both breathless.

"Let's get the hell out of here," Sayer said harshly. "I don't know what made me come here again today. This place makes me feel—"

"As though every minute here could be our last?"

The savagery of his expression made Aramanda catch her breath.

"Murderous," Sayer said, the hardness of his tone matching the rigid tension in his body. "And the first thing I want to kill is your memories."

He gave her no time to reply, taking her hand and leading her back to the rover.

But as he sped from the mine site, Aramanda glanced back, compelled to look once more at the place where they had found and lost each other, wishing she could believe their past was not already repeating itself in this future.

Eleven

Aramanda sat on the bed, her knees drawn up to her chin, thinking about Sayer. After yesterday's tragedy, he'd withdrawn from her, retreating to the balcony outside their rooms, lost in his own dark thoughts. Sensing his need to be alone, Aramanda had let him be.

Instead, she had tried to sleep, and ended up lying in the blackness for countless hours, with only her koala for company, listening to the small and shallow sounds of the night. Now, unable to bear the isolation any longer, she slipped off the bed, wrapping a blanket around her thin, silk shift.

She found Sayer still on the balcony. Bent forward, his hands resting on the railing, he didn't move until she softly called his name.

"Have you been here all night?" she asked, moving to stand next to him. She saw he had the blue bandanna crumpled in one hand. He caught her curious glance at it, but said nothing.

"Most of it." Sayer straightened, running his hands through his hair. Without explaining its presence, he shoved the bandanna in his hip pocket.

He had changed out of his dust-smudged clothes of yesterday into a pair of worn, denim trousers and a loose-fitting white shirt. A day-old beard shadowed his jaw, and Aramanda saw the tiredness circling his eyes in blue-gray shadows. "There didn't seem much point in trying to sleep. I knew it wouldn't happen."

"Have you decided what you will do now? About the mine, and Dr. Breyer?"

"I made a few calls last night, but it's the weekend and I won't be able to get any reinforcements here until Sunday afternoon at best. The sheriff is taking his own sweet time investigating Malcolm's death—he doesn't want to offend the county's biggest taxpayers, no doubt, even though it's pretty damned obvious the Montclairs are involved. And no one from the government is going to show a face until Monday. Jim made that clear when I rousted him out of bed at 3 A.M."

He looked from her out over the gardens spread beneath them like a tapestry in shades of grays and greens woven in a milky mist. "The Montclairs are sure to have stepped up security around the mines by this time. Until I get some help, there's not much I can do in broad daylight on my own."

"Meaning you will try to go back there tonight to do your test and look for clues as to who killed Dr. Breyer," Aramanda said, giving him a small, knowing smile when he turned to her in mild surprise. "It is not what you said, but what you did not say. I know you will not wait for others to prove you are right about the mine and the Montclairs. You will find a way to right the injustices yourself, no matter the danger."

She thought of yesterday and yesterdays past; and fear, both old and new, swept through her. "You will chance losing your life—just like Dr. Breyer."

"No, not like him. He didn't realize the risk. I do."

"Perhaps. But you believe you can overcome it, no matter how impossible the odds. The danger is the same."

Sayer's face hardened. "Things don't get changed by playing it safe."

Aramanda shivered, pulling the blanket closer around her, and his expression softened. Reaching out, he rubbed the back of his hand gently against her cheek, the corner of his mouth twisting up in a rueful half-smile. "I seem to be doing my best to worry you, in this life and the last. Look—there's nothing I can do right now, why don't we get out of here, have breakfast, and spend some time looking around? We can probably find something to do to keep me out of trouble for a few hours at least."

"You can hardly expect me to believe that," Aramanda said

lightly, accepting his shift in mood for the moment. "But if you will wait for me to change into something more suitable, I accept the challenge of keeping you diverted."

"Oh, I don't know . . ." Sayer flicked the edge of the blanket with his forefinger. "I kind of like you in this. I find it very diverting."

"Do you now? I never knew you had such a passion for gray wool."

"I do when I can imagine what's underneath," he murmured, looking at her with an intensity that made Aramanda tremble with a wash of sudden heat. "Ivory silk . . ."

Aramanda loosed her hold on the blanket. "White." She let the blanket slip from her shoulders, revealing the fragile material that skimmed the curve of her breasts, reveling in the smolder of desire the sinuous motion started in Sayer's eyes. "Is this what you envisioned?"

He shook his head slowly, his gaze claiming her body as surely as a touch. "No . . . I couldn't have imagined anything so perfect." With provoking languor, he swanned his fingertips over the thin strap at her shoulder, tracing the edge of the silk to the hollow between her breasts. "If this is your idea of being diverting, I approve."

"I have other ideas . . ."

"So do I."

". . . but I believe you said something about breakfast."

"Did I? My mistake."

"Yes, but I will give you the chance to amend it—" Smiling, she gathered up the edges of the blanket and turned toward the bedroom. "—after breakfast."

She felt his eyes following her as she left the balcony. Desire tempted her to turn back, yet she resisted the enticement. She wanted Sayer to love her, needed him like a sustenance she could not live without.

Her desire for him had provoked her to boldly invite him to touch her; her remembrances of yesterday's anguish and loss stopped her from seizing her advantage and seducing him into giving her all she longed for.

An hour later, seated across from him at a corner table in the inn's dining room, Aramanda couldn't help regretting not taking that advantage. Studying his face, watching the motion of his hands as he thumbed through a pamphlet the desk clerk had provided him, she only half-heard his haphazard descriptions of the points of interest around the Schuylkill countryside, listening instead to the timbre of his voice.

"There's supposed to be the remains of one of the mining camps a few miles north of here." Sayer absently added nearly half the contents of the cream pitcher to his tea, his attention fixed on the pamphlet. "It seems to be one of the original Montclair mining settlements."

"It is near the main mine," Aramanda said. "That is what you wanted to know, is it not?"

"Mmmm . . ."

"I would like to see it—again. I spent so much time there. The memories . . ."

Sayer looked up at her. "Then we'll go. As soon as you've finished. It's a nice morning for a drive, and you can teach me a thing or two about mining history."

"Mining history. Yes. That will be interesting." Aramanda paused. "There is one place I would like to go first."

"Where?"

"It is not far. We can walk from here." Rising, she held out her hand to him. "Please, Sayer, it will not take long."

"I don't care if it does." Tossing a few bills on the table, he stood up and took her hand. "I'll follow you anywhere. I'm still thinking of ways I can rectify my mistake in suggesting food before pleasure," he whispered in her ear as he followed her out of the inn.

"I am certain you will think of something. You always do."

Outside, she turned left and led Sayer three blocks to a small side street. Following her memories and remembrances of the land, she at last stopped in front of a small rock church tucked in the clasp of several pink-blossomed tulip poplars.

Wordlessly, she walked up the few stairs and slowly pushed open the heavy oak door.

"How did you know this was here?" Sayer asked when they stood side-by-side inside the dimly lit entryway.

"I have been here many times. And the lay of the land has not changed so very much. A friend, Father Creeghan, was priest here before he came to the church in the mining town. I thought . . ."

Aramanda drew a breath and looked directly at him. "I wanted to come here to remember Dr. Breyer. You feel you must find out what happened to him because of your fight over the mine. I want to remember him for who he was, how he cared about the miners. I liked him, even in the short time that I knew him."

"So did I." Sayer paused, steadily holding her gaze. "You once told me I didn't see the faces behind my causes. Maybe more times than not I don't. Maybe because it's easier to focus on the injustices than the people affected by them. Caring about the people involved makes it harder to make the tough decisions. That sounds like an excuse—"

"No." Touching her fingertips to his face, she smiled. "I know you care. I know you do. You are only afraid to admit it. Just as I am afraid to take bold chances to force change in my life for fear of harming someone. Perhaps each of us can learn from the other. Perhaps there is a way for us to come from both ends to the middle."

"You're the only one who can convince me that miracle is possible."

"Miracles are possible. I know. I am here with you. That is truly a miracle."

Aramanda stepped back from him and turned into the sanctuary. The stained-glass windows broke the sunlight into a thousand colors, patterning the aisle as she walked up to the altar. There, she lit a single candle and knelt to offer a prayer for Malcolm Breyer.

Sayer, sitting in the first pew, watched her in silence. Kneeling before the altar, the pale light enveloping her in an ivory haze, she looked unreal, like an angel who had come in answer to his prayers.

He had to resist the urge to leave his place and go to her, to touch her, to reassure himself she was here with him and not some apparition that would vanish if he dared break the spell by moving.

When she rose and sat down next to him, he took her hand again and looked at the tiny flame she left behind. "You once told me Malcolm reminded you of someone from your past," he said. "Whom?"

"Scully McGehan, a good friend to both of us. He was very gentle, a scholar like Dr. Breyer. He believed he could bring about changes by exposing the facts and appealing to reason, but he, too, underestimated the risks because he thought he had little to lose. He took rash chances because of it. I do not think he was ever at peace with the choice he made to fight with Roarke."

"No . . ." Sayer looked down at her. "I'm glad we came. It's helped me to see things more clearly. I needed to remember Malcolm, too, and what he tried to do." He glanced at the candle flame. "I hope he's found his peace."

Aramanda nodded, knowing she needed no words for Roarke to understand how she felt. They sat together in the quiet of the sanctuary for timeless minutes, hands touching, sharing a communion of soul and emotion that needed no explanation or reason.

"Thank you for coming here with me," Aramanda said at last. "For the first time in days, I feel a . . . a serenity. I am no longer afraid of this reality or of sharing it with you for however long destiny grants us."

Sayer studied her a moment, then slid his fingers under her chin, tipping her face toward his. "Then why the tears?" he asked gently.

"I—I do not know. I . . . the feeling is also sad, like grief, as if something precious is ending . . . oh! It makes no sense, I know." Shaking her head in frustration, Aramanda dashed away an errant tear.

"It's probably not supposed to make sense; nothing much does these days.

"That is true. At times, I do not even understand my own feelings. I think I will wake up in your arms and it will all have been a dream, and none of it, in the past or now, will have happened. I sound like a child, wishing for a magic spell to make it all better again," she added, trying a small smile.

"If that's childish, then we're both guilty." With a last glance toward the altar, Sayer took both her hands in his and guided her to her feet. Aramanda expected him to lead her out of the church, but instead he looked down at her for several moments, saying nothing.

"What is it?" she asked at last.

"I don't know." Gathering her into his arms, he held her tightly, his face buried in her hair. "I don't know. You said you felt more peaceful. I feel . . . uneasy. I feel torn, pulled in two different directions, and I can't go both ways. But I want to. I want to, but I can't."

"And I cannot choose for you. I cannot decide what compromises you are willing to make," Aramanda said softly. "You know I love you. That is all I can offer. It is all I could ever offer."

Though he made no reply, Aramanda knew the struggle within him was the eternal conflict between them. She had been brought here, given another chance to resolve it.

Except she feared they would never find their redemption here. She could only pray that, in time, Sayer would choose to return with her and love would be stronger than destiny.

Several cars were parked haphazardly at the edge of the restored mining town. Sayer pulled the rover into an open slot next to a battered pickup truck, glancing at the row of rough wood buildings as he switched off the ignition and pocketed the keys.

"It doesn't look like much."

"What did you expect, after so many years?" Aramanda asked, smiling and shaking her head. "It is not Philadelphia. Even when *I* knew it, it was little better than this. The miners and their families were poor and most so in debt to the company store they had no means of ever improving their conditions. My uncle certainly had no intention of doing so on their behalf."

"Yet you kept coming back, when you could have stayed away."

"I had reason." Her eyes suggested several things, all of them provocative. "As I have reason now."

Resisting the temptation to ask for a demonstration, Sayer opened his door and walked around to hand her out. "Someday, you're going to have to explain those reasons to me. In detail."

"Perhaps." Giving him the secret, knowing smile that always drove him crazy, she turned and slowly, gracefully started walking up what once had been the main street of the mining community.

Sayer caught up to her in a few long strides, and they walked hand-in-hand up the street, pausing once or twice to glance inside this building or that. As they passed a small gray stone church, he saw Aramanda glance in its direction, a wistful smile curving her mouth.

She flushed when she discovered him looking at her. "I was thinking of the hours I spent there, simply talking," she said as they continued their leisurely walk. "It was one of the only places where we—Roarke and I—could be alone. Father Creeghan was quite kind about it. I think he fancied himself a matchmaker."

She felt Sayer stiffen beside her and knew the mention of Roarke's name had provoked it. She could accept he had the soul of the man she loved, but he only thought of Roarke as a rival.

It left her divided between two men—loving both, loving them as one. Yet she could never explain it to Sayer.

Wanting to distract him, she stopped in front of a squat, two-story structure and, giving the door a shove, peered inside. "Ah, the tavern. One of the miners' favorite places to spend the evenings, although I confess I never understood their preference for Tansie Caitlan's bad ale."

Sayer knew she was deliberately trying to divert him, just as he knew she sensed his anger every time she mentioned Roarke Macnair's name. He rewarded her with a smile that didn't quite disguise the tenseness still in him. "Why, Miss Montclair, how do you know it was bad?"

"I was persuaded to try it—once. After which, I sat in on a hand of cards and proceeded to lose half-a-night's winnings."

Sayer laughed despite himself at the merriment dancing in her eyes, though she made a vain attempt to keep her mouth from twitching upward.

"The miners seem to have been a bad influence on you," he said, the laughter abruptly gone. He knew they were speaking of Roarke Macnair, and it irritated the hell out of him. The fierce possessiveness he'd never felt for any woman returned tenfold. If he never heard that name again, it would be too soon.

"Very. But I did learn the difference between a straight flush and a full house—something Mama and all my governesses overlooked in all my lessons."

"A very useful skill. Particularly if you're playing with someone else's money."

"They seemed to think so. I suspect, though, they dared me to play simply to see if I would be brazen enough to do it." She slanted him a provocative glance through her lashes. "Just as you do."

"Me?"

"You always encourage me to do things no proper lady in her right senses would consider," Aramanda said, laughing back at him before she stepped into the tavern. "I have discovered many things about myself because of you . . . and learned many pleasures."

The soft, longing note threaded through her last words plucked at Sayer's heart. Leaning against the door frame, he watched her move about the room, drawing her fingertips slowly down the bar, lightly touching a chair or table.

Sunlight, muted by the layers of dust on the window glass, lent her a pale, golden aura, reminding him of the first moment he had seen her, a vision of perfect beauty, conjured from his need. As she weaved her way through the room, she began humming a bittersweet, lilting tune, her body swaying in time to the rhythm.

"What's that song?" he asked, certain phrases sounding familiar, but the whole of it just out of the reach of his memory.

The feelings it evoked teased him—a warm, bright river of them, happiness and pleasure tinged with poignancy.

"Scully used to play it for me on his fiddle when we came here together," she said. "He said it was an old Irish ballad his mother had taught him and that it reminded him of me. I never asked him why."

She hugged her arms around herself, spinning about in the center of the room, momentarily caught up in the enchantment of her memories. "Roarke and I danced to it once, the first and only time. It was late, and almost no one was here but Roarke and me and Scully, and Tansie at the bar, and I asked Roarke if he would. He laughed at me because he was sooty and rumpled, but none of that mattered. I have never forgotten that night. It was the first time . . ."

"The first time you loved him?" Sayer asked harshly.

Aramanda stood still, staring fully at him, the expression on her face a mixture of longing and hesitation. She had hurt him, and it hurt her in return to see it in his eyes.

"The first time that I knew your soul and mine were destined to be together," she said at last, so softly the words whispered in the quiet. She added almost at once, "I should not have told you."

"Why?"

"Because it troubles you to hear me speak of the past."

"It troubles me to hear you speak about him," Sayer said. Walking toward her, he stopped a hand's breadth away. "I don't want to know how much you loved him."

Sayer looked at her for a long moment, fighting the conflict of primitive fury and possessiveness threatening to overcome the civilization Aramanda credited him with. He had never felt less civilized. The violence Roarke Macnair advocated didn't seem so forbidden when she said his name with such tenderness and so many dreams in her eyes.

Aramanda saw the battle in him and wanted to scream to break the silent bonds holding them captive between past and present. But she stayed quiet and waited for him, not willing to unwittingly hurt him again.

Finally, in a gesture slow and poignant with meaning, Sayer

offered her his hand. "You told me about a night of firsts, but I think there should always be seconds. You asked him then; I'm asking now. It's a shame to waste the music. Would you dance with me?"

Wordlessly, her eyes a mirror of a thousand words and one pure feeling, she laid her hand on his with a sense of doing an act of great import, coming into his arms as he moved to guide her into the first steps of their timeless dance.

Holding her, breathing in her essence of warm roses, feeling the motion of her against him, Sayer heard their music. It sang inside him, a melody he had always known but had lost and then regained only when she touched him.

No matter what her past, whom she believed him to be, or all that lay between them—with her, Sayer could believe in forever. This was Aramanda, his woman, his soul, and he could forget the anger, the pain of her loving another when he held her in his arms.

Overwhelmed by emotion, Sayer pulled her closer, grazing a light kiss on her temple, then her cheek. When he tasted a faint dampness, he looked down. Sliding his fingers under her chin, he lifted her face to his. "What's wrong?"

"Nothing . . . nothing is wrong. Everything is right."

"Then—"

"I am afraid. I am afraid it cannot last, that I truly do not belong here. I feel I must return, too soon. And I do not want to leave you again. I do not want to go back to a place where there is no tomorrow."

"Then stay. Stay with me."

The look of wonder on her face blunted the shock of realization that came a split second later—the realization he'd just offered her his heart.

But he would not turn back now. He didn't want to turn back now. He wanted her.

"Sayer . . . I cannot. I—"

"Stay with me, Aramanda. The only tomorrows I have are with you." Taking her face between his hands, Sayer kissed her, long and deeply.

She responded with a fervor that left no room for doubt, giving herself, heart and soul, to him alone. This was his woman, no matter what lifetime she came to him from, no matter what cause or time divided them.

"Let's get out of here," Sayer said when he finally summoned the strength to drag his mouth from hers.

"Must we?"

The fine tremble in her; the quick, shallow sound of her breathing; the taste of her on his mouth; the huskiness of her voice combined in a passionate assault on his senses, nearly causing him to take back his words.

"Either we go or we give the next people who walk in here a lot more than they bargained for."

"Perhaps it would be best if we left," Aramanda said, a faint flush coloring her face. "Where are we going?"

"I don't know. The hotel, Philadelphia, London—come back to Colorado with me, it doesn't matter. Anywhere we can be together."

"Anywhere?"

"Do you have a preference?"

"I do. And it is not far from here. Will you let me take you there?"

Sayer stopped in the center of the street, ignoring the glances they drew from several passing tourists.

"You've already taken me farther than I ever expected to go. I won't stop now," he said, claiming another lingering kiss. "I have a feeling we've just gotten started."

The last of the afternoon sunlight, shaded yellow-green and gold, filtered through the canopy of pine and oak, making patterns of cool and warm on the forest floor. Carrying the handful of wild roses Sayer had picked for her, Aramanda slowly walked up the familiar path. She listened to the whisper of the woods, content to simply be with him in this place.

"This is so far away from everything, past or present," she

murmured, glancing up at him. "There is no time here. I think that is why I love it so much."

Sayer squeezed her hand. "I understand. It reminds me of some of my favorite places in Colorado. I've always felt more comfortable in places with no boundaries, no expectations."

"It is where we belong, not one place or the other but in between, where there is only space for us."

"You've been here before." He didn't ask, but stated it with surety. Aramanda nodded, and Sayer looked around them, his gaze abstracted. "It doesn't make sense, but it looks vaguely familiar." He frowned. "I remember—the first time I touched you, in the shop. I had a dream, a vision of you. We were here—together. But that's impossible."

The husky edge to his voice, his soft emphasis on the last word *together* caused a quiver of awareness under her skin.

"Is it? I remember it very well. Though this is not quite the place I remember best. It is there—" She gestured ahead to a point several yards away where a phalanx of silver maples seemed to stand in an impenetrable barrier at the end of the path. "Just beyond those trees, a little to the left there is—"

"—a path that leads into a small grove." He said the words with both wonder and doubt, with surprised pleasure and disbelief that he could recall something unfamiliar to him. "This feels weird."

"What is weird?"

"Strange. Uncomfortable."

"Oh. It does not feel *weird* to me," Aramanda said softly, holding his hand more tightly. "I feel peaceful here with you, as if time has granted me a a brief reprieve."

She did not give him a chance to answer but started in the direction of the secret grove. "I am surprised at how little the forest has changed," she said, glancing around her. At the end of the path, she ducked under the branches Sayer held aside for her, parting the leafy screen that separated them from the other side.

When she stepped out into the circle of trees, she drew in a breath in sudden awe. "It is exactly the same." She walked into the knee-high grasses and their litter of wildflowers, half-expecting it all to shimmer and fade like an illusion. "How can it be? How can it be so . . . so untouched? Everything else is so different."

Coming up behind her, Sayer put his hands on her shoulders, standing close, sharing her wonderment. "Maybe because there are some things time never changes," he said. "Places. Feelings."

"Do you believe that?" Aramanda whispered, not daring to believe it herself.

"With you, I can believe anything."

She turned to him, all her hopes in her eyes, offered to him with her heart. "Can you? Truly? Or is this only another of my dreams?"

"It's not a dream." Sayer looked at her, trying to find words for feelings he had never given a name to in this lifetime. "I thought I had everything I needed to be complete," he said at last. "Challenge, success, respect. But it was never enough because I was never whole. I can't be without you."

He touched her face, wanting to imprint the contour and nuance of every feature on his skin. "The power of what I feel for you scares the hell out of me. I don't understand it; but lately, I can't think of anything but you, I don't want to do anything unless it's with you. I thought I had everything, but I had nothing until you. I can say I love you, but it doesn't describe what I feel. It's beyond that, and I don't know how to tell you."

"You do not have to tell me," Aramanda whispered. She felt shaken to the core of her soul, forever changed. "I never thought to hear you say those words to me, not in this place, this time. I thought you were lost to me, that your causes in this life were even stronger than in the last."

"I've found a new cause—in you."

For a moment, Aramanda could say nothing, too moved by his admission to tell him what was in her heart. "If this were the last place God made, the last hours I had in any place in time, it would be the only place I would ever want to be. I would forsake every moment of the past to stay here with you."

"Then stay. We don't have a past anymore, only a future."

"I want that. I want to stay—"

"But?"

"I—I feel there is no time left to me here, only these few stolen moments left with you. I do not belong here. I am afraid . . ." Fear and a desperate need swept through her, uncontrolled. "Show me, Sayer," she said, suddenly possessed by them. "Show me it is real."

Aramanda reached for him as he pulled her into his arms, bending her body to the strength of his. The hunger came upon her, fast and furious, pushing out of her mind any reason or emotion but that of wanting him, purely and forever.

The roses slipped from her hand to the ground, scattering petals over the soft grass. Returning his kiss, she slid her arms around his neck, holding to him as if he were her one light in a depthless night.

Sayer felt overwhelmed. Touching her, feeling the intimate press of her against him, the promise and plea in her kiss, he could only step into the fire with her, relying on blind faith to overcome all the obstacles destiny threw in their way.

Caught up in the urgent desire she spoke with every caress, he knelt in the thick grass, gently bringing her with him. He ran his fingers over her face, along the delicate line of her throat, feeling her quiver at the slight touch.

"I want to love you," he murmured.

"Yes . . . yes, now, before it is too late."

"It will never be too late. We have forever to be together, I promise you that. But I want it to be us, Aramanda."

Sliding his hands into her hair, he lifted her face to his, his touch gentle, his eyes burning with a fierceness that was only partly passion. "I don't want you to be loving a ghost of your past. Whatever happened then, whatever you and Roarke Macnair were or weren't to each other, is over. I'm not Roarke. I'm Sayer. If you want us to be together, then it has to be in this time, in this place."

"I know who you are," Aramanda said softly. She slipped her hand inside his shirt and laid her palm against his heart. "You are the man I love. In this time, in this place." Leaning into him, she kissed him softly, then with increasing passion when he responded.

This time, swept up in the tempest they created from desire, he held nothing back, left no room for either of them to doubt. His fingers caressed the curve of her back, tracing her spine up to her nape, then gradually moving down again as he parted the fastener of her dress, leaving only the delicate silk of her chemise between her skin and the warmth of his hand.

Lowering her to the bed of grasses and crushed roses, he slid the dress from her body with a maddening languor, finally tossing the billow of gauze aside.

Aramanda felt a slow heat tremble over her body as his eyes roamed over her. Seeing the hunger in his gaze, she expected him to remove the last barrier of her clothing. Instead, he left the fragile material between them, stroking, touching, tasting her through the whisper of silk until she wanted to beg him to assuage the aching need he evoked with the barest caress.

With all that had happened between them, she half feared she would feel shy with him. This was the first time they would love each other . . . the first time she would touch this man's body, give herself completely to him, and surrender her heart.

Yet passion, as strong and enduring as her love, made nonsense of her doubts, drawing her to him, into him, so she lost herself in the timeless world only they could create. It felt as new and wonderful as his first caress of yesterday, as powerful and spellbinding as the ageless love between them.

It lasted an eternity, yet could never be long enough.

Finally, with desire coiled tight and hot in the deepest part of her, Aramanda touched him with a wanton abandon, feeding his need with her own until he pulled apart from her long enough to strip away the rest of their clothing.

The warm softness of her in his arms, the wild taste of her passion pushed Sayer to the limit of his control. Sliding his hand under her neck, he brought her fully against him, taking a long moment to simply look at her face.

"If I lived a thousand lifetimes, I would never find anyone as beautiful as you," Sayer whispered. "I know you aren't a dream, because I couldn't have imagined anyone so perfect."

Her lips parted as if to deny him and he stole the first breath of sound with his mouth, deepening his kiss as he joined their bodies, completing their union of souls.

He made love to her so tenderly, yet with such passion, Aramanda felt herself reshaped and made whole by the love he poured over her, into her. Joy tasted sweet; passion burned through her; heaven sang in her ears.

When he finally brought her to the peak of fulfillment, to a place of dizzying height and brilliant light, for what seemed an eternity she learned to fly without wings before gently drifting back to earth in his embrace.

Afterward, lying with Sayer in the twilight stillness, Aramanda clung fast to the fragile, elusive sense of completeness wrapping them both. "I will never feel this way again," she murmured at last.

Sayer's laughter rumbled in her ear. "Wanna bet?"

"How could you improve on perfection?"

"Oh, I have a few ideas. Besides, that sounded like a challenge to me and I never turn down a dare."

"No . . . not a dare." She smoothed back the hair from his brow, smiling into his eyes. "Only my most cherished desire."

"And mine. Always mine, Aramanda. Now and forever."

Gathering her back into his arms, he made love to her again under the first glimmer of starlight, the depth of feeling he communicated in his touch eclipsing the nameless apprehension still plaguing Aramanda.

Sayer gave her all she desired and more before taking her back to their rooms and to his bed, inviting her to join him in creating their forever magic once again.

It was hours later, in the waning moments before midnight, that Aramanda stirred from a restless doze, awakened by a clear sense of urgency.

She pulled herself to a half-sitting position, glancing around the shadowed room.

"Sayer?"

He lay beside her, the sheet flung over his hip, his arm curved against her waist. At her whisper of his name, he shifted, murmuring something unintelligible in his sleep.

Aramanda tried to push away the uneasiness creeping over her, but it grew stronger, more insistent with each passing minute. Though she had not thought of them in days, she suddenly felt the presence of the odd couple from the travel agency, as strongly as if they stood beside her.

She looked at Sayer and reached out a hand to touch him, to reassure herself they were together. As she did, the moonlight from the open window shone through her hand, making it appear as insubstantial as fairy's flesh.

The feeling of displacement that had plagued Aramanda for so long hit her with its fullest force, dizzying her so that she clutched at the side of the bed, trembling, helpless in its tightening grip.

No! It cannot be time. It cannot come now!

Aramanda struggled fiercely against it. "No, I must stay!" she cried softly, defying a destiny that would rip her again from the man she loved.

A sudden, vivid vision of Lila came to her.

You do not belong here. You must return.

"I cannot!" Anguish consumed her, the pain of it ravening, merciless.

The past is the only path to the future.

"How? How can I leave you?" Aramanda whispered to her lover, not trusting herself to touch him, to wake him, for fear she would succumb to begging Sayer to take her back to the only place they could find the future together.

If you return alone, you have no future.

"How can I return without you? Sayer . . ." A feeling of near-panic assailed her, coupled with a deep-reaching faintness that made her body weak and her head whirl.

"How can I return at all?"

You will know how, from whence you came.

From whence I came . . . Aramanda looked at Sayer once more. He asked her to stay, yet she could not. No more than she could beg him to return.

She could only do what she must and pray and hope and trust with her heart that his soul would remember their love, that his heart would cause him to follow . . .

That their love was powerful enough to defeat time.

Careful not to disturb him, she slipped out of his bed and into the clothing he had carelessly tossed onto the floor. Then, hesitating, she stepped next to the bed and looked down at him, love and sorrow and the strange fear clashing inside.

"I must go, Sayer, back once more. Please try to understand," she said softly. "I will find my way back to you. I vow I will if it is all I ever do, in this lifetime or the next. But I must do this now. There is no other choice for us, no other chance for redemption."

Tears blurring her last vision of him, she leaned over and gently smoothed back the hair from his forehead before brushing a kiss against his mouth.

The touch of him, intensifying all she felt for the lover she had lost and found and now lost again, at odds with the force pulling her away, threatened to rip her soul in two.

Catching her breath on a sob, Aramanda turned and rushed from the room, leaving Sayer in unknowing darkness.

Sayer stretched out his hand, reaching for her. Instead of warm flesh, his fingers curled around rumpled sheet. The unexpected sensation jolted him into wakefulness.

"Aramanda?"

Nothing.

No reply, no sound—nothing but the impression left on her pillow and the scent of wild roses to indicate she had ever been there at all.

"You can't have just disappeared," Sayer muttered to himself, throwing back the sheet and hauling himself out of the bed in one motion. Even as he said the words, though, he was attacked by a sudden fear she could do just that.

I feel there is no time left to me here, only these few stolen moments left with you . . .

With her in the forest, he'd discounted her words, concerned only with what they shared at that moment of time. He'd never truly believed her story of cheating time to find him, despite her insistence and what the weird couple at the travel agency claimed. It seemed too impossible.

Now the only impossibility was the thought of living without her.

"Aramanda! Dammit, woman, where have you gone? Where could you go without me?" Quickly jerking on his jeans and shirt, he made a fast search of their rooms, knowing it was useless.

Grabbing his keys, he ran downstairs and rousted the front desk clerk out of a comfortable slouch. "Did you see a woman leave here within the past hour or so? She was with me—"

"Miss Montclair? She asked for a cab, said something about having to go to one of her family's mines tonight. I thought it was kinda weird, but—"

Leaving the clerk in mid-sentence, Sayer turned and dashed out the door to where he'd left the Range Rover parked. He shoved the rover into gear and headed in the direction of the mine.

What seemed like years ago, he'd planned to make this midnight jaunt on his own to get the soil samples he needed.

The samples, the trouble at the mine, any and every cause he'd ever fought for, now seemed small and insignificant compared to the strength of his need to find her.

She'd left him and taken his soul, and he'd walk into hell to get her back.

Sayer expected trouble at the mine. There was the perimeter fence; and he knew the Montclairs had left a guard on duty at the front gate, the sheriff had told him that. The back of the property was a different story.

To hell with the risk. I've got to find her.

Choosing a quiet spot out of the line of sight of the guard and near the mine opening, Sayer parked the rover near the fence, headlights on, to shine into the dark maw of the mine entrance. He didn't think twice about scaling the fence and used the hood of the rover for a lift up.

On the other side, he strode into the mine, thinking only of her. What remained of the rational part of his brain told him he was insane to think she would be here; his heart knew it was a certainty.

"Aramanda!"

His own voice echoed back at him.

The acrid smell of coal hung heavy in the warm, clammy air. A sheen of sweat broke out on his brow, but he felt cold. Sayer walked farther into the shaft, swiping his forearm over his face, then he remembered the bandanna.

He reached in his back pocket, drawing it out. But when his fist closed around the frayed cloth, his fingers went numb.

Sayer stared at his hand, a wave of dizziness making his head swim. Before he knew what was happening, the dull, tingling sensation spread up his arm, across his chest, and down both legs.

He tried to move, to turn, and couldn't. Paralyzed, he watched the faint light from the rover's headlights slowly give way to blackness.

Then he saw her eyes.

Twelve

Those eyes . . .

If he knew nothing else, Sayer knew her strange, beautiful amber eyes. How long he'd been standing here in this twilight purgatory, reaching for her from afar through their silent exchange, he had no idea.

She stood so far away, in back of so many faceless people, he couldn't talk to her, couldn't reach her.

Don't walk away, for God's sake. Don't leave until I get a grip on myself!

His senses returned, slowly, painfully, bringing the realization there was a crowd in front of him, all staring up at him in anticipation.

Up?

Sayer started. His mind seemed to have taken flight. Nothing made sense. A moment ago he'd been alone in the mine. What was happening here? And why did he feel like he'd taken the worst in a fifteen-round fight? Unwillingly, he pried his gaze away from Aramanda to stare around him.

His vision blurred, refocused.

Too clearly, Sayer saw he stood on a raised platform—a table—his arm lifted, waving a blue bandanna like some rebel flag.

What the . . . Sayer tried pulling his arm down, winced at the sharp pain of lowering it.

He struggled for logic. He wasn't scheduled to give any speeches until Europe. . . . His body ached all over, felt like he'd run a marathon.

Where the hell am I? And what the hell am I doing standing on a table in front of all these people?

A wild flood of confusion shot through him, a chilling adrenaline rush like ice through his veins.

Sayer glanced from side to side, recognizing nothing about the place or the men. Looking around the room, dimly lit with flickering oil lamps, he focused on the group of faces, their eyes fixed on him.

An audience? He swept the crowd, searching. Nothing and no one looked familiar.

The narrow room was unevenly constructed of rough, dark timber, a long bar at one end and crudely fashioned tables and chairs haphazardly crowded together. It smelled of sweat and dirt and old beer, all simmered together by the uneven heat of a hissing wood stove.

The men themselves looked like the cast from a period movie with their bushy sidewhiskers and beards, dressed in coarse, faded vests, shirts and trousers blackened in hues of soot and gray and thin from too many washings. He felt the expectation racing hot and tense in them, as he had so many times in the past when he'd used his voice and his passion to rouse a crowd to action.

But he didn't know any of this.

Except the eyes of Aramanda Montclair.

She watched him with the same look in her eyes she'd had the first time he'd seen the vision of her in the auditorium—sadness, longing, expectation.

The same day she'd told him she had cheated time to be with him.

If she could come forward, I could go back . . .

Sayer shoved a hand through his hair, shaking off the unimaginable thought.

Dammit, that's impossible. Why are they staring at me like that? What do they want from me? What does she want?

"Roarke! Get down. Don't say anything else!" A short, burly man with rumpled black-and-silver hair, wearing a stained vest over his shirtsleeves, tugged at Sayer's pant leg. His faded blue eyes reflected concern and a touch of apprehension. "Come now, man, that's the Montclair girl standin' back there. You're goin' to bring trouble on yourself. You all right, Roarke?"

"Ye—" Sayer cleared his throat. "Fine. And I see her. I've said all I had to say for now, anyhow."

Is that my voice?

If so, it had dropped an octave and was strangely accented. His voice had always been considered deep, but now he almost growled. Had the man called him Roarke?

He continued to stare and stare at the crowd in disbelief. A rumble was beginning to move over the room, an unsettled excitement; the men began pressing in on him, saying things that in his dazed state sounded like a confused mutter.

I have to get to her!

"What the devil is she doing here?" another man at his side asked. The voice, diffident, slightly hesitant with an odd musical lilt, sounded strangely familiar. Sayer, his eyes fixed on Aramanda, didn't spare him a look.

"I don't know, but I'll find out," Sayer heard himself grumble, then abruptly he turned and jumped down off the table. His knees gave out and the man grabbed his arm.

"Steady there. You've gone white in the face, friend."

Sayer briefly accepted the support and this time glanced to put a face to the voice. Surprise shot through him.

The man, save for the mutton chops and scraggly, longer hair, could have been Malcolm. A ragged woolen coat hung from his bony shoulders, and he wore a cap pulled low on his gaunt face. He seemed not to notice the astonishment Sayer felt sure must be clear on his face.

The would-be Malcolm pushed him onto a chair. "Sit down, man. Dawn to night in the mines and too many nights of this without sleep are going to kill you before Montclair gets his chance. I'll go see what the lass wants and get you an ale. And for the love of heaven, put that damned bandanna away!"

Sayer automatically stuffed the scrap of cloth into his vest pocket. *I don't wear vests . . .*

"Thanks," Sayer muttered as he watched Malcolm's clone pick his way to the front of the room.

Struggling against an insidious light-headedness, Sayer shook his head to clear it, then shoved to his feet. He had to get to Aramanda, the only reality he knew.

"We're with you all the way, Roarke," someone he passed said, punctuating the comment with a hearty slap on Sayer's back. "You know we'll follow you to hell and back."

Thinking it was likely going to be hell for a long time, Sayer muttered back something unintelligible. Other men spoke to him, but as he neared Aramanda, he tuned out every voice but hers. Malcolm—or someone who looked startlingly like him—stood next to her; she spoke to him in hushed tones.

Aramanda gripped Malcolm's arm, and Sayer saw him shake his head and push her hand away. Then he abruptly pushed through the men and shoved open the heavy front door.

She turned to follow, but another man standing next to her stepped in front of her, blocking her way. He swept his cap from his head.

"Good evenin' to you, Miss Montclair," Sayer heard him say as he drew near them.

Aramanda nodded kindly to him, but Sayer saw strain disguised by her gracious facade. "Good evening, Mr. Dobson."

"Best be careful walking out alone at night, Miss Montclair. Can I see you home?"

"No. Thank you, but I will be fine on my own. Now, if you will excuse me."

"The missus says to thank you for the needles and yarns."

Aramanda smiled gently. "Tell her to let me know when she has used them all. I will send more along as soon as I am safely able to."

"You're a good soul, miss, just as your father was, God rest his soul." The miner fiddled nervously with his cap.

His legs and arms gaining strength and coordination as he strode quickly through the crowd, Sayer caught up with Aramanda just as she lifted the hood of her heavy dark cape to cover the gleaming red-gold of her hair, readying to leave the tavern.

"Wait! Ara—Miss Montclair, I need to talk to you!"

Aware every eye in the bar suddenly turned on them, Sayer ruthlessly ignored them and reached out for her.

"Roarke, let the girl be," the burly man who had talked him down from the table called out. Now behind the bar, he snagged Sayer's sleeve as Aramanda, after one disbelieving glance at Sayer, turned and pushed the door open.

"I have to talk to her."

"Aye, I'll bet you do," grunted one of the men, pushing to the bar for a tankard. "It's no use arguin' with him, Tansie. You know how Roarke is once he's set his mind to do somethin'."

"I know how he is." Tansie leaned over the counter and took a harder grip on Sayer's arm, pulling him close to his face with an easy strength.

"You're making the men nervous with your fancy for that girl," Tansie whispered harshly. "What she seems to be and what she is are two very different things, friend. Don't matter how much charity she gives out, there's no guaranty she's her father's daughter. Some of the men are wonderin' if that beautiful face of hers is making you forget that!"

Sayer faced Tansie squarely. "I know exactly what and who she is."

"We don't trust her."

"If I say she's trustworthy, that's all the proof you need."

"It had better be, Roarke. It had damned well better be."

"It is." Sayer jerked his arm away and shoved out of the bar into the chill, bleak night, leaving in his wake raised stares and dark mutterings.

The air, heavy with the smell of coal and dust, assaulted his lungs, making him cough. He darted a glance to both sides of the street. What little pallid light seeped out into the street from the rows of windows along either side the smoky air was muted so it was of no use to him in locating Aramanda. There were no street lights, no flashing neon signs, no cars whizzing by, no sirens or horns. The darkness was eerie, the silence completely unnerving.

A short way from the tavern, though, Sayer spied the soft

amber glow of what might have been a lantern swinging from side to side as someone hurried off into the still, cold night.

He ran to catch up with the teasing light, cursing this body that moved awkwardly and slowly compared to his customary pace. "Aramanda! Wait, please. I have to talk to you."

The figure in the black night turned briefly back, then quickened the pace.

Finally Sayer caught up enough to recognize the cloak Aramanda wore. "Aramanda, stop! Why are you running away from me?"

She did stop, suddenly, whirling to glare at him. "What would you have with me, Mr. Macnair? We have nothing to say to each other."

"Wha—Aramanda, it's me." He put both hands to his chest. "Sayer. We have a hell of a lot to talk about."

She held the lantern to his face, peering at him closely. Her mouth twisted in a deriding line. "You are drunk, Mr. Macnair, and I am hardly surprised. Go home. You are of no use to your brother in this condition."

"My brother—I am not drunk! I'm having a nightmare!" Sayer reached out a hand to her. "Aramanda, don't you remember? We were at the inn. You left; I came after you—"

A stinging slap to his cheek cut him short.

"How dare you insinuate such things! For that matter, how dare you call me by my first name!"

Sayer rubbed his cheek—and found hair. Sideburns? He hated sideburns. "This has gone too far."

"Have you no decency at all? On this of all nights, when your own brother's family grieves for the loss of their child, you stand here insulting me with your indecent insinuations. You disgust me, sir! Good night!"

"Wait! Their baby died? Nina? No, it can't be. Liz said they'd waited so long. . . . I saw her only yesterday."

"And I saw Rose only an hour ago, while you were in the tavern obviously getting deeper and deeper into your cups."

"I am not drunk, dammit."

"Then you have no excuse for your insolence."

"I—" Sayer shoved a hand through his hair. "I'm sorry for what I said. I don't know what happened . . ."

But with a growing uneasiness, he started to realize this nightmare was all too real. Aramanda's manner and clothing, the tavern, the men, the lantern, the smell of coal and lamp oil in the cold night—no one could manufacture such a texture of reality. It all spoke undeniably of another time.

Her time.

The thing he had sworn to her could never happen was his reality now. He hadn't believed her. Why should she believe him?

"Tell me one thing, please. What year is this?"

Aramanda glared at him. "Your brother's child is dead, and you wish to jest?"

"No, I—please, just tell me the year, then take me to my brother's house."

"It is the year of our Lord, eighteen hundred and sixty-seven, the month of March, if that is any use to you," she snapped. "And you are quite able to find your brother's house on your own."

Sayer felt the blood leave his face in a rush. His head throbbed with the struggle to resist what he couldn't accept as truth.

Except, in his gut, he knew it was the truth. He had returned to her time, just as she had begged him to. It could not be; but it was. She had told him she did not belong to his time; and now, with sudden, dizzying force, he knew exactly how she had felt.

His knees started to give way and, instinctively, he reached out, groping for some support. His hand grazed her shoulder.

"You are drunk. Take your hands off me at once."

"No," he said, his voice barely a graveled whisper. "I swear I'm not." What else could he say? She would think him insane if he tried to explain. Just as he had when she'd tried to tell him.

Aramanda, I didn't realize . . .

"I'm sorry, Miss Montclair," he said, trying to sound apologetic, gritting his teeth against an overwhelming desire to take her in his arms and hold her to his heart until she admitted she recognized him as the man she loved.

Something in his voice, some entreaty he couldn't keep out, paused her. She cocked her head at him, her eyes appraising him.

"You do not sound as if you are sorry. But I believe you. You are not drunk." Aramanda frowned. "Perhaps you are coming down with the fever. It sometimes manifests itself in strange delusions. You, though," she added with a sardonic cant in her voice, "probably defy illness as you do everything else that does not please you. You do not even have a coat."

"I'm fine." Straightening, Sayer fought back a wild temptation to run blindly into the night, to try to escape the bizarre truth that he'd just gone over a hundred years backward in time.

"I'm just . . . tired," he said. He focused hard on her beautiful, familiar eyes to force himself to reign in the impulse. "Were you on your way to my brother's house?"

"Yes."

"May I walk with you?" Sayer asked, needing to stay near her, to have her by his side to anchor him into this new reality.

"If you keep your tongue. And your distance."

"You have my word."

"Then hurry along. I must return home soon or my uncle will find me missing from my bed."

"You escaped to come here tonight?"

"Of course," Aramanda said, glancing at him in some surprise. "Do you imagine he would allow me into the miners' camp after dark? He does not know most days when I come visit."

"You're either very brave or very crazy."

"I could say the same of you, sir. I saw you there at Tansie's tavern, making your speech to your rebels, brazenly waving that wretched blue cloth of yours without regard for any consequence. What if one of my uncle's guards had walked into the tavern just then? You take foolish chances with your life, Mr. Macnair. Or does it not matter to you?"

"I—I was only speaking my mind." Sayer was guessing, of course, but it had been obvious the crowd had gathered to listen to him.

Or to Roarke Macnair, the infamous rebel leader.

Sayer tried to assimilate the thought, then thrust it aside as the implications started to soak in. "Why shouldn't I wave a piece of cloth?" he muttered, more to himself than to her.

"Do not believe I am stupid or a fool," Aramanda said, lifting her chin. "You know my uncle's edict as well as anyone—death to those who stand behind the symbol of your rebellion. That secret has been poorly kept."

"Death?" Sayer repeated the words half in disbelief, half to convince himself of the truth in them. He stuffed the bandanna deeper into his pocket.

"What happened to my brother's baby?"

"Are you such enemies with Liam now that you cannot even speak his name?" Without waiting for his reply, Aramanda went on. "You would know, if you had been home instead of at the tavern creating trouble among the miners. They lost Rose to the cold. She was always a fragile child but even a strong child cannot endure a lack of heat for long in winter."

"Are you saying my brother—Liam—had no heat in his house?"

Aramanda eyed him curiously. "Are you so surprised? It is a common-enough circumstance in the camp. Have you never run out of coal?"

"Hell no. My God—this isn't the middle ages!"

"I will not hear you take the Lord's name in vain or use such language with me!"

Sayer shook his head impatiently. "I only meant I wish my brother—Liam—would have told me. I would have shared all I have with him."

"He is proud. And from what Bridget tells me, you and your brother share little more than a last name."

"Bridget says so, does she?" Sayer asked, taking note of his sister-in-law's name. "I'm sorry to hear that."

Aramanda had no reply for him, and they walked on in silence.

Sayer used the quiet to try and dredge up every bit of information he could recall about Roarke Macnair from what Aramanda had told him and from his own brief research with her at the library.

Obviously, however he'd gotten here and for whatever reason, he was accepted as Roarke. And he'd come to this place before the love between Aramanda and her rebel leader had begun to blossom. Before Roarke's death.

Had she willed him to return with her? If so, why couldn't she remember him? And what the hell was he going to do if she never remembered?

How could she? In this time, this place, none of it had ever happened. None of it would happen for over a hundred years.

Sayer let the thought sink in. It brought with it a gaping emptiness and something akin to grief.

He shook both off, though the feelings only retreated. For right now, it appeared he didn't have much choice but to play out this bizarre twist of fate. To pretend he was Roarke Macnair and pray destiny saw fit to give Aramanda and his future back to him.

Over the next slope of the rough dirt street, the air cleared some and in the moonlight Sayer saw the tops of dozens of tiny shacks. They looked like row houses or low-income, inner city, cracker-box houses crammed together along both sides of the dirt path. Somewhere in the distance, a dog barked and a flurry of chickens cackled into the night.

But these weren't frame houses with brick facades or even vinyl siding. Plain, unpainted clapboard shacks with tin roofs, they reminded Sayer of the poverty-stricken neighborhoods in the Bahamas. The places tourists avoided.

As they walked down into the village, the stench of rotting vegetables and human waste hung heavy around them. Sayer coughed and breathed through his mouth to avoid the smell. He couldn't keep his eyes from the vista he wanted to deny existed.

This was reality, though. Through one front window he saw a woman in a long woolen skirt and badly stained apron, her hair falling out of a tattered scarf, bent over a huge barrel, scrubbing clothing against a washboard. At the next, several little ruddy-faced girls in torn ankle-length cotton gowns sat on the rough, planked floor in front of a hulk of a stove, braiding each other's hair and tucking it under yellowed nightcaps.

"Wait a moment," Aramanda interrupted his thoughts. "I must stop here."

Sayer followed her to the doorstep of one of the smallest

houses, hanging slightly back. She rapped on a door and, after a moment, an elderly man peeked out around the door.

"I am sorry to call so late," Aramanda said softly, "but this was my only opportunity to check in on Mrs. Ryan today." She smiled, and the tenderness of the gesture made Sayer's heart twist. "If it is presumption on my part, then I will leave it until tomorrow."

"Nonsense, lass, you're always welcome," the man said. He scrunched his nose, the gesture lifting his upper lip to reveal blackened, jagged teeth. He stepped aside to welcome Aramanda in the door and caught sight of Sayer.

"Mr. Macnair very kindly offered to escort me this night," Aramanda said quickly, to Sayer's surprise.

Staring warily at Sayer, the man grumbled, "Oh, all right, the both of you, then, come in."

Inside the tiny front room with smoke-blackened walls, thick with the smells of coal dust and boiled cabbage, a frail old woman wrapped in a tattered blanket sat in front of a small stove. One spindly leg was propped up on a rustic oak stool slightly to the side. She glanced up at them, and a faint color came into her sunken cheeks when she saw Aramanda.

"Good evening, Mrs. Ryan," Aramanda said gently, as though speaking to a frightened rabbit. "How is your leg today?"

The woman pulled her blanket taut around her thin shoulders and slanted a cold look at Sayer, making him distinctly uncomfortable. "Swellin's gone down some," the woman answered after a long, uncomfortable pause.

"Good. I will bring new wrappings over tomorrow. It is time they were changed."

"Don't take no chances on our account, miss," her husband said, a deep frown worrying a furrow between heavy rust-colored brows.

"I will do as I see fit and you know it," Aramanda told him firmly. She turned her attention back to the woman. "You must not put your weight on your leg until it is healed. Remember that."

"She will. I'll see to it," the old man said. His mouth briefly lifted in a semblance of a smile. "I need her help with the garden this spring."

"You do not fool me, Michael Ryan," Aramanda said softly. "Good night to you both."

Sayer nodded his retreat and followed her out. He drank in what now seemed comparatively clean air. "I see you're a nurse as well as an angel of compassion."

Aramanda laughed. It was a sound he knew well, rich and melodious; it salved his nerves. "Of course not. I only make do with common sense." She pointed ahead. "Look. The lamp is still lit at your brother's house."

"How can you tell which house is theirs? They all look exactly alike."

Aramanda peered up at him and shook her head as though he were mad. "You truly are blind, Roarke Macnair. Bridget always keeps a violet in the kitchen window."

Sayer followed Aramanda's gaze to where the tiny flower sat on a stark wooden sill, barely visible through the square of clouded glass. He could only admire the indomitable spirit Bridget must possess to care for the life of a single flower when her own life and that of her family were so fragile.

In answer to Aramanda's knock on the front door, an old woman in faded gray pushed it open to them. "Mrs. Donahue, you are still here—"

"Oh, thank the Lord, you've come back!" Tears, left untouched, stained the other woman's creased face. "Liam's gone to take the other children to Mrs. McKinney's for the night, poor mites. But she's in the bedroom. She won't give her up! I've tried, but she won't let her go."

As he neared the light from inside, Sayer guessed the woman to be years younger than the lines of strain around her eyes and mouth made her appear. He noticed the hand clutching the door was callused and red, her nails dry and broken and splintering.

Aramanda led the way into the stark, cramped room. She turned to Sayer. "You had best let me see her alone."

"Of course," Sayer told her, welcoming a few moments to gather his thoughts.

"Father Creeghan said he would be here. Please send him to us when he arrives."

"I will." *A priest should be easy to recognize.* "Is there anything else I can do?"

The look she gave him, a mix of some complex emotion Sayer couldn't decipher, made him feel uneasy. "Speak to your brother when he returns, without angering him if that is possible."

With that, she lifted her heavy skirts and followed Mrs. Donahue from the room, leaving Sayer alone.

The squeak of the rockers against the rough wood floor and the softly sung lullaby made the only sound in the cold silence. Aramanda, kneeling at the foot of the rocking chair, watched helplessly as the young mother swayed back and forth, crooning to the lifeless child in her arms in a high, cracked voice.

"Bridget, please," Aramanda whispered. "Please let me take her now. There is nothing more to be done."

"Oh no." Bridget Macnair, her lank blond hair hiding her face, touched the bright red tuft of hair on the baby's head, the only spot of color in the pallid morning grayness. "Oh no, she's sleepin' so soundly now, you wouldn't want to wake her. She's such a good little lass, our Rose—never a peep from her once she's closed her eyes." She began humming the notes to another lullaby, cradling the infant close in the bitter chill of the small room.

Tears running unheeded down her face, Aramanda turned to Mrs. Donahue standing behind. "I cannot leave her like this. Not with Rose . . ."

The name caught in her throat. She turned back, fighting to find a word or a touch that would reach Bridget in her grief. Reaching out, she laid her hand on Bridget's, feeling everything, unable to say anything.

Bridget lifted wet blue eyes. "You're crying. Don't cry, Aramanda. Don't cry. Rose isn't crying. See? She isn't crying." She began to shake, her body sagging as she bent over the baby. "Please don't cry. Please don't . . ."

Aramanda put her arms around the younger woman, crying with her as the sobs racked Bridget's thin form. The sorrow she shared as she held her friend went so deep, she felt it brand her soul, marking it forever with the unbearable memories of discovering Rose frozen to death in her mother's embrace.

Finally, spent and pale, Bridget straightened enough to gently put the tiny body of her daughter in Aramanda's arms. "You take care of her now. You and the father. Rose loves you. You know how to take care of her. I can't anymore. I can't."

Letting Mrs. Donahue take her place at Bridget's side, Aramanda struggled to her feet and held the baby close to her bosom. A light knock sounded; then Father Creeghan stepped quietly into the dark, little room, easing the door shut behind him. Tall, spare, the black of his cassock accentuating his pallor, he let his deep gray eyes express the same defeat that consumed Aramanda.

The wintry wind seeped through the cracks in the walls, slicing through the wool of her dress, but Aramanda felt nothing except the icy blackness of grief and pain. She huddled over the baby, her straight fall of auburn hair sheltering Rose from the chill. As if it could matter now!

Father Creeghan held out his hands in an offer to take the baby. "You've done all you can, child."

Aramanda took one last look at the little girl. Bending to her again, she pressed a kiss to her forehead, resting her cheek against the small, cold one for a long moment. Then, wordlessly, she handed the baby to Father Creeghan.

Aramanda walked to the bedside and stared at the faint, flickering light of a single candle.

She heard Father Creeghan pray over the baby and hand her to Mrs. Donahue. "I'll have Fred start on the coffin tomorrow," she said before leaving the room.

Turning from the hypnotizing flame, Aramanda eased a blanket around Bridget's shoulders. "Try to rest," she whispered, motioning for Father Creeghan to join her outside the room.

He ran a gaunt hand over his sparse gray hair, sighing heavily. "A moment with Bridget and I'll be out."

Before she left them to their private prayers, Aramanda drew in a long breath and fixed her gaze on the waning flame once more, the unusual gold of her eyes reflecting the flame.

"So fragile," she whispered, "life is no more certain than that flame."

She shut the door behind her and moved numbly into the room where Roarke Macnair paced in front of the window. He looked weary, his dark hair ruffled as if he'd repeatedly shoved a hand through it.

"Liam should have been home by now."

He stopped and looked at her. "No sign of him yet," he said softly. "How is his wife?"

"His wife?" Aramanda wondered at his formality. "Bridget is with Father. If anyone can bring her a measure of comfort, it is he."

"Good," he said, his gaze steady and intense. "And how are you?"

The question, that he would even think of her feelings at this time, the concern in his voice, touched her somewhere deep and private. "I—I only wish I could be of help."

"I was thinking the same thing." He offered the barest hint of a smile then bent toward the window to peer out again.

As if they had a will of their own, her eyes lingered over his powerfully built shoulders and long muscular legs. His hair, the color of strong coffee, had just the right touch of boyish wave to make her fingers ache to curl into the thick wave of hair at his nape. He had eyes like blue flames, full of the fire of rebellion, full of passion. His strength, power, and spirit were carved in the clean lines of his face.

A dangerous man. A man she feared yet, in a secret place in her heart, found impossible to resist.

He towered over her own considerable height, at least a full head taller. Not many men in her acquaintance were tall enough to make her feel sheltered or protected. But this outspoken rebel did somehow. She ought to avoid him for his reputation alone, his volatile temper.

And yet she was ever more drawn to him.

He turned back to her then and without a word, without a touch, held her in his gaze, rendering her powerless to move, to speak, to flee. An intimacy she could not have explained passed between them, as if for some reason he knew her better than she knew herself.

Her heart responded, quickening in an excited fear with each passing moment. Her palms began to sweat; she swept them down the sides of her skirts.

The door to the bedroom closed then, and Father Creeghan moved silently into the room, breaking the strange enthrallment.

"I see Liam has not returned."

Struggling to hide the blush she felt in her cheeks, Aramanda turned aside and shook her head. "Mrs. Donahue said he took the children to the McKinneys' for the night." She hesitated then added, "Perhaps he stopped at the tavern. Ale is a small solace, but it is often the only comfort he has."

" 'Tis his worst enemy as well, my dear." He nodded to Roarke. " 'Tis the worst evil for all of you."

"No doubt," Sayer said.

Aramanda saw the black expression in his eyes and wondered whether his anger was directed at Father Creeghan, Liam, or himself. "I am certain you are right," she intervened. "But on a night such as this, perhaps it will numb the pain. I only wish I would have known sooner. Perhaps I could have . . ." She trailed off, not knowing what she could have done.

"There was nothing anyone could have done for poor little Rose. 'Twas too late." Father Creeghan shook his head. "I suspected Liam had sold his soul to the company store, but I never knew it had gotten so bad they were without coal again. He's too proud to tell anyone, to take anything like charity. But Rose was just too young to take the cold, poor little lass. She never was a strong child, and with no heat in the house for two days . . ."

"That is three this winter," Aramanda said woodenly. She abruptly turned to him, tears unchecked. "Liam and Bridget have been friends to me, even though my name is Montclair. Why did they not tell Mr. Macnair they needed coal? How can you bear these sorrows? I cannot. Each time, it feels worse to me, especially knowing my family is the cause and there is nothing I can do to stop it from happening over and over again."

"I have seen so many tragedies that there are times I would give my eyes not to see at all. But work 'tis next to impossible to find these days and conditions at many of the other mines are no better—"

In their shared grief and anger, the pair seemed to have forgotten Sayer.

"That does not excuse the way my uncle runs those with the Montclair name! I have tried again and again to make him see the misery he causes. But he refuses to listen, particularly to a mere woman he considers hysterical."

Aramanda's hands clenched at her sides. "The miners can never seem to unite enough of an effort to fight back. If only there were someone who could lead them, someone who believed strongly enough in the need to change."

" 'Twould take a strong man, one with more than his share of courage and vision," Father Creeghan said. "A man not afraid to dream, and there are precious few of them left in the mines. The work and the hardships beat it out of them 'til nothing's left but the comfort of a long ale and a few hours' sleep."

"I have heard there is one man, in fact, who seems to wish to take on my uncle." Aramanda turned to look at Roarke, her meaning clear.

A deep frown creased his brow; his eyes shifted from her to Father Creeghan and back to her.

"Yes. 'Tis so. But I fear Mr. Macnair is more a danger than a help to us. We need not mince words, we three." He faced Sayer. "We both know you are being blamed for the recent rash of explosions and thievery of Aramanda's uncle's property."

"Am I?"

"Perhaps your methods are wrong . . . but conditions must change!"

"I agree. Absolutely." There was no pause in his conviction.

His eyes stayed on Aramanda, intent, unwavering, a fire of his soul reflected in their midnight-blue depths.

Father Creeghan raised a brow, looking from Aramanda to Sayer. He then moved beside Aramanda, laying a hand on her shoulder. "You cannot make the whole world your responsibility, child. You only leave yourself open to heartache."

"I do not care! And I do not care about the whole world right now, only this one. I have tried and tried to think of a way to bring about some change, any change. I cannot bear to see such cruelties inflicted by my uncle here, nor more than I can see them inflicted on my own family. Gervase would see us all suffer for no more reason than it pleases him."

She shivered and wrapped her arms around her body to fend off the cold inside her heart. "But I am a woman, without status even in my own family, and the Montclair name itself has become a great hindrance to me among the miners and their families. Gervase has ruined the memory of my father's good name. The miners trusted my father, relied on his compassion. Now they shudder at the mention of my uncle's name."

Trembling with anger and frustration and renewed grief, Aramanda bowed her head, a plea in her heart for an answer. "Yet there must be a way. There must be!"

A moment's hush followed her entreaty to heaven; and in the perfect stillness, the lights of the oil lamps flickered and dimmed as if caught in a draft.

She felt suddenly dizzy, her vision clouded. For an instant, she saw through new eyes the view of a great audience from a place high above the crowd and a man, dark and charismatic, swaying the multitudes with the passion and power of his voice. He paused and looked up and their eyes met, and for a flicker of time, she felt their destinies cross and link.

It ended so quickly, the familiar sights of the sanctuary before her again with startling clarity, that Aramanda doubted it had ever happened.

"Are you all right, child?" Father Creeghan's hand briefly tightened on her shoulder. "You've gone pale. Perhaps you should sit down."

"No . . ." Aramanda brushed her fingers against her temple. "No, I am fine. It was only a moment . . ."

"You're allowed that, and more. You've spent too many hours worrying over others and none worrying over yourself," Father Creeghan said. "And don't try and tell me you haven't. You've done more to help the families here than anyone. No one holds your uncle's wrongs against you. They know it will take little short of a miracle to better things in their lifetime."

Dashing the tears from her cheek, Aramanda turned not to him, but to Roarke, determination and despair gripping her heart in equal measure. "Then I will have to find a miracle."

"No less than a miracle would help," Sayer agreed, meeting the challenge in her eyes.

It seemed natural, a thing he had done many times before and not balked at.

But inside the challenge what she was asking of him hit like a truck. He wanted to drag her aside and tell her she put her faith in the wrong man. He wasn't Roarke Macnair.

He was Sayer, with a hundred years of civilization between him and the fiery rebel leader. In his own reality, he'd crossed the legal lines a time or two, but not with the hard, brutal violence Roarke Macnair apparently considered his right.

Yet he couldn't turn away from her, his Aramanda, any more than he'd been able to abandon her in his reality.

The slam of the front door jarred the silence between them, making Aramanda start and Sayer turn quickly.

A tall, muscular man with unruly brown hair and hot dark eyes shouldered his way through the narrow door. Taking one bleary glance around, he winced, then stumbled to a chair, falling on it more than sitting down.

Sayer stared at him, getting used to meeting people who looked like someone from his time. This man, apart from the bushy sidewhiskers and miner's dress, could have easily passed for his brother Will.

"Liam," Aramanda began, "we have been waiting—"

"Get out! All of you! I want to be alone with my family!"

Aramanda walked over to him and stood stiffly before him.

"You want to be alone with your ale. Go to bed, Liam; you are not yourself and certainly no help to Bridget in this state."

"I'll give you a hand," Sayer said, following Aramanda to Liam's side. He stretched out a palm.

Liam shoved away Sayer's hand. "Get away from me."

Father Creeghan sent him a no-nonsense look. "They are here to help. As am I, my son."

"Well, well, Father, now that you mention it, maybe Roarke will help us." Liam's voice sounded angry, slurred. He speared Sayer with a glare. "You make noise about changing things around here enough. But can you do any more than blow up bridges and burn down Montclair property? Can you raise the dead?"

"Liam! Don't!" Bridget appeared suddenly, rushing at her husband. "I won't stand for your fighting with him now."

Sayer bent to pull her gently away at the same time Aramanda reached out to put a restraining hand on Liam's arm. Bridget leaned into Sayer, her tears wetting his shirtfront.

"We understand," Aramanda soothed. "Of course we do." She looked pointedly at Sayer.

Sayer heard the warning in her tone, but something, a mixture of animosity past and present, compelled him to speak his mind.

"I wish I could bring Rose back," he said, gently stroking a hand over Bridget's hair. "But all I can hope to do is change the horrors so tragedies like this don't keep happening."

"Explosions and fires aren't my idea of help!" Liam shot back. "You never think of how your reckless attacks on Montclair's property affect us. Why should you? You don't have a wife and children to clothe and feed. You don't even care for your own life. All you worry about is your damned ideals. Well, your ideals didn't save my Rose, did they?"

Liam put a shaking hand over his eyes as if to block out the vision of the daughter he had lost. "To hell with you, Roarke. It's only gotten worse for us since you started making trouble, since you started stirring up everyone's hopes. Montclair's only stepped down harder to stop your damned rebellion. We've only gotten more of hell because of you."

"That wasn't my choice. I hope one day I can convince you we can work together instead of against each other. I don't want us to fight anymore . . ."

Sayer heard his own words like an echo of so many similar arguments, harsh words he and Will had exchanged. All at once, the determination he'd always had to convince Will to see things his way seemed irrelevant.

All that mattered was that an innocent child, a family's cherished little girl, had died. A new life senselessly, cruelly ended for lack of something as basic as a few lumps of coal.

"This isn't the time to talk about any of this," he said flatly.

"I think it's the perfect time."

"No—Liam." Bridget pulled out of Sayer's protective hold and whirled on her husband. "No more fighting tonight. I can't bear it." Her face crumpling, she turned and rushed out of the room.

Sayer looked to Aramanda, his expression hard. "My being here now is only making matters worse. I'll go."

She nodded, her amber eyes shimmering with tears.

Sayer headed for the door, closing it softly behind him. He hadn't mentioned going home because he had no idea where home was.

Thirteen

Sayer had no trouble finding the church. He supposed Roarke Macnair lived in the mining town, but he could hardly ask directions.

Instead, he went to a place he recognized, surprised to find it looked almost exactly the same as it had when he and Aramanda passed it yesterday.

Except yesterday won't happen for over one hundred years. If it ever happens.

Pushing open the door, Sayer tried to force himself to accept the thought. But his mind was already maxed out trying to accept several dozen impossible things.

He thought of Aramanda and all the times she'd tried to convince him she had come to him from another reality. Now, with their situations reversed, he wondered how she would react if he told her the truth.

Probably better than I did. And she handled the whole crazy mess better than I am, although she, at least, wasn't trying to live someone else's life.

She only had to make me believe I loved her.

His throat constricted and Sayer swallowed hard to get past the pain. If this was destiny's idea of matchmaking, it sure as hell fell far short.

He supposed, considering the twisted logic of everything that had happened so far, he should expect history to repeat itself. Aramanda would fall in love with Roarke Macnair once more and . . . and then what?

Inside the doorway, Sayer stopped. What was he doing here? *The past is the only path to the future.*

The remembrance of Lila's voice speaking those words to Aramanda suddenly came into his head as clearly as if Lila were speaking in his ear.

So, was he supposed to fix things in this lifetime and keep his fingers crossed everything would right itself in the next? A nice theory, except he had no idea what to fix and what to leave alone. No one had bothered to give him any directions for changing realities.

"Use the force, Sayer," he muttered and strode blindly into the sanctuary. He sat down on the front pew, welcoming the solemn silence as he tried to make some sense out of madness.

The reprieve didn't last long.

"Roarke!" The gentle voice with its soft Irish music echoed startled surprise through the sanctuary.

Twisting in his seat, Sayer met the direct blue gaze of Father Creeghan as the priest came down the aisle toward him. " 'Tis a rare day when I see you in church, except to try and cajole me into accepting your latest scheme—or to at least look the other way. Have you come about Rose?"

"Rose? No . . ." Sayer said, remembering the name of the child Liam and Bridget had lost with an inward hollow ache. "No, I—I needed some place to . . . think. Do you mind if I stay?"

"You've never asked permission before. 'Twould it make any difference now if I said no?"

His thin face creasing in a brief smile, Father Creeghan laid a hand on Sayer's shoulder. "Stay as long as you need. Despite the differences between you and your brother, I know Rose's death must have hit hard. You've worked many a day to force change to keep this very thing from happening, and this time it was your flesh and blood. I haven't agreed with your methods, but when I held that little girl in my hands today . . ."

He shook his head, an ageless sorrow in his eyes. "Well, I could see how a man might be tempted to violence."

"Aramanda—Miss Montclair apparently thinks I'm tempted too often," Sayer said lightly, hoping to elicit some useful information about Roarke Macnair, something more personal than the black-and-white words he'd read in a library book.

The hand on Sayer's shoulder tightened, then slipped away.

"She's a wise lass; you could do yourself no worse in listening to her. She has her father's kindness in her and his courage. I can understand how you feel about the injustices against the families here, but there've been too many accidents, Roarke. Gervase Montclair is neither a patient nor a forgiving man. I fear you may have started a fight you can neither control nor win."

"That will not stop him from carrying on with it," a voice spoke from the far end of the sanctuary. When Sayer turned, he looked directly into Aramanda's eyes.

She wore her cloak thrown loosely over her shoulders, and the wind had torn her hair free from its braid, tossing it in coppery streams over the midnight wool. Defeat made her pale and painted violet shadows under her eyes. Conviction put fire in her eyes and held her proudly.

"It will not stop you," she repeated, "will it, Mr. Macnair?"

"Probably not," Sayer returned, getting to his feet. He ignored the curious glance Father Creeghan flitted between the two of them. "Would it stop you from caring about the families here?"

Aramanda started down the aisle. "It is hardly the same thing."

"Isn't it?" When she hesitated, looking as if she thought she had said too much already, he prodded her. "Go ahead. Say it. You aren't going to hurt my feelings."

"That I can believe. I was only going to say that I am not the one destroying property and risking lives to make my point."

"You aren't making a point at all. You just come here to patch up misery the best you can, but you don't do anything to stop it."

"That is not fair."

"Isn't it?"

"No. I would stop it this instant if I could. But the matter is not as simple as you portray it. I have *people,* not merely causes, to consider."

Standing a few steps from him now, Aramanda held out a hand to him. Neither of them noticed Father Creeghan rise and quietly leave the sanctuary. "Can you not see you risk doing more harm to them than good when you challenge my uncle in this way?"

"No, I can't! I—" Sayer stopped, hearing the words that came out of his mouth, but suddenly feeling they sounded as if they belonged to someone else.

Someone instead of the man who had jeopardized all his causes and thwarted time because he loved Aramanda Montclair. At the same time, most disquieting of all, the words sounded familiar, apparitions at the back of his mind that lent a strange conviction to his voice.

When she had been lost in his reality, Aramanda had told him she felt an unsettling sense of displacement. Sayer felt angry and uneasy at being forced to play the role of a man he'd hated because Aramanda had given him her heart and soul.

Inexplicably, though, he felt no more displaced than he would have returning to a place he had not visited for many, many years. It was unfamiliar and hard to make his mind accept the impossibility of being here.

But at times, it was disconcertingly easy to slip back into a role that should have been totally alien.

Shoving a hand through his hair, Sayer sat down again. "I haven't had time to think it through," he finished. That, at least, was the truth. "Sometimes a good fight is the only way to win the war."

"Sometimes?"

"Yes, sometimes. I don't go out begging for a battle."

"Ah, I see. I suppose all of the *accidents* at the mines are merely coincidence and your reputation as a radical and a troublemaker is greatly exaggerated, to say nothing of your supposed preference for gambling and Tansie Caitlan's ale."

Aramanda stopped, shaking her head before sitting down a few feet away from him, folding her hands neatly in her lap. Staring fixedly at her crossed hands, she said low and fast, "You have even managed to make me forget my own manners. I am not accustomed to stooping to insults."

"What you're not accustomed to is speaking your mind. It's not criminal, you know."

"Unless you are encouraging mayhem and disobedience," she said, flashing him a wry smile. "I am surprised, though, to hear you confess to some uncertainty. When I listened to your speech this evening, you seemed determined to carry out whatever violence was necessary to gain your end. Now, you seem less adamant. Is it because of Rose?"

"It's because of a lot of things. You wouldn't believe me if I told you," Sayer said honestly.

He recalled again his own lasting disbelief when she had come to him from seemingly nowhere. How could he ever explain his presence to her? Did he even want to try?

"Perhaps in time you will tell me," she said softly.

"In time . . ." Sayer nearly laughed at her unknowing choice of words. "In time—I'll probably tell you a lot more than you want to hear."

Aramanda frowned slightly. "Will you? You sound . . . strange." She brushed her fingers against her temple, glancing at the altar.

"Is something wrong?"

"Yes—no. I was only thinking of when I was at Liam's home, earlier, after Rose . . ."

Her words faltered to a stop and she looked at him, a faint sheen of tears in her eyes. "When Father Creeghan said it would take a miracle to find a leader among the men here and I told him I would find a miracle. I do not know why, but my first thought was of you. I heard you speak, and while you talked, I believed every word, I believed you could be my miracle. But when I listened to those words, I was afraid. You may lead, but to where, to what end?"

"To whatever end improves working and living conditions and puts some of the profits in the pockets of the men who spend the better part of their lives making your family's fortune," Sayer said.

The words slipped out before he realized they had. The fervor they inspired flashed in her eyes. He swallowed hard. To her he was as much as announcing his commitment to make the coal mines his cause once again.

Again? How can it be again? I'm not Roarke Macnair.

"And you will pursue those ends no matter what the risk, no matter how many are hurt because of it?"

"How many are being hurt now?"

"How many will be turned from their homes or literally starve if my uncle decides to close down the mines until he breaks every last man to his will?"

"Maybe fewer than are now. Your ideas of compromise didn't help Rose. I'm sorry," Sayer said quickly, regretting the words as soon as he had said them.

Pale, her hands clenched in her lap, Aramanda stared at him with an expression of pain and censure. "I shouldn't have said that," he said gently. "I didn't mean it."

"I have no doubt you did," Aramanda said so softly he scarcely heard her voice. "I do not believe you are a man given to saying what you do not mean with all your heart and soul. And you are right; I could not help Rose. But you will not help the other children, either, with explosions and murders and by terrorizing those who do not share your views."

"I don't want to terrorize anyone." Sayer reached out and took one of her hands in his, feeling her faint tremor at the touch. "Especially you. I only want to make things better, for everyone. I can't tolerate injustice, no matter what lifetime I find it in."

"Are you planning to wage your wars from beyond the grave now?" she asked, a faint amusement in her eyes. "You are truly dedicated to your causes, Mr. Macnair."

Sayer shrugged off his slip. "I want you to understand—"

"And approve? I do not approve. But . . ." She looked down to where he still held her hand clasped in his. "But I do admire your dedication and your courage, however misguided they may be."

"I'll choose to take that as a compliment. It's probably the best I can hope for under the circumstances."

"That may well be," Aramanda said, attempting to draw her hand away. Sayer held fast. "Let go. You are—"

"A scoundrel? A rogue? A blackguard you'd rather see horse-whipped and hung rather than trust?" He looked straight into her unusual eyes, compelling her to look back. "Or touch?"

A faint flush colored her cheeks. "It is not that. It is . . . I was going to say, you are—you are making me nervous."

"Nervous? Mmmm." Sayer rubbed his thumb over the delicate skin of her inner wrist, feeling the quickened throb of her pulse. "That's interesting."

"It is not proper, sitting here, alone like this."

"Does it matter?"

"Perhaps not to you."

"Oh, it matters to me. It matters very much," he said softly. Moving slowly, he lifted his free hand and gently grazed his fingertips over her face, tracing along the familiar proud, delicate features. "But not whether it's proper. I don't give a damn about that. I want you to trust me. I need you to trust me. I can't accomplish whatever it is I'm supposed to do without that. Without you."

Aramanda stayed motionless under his touch save for the faint quiver of her skin, but she made no attempt to move away. "You know what it is you wish to accomplish; you have always known. But you have known me for a short time. How could I—my trust mean that much to you?"

"A short time . . . no." Sayer shook his head, suddenly filled with a longing so intense he wanted to blurt out then and there the whole truth of his coming, to make her remember a love she had no memory of, could not have memories of in this world.

"I've known you a lifetime, an eternity. Even if it's only been hours, it feels like forever."

Seeing the denial start in her eyes, Sayer leaned toward her and kissed her, gentle, coaxing at first, then with increasing passion when he felt her hesitant response.

Tentatively, Aramanda laid her hand on his shoulder, her fingers tightening as his kiss deepened. Her hand slowly crept up to his nape, pulling him closer.

Desire swept aside his apprehension and confusion. Sayer let go her hand and wrapped his arm around her waist, bringing her against him, not caring in what time they had found each other again, only that they had.

He forgot she now considered him nearly a stranger and a dangerous, unpredictable one at that. All that mattered was that he was holding her, loving her once more.

"No! I cannot—" Aramanda abruptly broke their embrace, shoving back out of his arms and jerking to her feet. "I hardly know you. . . . We cannot. I do not—this feeling, it is . . ."

Her hand flew to her mouth. Giving him a stricken look, she whirled and fled out of the church, letting the door slam closed behind her.

The sound reverberated through the sanctuary. But the echo of her voice, her scent, her touch lingered much longer as Sayer stared into the emptiness she'd left, feeling the hollowness inside him more strongly than ever before in any time.

Aramanda rode back to the Montclair estate at a full gallop, uncaring of the cold wind whipping at her face. She felt shaken to the very core of her soul, unprepared for the shock of feeling she'd felt when Roarke Macnair had held her in his arms.

He'd told her it felt like forever and it had—it had. For those few moments, he hadn't been the rebel miner who frightened her with his brashness and his bold plans for violent change, but a man, a lover she had waited an eternity to find.

Never moved by passion before, she had wanted more, much more, than his kiss; and the raw fervor of that desire frightened her more than any mayhem he wrought ever could.

She left her mare with the stable boy and ran headlong to the house, only stopping once she reached the quiet haven of the sitting room.

She rushed inside, flinging the heavy mahogany door closed behind her. Her sister Jessalyn, seated in the supple leather chair by the fireplace, looked up from the embroidery in her lap, her large dark eyes wide and startled.

"Good heavens! Aramanda, whatever is the matter? You're as

white as paper! You look as if you are being pursued by Satan himself."

Putting down her needlework, Jessalyn hurried over, taking Aramanda's hands in hers. She tilted her head to look into Aramanda's face. "You're frozen! Here—"

Jessalyn guided Aramanda to a seat by the fire. "You've been to the wretched mining camp again, haven't you? What has happened? Why are you so upset?"

Aramanda looked at her sister, at the thin, pale face with its corona of light auburn hair, the features gently drawn in delicate lines of courage and humor. Jessalyn's smoky brown gaze held hers with a straightforward question in them; and Aramanda knew, as always, that she could not evade Jessalyn's need to know.

She tried to focus her thoughts, to force a calm she did not feel. For a moment, she could not speak. Drawing her woolen cloak more tightly around her, she glanced into the burning heart of the fire, seeing Roarke Macnair's face, tasting his kiss.

She shivered, closing her eyes to visions and feelings she could not escape.

"Are you ill?" Jessalyn's clear voice sounded like a bell into her thoughts. "Perhaps I should call Mama—"

"No! No," Aramanda said more quietly, laying a hand on Jessalyn's arm. "No, I am not ill. I am sorry for worrying you. I . . . it has been a—a truly terrible day."

"You should not keep going back there," Jessalyn said, taking the chair across from her.

"I will. As long as they are in need."

Jessalyn shook her head. "I do not have your courage, Aramanda, or your stubbornness, and at times I am grateful. I know you care for the miners and their families, but perhaps you care too much. As long as Uncle Gervase controls the mines, things will never be different. Mama allows these visits of mercy, but Uncle Gervase is so angry over them I fear once he and Mama are married—"

"I cannot let that happen."

Jessalyn looked at her with a mixture of disbelief and hope. "How will you stop it if it is what Mama wishes?"

"It is what Gervase wishes. I cannot allow him to divide our family. He already has inflicted too much misery on the mining families. I will not allow him to do the same to all of you."

Studying her sister's face, Jessalyn got up from her chair and knelt by Aramanda's side. "What happened at the camp this morning?"

Aramanda stared steadily into the fire, not trusting herself to accept the comfort Jessalyn offered. She did not think of hiding the truth from her sister. Although two years younger than she, Jessalyn had a strength that refused to flinch from reality, no matter how dark or disturbing.

"Bridget and Liam's daughter, Rose, died of cold. I found Bridget holding her, rocking her close, as if she were still a living child. There was nothing I could do, nothing at all . . ."

The remembrance flooded over her, and she let the tears come with it, a release for the pain and despair.

Jessalyn put her arms around her, hugging her tightly while the storm of grief shook her until, spent and trembling, Aramanda pulled away, wiping the wetness from her face.

"Forgive me. It was too recent."

"There is nothing to forgive," Jessalyn said quietly.

"I have only known them less than a year, but they have become almost family to me since the time I helped nurse Bridget through the fever. Bridget has taught me so much of the courage needed to keep a family together amid such hardships. And how all this—"

Aramanda waved a hand at the opulent comfort around them, the wealth that showed in the fine fabrics, heavy velvet curtains, the thick rugs in rich tones of red and blue, the polished wood and brass. "—how this means so little when a woman is loved."

Jessalyn stroked a soothing hand over her sister's hair. "You are loved, Aramanda, by your family here. And I welcome the chance to take care of you for once. You are forever fretting over the rest of us—and everyone else you pass on the street. You are just as Papa was, worried more for the miners as men than their worth to the business."

Jessalyn's hand faltered and a small frown came between her

eyes. Her gaze looked beyond Aramanda. "I sometimes think it was not a good thing for Papa to have taken you to the mining camps when you were so young."

"Papa thought it his Christian duty to help those in need. I saw the horrors there and I could only think it was something I *must* do." Aramanda managed a faint smile and added lightly, "Besides, you know that for me to sit as you do—though mind you, I admire your patience to no end—by the hour with only your needle and yarns for companions is a sentence worse than prison to me."

To her surprise, Jessalyn did not respond with her usual quip. She looked distracted, worried.

"What is it? What troubles you so?"

Getting to her feet, Jessalyn slowly sat down in her chair again, catching her lower lip between her teeth as she contemplated her next words.

"There was another explosion at the main mine today. One of the miners was killed and two of the watchmen Uncle Gervase hired injured. Uncle Gervase ranted on about it for nearly an hour at luncheon. He accuses a secret society, the Molly Maguires. Uncle Gervase says they are a group from an ancient Irish order, one that demands complete loyalty and will use any means to assure it among their own."

She paused, then added, "He suspects Liam's brother, Roarke, of leading them."

"Does he?" Throwing back her cloak, Aramanda stood up, pacing in front of the fire, the gray wool of her skirts whispering with her steps. She hoped Jessalyn would attribute the sudden color in her face to the warmth of the flames. "What does Gervase know of secret Irish societies in the mining camp?"

"I do not know. He probably has spies within the mines. Aramanda—"

Aramanda turned to her sister, guessing Jessalyn's next question. Her heart skipped, catching on a queer beat.

"You know Roarke Macnair, don't you?"

"I know most of the families in the camp. It is a small community."

"That is not what I asked."

"Yes, then, I know him."

"Well?" There was demand and concern in Jessalyn's voice.

"No . . . not really." Clasping her hands together, Aramanda looked back at the fire. "We have spoken several times, little else."

When Jessalyn stayed silent, Aramanda looked to her. "What did you expect I would say?"

Jessalyn's shoulders lifted in a tiny shrug. Her direct gaze made Aramanda feel hot all over. "What you are not saying now. The little else."

"I—he kissed me," Aramanda suddenly blurted out, her confusion of feelings spilling over into words. She spun away from Jessalyn. Over shame and uncertainty and embarrassment raced a strange heady excitement.

"We were at the church together, after Rose—and . . . and, I do not know. He was very gentle and I did not think of stopping him until—until after he had touched me."

She looked fully at Jessalyn. "I did not think of it because I wanted him to touch me."

Jessalyn looked shocked. She glanced away, running her tongue over dry lips before turning back to Aramanda. "I have never heard you speak so boldly before. Do you care for him?"

"No! No, of course not. I . . . I cannot care for him. He is an arrogant ruffian, reckless and too bold, completely dedicated to using whatever means he must to win his battle with Gervase. How could I care for such a man?"

"I saw him, once, when I dared to ride past the mines," Jessalyn said. "Patricia pointed him out to me. He is very attractive."

"So are tigers, but I do not care for them."

"I hope you are speaking the truth, Aramanda," Jessalyn said, moving to her sister's side. She touched Aramanda's arm so Aramanda would meet her eyes.

"Roarke Macnair is a low-bred miner, and, if Uncle Gervase is correct, he is also a thief and a murderer and the man responsible for trying to ruin our family's business. I sympathize with the plight of the mining families, but I am not willing to sacrifice the people I love for them. If you do care for him, you could well find yourself being forced to choose between your loyalties to your family and a man who wishes to destroy us."

Aramanda turned from the dark, steady gaze that saw too much. The fire flared up briefly, searing a vision of flame on her eyes. "That will not happen. Roarke Macnair means nothing to me."

Jessalyn said nothing in reply, and Aramanda sensed her doubt. Yet she had no defense against it because, in her secret heart, she feared Jessalyn's warnings were truer than her own words.

The next morning, Aramanda set out early for the mining camp, taking the dogcart instead of her mare. Although it was a Saturday, she knew many of the miners would not report to work.

Rose Macnair was to be buried this morning, and they would attend the services. Her uncle planned to spend the day in Philadelphia, seeing to various business matters, so Aramanda took the opportunity to slip out just past dawn, hoping in the few hours before the funeral she could be of some small service to Bridget and Liam.

A fine, icy drizzle started to fall as she steered the pony down the main street of the camp. Nearing the church, she slowed, intending to say a few words to Father Creeghan about the services.

She pulled the cart to a halt in front of the church, and at that moment, the door to the sanctuary opened and Roarke Macnair started down the front steps.

When he recognized her, he stopped midway, staring.

"You look as if you slept here last night," she said, the words tumbling out before she could stop them. Her pulse started jumping, the blood leaping in her veins.

The corner of his mouth twisted up. "Good morning to you, too, Miss Montclair."

"I-I am sorry. It is just—why did you not go home?"

He trotted down the remainder of the stairs, and Aramanda saw more clearly how haggard and drawn he looked. He was coatless, and the light rain made the thin cotton of his shirt cling to his broad chest and shoulders. He stopped at the last step and

stared v...
as thoug...

"Your...
you are. I...
stayed up...

Sayer sh...
of dark hai...
here."

"I did no...
a walk," she...
of hurt she im...

"Now?" Hi...
exactly."

"Are you lo...
when he looked...

"How could I...

"I do not kno... to stand about in the rain withou... ...gging to catch your death of cold. You are beha...ng rather oddly."

"I was just leaving," he said, turning away from the cart.

"Your house is that way," Aramanda said, pointing in the opposite direction.

Sayer stopped in mid-step and slowly pivoted to look at her. "I know that."

"Would you like a ride? I came here to see if I could help Bridget and Liam in some way, but it appears as if you are the one who needs help. You shall freeze to death if you stand there gaping at me much longer," she added tartly when he made no move to climb up onto the cart-seat. "I believe one funeral is enough for today."

"More than enough," Sayer said darkly. Without another word, he hefted himself onto the seat beside her, looking anxiously from side to side as she set the pony in motion again.

Aramanda watched him curiously. The man was acting like a visitor who had just come to town rather than someone who lived and worked there day in and day out.

Pulling up a few minutes later in front of a square, ramshackle

the others, she de-
her hands. "I suppose

down off the cart and walked
palm up. "Come inside and have
he said, staring distractedly at the
palms. "You're probably near frozen
can leave your pony . . . somewhere for a

accustomed to the weather. It is you who seems to
g. Go inside. I'll put the pony in the shed if you will
t," Aramanda said, only then realizing that, in doing so,
had accepted his invitation. It was highly improper, being
alone with him in his home.

Yet, today of all days, she doubted anyone would bother to notice. Laying her smooth palm on the roughness of his, she allowed him to hand her down. He waited, for some reason looking uncomfortable, as she deftly unhitched the pony from the cart.

"I'll take him around," he said when she had finished. "You've done all the work. Go on inside. I'll only be a minute."

Nodding, Aramanda pulled her cloak more closely around her and walked the few steps to the front door, drawing in a long breath as her fingers closed on the handle and she pulled the door open.

It was gray and chill in the main room, smelling musty and neglected. There were no carpets, the only furniture a rough table and a few benches. She shivered, not so much from the coolness as from the lack of feeling in the house.

Not waiting for Roarke's return, Aramanda checked the coal in the grate, then kindled a fire. She was lighting one of the oil lamps when he came in the door, rubbing his hands together to stave off the cold.

"It is a wonder you have survived this long on your own if this is how you live," she said, setting the lamp down on the table. "Perhaps that is why you court trouble. A prison cell might be preferable to this."

"You may be right," Sayer said, glancing around the room for the first time—in over a hundred years.

"Then why do you stay here like this?"

"At the moment, I don't seem to have much choice."

The irony in his voice struck her like a slap. "You are right," she said quietly. "With the company owning all the homes, as well as running the store, there is little alternative to this. It is just that this house—"

She looked around the room again. "This house feels so empty. So . . . hollow." Her eyes met his again. "I am sorry."

"Don't be. I brought this on myself. I'll make the best of it." Moving farther into the room, he opened the cupboard near the grate and began poking around inside. "There must be something worth brewing in here somewhere."

"Let me." She stopped his haphazard search by laying her hand on his.

Instantly, she felt a warm flush of awareness spring between them, bringing a familiar intensity into his eyes. She drank in his earthy scent. It surprised her to find that the dark shadow of his day-old beard enticed rather than repelled her. "You should change out of those wet clothes," she managed at length. "You cannot go to Rose's funeral like this."

"No . . ." Lifting his hand, he slowly drew the hood of her cloak away from her face, letting the material pool around her shoulders. He searched her face, then shook his head, as if throwing off a daze. "No—I can't."

Stepping around her, he strode quickly up the narrow stairs leading to the upper rooms, leaving behind the cold and the emptiness.

Aramanda stared after him, held motionless by the magic and confusion he left in the wake of his touch. His lightning shifts of mood unnerved her.

In the short time she had known him, he had seemed focused, hard, dedicating all his emotion and energy to his cause. Now, that intensity seemed diffused, divided by some inward vision she could not fathom.

She heard him moving about the upper rooms, the firm tread

of his footsteps, the bang and shuffle of opened and closed drawers, the slapping sound of wet clothing being carelessly tossed on the floor.

Reaching for the teakettle, her hand trembled. She didn't want to imagine . . . but an insidious heat curled through her as she remembered their kiss at the church, the taste of fire and temptation, the strength and tenderness in his hands.

"I think it's hot."

The crude tin tea canister slipped out of her hand and clattered against bare wood. "Do you make it a habit to sneak up on visitors?" her abrupt awareness of him made her snap. Bending down to retrieve the canister, Sayer handed it to her with a smile. "Not usually. What were you dreaming about?"

"I—nothing. I am sorry. You startled me. I did not hear you on the stairs."

"I'm not surprised. You looked as if you were somewhere else. In another time."

"No, I . . ." The intent way he looked at her, as if he were trying to say more than his words allowed, made her stop and stare back at him, searching his expression for a clue. "What is it? What is wrong? There is something so different about you now . . ."

"Is there?"

"You know there is. You speak so . . . strangely. It is your voice, and yet it is not. And since I saw you at the meeting, you have looked at me differently. As if—"

Aramanda dropped her eyes, suddenly unable to say more.

"As if I'd found what I'd been searching for?"

"That is not it."

"Then what is?" Sayer slid his fingertips under her chin, lifting her face to his. "What is it?"

"I cannot talk to you like this."

"Why not?"

"Because it is too—too intimate." She flushed. "Too unsettling to say such things to a man who is little more than a stranger to me."

"A stranger? Is that what you feel I am, Aramanda?"

"Yes, of course."

"You're a terrible liar."

Bending to her, he lightly brushed his mouth against her temple, her cheek, then swanned a bare kiss at the edge of her lips.

"Now how do you feel?" he whispered. "Tell me now I'm a stranger."

"You are. You—" Before she could finish her protest, Roarke's hand slid from her chin to her nape, pulling her into his kiss.

There was nothing chaste about the long, slow caress or the feelings it evoked. Passion, never before tried, flared in her, as sure and deep as if it had already lasted an eternity.

"Now." Roarke's voice came soft and hot in her ear. "Say it now."

"Roarke . . ."

"If you can tell me now, I'll believe you."

"No . . . not a stranger," she told him on ragged breath. "I cannot lie. But I do not understand."

Trembling, she let him gather her close, resting her head against his heart. She heard his own, like thunder. His warm, male scent filled her and heated her blood.

"I am frightened by it. It is impossible and yet—it is. I cannot deny it."

"Nothing is impossible. Trust me, I know."

"You are a dreamer," she murmured. "You see things the way you want them to be, not as they are."

"Maybe because there are a lot of things I want to be different."

Aramanda raised her head and looked into the midnight-blue eyes so near her own. "And you will fight to change those things, no matter what the cost."

"Sometimes the end is worth the cost," he said softly. He held her for a moment longer, gently touching her face as if he were memorizing her features with his fingertips.

Then, releasing her, he stepped back, his expression clouded again. "Shouldn't we be going?"

"Going? Yes—yes, of course." Aramanda tried to keep her

own expression smooth and calm as she pulled up the hood of her cloak and turned toward the door.

But, inside, she felt battered by a turmoil of emotion that seemed to have no beginning and no end.

Sayer stood near Bridget and Liam and their three sons, Aramanda at his side, listening to Father Creeghan intone the final words of the simple service.

Two men stepped forward to toss spadesful of wet earth on the tiny pine coffin, and Sayer had an involuntary vision of his brother Will's daughter Nina. In all the battles he'd waged, he'd never felt more powerless than he did now to affect any positive change and he began to see clearly what drove Aramanda to fight so passionately for the people behind his causes.

He wanted to change circumstances. She wanted to change lives.

"Come home now, Bridget," Aramanda said, putting her arm around the other woman's shoulders and gently guiding her to the dogcart waiting several yards from the grave site. "There is nothing else to be done."

"Nothing else but for you to go back to your fight, Roarke," Liam said as Aramanda settled Bridget and the children into the cart.

Liam stared down at the new grave, his face taut with pain. "None of this will matter to you. You don't have anyone you care for; so if you lose work or are thrown in prison, no one is hurt by it. I wish to God you could see how much it did matter to me, and any man with a child to feed and keep warm."

"It matters to me, too," Sayer said, feeling the true grief of loss, not knowing whether it came from a past he once knew or inside him now. "Not just the fight anymore, but this. This more than anything."

Ignoring Liam's initial stiffness, he put his arms around the brother he had found in this life, holding on hard until finally

Liam returned the embrace, his body shaking with the grief he could no longer contain.

They stood long minutes in the quickening rain until Aramanda finally came to them, wordlessly bringing them to the cart and back together as a family.

An hour later, Sayer sat on a bench near the grate at Bridget and Liam's house, holding their youngest son, Kinny, on his lap. Wrapped in a thin blanket, the toddler curled against his chest, drifting in and out of sleep.

Hearing the sound of light footsteps on the stairs behind him, Sayer twisted his neck to look over his shoulder. Aramanda gave him a faint smile as she came to sit beside him.

"You are both very quiet."

"He was pretty well worn out. I doubt any of them have gotten much sleep in the past few days."

"No . . . and it will not be much better in the next few days. I thought—"

Stopping, she looked down at her clasped hands, her unbound hair falling like auburn rain around her face and shoulders. The black of her gown accentuated the pale ivory of her skin and the gold fire of her eyes.

"I thought perhaps we could take the boys to your home, just for tonight. I could stay with you until evening and then come again in the morning," she said quickly, darting a hopeful glance at him.

"There is no work tomorrow and I had the idea of bringing them to the estate to spend some time in the gardens away from here. My youngest brother and sister are near their ages and they would adore the company, and it would give Bridget and Liam some time alone." She ducked her head again. "I told them you had agreed."

Sayer nearly laughed at her combination of bravado and uncertainty. "You look as if you expect me to tell you no."

Her head shot up, a fight kindling in her eyes. "Mr. Macnair—"

He flashed her a smile. "I'll say *yes* to anything if you'll promise me one thing."

"I knew you would want something."

"Did you now?"

"Yes. And I would advise you not to tempt your good fortune too far."

"That sounds like a dare to me," Sayer teased. "But I'll let it pass this time. What I want is simple. Stop calling me Mr. Macnair."

"And call you what?"

Sayer just stopped himself from telling her his own first name. He wanted to, badly. He wanted to hear her say it again, in the soft, broken tones that spoke of passion and love.

Instead, he said, "Roarke is fine. That's what everyone else keeps calling me."

Aramanda raised a brow. "What would you prefer?"

"Several things. But I don't think you'd be willing to call me any of them."

"I see," she said, her tone clearly saying she didn't.

"You called me *Roarke* this morning," he prompted, his voice husky.

"And you are quite the gentleman to remind me."

"I never claimed to be a gentleman. Uncivilized, I think you've said several times."

"I meant it."

"Does that mean you agree?"

"You have left little room for compromise. But then, you never do."

"You're getting pretty good at this speaking your mind thing."

Aramanda flushed, averting her eyes. "It is you." Lifting her gaze, she looked full at him. "For some reason, I cannot hold my tongue with you. You make me forget myself."

I wish I could make you remember yourself as my lover, Sayer wanted to tell her. *Except you have no memories of me, do you? You're waiting for Roarke to awaken your heart, not me.*

Sayer thought of this morning—the desire he had felt in her response to his kiss and the confusion and fear he had seen in her eyes—and, shoving aside every impulse he had to speak the truth, offered her a crooked smile.

"Maybe I just make you remember that it's okay to have your own opinions. Maybe in your circle it's socially unacceptable for a woman to speak her mind; but where I come from, it's unacceptable for her to sit back and say nothing. You don't have to feel and act the way your uncle or anyone else tells you is right. Trust yourself."

Kinny stirred in his lap with a whimper before resettling himself into a tighter ball.

Sayer glanced down at the small boy, drawing the blanket more snugly around him. "And you can start by trusting your decision about the boys. Let's get them packed up and ready to go. You can practice saying my name on the way to the—my house."

Aramanda looked at him a long moment, as if she were considering all he said and weighing his sincerity.

Finally, her gaze steady on his, she smiled, softly and fully, a new light in her eyes.

Without a word, she rose gracefully to her feet and moved toward the stairs to fetch the other children, leaving Sayer filled with a profound pleasure that suddenly made him feel he was already home.

Fourteen

A high-pitched squeal greeted Aramanda at the door to Roarke's house the next morning. Startled, she stood with her hand poised to knock. "What in heaven . . ."

Before she could answer her own question, the door was flung wide open.

Sayer, his hair ruffled and shirt half-open, stood with one hand braced against the door frame, Kinny propped on his hip. Teague, his arms wrapped around his uncle's neck, hung off Sayer's back, and Galen held fast to one leg.

"Good morning," he said with a raffish grin. "We saw your cart pull up and thought we'd beat you to the door."

"Under the circumstances, I would say you did a marvelous job of it." She eyed him up and down, shaking her head. "I worried over how you would be with three active children, but I see it was all in vain. They seem to have taken good care of you."

"I dressed Kinny," Teague told her with a five-year-old's eager pride glowing in his dark eyes.

"And I cooked eggs and potatoes for breakfast," Galen put in. Like his brothers, he took after Liam in looks. All three youngsters had the same dark brown, unruly hair and brown eyes and showed signs of one day matching their father in height and muscle. "Uncle Roarke kept burning the pan. He did make tea, though."

"That's only because Aramanda showed me how first," Sayer said, flashing her a devastating smile. "Besides, for a seven-year-old pup, you're not a bad cook," he added, mussing Galen's hair. "I couldn't have done any better even if I hadn't burned the pan."

Flustered from a full hit of Roarke Macnair's wicked Irish charm, Aramanda pulled her dignity around her and tried to appear the one in control of the situation.

"It is a wonder you have survived this long on your own without starving or burning down your house. I promise you, Galen, you will not have to cook luncheon."

"I don't mind. I like it here. Uncle Roarke told us stories about dinosaurs." He drew each syllable of the word slowly, then glanced up at his uncle. "Did I say it right?"

"Exactly right."

"Dinosaurs?" Aramanda stared at Sayer in wonder. "You surprise me."

"Why? Because it doesn't seem a subject for a trouble-making, ruffian coal miner? Stick around, Miss Montclair. I'm full of surprises."

His tone was light, but Aramanda sensed an underlying note of sardonic humor she didn't understand. For a moment, she felt a strange uneasiness, an odd shift in time and space, the same feeling she had experienced at the church when she imagined she saw him.

Brushing it off, she met his eyes. "I have no doubt of that. And I am also certain there will be more of them before the day is out. So, shall we go? I hate to waste any more of such a lovely morning. It feels almost warm today."

Sayer slid his eyes down and up her body, the expression on his face so eloquent Aramanda didn't need an explanation of his thoughts.

"Very warm," he agreed, bringing the color rushing to her face.

Sayer briefly flirted with the idea of provoking her further. The delicate flush blossoming on her skin and the confused mix of pleasure and chagrin in her amber eyes started a warm tenderness in him, and feelings not so tender . . . something heated and hungry and fierce.

Before he could say something he certainly would regret and

before she could recover, Sayer flashed her another grin and packed the boys back into the house, sending them scurrying for shoes and hats and coats.

When they were ready, Aramanda let Sayer take the reins of the cart, relaxing as she shared the boys' pleasure in the short drive to the estate. They avoided the main road leading to the house, instead taking one of Aramanda's favorite shortcuts, a narrow sunny lane leading directly to the back boundaries of the extensive gardens.

The fickle spring had decided to be gracious, and Aramanda took a sensuous pleasure in the tentative heat of the sun and the dappling of cool and warmth on her skin as Sayer guided the cart through the canopy of trees.

She also took pleasure in watching him with secret sideways glances. The flex of his hands on the supple leather, the sound of his voice, rough-edged and rich velvet, the brush of his shoulder against hers as the cart jostled along the rutted dirt road—the texture and taste and scent of Roarke both filled her and created an aching hollow in her.

It defied reason, as did the mix of relief and regret she felt when she spied the edge of the estate's back lawn. Jessalyn, Oliver and Penelope in tow, waited for them near the smallest pavilion, an airy structure of sun-bleached cedar with a greening copper roof.

Aramanda raised a hand in greeting, calling out to Jessalyn, and Sayer snatched a moment to study the trio.

The sister she'd called Jessalyn had a charm about her—not Aramanda's vivid beauty, but a gentle loveliness like the luminescent inner petals of the palest of roses. Her features were softer, with more laughter in them, her strength showing in her large golden-brown eyes. She stood tensely, holding tightly to the hands of the children on either side of her.

The two littlest ones he guessed were close to Kinny and Teague in age, both with smooth hair an indeterminate shade between auburn and blond, the boy with Aramanda's amber eyes. He stared at the newcomers with undisguised interest, hugging a tattered stuffed bear to his chest.

Jessalyn's gaze flicked between Sayer and her sister as Sayer handed Aramanda down from the cart. He caught her glance and smiled slowly.

Jessalyn blushed, quickly dropping her eyes. She smoothed her hand down her skirts, wetting her lips with a dart of her tongue.

"He is much different than I expected," Jessalyn whispered to Aramanda after her sister had made introductions.

Aramanda followed Jessalyn's glance to where Sayer knelt between Kinny and Teague, listening with due solemnness while Oliver showed them his bear, explaining how the kitchen cat had mangled his favorite companion's ear. Penelope, never shy with strangers, had already dragged Galen off to explore the duck pond.

"And what did you expect?" Aramanda asked.

"I am not certain," Jessalyn said, looking again at Sayer. "I have only seen him once or twice before in passing. He is much more dangerous-looking at close hand. He seems so much taller, more powerful. That kind of strength frightens me. And yet he is quite gentle with the children and with you, not at all like the murderous rebel Uncle Gervase portrays him as." She shook her head. "It is confusing."

"Yes," Aramanda said softly. She let her gaze wander to him again, watching the supple motion of Sayer's large hands, the play of muscle under his coat as he examined the injured bear. "Yes, it is very confusing."

"It was kind of you to bring the boys here. I'm sure Oliver and Penelope will enjoy the visit also."

The twist in Jessalyn's conversation turned Aramanda's head. "After all that has happened, I thought—"

"Apparently Roarke thought the same."

"The idea was mine."

"No doubt. I only hope you have considered where such thoughts may lead."

Something in Jessalyn's tone made Aramanda defensive. "If you are worried about my reputation—" she began hotly.

"I was not inviting one of your lectures," Jessalyn said with a small smile. She laid a hand on Aramanda's arm, all humor vanishing. "You may ignore the social differences, but you cannot so easily forget your name is Montclair. No matter how much you care for him, that alone will always divide you. Would you be willing to forsake your family, your life, for those miners? For him?"

"How can you ask me that?"

"How can you think you will not one day have to answer that very question?"

"Because I have no feelings for him that would force me to choose," Aramanda said, hearing the lack of conviction in her voice and knowing Jessalyn heard it as well.

She felt his eyes on her and her throat tightened with a bittersweet emotion.

"You will have to answer, one day," Jessalyn said quietly.

"I—"

Aramanda looked to Sayer, and he held her gaze for a heartbeat, the intensity in his midnight-blue eyes an almost palatable fire. There was challenge there, too. A challenge Aramanda felt inadequate to answer.

Catching her breath, she broke their linked gazes, still as keenly aware of him as if he were touching her.

"I think Oliver would enjoy showing Teague and Kinny the duck pond," she said. She could not quite keep the tremble from her voice. "I will take them down."

"I will do it," Jessalyn said, starting forward. "There is a sunny spot just inside the pavilion you would enjoy."

She walked over to Sayer and the boys, smiling at the children and saying a few words to Sayer. Gesturing back to Aramanda, she took Oliver and Kinny by the hand, nodding for Teague to follow.

Aramanda stood motionless as Sayer strode toward her, shedding his coat as he came.

"I don't think she believes I'm quite tame," he said, slinging the coat over his shoulder. Pushing the hair off his forehead, he grinned at her. "Then again, she did trust me enough to be alone with you."

"Perhaps it is me she trusts," Aramanda said lightly.

Turning away from the potent attraction of his smile, she walked into the garden, stopping to finger the barren ends of a rosebush. "She thinks you are dangerous."

"And what do you think?" Sayer asked, walking up behind her.

"I think you are dangerous, too." She turned to look at him. "Dangerous to my family, to all the Montclair name stands for."

"And to you?"

"Yes. To me. Because you make me forget who I am."

"And who are you, Aramanda Montclair?" he asked gently. "Who do you want to be? The Montclair heiress, the pampered daughter learning to embroider and talk prettily and to defer to anyone you might offend by speaking your own mind? Or do you want something more?"

Tossing his coat aside, Sayer reached out and slowly trailed his fingers down the side of her throat, shivering her skin. Then, looking into her eyes, he unfastened the tie of her cloak, slipping it off her shoulders and letting the light wind fully clasp her body.

"Do you want to feel something more?"

"I am both," she said, her voice barely escaping a whisper. "I cannot stop being a Montclair, yet I want more than being a Montclair can offer me. That is why I keep returning to the camp. I want to help, but I also want to feel. I want to know what it is to truly be alive, to feel so strongly and deeply that only the feeling matters."

She caught her breath, shocked at herself for confessing to him desires she had told no one else, yet at the same time needing him to know.

"You," she said softly. "You make me feel that way."

"You make me feel . . . found."

Something deep and longing in his voice made her feel the same strange sense of stepping out of time, as if she had left this reality for one they had created.

"How can you be lost? You are a natural leader, always so determined, so focused on your cause."

"I don't think I can make you understand." Sayer paced a few steps from her, raking both hands through his hair. "I don't be-long. I'm in the middle of nowhere and I can't see the way out. With you—"

In a sudden motion, he looked back at her. "With you, I know there's a reason for all this. You're the reason."

"No, how can I be? You carry yourself so lightly, you can laugh even when it seems all that is left to you is defeat."

"And you can cry." Walking up to her, Sayer put his hands on her shoulders, holding her with strength. "You care when no one else can or does."

"But I cannot convince others to sacrifice all for my cause," Aramanda said, a keen sorrow stabbing at her heart.

She pulled away from his hold, facing him with a defiance of her own. "Gervase is convinced you lead the Molly Maguires. Is it true?"

A puzzled frown crossed Sayer's face. "And if it is?"

"Two men were injured and one killed yesterday at the mine. The Molly Maguires are being blamed, for that and the other violence at ours and other collieries and against the railroads. I have heard the men speak about the Mollies, how their only weapon against the conditions the mine owners foster is violence. They organize for a better life, yet terrorize those who do not belong to them."

Filled with anger and a grief she could not describe even to herself, Aramanda sucked in a hard breath and held it for a mo-ment to keep herself from shedding the tears in her heart.

"How can I trust you?" she said when she could trust herself to speak. "How can I believe you care for anyone or anything other than your cause if you not only condone such acts but initiate them as well?"

"Do you believe I did?"

"Tell me you did not," she cried fiercely. "Tell me you know nothing of secret societies, that you do not plot to bring the Montclairs to their knees."

Aramanda held her breath, her heart pounding so loudly in her ears she wondered if she would hear his answer.

Sayer hesitated, and she saw the struggle in his expression.

"I can't," he said at last.

"Then it is true."

"I didn't say that."

"No," she said in a flat tone to keep from crying out the hurt she had no right to feel. "You told the truth in what you did not say."

"It's not that simple."

"It would have been simple enough to tell me *no.*" Aramanda turned away, shutting her eyes against the tears. "But you could not lie to me."

"I'm not lying to you now. The truth is something so complicated you can't begin to imagine it," Sayer said.

His voice held a note of torment that surprised her. But she could not afford to respond to it, to respond to him. What she felt for him demanded everything, and she did not have all, heart and soul, to give.

She felt him close, a breath away from touching her, and his hand brushed her hair as gently as a whisper. Her doubts retreated, replaced by a longing that tempted her, like a siren's song, to surrender. Everything.

"All I can ask is that you trust me," Sayer said softly near her ear. "I won't do anything to hurt you or your family."

"I cannot," Aramanda whispered. She closed her eyes and tried to breathe deeply to steady herself. Instead, she breathed in him. The scent of temptation made her fire and water. "You have started something you cannot stop. It will always be between us."

"It doesn't have to be. It can be different this time."

"This time?" Aramanda twisted to look at him, overwhelmed by despair and anger at him, at the situation between them, at her own feelings for him that refused to grant her peace. "There is only this time. Do you believe we will have a second chance?"

Whatever answer he might have given her was lost when a gentle rustle of cloth against the hedges brought them both sharply back to the realization of where they were. Aramanda turned as Sayer looked behind her and started in dismay when she saw her mother moving slowly toward them.

"I am sorry to disturb you when you are entertaining, Aramanda," Cordelia Montclair said, her beautifully modulated voice giving slight emphasis to the word *entertaining*.

She carefully picked her way to within a few feet of them, stopping to appraise them both for a long, awkward silence.

Cordelia was a reflection of what Aramanda would see in her mirror many years ahead: smooth dark auburn hair threaded with silver, smooth skin loosened at the edges but the delicate features retaining their ethereal loveliness. Except that, in Cordelia, there was a hint of weakness around her mouth and the amber eyes were more inclined to slant away.

She was dressed in a flawlessly cut gown of fine, gray wool, a lacy shawl of elaborately spun silk around her shoulders. Aramanda thought her mother might well be having company to tea rather than confronting her daughter and the rebel who threatened her family's livelihood.

"I thought it best to find you before your cousin Patricia did," Cordelia said at last, glancing at Sayer though the comment was meant for Aramanda. "She has just arrived from the city, and I suspect your uncle is close behind her."

Aramanda flushed. "How did you know we were here?"

"There are few secrets in our house I do not know. Your sister was indiscreet in asking cook to prepare an inordinate amount of jam cake for tea."

She looked pointedly at Sayer again, and Aramanda hastened to make introductions. "My mother, Cordelia Montclair. Mother, this is—"

"—the infamous Roarke Macnair. Yes, I know." Cordelia studied the rosebush nearest her, fingering a dead bud. "Gervase has spoken your name in vain quite often these past weeks. I must say, I was surprised to discover you had accompanied Aramanda here. Surely there are more—hospitable places for you to spend a Sunday afternoon."

"Oh, I don't know." Sayer smiled at Aramanda, his eyes caressing, making her feel she would like to kick him for his arrogant confidence. "Aramanda has been very hospitable."

"Indeed." Cordelia's eyes swiveled quickly to her daughter,

then, unexpectedly, her expression softened. "Aramanda of late has developed a most unflattering habit of doing as she pleases, no matter how unpleasant things become because of it. She drives me to distraction, just as her father did."

Cordelia glanced back at Sayer. "I suspect you have been encouraging her, Mr. Macnair. You do have a flair for making trouble."

"If I do, it's because there doesn't seem to be any other way to bring about change," Sayer said, all trace of the charming rogue vanished, "whether in people or circumstances."

"Your changes would destroy my family."

"You're destroying the mining families by the way you do business."

"The way *I* do business?" Cordelia arched a brow. "Surely even you realize it is my brother-in-law who oversees our family's collieries."

"But you have a controlling interest in the mines."

"Yes . . . but I am a woman. It would hardly be seemly for me to intercede in matters that are better left to men."

Aramanda saw the anger sweep Sayer's expression. "I suppose it is more *seemly* to ignore the misery and corruption," he said tightly. "And when you marry Gervase, it will be more seemly to let him have total control over both the Montclair business and your family. That's certainly a much better solution than mine."

"Roarke!" Aramanda stepped between him and her mother. "Please . . . this will not help."

"No. Let him speak his mind, my dear," Cordelia said, waving aside Aramanda's protest. She smoothed her skirts, and Aramanda noticed a slight tremble in her hand. Her eyes slid to the hedges at her side. "It appears Mr. Macnair thinks I can work miraculous changes with a snap of my fingers."

"Not quite so simply," Sayer retorted. "But you could have influence, if you chose. Just as your husband did."

"What my husband was or did is not of your concern. And I do not choose. I have my children to consider. I suggest you consider the same. Fighting Gervase will gain you nothing but a rope around your neck. Believe me, Mr. Macnair, I have known Gervase far longer than you. There is no mercy in him."

The color had faded from her, and the hand Cordelia reached out to her daughter trembled. "I hesitate to speak so frankly, but it is better to know the truth than to believe you can achieve the impossible."

"It isn't impossible that you should refuse to marry Gervase!" Aramanda blurted out. "Roarke is right. If you become his wife, we will never be free of him. He will own us—fortune, body, and soul."

"Aramanda!"

"I am sorry, Mother, but you know it is the truth as well as I."

"I know I will do what I feel is best. I will not allow myself to be influenced by sentiment. Or by threats."

"I wouldn't presume to threaten you, Mrs. Montclair," Sayer said, a little of the tension leaving his body. He smiled, although Aramanda noticed the expression did not reach his eyes. "Then again, if I dared, you might feel compelled to use some of that influence you would rather ignore."

"If I thought you would harm any of my children—" She looked from him to Aramanda and back again. "Then, Mr. Macnair, you would discover how willing I am to use whatever influence I possess."

"Roarke would not harm me or any of us," Aramanda broke in, unable to stop herself and encouraged by the admiration she saw in Sayer's eyes. "He is only trying to help and he is right: You could have influence on the business. You do not need to marry Gervase to protect our family."

"That is enough, Aramanda," Cordelia said quietly. A muscle twitched in her cheek though her expression remained unreadable.

"I am sorry, Mother," Aramanda said, "but you must know—"

"I know it is important to me that you remember who you are and where your first loyalty lies," Cordelia returned sharply.

She turned again to Sayer. "I have tolerated your presence here because of the children and because Aramanda wished it.

And I will admit also to having a certain vulgar curiosity about the man who has caused Gervase such grief. Now, though, I believe you have outstayed my patience. I suggest you leave before Gervase discovers you are here. He, I assure you, will have no tolerance for the man who brazenly avows to destroy him. Good day, Mr. Macnair."

With a sharp nod to him and a hard glance at Aramanda, Cordelia made her way back up the path leading to the estate house.

Helplessly, Aramanda watched her leave, tears of frustration and regret starting in her eyes. "How can I make her understand?" she whispered.

"Maybe you can't," Sayer said. He stood a little away from her, and Aramanda heard her regrets at upsetting her mother echoed in his voice.

"I must," she said. "It may be the only way I can stop this madness. If I cannot convince her to listen, I fear we both may lose this fight."

Not waiting to hear his reply, Aramanda hurried past him, gathering up her cloak and walking quickly away from the estate to where the children played together.

Sayer followed her to the pavilion near the duck pond, feeling an uncharacteristic hesitation. He had never before shied away from jumping headfirst into a battle, and this cause was as compelling as any he'd ever been drawn into.

Except the more he became involved, the greater the risk grew he would hurt Aramanda—and this time, lose her forever.

If I only had some idea of how to change things in this time . . .

Inside the small shelter, he stood opposite from where she sat, leaning his palms on the railing to look out at the children romping at the edge of the pond.

"I should take the boys back to the camp. I don't want them involved in the trouble that's sure to come up if your uncle finds us here."

"Yes . . . just a few more minutes, though." Her eyes softened as she watched the light play. "They have no idea of all that divides us. For them, this is simply a Sunday afternoon to be savored before they return to the strife and sorrows of home."

The longing in her voice made Sayer turn to her. She looked at him and he saw all the need, the sadness, the stubborn hope in her eyes finding a reflection in his.

Striding to her side, he sat down next to her and took her hands in his. "None of it should matter, but it does. It only makes it more important we find a way through it."

"I do not see how it is possible. There seems to be no possible end to it all—only more heartache."

"No." Startled at the force of the word, Aramanda started back.

Sayer forced a softness into his voice, layering it over his conviction. He rubbed her hands between his as much to ease her tension as his own.

"I won't let that happen. It will be different this time. I know it. There's no other reason for all this to have happened if it doesn't end differently. I'm going to be really unhappy if this is some cosmic joke."

Especially if I end up dead again. Once in a lifetime is enough.

She looked at him with disbelief. "And are you a seer now, with a crystal ball to look into our future?"

Sayer shrugged. "Something like that. You'll just have to trust me."

Her brows lifted and she shook her head. "You make it very difficult sometimes."

"I know. I'm not very good at this sort of thing."

"At what?" Aramanda's expression wavered between exasperation and laughter. "Being a hero? Perhaps you need more practice. You have only just begun to earn your reputation as a leader of the miner's rebellion."

"If I didn't already know what an angel you are, I would say you're laughing at me," Sayer said, feeling a warm rush of satisfaction when he drew a smile from her. "Now I know you're laughing."

"I am sorry," Aramanda said, her eyes dancing. "It is just you are so unlike any hero I have ever imagined. You must admit, a gallant knight from the coal mines is rather improbable."

"You've been reading all the wrong fairy tales," he murmured. Sliding his hands up her arms, Sayer pushed her hood back again, threading his fingers through her hair. "In my fairy tale, the hero can come from anywhere. Or from out of nowhere."

Her lips parted to reply and he seized the advantage and kissed her, fiercely and passionately, until the feeling sang in his ears and pounded hotly through his veins.

She was honey and silk and the essence of summer roses and autumn fire in his arms, and touching her was an intoxication. Surely this was all that mattered, not rebellions or family divisions, but this vivid, elemental feeling, this timeless emotion he felt only for her, always for her.

When they parted, Aramanda made no move to pull away from him. Instead, she simply stayed near him, looking at him with a bemused expression in her eyes.

"I'll find some way to work this out," Sayer whispered against her mouth, his breath coming in ragged gasps. "I promise you."

"For some reason, I believe you, Roarke Macnair," she said softly. She reached up and brushed the errant wave of hair from his forehead. "Although I have no earthly reason to do anything of the kind."

"I could make some suggestions."

Aramanda blushed. "No doubt. Did you not say something about taking the children back?"

"My memory's not what it used to be."

"Ah, so that is why you could not find your house the other morning," she said, laughing. "All this time I have been thinking it was Tansie's ale. Now I see it is—"

The clash of raised voices—one Cordelia's, the other a black rumble—sounded behind them, turning both Sayer and Aramanda to the direction of the estate house.

Aramanda's fingers tightened on his, and she paled. "Gervase! The children—he cannot find them here."

"Go and warn Jessalyn," Sayer said, pulling her to her feet, and taking her with him out of the pavilion. "Tell her to take the boys to the start of the path we came by and to wait for me there."

"You cannot be thinking of confronting Gervase!" Aramanda cried. "It is madness!"

"Probably. But you're the one who favors sitting down and

talking things over. Here's my chance to try it. Go on." He prodded her in the direction of the pond, adding lightly, "It'll be all right. I'm bigger than he is."

At least I hope I am.

"I will be back. I will not leave you to face him alone," she said. Suddenly raising up on tiptoe, Aramanda took his face between her hands and kissed him hard, then whirled away and ran down the hill toward the pond.

Sayer watched her for a moment, before striding up the path to the place where they had met Cordelia. Gervase had to pass this way to find them, and he wanted to stall him long enough for Aramanda and Jessalyn to get the children safely away.

He didn't have long to wait.

Gervase Montclair came stalking down the pathway, slashing at an errant piece of shrubbery with the walking stick clenched in his fist. He was a big man, easily Sayer's own height and thickly built. There was nothing soft about him, though, no pity or humor etched in the chiseled lines of his mouth and nose or the flint of his eyes.

When he saw Sayer, his face turned to stone.

"Cordelia told me you were here, but I half-expected it to be another of her idiotic imaginings," he snarled. "I know my niece has been a fool over the rabble in the camp, but I see she has now completely lost whatever wits she had left to her."

Flexing and unflexing his hand so tightly he felt the tension all the way up his arm, Sayer fought a surge of primal anger. He'd never been the best at holding his temper; but in this time, he seemed to have an even more precarious grip on it.

"I came to her. She seems to be the only one of your family willing to listen to reason, and with any compassion."

"Compassion!" Gervase slammed the point of his stick into the ground. "You are trying to destroy me, piece by piece. There is no reasoning with you or any of the gutter-bred mongrels who are too stupid to know better than to follow you. Is that your notion of compassion?"

"And what is yours? Destroying men and their families to squeeze one more ton of coal from your mines?"

"I could care less for the families you say suffer so much. I am not my brother, coddling them as if they were children. The men are paid to do a job—let them go find other work if it is so terrible here. After a month on the streets, they'll be back, begging for the lowest tasks I have at any wage!"

"You may not have many jobs to offer," Sayer said through gritted teeth. "Your mines don't seem to be the safest places to work these days."

"Because of you."

"You'll have a hard time proving that."

"I will have all the proof I need—soon. And when I am through with you and your band of ruffians, yours will be a camp of widows and orphans. I'll see every last one of you hanged before I run my business by your whims. And I'll take the greatest pleasure in breaking you."

"We'll see who breaks first. I have nothing to lose. You have everything."

To his surprise, Gervase's face creased in a parody of a smile. "You're not invulnerable. You came running to her."

He stabbed his stick at a point behind Sayer, and Sayer twisted to see Aramanda running toward them, her face white with fear.

"What are you doing here?" he asked when she reached his side, refusing to touch her, to show any feeling Gervase might seize on and exploit.

"I came to—"

"Try and tell me how wrong I am once again," Sayer put in before she could finish.

She flinched from the whip of his words, hurt starting in her eyes, and he wanted to reach out to her and tell her it was all a lie . . . to enfold her in his arms and never let her away from his heart again.

For her sake, he forced a coldness into his voice. "Your uncle's been doing an excellent job of that all on his own. It seems you and he share the same opinion of me."

The pain on her face was quickly replaced by understanding. "He and I share nothing," she said firmly.

"Aramanda—"

"No! No, Roarke," she said, looking to her uncle. "I will not pretend I am allied with you," she told Gervase.

"I care less for your opinion than I do for his," Gervase snapped. "You have let your emotions completely rule you in this matter. Your mother should have taken you in hand months ago. When I am her husband, I will not be so tolerant."

"Tolerant!" Sayer gave a derisive laugh. "You're as tolerant as you are compassionate. I don't know why Aramanda thought you would ever consider compromise."

Gervase's eyes narrowed and his hand clenched around the head of his stick so hard his knuckles showed white. "This is my compromise: Disband the Molly Maguires and cease your war against me or I will have every last one of you hanged, guilty or innocent. It makes no difference to me. Now get off my land."

Turning his back on them, Gervase stamped back up the path to the estate.

As Gervase disappeared in the maze of bushes and shrubbery, Sayer caught a flash of royal blue and the figure of a fair-haired woman hurrying up the path behind him.

"My cousin Patricia," Aramanda told him, a hint of scorn in her voice. "She most likely eavesdropped on every word. Patricia is a collector of other people's miseries. I suppose with Gervase as her father and no mother to guide her, she could have learned little else."

"Nice girl," Sayer muttered.

"Oh, Roarke . . ."

Aramanda looked at him, tears welling in her eyes. Her fear shivered through her, making her pale and her mouth tremble. "He means what he says. He will do all he can to break you. You truly have started a war you cannot win."

The blind, determined anger he always felt when faced with a seemingly unconquerable injustice flared inside him with a familiar intensity. "I'll find a way."

"Then you are lost to me."

"What . . ."

Tears slipped down her face. "I thought . . . I believed, for a few moments when we were together, that we might one day find each other in a place where nothing and no one divided us. But you are ruled by your cause. There is no room for you to . . . to care."

"You're wrong," Sayer said. "This time you're wrong. And I'll prove it to you, that I can promise you."

Touching his fingertips to her tears, he turned and strode swiftly down the incline to where Jessalyn waited with the children, hoping he had made her a promise he could keep.

Fifteen

"You sure that door's locked?" One of the miners stole a nervous glance over his shoulder toward the front door of the tavern.

"Go check it, Tansie. We sure as hell don't want that Montclair girl struttin' in on us again."

"I tell you, it's locked up tight," Tansie growled at the skittish men. He wiped a spill of ale off the bar, shaking his head. "The lot of you's so jittery you're jumpin' at your own shadows."

Sayer, sitting at the head of the table in the farthest corner from the front windows of the tavern, found it easy to catch some of the men's uneasiness in the dimly lit shadows of the room.

To any watchmen or police who passed, the tavern would appear closed for the night. But inside, speaking in hushed voices, the tightly knit group of men who called themselves the Molly Maguires sat close around the light of a single candle, waiting for him to speak.

They'd lingered after the usual night's crowd had dwindled to meet in secret, expecting him to give the word on their next move against Gervase Montclair.

Lead . . . he knew how to rouse a group to action well enough . . . to inspire passion, foster resolve. It had always come naturally to him. And fortunately, he'd figured out as early as grade school, most people were much happier following than leading.

But in this time and place, without a safety net of human rights laws and government regulations and a police force to enforce them—as much as all of those had often been the bane of his existence—Sayer now found himself thinking almost fondly of paperwork in triplicate and the frustrating maze of government bureaucracy.

These guys were dangerous.

They blew up trains, burned down houses and barns and stores, shot men in cold blood. Often, apparently, at Roarke Macnair's command.

And now they'd gathered, waiting with flames in their eyes and the taste of blood on their lips, to listen to *his* next plan.

Sayer thought of all the times he'd been tempted to break the law to win his battles, even the few times he'd bent it severely and ended up spending uncomfortable hours in a county jail. Most of the time he'd wanted nothing more than to chuck the red tape and the bureaucratic bull and force people to do what he knew was best.

Now, he had the chance. He could demand reform, any way he wanted.

Somehow, though, reality fell far short of fantasy. Murder, destruction for a cause, so noble-sounding in history books, didn't translate well when he knew the people that would be hurt.

The problem was, he had to convince these bitter, angry men of it. Even more important, he had to give them hope.

Why he was here didn't matter anymore. He couldn't walk away from this fight any more than he could walk away from Aramanda.

"Montclair!"

The name, snarled out, pulled Sayer away from his thoughts.

"He won't give up this fight 'til he's in his grave, I tell you. And the girl—" Jack O'Keefe spat at the floor. His thin lips curled back. "She thinks she owns us, just as her uncle does and will do 'til he's buried six feet deep!"

A hushed grunt and mutter of agreement went around the table as men lifted their tankards to the notion of putting Gervase Montclair in an early grave.

Sayer glared at Jack. He considered O'Keefe the most volatile of the group. Too many years spent in darkness—hacking, loading, breathing coal and for a debt to the company store that couldn't be paid in three lifetimes—had twisted O'Keefe until nothing was left but a naked brutal desire to take compensation in blood.

Bitterness had twisted a face that might have once been attractive into a sneering mask. A lifetime of sweat and drudgery with scarcely the shirt on his back to show for it had left him hard and lean, and many of the men feared his strength and his vile temper as much as they respected him for it. No one knew exactly what Jack O'Keefe was capable of, and few wanted to find out.

"This talk is getting us nothing but an early grave ourselves," Scully McGehan cut in before Jack's idea could catch fire. "Let Roarke tell us his plan."

Immediately, the men turned to Sayer, anticipation in their expressions, their eyes fixed on him, intently awaiting his next words. Sayer mustered his resolve.

Before Sayer could begin, Jack's graveled voice broke in.

"Go straight for Montclair. Threats won't move him. Unless, of course,. you ain't got the stomach for it, Macnair," he added with a deliberately provoking sneer.

Sayer's jaw tightened, but he reined in his temper, knowing Jack only needed the wrong word to come up swinging. A fight here, when he needed the miners rallied behind him, would only get them all tossed in the local jail.

He stood up, resting both fists on the table. "I've got the stomach to do whatever needs to be done. Including taking both you and Montclair on, if that's the way you want it."

"Since when did you start asking me the way I want it?" Jack growled. He took a long swallow of ale and slammed his tankard back on the table. "You're the man with all the damned answers, ain't you? You strutted back in here after the war with everyone callin' you a hero and took over what I had started, convinced everyone with your fancy words that you knew more than I did about changin' things 'round here—"

"Aye, and got a lot more done than you ever started," Scully spoke up, not backing down when Jack shot him a fierce scowl.

"And where's all his talk got us? Tell me that." Jack swung his glower to Sayer. "You seem to be doin' all right for yourself; you even got the Montclair girl smilin' for you. But what about the rest of us? We got nothin' but kicked harder by Montclair and his guards."

Several of the men muttered in agreement, and a rumble of low-spoken conversation rippled through the gathering.

"You side with me, don't you, Liam?" Jack prodded the large silent figure in the farthest corner. "Why your little lass Rose might still be livin' if Montclair hadn't cut the coal rations because he didn't like the way Roarke does business." He barely hid the smirk on his lips.

A ripple of tension went through Liam, and his hands clenched. Sayer feared Liam would attack the bastard then and there, and he braced himself to lunge out and stop him. Jack would slit his throat without a thought before Liam even knew what had hit him.

Liam stood and gripped the table, white knuckled. "Leave my Rose out of this! All I want is a decent day's wages for a decent day's work. I don't want any more trouble." He shot a black glare at Sayer. "But maybe Jack's right. Seems to me things all the way around are just gettin' worse since you started causing trouble."

"I don't mind trouble, but I'm all for causing as little of it as possible to get the job done," Sayer said tightly.

"That ain't what you used to say," one of the miners sitting nearest Jack spoke up. "Up 'til now you've been all for making things as tough on Montclair as he's made 'em on us."

"Are you going soft, Macnair?" Jack taunted. "Let's hear the truth. We've all seen you with the Montclair girl. Seems maybe your loyalties are goin' a different direction."

"Leave her out of it." Sayer never raised his voice, but the low, dangerous tone made Jack drop his eyes and reach for his tankard.

"We got enough problems without this fightin' among ourselves," Tansie put in. "So? What's it going to be, Roarke?"

"I can tell you that!" Jack shoved to his feet. "Take the train off Schuylkill Bridge!"

Several of the men nodded their approval and raised their tankards in support.

"Are you with us or with her, Roarke?" Tansie asked.

"I'm with you," Sayer said, with a grim feeling of taking a step onto a high wire over an abyss. "And so is she. Why the hell do you think she spends so much time here? Not for the pleasure of your company, I'd say."

"Roarke's right." Liam spoke up unexpectedly. He sat hunched over the table, cradling his hands around his tankard, not looking at the rest of the gathering. "Aramanda's got nothing to do with her uncle. She's only trying to do what's best, like her father did."

He glanced to Sayer, and Sayer flashed him a look of gratitude. Liam shrugged and dropped his eyes back to his ale.

"Unless she's spying for him," Jack sneered.

A few of the men made noises of agreeing with Jack. But Sayer saw more lowered eyes and faces that refused to condemn Aramanda. Many of the men in the room knew their families had food and coal only because of her kindnesses, and the ones who had been here for more years than they cared to recall also remembered her father's charities.

"If she is, then I ought to be the first man hung," Sayer said. "She knows more about what I'm doing than most of you. If she wanted us dead, she'd have had proof enough by now."

"No one can trust a Montclair since Gervase took charge of the mines," Tansie insisted. "I hope for all our sakes, Roarke, you aren't betting our lives she'll choose you over her family."

Scully pounded a fist on the table. "Enough about the girl. We have to settle on the train tonight. It's crossin' the bridge tomorrow morning loaded with Montclair coal. Do we stop it or not?"

"I say we take a vote," Tansie suggested.

"In favor of stopping it. No more." Sayer glared at Jack, who stared back at him, hatred in every line of his expression.

Every hand at the table went up, but Sayer caught the glances exchanged between Jack and three of the miners. A flicker of uneasiness sliced through him. O'Keefe's agreement had been too ready.

"Then it's settled," Jack said. His hard eyes stayed on Sayer. "I didn't see your hand go up, friend. Are you plannin' on letting us do your dirty work?"

"I'll be there," Sayer said with a conviction none of the men could doubt. "You can count on it."

Clouds heavy with the threat of rain hung in a huge dark mass over the men hidden and scattered strategically in the hills around Schuylkill Bridge. They obscured the last of the day's light, smudging shape and form with a charcoal grayness.

Sayer, crouched nearest the bridge behind a small hillock, grappled with a growing sense of uneasiness. At the last minute, he'd gotten word that the train's schedule had mysteriously changed to early evening, the time of day the miners ate supper with their families before heading out to the tavern.

The change seemed coincidentally timed with the Mollies' plans. Sayer didn't like it. But he had committed himself to going through with it and he wouldn't turn back now.

It had taken all of the dozen or so men who'd come for this little party to block the track atop the bridge with rock and other debris. After the barricade was set, they'd all scattered and hidden to watch.

Sayer waited in silence. Behind him, Scully fidgeted, anxiously looking at his pocket watch for the tenth time in the last half hour.

"Train's late. Five minutes."

"Just keep your eyes on the track. I've got a bad feeling about this."

Scully hunched down nearer to him. "Seven minutes."

A whistle, long and loud, sounded at the far bend.

Sayer stood swiftly, Scully with him. Almost simultaneously, they spotted the three men, clinging to the underside of the bridge beneath the barricade.

"What the hell!" Sayer exploded. "It's Jack, damn him!"

Scully put a restraining hand on his arm. "There's nothing you can do to stop him now. We're in for a night of it, friend."

A wild, triumphant laugh mixed with the shriek of the train's whistle.

Jack lifted an arm, waving a cloth like a flag to a bull. "We'll blow her clear off the tracks!"

"Damn!" Not hesitating, shoving aside Scully's hand, Sayer navigated the rocky hillside with quick, sliding steps toward the bank of the river.

The whistle sounded again, louder. The clackety rhythm of the train's wheels started blending into the shrill sound.

At the next whistle's blow, a half-dozen men with bandannas covering their faces sprang out from hiding and dashed down the hillside toward the bridge.

Sayer snagged one of the men as he ran by, pulling him up short with an iron grip on his arm. With the man's face close to his, Sayer noticed the bandanna he wore was red, not the blue symbol of the Mollies.

"All you're going to do is get us killed, and for nothing!"

"We're ready for a fight, friend," the man growled from behind his covering cloth. "We want the spoils as much as you and your chosen few have been takin' all along."

"There won't be any spoils. There never have been."

"We'll see about that!" The miner yanked his arm from Sayer's grip. "We'll just see about that. Look—there she is!"

Sayer spun around. He saw a flicker of flame beneath the bridge, then Jack and his companions scurrying down the support beams. Except for the rhythmic clatter of the train rolling along its track, there was only profound silence.

Once more the whistle sounded—this time, a long, desperate screech as the barricade swung into the view of the oncoming engine. The scream of brakes accompanied the smell of hot metal to metal.

Moments before the engine skidded into the barricade, the bridge exploded under the cars. Every man instinctively flinched from the roar of fire and debris.

Coal rained like black hail, pelting the river below and the ground beyond, and a plume of oily black smoke and red-and-orange flame speared the sky.

Several of the men flew into a wild frenzy of celebration, raising their fists in the air. Others, terrified, started to run.

Two of the coal cars teetered for long moments on the edge of the track then plunged into the river with a tortured cry of twisted metal. Water ballooned around them, hissing steam.

The engine, wrenched and crushed by collision with the barricade, managed somehow to stay on the track.

Sayer didn't wait for the mayhem to clear before bolting for the engine. Ignoring Scully's warning cry and the flying whirl of sparks and coal, he scaled the beam to the bridge and hoisted himself onto the track. His breath coming hard and fast, he ran for the engine and shoved his way inside.

The engineer, dazed, nearly unconscious, blood running down his face, huddled against the side of the car. Black smoke rolled through the car, and Sayer could feel the first heat of the fire below them.

The fireman stood, back to the wall, hands up in surrender, his eyes pleading. Soot and blood smeared together on his face. "Please, let us go," he begged. "We got families."

"Get out of here, fast," Sayer shouted over the pandemonium brewing outside the train. "I'll take care of him." He gestured to the engineer.

Hesitating, the man threw a glance at the engineer then turned and rushed out the back end of the car—at the same time Jack and two of his men jumped onto the engine, blocking his path.

They grabbed the fireman and held him struggling. "You better not show up working this train for Montclair again, or your wife'll soon be a widow," Jack threatened, his face pressed close to the fireman's.

"Let us go and you'll never see us again. Come on, man, your fight's not with us."

Sayer swung on Jack, fire in his eyes. "Let him go. Or you'll answer to me."

"You're outnumbered. Maybe it'll be you answering to me for a change."

"Then we'll finish it in hell."

"That we can do." Jack jerked a revolver from his coat and pointed it at Sayer. "But first I got some business to take care of. Grab a shovel," he ordered one of his men. "Get that fire goin'. I want it stoked up good and hot."

"Don't do it," the engineer said weakly, struggling to get to his feet. "She'll blow."

The man shoveling coal into the box stopped, glancing at Jack. "Maybe this isn't so good an idea."

"I'm not stayin' around for this," the other of Jack's followers shouted, releasing the fireman he was holding and darting out of the engine. Freed, the fireman jumped out of the train car in the miner's wake.

"Do it, damn you!" Jack yelled, waving his revolver at the man at the coal box. "I want this whole train blown to hell!"

Sayer moved to help the engineer, discovering the man had broken a leg in the collision. He eased him to a bench and whirled on Jack again. "You damned fool! Can't you see what you're doing. Montclair will hang us all."

Ignoring the threat Jack made with the revolver, Sayer lunged at the man still shoveling coal, knocking him back from the firebox.

He didn't see Jack aim the revolver.

"Not if he don't know who did it."

The shot caught the wounded engineer in the chest just as Sayer spun around.

"No!" he shouted, throwing his full weight into Jack and yanking the revolver from him, sending it skidding across the floor of the train car. The engineer slumped to the floor, blood pooling around his chest.

The man stoking the fire dropped his shovel. "I'm gettin' out of here. She's gonna blow!"

Dragging a half-dazed Jack by his collar, Sayer leapt out of the train. Behind them the boiler fumed furiously, steam and black smoke filling the wrecked cabin of the engine.

"Jump! We ain't got time to climb down," Jack yelled, twisting to free himself from Sayer's hold. "The river! Jump, dammit!"

Sucking in a deep breath, Sayer shoved Jack off the bridge then plunged into the icy water after him.

Slapping his baton repeatedly against his open palm, Hulsey Lloyd paced the windowless back room of the police offices, trying to decide how to best deal with the motley dozen men his constables had gathered there.

Decisions like these always left a bad taste in his mouth. He hated his job as chief in this godforsaken place and hated more the miners who made it hell with their continual violence against Montclair. They hated him as well, but they respected at least the strength in the short, bullish body and the large, callused hands. Several constables had suffered beatings at the hands of the rebels; but after one failed try left a man dead and another broken, few dared think about challenging Lloyd.

Lloyd had no love for Gervase Montclair, either. But without Montclair and his mines, Lloyd would be no better off than the men who worked from boyhood to death in the mines.

He looked at the group now lining the wall—bedraggled, wet, streaked with soot—and his eyes fixed on Sayer.

Sayer looked back without flinching, defiance in the very set of his shoulders indicating his refusal to be cowed by the force of authority.

After the disaster, both his and Jack's men had scattered in separate directions, making for home at breakneck pace. Less than half an hour later, the knock at his door had come.

He'd gone along without a struggle, seeing no need in delaying the inevitable. With Roarke Macnair's reputation as an ally, Sayer felt lucky the constables hadn't shot him on sight.

Not that it wasn't still a possibility, from the look on the police chief's face. Except Sayer didn't give a damn what the police or anyone else thought. He only wanted the chance to see Aramanda again, to tell her the truth, to convince her he wasn't a murderer. Nothing else mattered.

"You, Macnair, tell me what happened," Lloyd said finally. He held the baton stiffly at his side, his hand gripped tightly around it.

"I don't know."

"That's a poor lie. Everyone knows you lead this rabble. Tell me the truth."

"I don't know," Sayer repeated stubbornly. *Or I don't know anything you'd believe.*

The baton came hard across his mid-section. By sheer will, Sayer kept from staggering, clenching his jaw against the pain.

"Does that help your memory?"

"Can't say that it does," Sayer muttered through gritted teeth.

Lloyd gave him a derisive look and moved down the line to the next man. "Who gave you the order to derail that train?"

"I don't know nothin', sir. I was home with me wife."

With a quick motion, Lloyd slammed the baton against the man's stomach. Crying out, the miner doubled over, collapsing to his knees.

Two more men suffered the same before Lloyd reached Jack. He stood, eyes fixed on the floor.

"Look at me." Lloyd pushed his chin up with the end of the baton.

"Aye, I'm lookin'." From the corner of his eye, Sayer caught the flare of hatred on Jack's face.

"I know you. You make a lot of noise over at the tavern, don't you? A braggart and a troublemaker."

Jack ducked his head again. His hands clenched so tightly his knuckles whitened. "No, it ain't me you want." He lifted his head to glare at Sayer.

"What kind of a fool do you take me for?" Lloyd snapped as he brought the baton down over Jack's shoulders. Jack's legs buckled, and he flattened a hand to the wall to keep from falling.

Lloyd turned on them with a fury. "I know you're responsible; and if I prove it, you'll all hang, that I can promise you. Especially you, Macnair." He took a step closer to Sayer, red flags of anger staining his sallow cheeks. "You've been nothing but trouble to me since the day I set eyes on you. You planned the raid and you murdered the engineer. And I'll follow you into hell, if that's what it takes to prove it."

Before Sayer had a chance to answer, Lloyd struck out with the baton again, one glancing blow striking Sayer across the cheek. It brought him to his knees, gasping hard for control of the pain and dizziness.

His companions watched in sympathy and shared pain. Jack smiled.

Sayer hauled himself to his feet and swiped the blood from his mouth, determined not to give Lloyd the satisfaction of seeing him defeated by either beatings or threats.

"I'm no murderer," he ground out, "but after an hour in your company, I might reconsider."

"Try and I'll see you at the end of a rope. And I'll be the one to put it around your neck."

Before Lloyd could add to his tirade, the door burst open and Gervase Montclair pushed the constable aside to enter. He scowled at the men, his eyes murderous, then turned to Lloyd. "Well?"

"I'm investigating, Mr. Montclair, questioning these men," Lloyd said tightly, with the barest trace of respect. "I'll know more in the morning."

"What more is there to know? These men, Macnair—" Gervase stabbed his walking stick at Sayer, "—destroyed my property and murdered a man. I want him hanged."

"If he's guilty," Lloyd said.

"If! My God, man, who else could it have been?"

Lloyd stayed silent.

Gervase slammed the end of his stick into the floor. "I don't believe you can doubt his guilt! If I have to break every man in this town, including you, I will see this resolved—and quickly. No low-bred Irish ruffians are going to destroy my business simply because they would rather fight than work."

Lloyd nodded, standing stiffly. "You'll do what you must. And so will I."

Sayer kept his face expressionless; but inside, he felt a small measure of relief. At least Montclair didn't own the police. A small comfort, but he'd take it.

"You can be certain I will," Gervase snarled. With a final hard glare at Sayer, he strode from the room, leaving the door hanging open.

Staring a moment at Gervase's wake, Lloyd finally called to a few of his constables. "Get these men out of my sight."

"Where to, sir?" one of the constables asked, eyeing the men warily.

"To hell, if it matters. Except for Macnair." Lloyd turned a look of pure loathing on Sayer. "Maybe the view from a cell will take a bit of the arrogance out of you, if anything can."

Two constables grabbed Sayer and, none too gently, dragged him to a small, dank cell in a corner of the building. As the heavy metal door swung shut behind him, Sayer leaned a hand to the cold stone wall, grateful most of his body was still in one piece.

If he'd ever had any aspirations to be a dashing rebel leader of legend, he'd lost them tonight.

"But you must let me speak with him," Aramanda pleaded, repeating her entreaty to the constable at the jail for the third time. "Please, only for a few moments."

Standing outside the jail, her cloak wrapped tightly around her against the chill of the late-night air, she looked up at the constable, appealing to him with her eyes and her voice. "Please, I must speak to him myself."

Hearing her uncle's angry cursing as he'd slammed into the estate house less than an hour before, she had feared the worst. She had risked Gervase's wrath being turned on her and crept out her bedroom window, taking her mare on a fast and furious ride to the camp, going straight to Liam and Bridget's home.

Liam, angry and smelling of ale, had told her of Roarke's involvement in the train disaster, and of his arrest. She'd wasted no time in going to him, conflicting emotions whipping at her heart.

She had imagined him to be ruthless and idealistic enough to be capable of almost any act, if he thought it would further his cause.

Yet the man she had come to know could never be a murderer, she knew it in her heart though reason denied it. How could he hold her so tenderly, speak so gently to her, arouse such passion in her if he were capable of spilling blood so mercilessly?

"I must speak with him," she implored the constable again, desperate to see Roarke, to touch him, to convince herself her heart told the truth.

He cocked his head and squinted down to her. "Does your uncle know you're here, lass?"

Aramanda straightened, looking directly at him. "No. Of course he does not. He would sooner see me dead than in the company of Roarke Macnair."

The officer shifted uncomfortably. "Miss Montclair—"

"I will go to him. If you refuse, I will go to Mr. Lloyd myself and demand to be admitted. I do not think he would be pleased to be roused from his bed at this hour."

"That he wouldn't," the constable muttered. "Though I don't know he'd be any happier if he knew I was lettin' you speak to Macnair."

"Then you will let me in?"

The constable grabbed a lantern, shaking his head. "You're a good sort, lass. You care about the men and their families. I'll give you a few minutes, but no more."

Aramanda nodded, her feelings too raw to speak. She said nothing as he ushered her into the jail building, down a dark, close corridor to the cells. Toward the end of the hall, the guard stopped. He held the lantern up and rattled the metal grates.

"Wake up, Macnair. You've a visitor." The constable set the lantern carefully on the floor near Aramanda and, with a glance her way, moved back down the corridor toward his post.

Aramanda looked into the cell at the cots against the cold,

stone wall. She saw a man sprawled on one of them, his arm flung over his head. "Roarke?"

He muttered something unintelligible, shifted in the darkness. "Aramanda?"

"Yes, yes I am here. Roarke, please . . ." She heard the entreaty in her voice and did not know what she was asking of him.

Suddenly alert, Sayer shifted out of the cot, and Aramanda heard him groan as his feet hit the floor. "Damn, that didn't feel very good."

He limped his way to the bars, giving her a crooked smile. "It hasn't been a good day."

"My God, Roarke . . ."

His shirt hung open, and Aramanda could see the shadows of bruising on his chest and abdomen. Dried blood and dirt smudged his face and a nasty-looking purple-and-red swelling marked his cheekbone. Worse, she could see the tiredness in his eyes and body, the weariness of defeat so alien to him.

Uncertain where she could touch him without hurting him, Aramanda reached trembling fingers through the grates to brush a streak of dried blood from his temple. "You are injured. You should not be here."

"Thanks, I know that," Sayer said, wincing as he rubbed a particularly sore spot on his shoulder. "I was doing okay until I fell asleep. Now, I ache in places I didn't even know I had."

"Who did this? Gervase?"

"No, Lloyd and his bat. He ought to be in the major leagues. Never mind," he added hastily at Aramanda's puzzled frown. "What are you doing here?"

"I—I was worried for you. Do you wish me to go?"

Sayer lifted his hand to cover hers, his fingers stroking the back of her hand, savoring her warmth even through the thin material of her gloves. "Of course not. I hoped you would come. I just didn't think you would."

"You did not think I cared enough," Aramanda said softly. She held tightly to his hand for a moment. "It does not matter. I am here."

"So you are. But you shouldn't be. Your uncle—"

He left the rest of the sentence unspoken, but Aramanda knew from the anger that flared in his eyes all he meant to say. "Gervase does not know I am here. He spent the evening locked in his study with a visitor from Philadelphia, a detective from Pinkerton's."

"How do you know?"

Aramanda slanted a sideways glance away from him to assure herself the constable had left them alone. "I looked in his coat pocket after the butler hung it up."

Sayer stared at her, taken aback. "You what?"

"I checked his coat pocket and found his cards," Aramanda told him calmly. "Do not look so shocked. How else could I learn who he was?"

"Good point." Sayer gave a short, bitter laugh and shoved a hand through his hair. "I suppose Gervase is furious because Lloyd didn't beat us all senseless, then hang what was left."

"Do not say that!" Aramanda laid her free hand against his face. "I do not want to imagine what might have happened to you. If the disaster is only half as terrible as Gervase described—"

"You didn't come here to give me his version of it." His face tightened, his eyes intent on hers. "Did you?"

"No. I came because I want to know the truth."

"You want to know if I killed the engineer."

"Yes." She said the word bluntly, without emotion, steeling herself to hear his reply.

"No. I didn't."

Aramanda let go the breath she had been holding.

Sayer looked at her a long moment, then released her hand and took a step back. "Did you believe I was a murderer?"

"I . . ." She caught her lower lip between her teeth. They locked gazes, then Aramanda broke the silence with a sigh. "I believe you might do anything for your cause. But, no," she said clearly. "I do not believe you would kill for it."

Sayer raked a hand through his hair, closing his eyes briefly as if the memory—or she—had hurt him. When he looked at her again, Aramanda saw anguish, regret, and fury clearly mirrored in his eyes. "Things went wrong. We only intended to barricade the tracks. Jack O'Keefe and some of his men had a different plan."

"It does not surprise me. Liam tells me Jack has always been jealous of you and your ability to succeed where he fails," Aramanda said.

"Well, he got what he wanted tonight," Sayer said, not able to hide his bitterness from her. "I should have seen it coming. But I underestimated O'Keefe's influence. And it cost a man his life."

Aramanda did not try to comfort him with false solace. She understood that he would not welcome it.

She could think of nothing to ease the rage of emotions in him, nothing she could offer him but her heart's trust.

She reached out a hand to him . . . silent, steady. After a moment's hesitation, he moved near the bars again, taking it in his own. His fingers rubbed over hers in a slow rhythm.

Through a communication of the tension in him, his touch reassured her, promised her he was whole and alive. "I am afraid for you. After what has happened this night, Gervase will stop at nothing to see you hanged."

"I know."

The grim acceptance on his face frightened her. Aramanda clung to his hand more tightly. She felt cold inside, a deep, insidious cold that fire could not warm. "You know, but it will not stop you from continuing this madness."

"No," Sayer said with a resolve she could not doubt, "it won't."

Fear and grief stopped her from speaking. She waited, biting her lip, until she could voice what was in her heart without crying out for him to choose another path. "Then what must we do?"

"We?" Sayer looked at her as if she had offered him a chance to see paradise.

"Yes, *we.* I am here. I wish to help."

For a moment, Sayer said nothing, only stared at her, his eyes memorizing her face. "Thank you," he said at last, his voice husky.

The expression on his face made Aramanda feel both humble and fiercely glad she could rouse such emotion in him.

"You are welcome," she answered softly.

They looked at each other for several timeless seconds, both saying with their eyes and touch what they could not put into words. At last, Aramanda found the voice to speak. "I know you are not in a position to make plans now, but—"

"What will we do? Nothing, until tomorrow. I have a feeling Lloyd just wants me here for a night, to flex his authoritative muscle." Sayer reached through the bars and stroked her cheek with his knuckles. "Go home, Aramanda. I don't want Gervase to find you missing."

"I am not concerned with Gervase. My concern is for you. For us."

The last words, spoken so softly Sayer scarcely caught the meaning that trembled in the air between them. Sayer felt her skin shiver under his touch. "What is it?"

"I . . ." She could not look into his eyes. "At times, I have let myself have foolish dreams. Dreams I have no right to."

"Tell me."

She lifted her face to his and Sayer could see her dreams there, clear in her eyes. All she had told him when she had come to him in his reality was there for him to see, her hopes for love . . . a family . . . peace.

"I let myself believe we could find peace between us and—"

"And love?" Sayer finished for her.

Aramanda did not agree or deny him. "Yet, at the same time I have the strangest sense that . . ." She shook her head. "I cannot explain it."

"We're running out of time." It was not a question.

"Yes." Wonder filled her that he shared her emotions, leaving a pleasing warmth deep inside her. The cold persisted, though, tempering the pleasure, hovering at her side like a shadow.

"Yes, how could you know? It seems somehow larger than our present troubles encompass. Or . . . perhaps I am simply tired. Forgive me." She brushed her fingertips against her forehead, "I do not know what I am saying."

"But you do." Sayer took both her hands in his, his expression holding an urgency Aramanda had never seen in him before.

"Listen to your heart." He hesitated a moment, then added in a soft, low voice that spoke from his own heart, "For though our minds dream of the future, our hearts cannot forget the past."

The poignancy of the words, the eloquence and passion with which he spoke brought tears to her eyes.

"You are little more than a stranger to me, but I feel I know you better than myself," she whispered. "Why do I understand with my soul your strange words, although my mind refuses them?"

"I wish I knew how to explain," Sayer said, holding fast to her hands. "But I can't. All I can ask is that you trust me. Please, just trust me."

"I find myself doing that, even when I should not," she said, smiling though the tears slid down her face.

Sayer took her hand in his and, stripping off her glove, brushed his lips over the backs of her bared fingers, his simple caress shivering her skin.

"Go home," he said gently. With a tenderness that went straight to her heart, he wiped away her tears with his fingertips, then stepped back from her, letting the chill and darkness come between them. "There's nothing else you can do here tonight."

"I will go," Aramanda said, holding his eyes with hers. She pulled the hood of her cloak over her hair and gave him one last, long look. "But I will be back."

Spinning away, she hurried down the corridor, not wanting Roarke to see how leaving him made her feel more alone than she had ever before felt in her lifetime.

Morning slapped Sayer in the face with a freezing blast of air, accentuating every sore muscle and tender bruise. Squinting against the pallid streak of sun touching him through the prison grates, he groped for the scant warmth of the rough blanket.

"Get up, Macnair." A constable stood over him, dangling the tattered wool coverlet. "Seems you're a free man."

"I am?" Sayer looked at him warily, wondering if this were another of Lloyd's ideas of torture.

"Chief says so."

"Just like that?"

The constable scowled. "Count your blessings, Macnair. Get moving. You're not gettin' any work done here."

Feeling like he'd been run over by a fleet of trucks, Sayer followed the constable to the office, gathered his coat, and stepped out into the icy morning.

Outside, he covered his nose and mouth with his cloak. This place gave a new definition to pollution, he mused as a gust of wind blew a toxic salad of cinders from steam engines, coal dust from culm banks, and powdered clay from the unpaved streets right into his face.

He trudged down the street in the cold of the dawn—sore, tired, his head throbbing. The throbbing escalated to pounding with the onslaught of the noise outside the jail. Steam engines huffed and puffed in the distance from Montclair collieries around the county, hammering into his aching head the momentous power of that name. The morning steam breaker whistle sounded throughout town, ordering the miners to work. Somewhere in the hills behind the jail, circular saws screamed from the mill.

A few yards from the jail, he passed the blacksmith pounding away on his anvil. He restrained the urge to cover his ears with the palms of his hands. Turning to duck away from the noise, he walked into the company store. He decided to buy a loaf of bread and a jar of coffee, hoping the food and caffeine would help him feel human.

As he pulled a few coins from his pocket to give to the man behind the counter, an elderly couple walked up next to him. The woman asked for a dozen apples for a pie, and her voice sounded strangely familiar.

When Sayer glanced to the side, he found himself face-to-face with the couple from the travel agency.

"Good morning," Weldon said, tipping his hat to Sayer. "You've looked better, I must say."

Beside him, Lila smiled and nodded, handing Sayer an apple. "Don't skip breakfast. You'll feel better."

Before his stunned, foggy-headed brain could react, they turned and strolled out of the store.

"Wait!" he shouted after them. The shopkeeper spilled his coins. Sayer snatched the bread and coffee. "Keep the change," he called over his shoulder and chased out of the store after the couple.

But although it had only been a split instant, outside the store he found nothing but the increasingly familiar assaults upon his senses: the stench and noise from pigs grunting and running freely in the streets, cows mooing from every backyard, chickens cackling, roosters calling out the morning's alarms, legions of dogs who barked round the clock.

The ground vibrated under his feet from the firing of a gunpowder charge down in the mine. He clutched a post in front of the store to steady his feet, wishing the nightmare would end.

Sixteen

Sayer slept badly, dragging himself up at the sound of the steam breaker whistle long before dawn the next day, too physically sore and battered by his own thoughts to lie on the hard bed staring at the ceiling any longer.

On top of everything else, he was expected to show up for work at the mine by six, though he didn't have the first idea how he was going to fake his way through a job he knew little to nothing about.

He'd managed to avoid it yesterday after his stint in jail. Today, he'd run out of excuses.

Pulling on a rumpled pair of pants and a shirt, he grabbed his coat and trotted downstairs to make a cup of tea. As he sat in the grayness drinking the bitter brew, he felt an unaccustomed hopelessness settle over him.

How am I supposed to fight or even compromise my way out of this mess when I'm fighting blind?

Shoving a hand through his hair, he realized how tired he felt—not just physically, but soul-weary. He'd gone into the mine at the start of this impossible adventure to find Aramanda. But often, she seemed further apart from him than ever before, divided from him by time and cause once again.

And time was something he sensed he didn't have enough of to squander. Aramanda had had only a few short days in his reality. He couldn't hope he'd have much more time in hers.

He drained his mug and pushed back from the table, thinking

of making one more cup of tea to help clear his head when an imperious rap at the door commanded his attention.

Probably Scully making sure I'm on time for whatever mayhem I'm supposed to have planned today.

But instead of Scully, Sayer opened the door to a slight figure in a dark cloak. For a moment, he thought Aramanda had come to him and he felt an odd twist in his chest.

Then, slender hands drew the hood away, revealing a fall of honey-colored hair. Sayer recognized the unusual hair-color— that of the woman he'd seen after his confrontation with Gervase at the Montclair estate.

"I was hoping I would find you here," she said, slate-gray eyes slowly sweeping him in obvious appraisal. Her voice was perfectly modulated to be both courting and importuning, yet Sayer could hear the hardness underlying it.

It matched her mouth—full, sensuous, as inclined to twist and pout as it was to smile. He could see a reflection of Gervase Montclair's determination in her smooth features. It suited the woman better, disguised with softness, but Sayer wasn't lulled into thinking Gervase's daughter would be any less ruthless.

"It is a terrible hour," she said, smiling up at him, "but it was my only chance of finding you alone."

Sayer made no move to usher her into the house. "Why would you want to find me alone, Miss Montclair?"

"It is Mrs. O'Cafferty, actually. Patricia." She drew out the syllables of her name like an invitation. "May I come in? It is so cold." Without waiting for his answer, she glided past him, her smooth skirts brushing his leg.

"I had to speak with you, Mr. Macnair. I realize I appear unflatteringly bold coming here at this hour, without an escort, but my father is quite upset over your recent actions. I am worried over the results of this battle you insist on waging against him."

"Have you come to plead for mercy on his behalf?" Sayer asked coolly, closing the door and standing in front of her, his arms crossed over his chest. "If so, you lost several hours of sleep for nothing, Mrs. O'Cafferty . . . to say nothing of risking several embarrassing questions from your husband."

"My husband is in Philadelphia. My affairs are hardly his concern." Patricia flung back her hood, and her soft wave of fair curls fell artfully over her shoulder. She slowly unfastened the tie of her cloak and took her time in draping it over the table. "And I did not come here to plead. I came to offer you the chance to end this foolish rebellion of yours, quickly and to your benefit."

"How kind of you. Does your father know you're here?"

She smiled slightly. "Do you think he would approve?"

"I have no idea. Would he?"

"You are hardly his idea of an acceptable acquaintance."

"It doesn't seem to bother you," Sayer said, giving up on expecting a direct reply to his question. Her determination to avoid it already gave him the answer.

"Why should it? I do as I please."

"Am I supposed to believe, then, that you've an altruistic motive for wanting peace? Forgive me, but you don't seem the charitable type."

"You have been listening to my cousin's estimation of me," Patricia said, her mouth pulling in a tight line. "Perhaps I can change your opinion." She closed the distance between them, laying her fingertips on his arm, the touch just a hint of a caress. "I will be frank with you. I will not pretend I have the same affection Aramanda professes for the miners and their families. My father's fortune is in the Montclair collieries and I don't wish to be deprived of it."

"What about your husband?"

"What of him? He is a musician. I married him for amusement, hardly for what he could provide me."

Sayer wanted to push aside the hand on his sleeve and step away from the intimate suggestion in her eyes. But instinct told him Gervase Montclair was behind his daughter's visit and he wanted to know why. "You said you wanted to give me a chance to change my mind."

"About me?"

"About my fight to improve the conditions in the mines."

"Yes. That." Her hand slipped away. "I believe we can come

to some agreement. If you put a stop to this mayhem, then I will see to it you are paid well enough to leave this place and start over elsewhere, perhaps in a profession more suitable to your talents than mining. My father need never know."

"I have my doubts about that," Sayer said. "But what makes you think I have that much influence over the miners?"

"Don't insult my intelligence," Patricia snapped. "Father knows you lead the Molly Maguires; it is only a matter of time before he has the evidence to prove it. You know he has spies within the mines—you've killed three of them, although the accidents you devised were quite clever. Apart from that, there is no other man among this wretched group with your boldness and courage. You are the only one who could lead."

"Very flattering, but don't expect me to hand you a signed confession."

"I don't care whether you admit it or not. Only that you consider my offer."

"And what about the families here, the other men? How do they figure into your—offer?"

"They don't. I'm not concerned with them; and if you were so dedicated to them, you would not continue to let them be imprisoned or killed because of your actions." She looked hard into his eyes. "I only want this wretched business over and done with. You are the man who can end it."

"Am I?"

Patricia's eyes narrowed, then her full mouth curved in a cat's smile. "You are toying with me. I see why Aramanda has made such a fool of herself over you. You make it difficult for me to remember why I am here."

She reached out her hand again. This time Sayer stopped her, stepping back. "You're here to make me promises I'm sure neither you nor your father have any intention of keeping. Sorry, Mrs. O'Cafferty, you're nicer to look at than your father, but you should have stayed in bed. Tell Gervase he gets points for a good try, though."

"You are as arrogant and uncivilized as my father says!"

"I thought you liked that about me," Sayer said, flashing a pirate's smile. "I'm disappointed."

"So am I. But I assure you, you will be more than disappointed once this has ended." snatching her cloak off the table, Patricia pulled it over her shoulders again.

"I could have made your life much easier. I can also make it much more difficult. I can hurt you in ways you have not considered. Aramanda has been generous with the families here. Without her influence, the suffering would be doubled. Consider that when you congratulate yourself on so nobly turning down my offer."

Turning toward the door, she paused with her hand on the handle and glanced back at him. "My father can be cruel; but I assure you, I will make you wish you had chosen more wisely."

She left the door wide open on her way out, letting the cold air draft into the nearly empty room. Venting his frustration, Sayer kicked it closed behind her.

Scully had told him to expect more trouble and he knew Patricia O'Cafferty was going to be it.

Aramanda sat sideways on the large upholstered chair nearest the fire in the morning room, idly stirring honey into her tea, her chin resting on her free hand. She'd risen early, long before any of her family, her pent-up conflict of feelings stealing any hope of peaceful rest.

Vivid images of Roarke—imprisoned, in danger of being hanged, yet defiantly refusing to back away from his fight—had plagued her all night, so this morning she felt exhausted and on edge. She'd retreated to the solitude of the morning room, hoping the strong tea would revive her enough to face whatever the day had in store.

A light tread sounded in the hallway, and Aramanda lifted her head just as Jessalyn opened the door.

"You look as if you've been awake the whole night," Jessalyn said, eyeing her critically as she moved to sit in the chair opposite her. "Are you ill?"

"No. I did not sleep well," Aramanda admitted. She tasted her tea, making a face when she realized it was cold, and set it back down on the table at her side.

"I don't doubt it. Spending any time with Roarke Macnair seems to have that effect on you."

"It is not that!"

"Isn't it?" Jessalyn shook her head. "You are a terrible liar, Aramanda."

Instead of giving in to the prick of irritation she felt at Jessalyn's bluntness, Aramanda saw the humor—and the truth—of it.

"You are right," she said with a smile. "I have never perfected the skill of pretense, no matter what the situation. Mama feels I am quite hopeless."

"She should be proud of Patricia, then," Jessalyn said tartly, then gave a rueful smile of her own when Aramanda raised a brow. "Oh, do not pretend you have any affection for her. None of us do. She and Uncle Gervase are too much alike for any of us to feel even charitable about her. I hate the idea she may someday be living here with us."

"How kind of you to say so. You should learn to leave your doors closed if you wish to be malicious, cousin."

Both Aramanda and Jessalyn turned as Patricia swept into the room, her smile hard. "Please don't bother to apologize," she said when Jessalyn glanced to Aramanda, flushing.

"I was not about to," Jessalyn said, regaining her composure. "I am certain you have been as malicious about me, about all of us, and with less discretion."

"How petty you are, Jessalyn."

"While you, of course, are above such behavior," Aramanda said, coming to her sister's aid. "Jessalyn may have spoken out of turn, but neither of us expected anyone in our household would stoop so low as to eavesdrop on private conversations. Although, perhaps I should not be so surprised," she added pointedly, refusing to back down from Patricia's icy stare. "You went far below pettiness, spying on us in the garden the other afternoon."

Patricia gave a tiny shrug. "My father's business concerns me. You were in the gardens, where anyone might overhear your battles—or any other of your affairs you choose to conduct there."

"Any other of my affairs are certainly none of your concern," Aramanda said, rising to her feet. Jessalyn stood up and moved beside her.

"Perhaps." Patricia walked slowly to the windows, twitching the curtains aside to glance outside. "Perhaps not. I paid a call to the mining camp this morning."

Jessalyn stared. "At this time of the morning? Whatever for?"

"To see Roarke Macnair."

"Patricia—" Jessalyn began, looking from her sister to her cousin.

Aramanda willed herself to say nothing, though a warm flush started up the back of her neck. She would have dearly loved to have cut Patricia with a scathing comment, to smack the smirk off her face, anything to stem the tide of hateful words she sensed were coming. But she clutched her dignity to her instead, determined not to let Patricia have the pleasure of humiliating her.

"You look quite pale, Aramanda. You must be shocked. Oh, I know it was brazen of me. I am sure Father would be appalled," Patricia said with a small smile. "But I have been terribly concerned for Father. He is so distressed by the mayhem caused by these wretched miners he has even let it interfere with his plans to wed your dear mother. I thought it my duty to try and suggest some compromise. You understand, I am sure."

"No," Aramanda said clearly despite the tightness in her throat. "I do not."

"Of course, I realize you are infatuated with Roarke." She said the name deliberately, making it the sound of an intimate endearment. "He is quite attractive, rather like a brigand. But so unscrupulous. I do not know how you can bear it, Aramanda, how you can be so charitable to all of them when they are laughing at you the moment you turn to leave."

"What are you talking about?" Jessalyn demanded. She reached for Aramanda's hand, squeezing it tightly. "Aramanda has done all she is able to to ease the suffering there."

"Such a noble endeavor, it makes it all the more tragic."

"If you have something to tell me, Patricia, then say it and be done," Aramanda said. She felt a faint sick sinking feeling pass over her, but refused to show any weakness in front of her cousin.

"I am only trying to spare you any further humiliation, cousin. If you lose yourself to this man, it will reflect badly on all of us. I do not wish the Montclair name to be tarnished, particularly for so little cause. Your father did quite enough of that while he lived."

Patricia smoothed a hand down her skirts, stroking the sleek silk. "I told you I went to see Roarke. He was quite willing to speak with me about a compromise. He, in fact, said he would abandon his fight and leave us be, if I would . . . pay him. Handsomely, of course."

"You are lying," Aramanda whispered. "Roarke would never give up his cause so easily."

"And you are a besotted fool," Patricia countered with a vicious thrust. "He cares nothing for the miners' families—or for you. He is only interested in ending this fight to his advantage, no matter who is hurt in the bargain or what the cost. The miners know he is only using you to reach his end. They take what you offer and pretend to be grateful when they, in truth, despise you for being a Montclair."

"I do not believe you. I do not believe any of it! I know the families; I know Roarke better than you could ever hope to know him. I know how he feels for me."

"Do you? Truly? I think not, else you would be wholly on his side and not forever trying to mediate between him and my father. You have doubts, Aramanda, or you would be with him and not here, clinging to your family and the security of the Montclair name. You do not want him to destroy my father's empire any more than I do."

"I do not want him to destroy my family and those I care for. You are welcome to the empire, Patricia, if that is what you love best."

"I do not need your permission to take it," Patricia said, her eyes hard. "My father will see to that. And you will end up with nothing—from either your beloved family or the wretched mining families, and certainly not from Roarke Macnair."

Whirling about, Patricia swept out of the room before Aramanda could refute her, leaving behind a wave of insidiously rich perfume.

Aramanda stared after her, her hands clenched at her sides, willing herself not to give way to tears of anger.

"Aramanda . . ." Jessalyn stepped in front of her, taking Aramanda's cold hands in hers. "I am sorry. I should not have said what I did about her. It only made her more determined to be cruel."

"It is not your fault," Aramanda said, pressing her sister's hands lightly in return. She managed a weak smile. "Patricia has determination enough without being prompted. She knows I care about the families—and about Roarke—and she tried to hurt me with it. I suspect Gervase had his hand in it, also. My involvement with the miners is an embarrassment to him, and he does not take humiliation lightly."

"You are right, of course," Jessalyn said. She held her sister's eyes for a moment, then her own dropped and she stepped back, turning to look into the fire. "And yet . . ."

Aramanda waited and, when Jessalyn said nothing, she prompted, "And yet? What is it?"

Jessalyn looked back at her with her straight, unwavering gaze. "What if she is telling the truth?"

"She is not!"

"What if she is, even in part?" Jessalyn persisted. "You said yourself you were at odds over Roarke's methods of trying to force changes at the mines. And she is right: You are a Montclair. Can Roarke forget you are? Can any of them? Do they love you that much?"

Does he love you that much? Aramanda heard her sister's unspoken question and had no answer. She wanted no doubts, and yet she had them, stirred to cruel life by Patricia's scathing assessment. *Trust me,* he had said; yet did she?

You have doubts, Aramanda, or you would be with him and not here.

"I must go to the camp," Aramanda said suddenly, startling Jessalyn into an expression of astonishment.

"Now? What good will it do? Roarke will be at the mine, and you cannot see him there. Even if you do find him, how can you be certain he will tell you the truth?"

"He will. If he does not, I will know. And I must know. I will not let Patricia determine how I feel in my heart." Giving her sister a quick hug, she started toward the door. "I will decide that for myself."

Sayer swiped his forearm across his face, feeling the grit of coal dust and dirt eat into his skin. For nearly twelve hours, he'd worked alongside Scully and Liam in one of the dozen or so chambers of the mine. He found the lack of ventilation suffocating; the wet smell of rotting wood in the brattice work above and in the pillars all around, nauseating. Desperately, he missed his simple, cluttered office at the university in Boulder. In his mind's eye he saw his view from his window: tall timbers beneath the wide, open, powder-blue sky. He longed for a single breath of fresh mountain air.

At first he had had no choice but to watch and learn their techniques, developing a deepening respect for their expertise and their stamina by the hour. The boy assigned to him as his helper stood quietly by for the first couple of hours, staring silent and wide-eyed at Sayer's awkward, failed attempts to blast the coal from the face of the vein.

Sayer lamented that what his father had taught him about mining turned out to be of little use in a time over a hundred years earlier. somehow he had to learn from scratch in a matter of hours what he was supposed to have known since boyhood.

At one point early in the day, when he'd nearly blown his own finger off, it struck him as ironic that the men working beside him were actually looking to *him* to lead *them*.

In time, though, he caught on to using a hand bit and auger to drill holes. The hand-made explosive he learned to mix by eyeing the other men while pretending to busy himself breaking up large chunks of coal with a pick—a job he realized after rounds of disgusted grunts and curses from his companions was meant only for a miner's helper.

A couple of close calls reminiscent of those in his first college chemistry cab chastised him to go easy on the black powder he poured into a piece of brown paper then rolled up and pasted with soap. The little tube then had to be shoved into the hole in the vein with a long, thin, iron needle and the opening tamped with coal dust.

The last step was the tricky one. He had to stuff the squib—debatably known as a safety fuse—in the hole, light it, and run like hell over an obstacle course of coal, rail-car tracks, carts, picks, and miscellaneous tools before he was blown to smithereens.

But if the fuse failed, as it often did, it had to be relit or discarded. And that meant walking back to it when it might be quietly smoldering its way to a delayed explosion right in his face. The first time a squib did that, Sayer thought of his childhood and firecrackers and his mother warning him to stay back, stay back, until they had time to die or explode.

Only, here in the mine, if he waited too long, the mine boss came by with a club to his back.

At length he caught on to the basics of blasting coal from the wall of a damp, dark cavern. Gratefully, he let the miners' helpers load it into the rail carts for the mule teams to drag to the surface.

He'd never stayed more than a hour in the depths of a mine cave before, even though his father had spent more than thirty years working one of the largest Montclair collieries and Will still spent most of his days there. His memories, too, were nothing like this—dark, dank, cold, and permeated with the anger and frustration of the men who wanted justice and needed work.

"It's near time," Scully murmured to him. Bending close in the appearance of picking up a loose rock, he flicked his forefinger to the brim of his hard hat.

Sayer now recognized the sign as signaling the onset of some action. Tension crawled up his spine.

He nodded at Scully. Adjusting the waning light of his lantern's wick, he started to move past Liam, who kept his eyes fixed firmly on the task before him.

"What is it this time?" Liam muttered as Sayer began following Scully toward a crossroad in the shaft. "Did you find another spy or a watchman you're planning to bury? Or is this just another bit of fun with blowing up a shaft or two?"

"That's dangerous talk, friend," Scully told him. "Best you keep your opinions to yourself. There aren't many here who agree with you."

"Including my own brother," Liam said bitterly. "I'm waiting for one of your accidents to happen to me."

"Then you'll be waiting in vain," Sayer told him, laying a hand on Liam's shoulder. "But Scully is right. You're better off not talking too loud. There are a few down here who aren't too discriminating about who gets buried, spy or not."

Liam shook off his hand, turning to face him. "You're the one who had better watch your back, Roarke, or the next grave I'll be digging will be yours. Montclair isn't the only one who'd like to see you standing in the gallows."

"And who else might there be?" Scully asked. When Liam stayed silent, he shook his head, his face grim. "I see you've been listening to Jack O'Keefe again when he's full of Tansie's brand of courage."

"I've been listening to no one." Liam turned back to the wall, hacking fiercely at the rock. "I'm just telling you how it seems to me. I've had my fill of funerals these past days."

"I have, too," Sayer said quietly. "And if I have my way, there won't be another." He looked at Liam a long moment, but was answered by silence; then he pushed ahead of Scully, his face grim. "Let's go."

Several yards down one of the side paths, they met up with a small group of miners. Sayer recognized most of them from the fiasco at the train tracks.

"Looks like we're all here," Scully said, glancing around at the soot-smudged faces.

"And we brought a few friends," one of the men said. Reaching into a dirty burlap sack, he brought out a round metal container and handed it to Sayer. "There won't be no more loads going out the south shaft after a few of these. It'll be over with, fast and hot, just like you wanted."

"Will everyone be gone home by then?" Sayer asked, looking over the device in his hand. He didn't need to ask whether or not it was intended to spark an explosion. The paraffin and the long wick told him that.

The man glanced at his companions. "Everyone but Fred."

"Make sure he's gone."

"No need for that. He's a spy," the man added when Sayer flicked a frown his way.

"How can you be so sure?"

"Jack said he saw him talkin' not two days ago with the watchman after he left Tansie's. Why would he be doin' that? He's only been here a few weeks. There's no need for it."

"That's your evidence?" Sayer said, his frown deepening into a glower.

"It's always been enough for you before," the man muttered, not meeting his eyes.

"It's not enough now. You all are getting as bad as Montclair, ready to hang anyone who looks wrong, to believe anyone who's spreading the right rumor."

Hefting the explosive in his hand, Sayer weighed his words, thinking of Aramanda and how she would implore him to temper his action with concern for the miners. "I'm willing to fight, to do whatever it takes to change what's wrong and to bring down Montclair. But I don't have the stomach to kill whomever the lot of you happens to take a dislike to. If you don't agree, if you're willing to let Jack tell you what you should think, then say it now. I don't want men behind me I can't trust to turn my back on."

In the long silence that followed, the men looked to one another, sheepish, a few sending angry glances to the others.

"That seems to settle it," Scully said finally. Straightening, he brushed the coal dust off his pants, adjusting his coat. "Let's get on with it then. Most everyone will have started for home by now, and I want to be standing outside with them when the worst of it starts."

The men nodded in agreement, telling Sayer they would make sure the tunnel was clear before setting the explosives. Sayer went with Scully, watching the older man as he set their explosives and lighted the long fuses.

They'd started back toward the mine entrance when Scully stopped, glancing behind. "I'd best go check and make sure Fred has gone. There's a good ten minutes, probably a bit more, before this lot catches on."

"I'll do it. You go ahead. I don't trust them either, not about something like this," Sayer said, voicing Scully's unspoken fear. He motioned Scully ahead when the other man hesitated. "Go on. I'll be right behind you."

Pausing a moment longer, Scully started up the incline to the entrance, leaving Sayer to trot off in the opposite direction. It was only a short distance down the tunnel where Fred was supposed to be, and when he got there, the hollowed out chamber between the tunnels was empty.

Satisfied, Sayer turned to leave. A small stone, roughly the size of his fist, clattered down the dumping ramp in the chamber. Sayer whirled around, seeing nothing.

Shaking his head at his own jumpiness, he started down the tunnel again. As he did, a thundering roar, building speed like a locomotive, came rushing at him. With no time to think, he reacted instinctively, flattening himself against the chamber wall just as the load of rock hurtled down the ramp.

Smothered in a blanket of choking dust, he lost his footing as one of the larger stones sideswiped his leg and fell hard against the shifting pile of rock. As he did, the last of the jagged stone careened down the incline, half-covering him in rocky debris.

Momentarily stunned by the force of the fall, Sayer fought to both clear his head and wrestle free of the rock.

Ten minutes.

Scully had said ten minutes, but how long ago? Four, five minutes? If he didn't get himself out of this mess . . .

"Some second chance," he muttered, thinking for some reason

of the old couple and silently cursing their idea of tampering with destiny. "At this rate, I'll save Gervase the trouble of fitting me for a hangman's rope."

Pushing and flinging the rock aside, Sayer managed to free his legs from the debris; but he'd landed awkwardly, and the rock still pinned his left shoulder and side.

Ten minutes. Before, he'd worried about his time with Aramanda in this life running out.

Now, he only had a few minutes left to rescue himself or it was going to run out a lot sooner than he'd expected.

The reverberation of the explosion startled Aramanda, and she dropped the teacup in her hand, sending it crashing to the floor.

She'd spent the day with Bridget, helping her friend with small chores and spending time with the boys, taking comfort in the warm embrace of a family undivided by loyalties to business or cause. Bridget understood her dreams of one day finding such a love, of having peace, a family of her own. It soothed Aramanda's heart to share her dreams and listen to Bridget's in return, to talk with someone who understood and did not begrudge or belittle her hopes.

All the day though, Aramanda's thoughts had only partly been with her friend and the children. She had been waiting, waiting for Roarke.

At the violent sound, her heart gave a leap.

"What is it?" Bridget asked, looking up quickly from the bread dough she was kneading on the table. She put her hand to her mouth. "The mine. There's been another explosion." She exchanged a glance with Aramanda, half-fearful, half-horrified. "Do you think—"

"I'll go," Aramanda said, snatching up her cloak.

Bridget gathered up Kinny in her arms, hugging the toddler close. "Be careful."

"I will." Aramanda reached over and brushed her hand against

Bridget's. "Try not to worry. I am sure Liam is not involved. He never is."

Not waiting for Bridget to say the obvious, that it was Roarke who was always at the center of any mayhem, Aramanda rushed out the door, running in the direction of the mine.

Smoke billowed out of the entrance and a lesser explosion sounded from somewhere deep inside the mine as she neared the crowd of men milling outside it. She scanned the faces of the miners, desperate to find Roarke's among them.

"Best you not get too near," one of the men said, grabbing her arm as she started to move closer to the entrance.

"Where is Roarke?" Aramanda asked, clutching briefly at his sleeve, panic bubbling up inside her. "He must be here."

The man glanced toward the mine. "Still inside. Liam and Scully went after him. But you can't—"

His warning lost on her, Aramanda tore out of his grip and ran headlong to the entrance. For a moment, the belching smoke blinded her.

Then, like a vision of paradise in hell, she saw Liam and Scully emerge from the blackness, half-supporting, half-dragging Roarke between them.

A cheer went up among the men as they moved safely away from the entrance, propping him against the wheel of a cart. Bruised and battered, his eyes dazed, he succumbed to a fit of coughing. Liam and Scully dropped to the ground beside him, too spent for the moment to speak.

Aramanda flung herself on her knees at his side, both fiercely angry and sick with relief.

"I do not need to ask what happened. I should have known sooner or later you would bring this on yourself. First at the prison and now this . . ."

He stared at her, frowning, then started coughing again, plagued by the lingering effects of the smoke. She gently smoothed the hair from his face, touching his shoulder, his arm, his chest, tenderly probing for the worst of his injuries, worried by his silence.

"Are you all right?" she whispered. "Oh, Roarke . . . each

time I see you, it is worse. How can I bear seeing you like this, time after time? How long before I am the one standing at your grave?"

Sayer shook his head as if trying to answer, but another spate of coughing stopped him.

"Why do you keep doing this?" Aramanda's tears spilled over, and she took his hand, pressing it to her damp cheek. "What does it accomplish except to cause more violence, more danger to you?"

"It wasn't Roarke's doing," Scully said, his voice hoarse. "He would have been out in time. He went back to check to see that Fred had gone, and someone tried to bury him under a load of rock."

Scully's words sent a dark rumble through the men gathered around them. "Someone?" one of them sneered. " 'Twas Jack O'Keefe and his lot or I'll swear off ale for life."

"It's bad enough to be fighting Montclair; now we're fighting our own, too," another man put in.

"There'll be the devil to pay one way or the other," Liam said, gingerly touching his fingertips to a wide scrape on his cheekbone. "It won't take long for Montclair to hear about this, and he's sure to have the sheriff down this time. With the main shaft closed now, it'll near halve his production. He'll be filled with hell's fire to have Roarke's neck in the noose, and a few others with him. I wouldn't be surprised if Montclair decided to end this business between him and Roarke himself and damn the law."

"Gervase would never—" Aramanda began, shooting a shocked look in Liam's direction. Liam's gaze didn't waver, and she bit her lip, swallowing the bitter truth. "Yes, perhaps he would. He refuses to see another perspective, and he is angry enough."

"It won't do Roarke or us any good standing around here talking it over," Scully said, struggling to his feet. "We'll get him back and let Tansie take a look at him. When he's patched up, Roarke'll decide what's best to do."

Before Aramanda could protest, several of the men helped

Sayer to his feet and into the mule cart. With Liam and Scully riding behind with him, they started back to the camp, stopping at the back door of Tansie Caitlan's tavern.

Easing Sayer to a bench against the wall, Scully left Liam and Aramanda to tend to him while he fetched Tansie.

Sayer, slumped on the hard seat, rubbed a hand over his jaw, wincing. Aramanda felt a tiny twinge of relief steal over her when he glanced to her, the clarity back in his eyes.

"I hope one of you got the number of that cart that flattened me," he croaked.

Aramanda and Liam exchanged a bewildered glance. "Did you hit your head?" she asked tentatively.

"I hit everything. Or everything hit me. I think it was a little of both.' He tried to straighten and gave up the effort after the first attempt. "I feel terrible."

"That's not a surprise," Liam grumbled. "You look terrible, too."

Aramanda allowed herself a tremulous smile. She brushed the hair from his brow again, reassuring herself he was still with her by the feel of him. "You were nearly crushed by several tons of rock, from what Scully says. You were lucky not to have been killed."

"I don't feel real lucky right now," Sayer said with a groan. "I need a drink."

"Well, he can't be feelin' too bad if he's talking about drinking," Tansie said, coming into the room, Scully on his heels. "You look like you could use a bottle, friend. At least everything still seems to be connected in the right place."

Gesturing Liam and Aramanda aside, he checked over Sayer, probing for broken bones or other unseen injuries. Aramanda, her hands tightly clasped, watched his every motion, flinching every time Sayer winced.

"A couple of stiff whiskeys and a few weeks and you'll be in fighting form again," Tansie pronounced after several minutes, smiling broadly over his shoulder at Aramanda. She let go the breath she'd been holding in a painful release. "The lady's right. You were lucky, friend. This time."

"I'll take those whiskeys now," Sayer said, ignoring the implication in Tansie's voice.

"You should let Liam help you home and into bed," Aramanda said firmly. "You can drown yourself in whiskey there just as easily."

"I don't intend to drown myself. Just numb the pain enough so I can stay on my feet and upright for a while."

"On your feet?" Aramanda glanced at Liam, Scully, and Tansie in turn and received only shrugs and blank looks in reply. "Have you not done enough for one day? What do you intend to do? Finish blowing up the remainder of the mine? Surely you can leave that for later," she added tartly. "You will need something to occupy your time tomorrow."

"This has to be done tonight," Sayer said. Leaning a hand on Liam's shoulder and accepting his brother's arm of support, he managed to get on his feet. "Get the men together here," he told Scully. "I'm calling a meeting."

"Now?" Aramanda stared at him in disbelief. "Those rocks must have robbed you of what remained of your senses."

"He never had any to begin with," Liam muttered.

Tansie shook his head and started toward the bar. "I'll get you that bottle. You're goin' to need it."

"Are you thinking of going back to the mine tonight?" Scully asked, studying Sayer's expression.

"No, not the mine." Sayer looked from Scully to Liam and then at Aramanda. His face softened when she made no effort to disguise the plea in her eyes, and he reached out and took her hand, squeezing it tightly.

"Then where?" she asked. "And why?"

"Trust me." He gave her that smile, conspiratorial, rakish, like a man with a blade between his teeth. "I have a plan."

Seventeen

With a few stiff drinks in him, the pain from his assortment of bruises, scrapes, and cuts blended together until Sayer couldn't tell what hurt where. The alcohol blessedly numbed his aching muscles enough so he could detach himself from the damage caused by his untimely—or timely, as it seemed in retrospect—collision with the contents of the coal cart.

Nevertheless, as Sayer braced himself to speak, it took an effort of will to forget the past hours and concentrate on what he wanted to say.

He wished fleetingly that Aramanda could be with him. But he knew O'Keefe and his men would use her presence against him and he couldn't risk the distraction. This chance was too important.

In fact, he had the feeling it meant everything.

Sayer downed the last of the ale in his mug. Forgetting his usual precautions of locking the front door and closing the shutters, he used a chair as a step up to a tabletop in the middle of the tavern, commanding instant attention and more than a few startled looks.

Tansie, shaking his head, went to fasten the shutters, and Scully slammed his tankard on the table several times, silencing the scattering of mutters and grumbling.

"Quiet! Roarke's got something to say!"

A hush fell over the room, and the men pressed toward the center to gather around Sayer.

"I do have something to say, and some of you aren't going to like it," he started bluntly.

"I don't like it already," Jack drawled, directing a smirk at the men around him.

Several of them sniggered in reply, but they were drowned out by an equal number of angry calls for quiet.

Sayer pulled the blue bandanna from his vest pocket and held it high. "This is what I want to talk about," he said. "This and everything it means."

Liam, near the back of the room, scowled and shook his head. Many in the crowd shuffled nervously and glanced quickly at their neighbors. Scully wiped his face with a yellowed handkerchief.

With one eye on the front door, Tansie called out from behind the bar, "Roarke, some of these men don't belong—"

"If they don't belong, they know what's been going on. The Mollies are hardly a secret anymore. Montclair sure as hell knows about us. And he knows I lead you."

This time audible exclamations skittered through the crowd. A few men turned the collars of their coats up about their necks, avoided meeting any direct gazes, and made for the door. Some of them glanced at Sayer as if they couldn't decide whether or not he'd gone mad.

Sayer straightened his stance and pitched his voice with an equal measure of force and resolve. "If the cost of change is too high, then you'd better leave. I won't lie; it's not going to come cheaply. But it's not going to come at all if we don't stand together."

"And what are we standin' together to do?" one of the miners called up to him.

"To beat Montclair."

Sayer paused to let the words sink in.

"I'd be satisfied with a decent day's wage and with not having to spend more than I earn at the company store," Liam spoke up. "And I don't want my boys to have to start workin' the mines when they're barely past being babes. That's all most of us want, Roarke."

"It sure as hell is!" the man nearest Liam said.

"And we're never getting it from Montclair, that's for sure," Scully put in.

"From Montclair? You know we ain't."

"Montclair'll work us 'til we die of the black lung or are buried in one of his godforsaken holes," Scully said, "and we'll still be owin' a year's wages to the company store standing at the gates of hell."

Sayer let the men vent their anger for a few minutes longer, waiting for the right moment to speak the words he hoped would unite this group in a common cause.

He felt suddenly strong, invincible, as if this moment in this place was the precise time he'd waited for all his life.

He could sense Aramanda's presence, encouraging him, and as he lifted the bandanna again, he envisioned her with him. "Scully's right," he said. "But Montclair isn't going to make changes unless he's forced to. And not with violence."

"Are we just goin' to ask him nicely then?" Jack sneered.

"No," Sayer said. He paused, then put the force of conviction behind his next words, "We're going to stop working."

The silence in the room was so profound it was as if he'd instantly struck every man dumb with one simple phrase.

A full two minutes ticked past before Scully finally said slowly, "You want us to stop working?"

"Us, along with every other miner in this county and all the counties around us with large mines," Sayer said. "If we all refuse to work, mine owners like Montclair won't have any choice but to bargain with us. They won't have a choice because, without us, they're out of business."

Jack pushed his way through the crowd and confronted Sayer, glaring up with hate in his eyes. "What makes you so damned sure this'll work? There are plenty of men willin' to take hell from Montclair and anyone like him just to keep from starvin'."

"It will work," Sayer said firmly, his stance never wavering, "if we all stand together."

Jack started to speak again, but before he could mouth the words, the voices of the miners erupted around him.

Sayer caught their emotions—wary, uncertain, some angry—but he also felt the flicker of hope his words had ignited. Drawing the men's attention to him again by raising the symbol of their rebellion, he used the force of his words and the passion of his voice to hold them for the next minutes in thrall to the vision of the future he vowed could be theirs.

"But only if we stand together," Sayer concluded, his voice hoarse from the fervent intensity he had put into every phrase in his determination to convince them. "Unity is our weapon against Montclair and anyone like him. Without it, we might as well volunteer for hanging. With it, we have the power to force peace between us and shape the future we want."

He had them, Sayer could see it in expressions wavering between dismissal and a stronger desire to believe. Even Liam had emerged from the shadows and stood at the edge of the gathering, looking at him with something approaching admiration.

Sayer drew a breath and prepared to deliver the final thrust that would push them over the line. He started to speak, and the tavern door slammed open.

Gervase shoved into the room, followed by Lloyd and several constables. Lloyd pushed past Gervase and raised his hands as if to make a demand.

The gesture acted as a catalyst to chaos.

Jack immediately took a swing at the constable nearest him, connecting with a solid crack to his jaw. The constable staggered backward against the chest of one of the miners, and a melee exploded.

Sayer jumped down from the table and yanked back the arm of the constable before he could bring his nightstick down on Scully's shoulders. He twisted the stick out of the constable's hand, flung it into a corner, and sent the man sprawling into a chair.

Scully called out a warning and Sayer ducked just in time to avoid a flying chair. He cursed soundly and joined Scully in pulling two of Jack's men off a miner with a blue bandanna hanging half out of his coat pocket.

From the corner of his eye, he spotted Liam delivering a stunning blow to a constable who had tried to raise a club against him.

"Macnair!"

Sayer spun around.

Gervase stood unmoved amid the mayhem as if his sheer brute will held him inviolate. His face contorted in a feral grimace. In a swift motion, he yanked a revolver from inside his coat.

"No!" Without warning, Aramanda rushed into the tavern and flung herself at her uncle just as Gervase leveled the revolver at Sayer's heart.

Sayer lunged forward to push her away—the moment Gervase pulled the trigger.

The retort, like a small explosion in the close confines of the tavern, sent several men diving to the floor. A burning dart tore at Sayer's shoulder, pushing him back a step.

"Roarke!"

Aramanda, her face dead white, stared at him in horror.

Gervase cursed and fumbled with the revolver.

Stunned by the rapid action, Sayer felt a pain swell in his shoulder. He glanced at it in mild surprise. Blood flowered over the white of his shirt, spreading down his arm.

"Roarke!" Aramanda screamed his name again. She struggled to get past her uncle, past the snarl of men and broken chairs and tables. She wore no cloak over her ale-spattered skirts; her unbound hair was a wild tangle.

Gervase aimed the revolver again. But before he could try a second shot, Tansie's fist came down on his forearm, knocking the gun out of his hand and sending it sliding across the tavern floor.

With a vile oath, Gervase shoved into the crowd after it.

Ignoring his shoulder, Sayer forced his way around a quartet of scuffling men and constables and over barricades of broken wood and rolling tankards. Blood and sweat and ale slicked the wood floor, making his footing uneven.

Finally, at the edge of the wild crowd, Aramanda drew close enough to touch. Sayer reached out for her hand.

She reached back . . . then stopped.

"Did you cause this? Tell me."

"Now?" Sayer stared at her in disbelief. "In case you didn't notice—" He waved his good arm at the fighting around them. A broken bottle sliced close to his ear, smashing against the bar.

Aramanda stayed unmoved. Two spots of bright color stained the paleness of her face. "What did you say to them? I was with Bridget and I saw Gervase and Mr. Lloyd—"

"Dammit, I don't have time for explanations!"

Sayer took two strides to her and with his good arm swept her up and over his shoulder.

"Scully!" he shouted, catching sight of his friend.

Scully stabbed his arm in the direction of Tansie's back door. "Go! For God's sake man, go! It's you Montclair wants. We'll find you later."

Holding Aramanda firmly, Sayer ruthlessly ignored her indignant cries and struggles to free herself from his hold and shoved his way toward the back of the tavern.

Scully, Liam, and several of the miners moved almost as one to block the view of his escape out the back door.

Breathing hard, gritting his teeth against the pain in his shoulder, Sayer ran straight for the stable where Tansie kept his supply cart and horses.

"I will never forgive you for this, Roarke Macnair!" Aramanda cried. "Never."

"I'm beginning to regret it myself," Sayer muttered.

Whipping a bridle over the head of the biggest of the three horses, he tossed Aramanda across the beast bareback and hoisted himself up behind her. He locked her against him with an arm around her waist.

"Well, milady," he said before kicking the horse into a gallop, "welcome to the Molly Maguires."

A few miles down the road, fed up with having his teeth realigned and every bone in his body jarred by the rough, headlong gallop, Sayer jerked back on the reins, trying to bring his pur-loined steed to a halt.

"Whoa," he called out. "Stop, you stupid beast!"

He jerked harder, to no avail. The horse made a hard turn and Sayer slid sharply to one side, barely able to keep himself from losing his seat. "Stop, dammit!"

"Do you expect him to listen?" Aramanda shouted over her shoulder.

"Who's doing this?"

"You certainly are not."

"Then you stop him."

"It will be my pleasure!"

Snatching up the reins, Aramanda dug her heels into the horse's side and gave the reins a sharp pull and twist. Her action brought the horse to a sudden, sliding halt.

The unexpected motion caught Sayer off guard, costing him his precarious balance and flinging him off the horse's back to the ground. He landed with an ungraceful thud, face down in a muddy patch of ground.

"Son of a bitch. If I ever get my hands on that stupid excuse for an animal—"

Aramanda slid down from the horse and walked over to where he lay, looking at him a moment before putting a hand on his shoulder and rolling him over.

"Well! You are certainly a fine specimen of ruffian," she scoffed, her mouth twitching with the effort not to laugh. "You cannot ride worth a *faux* cent, Roarke Macnair. You do not even know how to put a bridle on!"

Sayer groaned. "Go ahead, laugh. I played soccer, not polo. I hate horses. I thought—"

"You thought what? Did your mother teach you dressage? You are a miner's son, not the son of a nobleman. Damn you, Roarke. It would serve you right if I simply abandoned you here. After all of your lies and contradictions—and then kidnapping me! What did you hope to accomplish by such a thing?"

"Wait one minute." Sayer clamped a hand over his still-bleeding shoulder, struggling to sit up. "So I can't ride. I'll

admit to that. But accusing me of lying is another thing altogether. And swearing! Really, Aramanda, I thought a lady
never—damn that hurts!"

"You are certainly one to throw stones." When he winced at
the word, Aramanda shook her head, sighing.

"Here, let me help you," she said. Tethering the horse to a
tree, she lifted her muddied skirts and stalked back to him, kneeling down beside him. "You are going to do yourself more harm
than good if you keep moving about like that."

"You know, this hasn't exactly been one of my better days."

She arched a brow. "Indeed."

"It's not easy being a hero. Your charming cousin threatened
to ruin my life, then your maniacal uncle nearly took it, right
after O'Keefe or his ruffians tried to bury me."

"Ah, yes, Patricia. I came to the camp earlier today to talk
with you about my cousin—before I discovered you nearly
crushed."

Aramanda's anger subsided and her heart softened toward him
as she looked up and down his bedraggled figure. She examined
his shoulder as best she could in the darkness, probing with her
fingers, feeling a tightness inside her ease once she had assured
herself he was not seriously injured.

"Do you have to do that right now?"

"Stop complaining. You sound like Oliver when he doesn't
want to take a tonic," she said, ripping a strip of cloth from her
skirt and gently but firmly tying it about his blood-moist skin.
"It is only a flesh wound."

"But it's my flesh." Sayer grimaced as she tugged the bandage
ends tighter. "Dammit, woman, if you want revenge for something, trust me, you're getting it now."

Aramanda finished and sat back, looking straight into his eyes.
"Tell me what happened."

"I think we might find a better place for explanations," Sayer
said with a sardonic twist of his mouth. "I don't want either
Lloyd or your uncle finding us here, and we're going to need
shelter for the night."

Aramanda said nothing for a moment, and Sayer thought she

would begin arguing again. Instead, her expression softened and she gently brushed the hair from his forehead.

"I was so worried for you," she said softly, not quite meeting his eyes. "When I saw Scully and Liam bring you out of the mine, I thought . . ." She stopped, unable to put her deepest fears into words. "And then when Gervase suddenly showed up at the tavern—I suppose I should be grateful there is anything left of you at all."

"You aren't the only one." Reaching up and taking her hand, Sayer curled his fingers around her in a protective gesture, gently stroking her skin. "I'm sorry. This isn't exactly the way I planned things to happen."

"I am certain it is not." She took her hand from his. "Not at the mine or the tavern—or with Patricia?"

Aramanda immediately hated herself for her weakness in mentioning her cousin's name. But the wound Patricia had inflicted was too fresh and she could not banish the uncertainties in her mind until Roarke convinced her she had no reason to doubt.

Sayer stared at her, his eyes appraising. The last thing he wanted now was to sit in the mud and give her an explanation about something that didn't matter.

Except he saw in her face it meant more to her than she would tell him and he was willing to stay here all night if it would ease her pain.

"She must have told you she came to see me—her own version of the visit, I've no doubt. What did she say? Never mind," he said when Aramanda's expression tightened and she glanced away.

Gently, he slid his fingers under her chin and turned her face back to his. "I can guess. No matter what she told you, she came to either bribe or blackmail me into leaving town."

"Well, you have left, and in dramatic fashion. Perhaps it worked."

"Do you believe that?" Sayer asked, his hand tightening.

"I . . ."

"Do you?"

"I do not know what to believe!" Aramanda cried, pulling out of his hold and turning from him to hide her tears in the darkness. "I want to trust you, yet I am afraid it will only lead me to heartache."

"Heartache? No." Sayer compelled her with his touch and the passion in his voice to look at him again. "Never. Patricia has nothing I want or will ever want. Neither love nor money." He flashed her a raffish grin, wanting to dispel the hurt in her eyes. "You're welcome to search my pants' pockets for bribes if you don't believe me."

Aramanda smiled in spite of herself. "Will that also convince me that you were not at the tavern tonight to call the men to more violence?"

"Listen to me," Sayer said, serious again. "I wish you had been there to hear it all. I think you would have been—pleased."

She drew back, startled. "Pleased?"

Sayer hesitated, choosing his words with care, wanting more than anything to convince her he meant to keep his promises. "I asked the men to stand together, not just here but with the miners at every colliery around . . . to refuse to work until the mine owners agree to compromise."

He took her hands in his and held her gaze fully. "You have dreams of families undivided, of peace and love. I want those dreams to come true. I want to make them come true, for the miners and their families." With infinite slowness, keeping his eyes on hers, he touched his lips to her hands, then said softly, his voice charged with emotion, "For you, Aramanda. I want to make your dreams come true."

Aramanda could not answer him. Blood rushed under her skin, making her warm and light-headed.

Was it true? Did he truly mean to give her the dreams she so desired? Could she believe he could work a miracle?

Sayer watched the emotions cross her face, leaving a bewilderment behind. "You don't believe me," he said flatly.

"I . . ." Pulling away from him, Aramanda looked down, then back into his eyes. "I do not know. Are you desperate enough to tell such lies to save your life, even though they would destroy me if I believed and they were untrue?"

Aramanda rose to her feet, trembling, not certain whether to run or stay, torn by her own traitorous heart. "And yet you are somehow different from the man I first judged you to be. These past days—oh, I do not know!" Turning away, she balled her hands at her sides, trying to control her feelings.

"Aramanda—"

Her back turned, she heard him stifle a groan as he got to his feet to come to her. Her heart pounded fast and hard, and she held herself stiffly to keep from turning into his arms.

"I am not the same Roarke Macnair," Sayer said quietly with an assurance that he could speak the truth. "You know that, Aramanda, in your heart, if not in your mind. And you know only you can help me to help the miners."

He was behind her then. Close enough for her to feel his heated breath on the nape of her neck. She sensed something inside her melting, though he had not as much as touched a hand to her back. The mere possibility that he could stole her reason away.

Her breath quickened and the blood raced through her, laced with lightning. "I do not know if I can help you."

"You can," Sayer murmured, his mouth so close to her ear she felt his lips brush her skin as he spoke. "Stay with me. Stay with me because it's what you want."

If he had touched her then, taken her into his arms, she could have refused him nothing.

But he only circled around so he faced her, his eyes intent on her, as if there were nothing and no one else in the universe that could take his gaze from her.

Bloodied and bruised, covered with mud, he still managed to exude the brash confidence and strength that made her heart beat faster and tempted her to abandon her role as the proper Montclair daughter and surrender to the wild, wanton feelings he roused.

"Aramanda . . ." Sayer's deep, rough-edged voice made her name sound like seduction.

Just missing a chance brush against her skin, he reached out and wound a tendril of her hair around one finger, slowly letting it loose.

Aramanda trembled at the look in his eyes, both desire and a deep-running need to have the answer he wanted.

He moved a step closer and her face lifted to his without thought, like a flower to the sun. "Will you trust me?"

Drawing in a breath, she held it for a moment before letting it go on a sigh.

"I give you this night," she whispered huskily, her lips a breath from his. "I will listen to your plan. And by morning I will know what sort of man you truly are, Roarke Macnair."

"So, how do you like living the life of a ruffian so far?"

Sayer tossed another log into the fire blazing in the hearth. He dropped back onto the heavy, green-velvet couch, propping his feet up on the armrest and rearranging the brocaded pillows at a better angle under his head.

Leaning back to look at Aramanda, sitting less than a foot from him, he added, "Not bad, wouldn't you say? . . . especially for my first try at being on the run."

Rubbing her hands up and down her arms to try to stave off the chill inside her, Aramanda pulled a face at him.

The house they had taken refuge in was several miles from her own family estate. Acquainted with the owners, Aramanda knew they customarily took their staff with them to town for the spring so she and Roarke would have safe haven, at least for the night.

And it would be a luxurious haven at that. The furniture was of excellent quality; the tapestries and rugs, rich glowing shades of greens and golds and blues; the house itself, an elegant construction of oak, brick, and stone. The slight mustiness of weeks of disuse had faded, at least in the sitting room where Sayer had lit a fire, adding a handful of fir cones for scent.

In the early hours of the morning, with deepest night around them and a gentle silence for solace, Aramanda felt, if not at peace, at least protected from the turmoil they had left behind.

With a small sigh, she shifted to the edge of her chair, moving closer to the fire. "We were fortunate tonight. I knew this house was vacant, but that by no means makes it forgivable."

"House?" Sayer gestured at the enormous room with its high ceilings and windows taller than he. "This place is palatial! I don't understand how anyone could abandon a mansion, furnishings and all. Except for the boards on the windows and the covers on the furniture, it's as though the owners expect to return home any minute."

"There are many houses such as this," Aramanda said, smiling at his disbelief. "My family owns one several miles south of here. It is only opened during the summer months, for house parties and hunts. The rest of the year we spend at the estate or in Philadelphia."

"Don't you worry about ruffians breaking in?" Sayer reached over his shoulder and drew a finger down her cheek, a rakish glint in his eyes. "Outlaws like us?"

Aramanda tried to ignore his touch, but her skin quivered at the wake of sparkling sensation he left behind. "You are the ruffian, Roarke Macnair," she said primly, her hands crossed neatly in her lap. "You kidnapped me. You pried the wood from the glass and broke the window. I have done nothing wrong."

"Yet."

Frowning, Aramanda rose to her feet, taking a few steps from him, out of reach of temptation. "You refer to this plan you hope to convince me to support, I suppose. I am ready to hear it."

She slanted a glance at him, her eyes sliding from the hair that fell over his forehead down his face and throat to where his half-buttoned shirt spread open.

"And I'm starving," he murmured.

Her eyes flew up to find the hunger in his. "You—"

Sayer smiled, slow and easy. "Do you think you can navigate our way to the kitchen? I'm sure you know far better than I where it might be. And you know what I'm like as a cook."

"About as skilled as you are at riding."

"Ah, but I do have other talents," Sayer said, his smile broadening as the color washed into her face. "Still, without you, I could easily spend the rest of the night meandering from room to room, only to die of starvation before dawn."

"Roarke—" she warned.

"I'm serious," he insisted, looking anything but.

"All right." Aramanda gave up the unequal fight between her reluctance and Roarke's fatal charm. "I admit I am hungry as well. Are you sure you feel well enough to accompany me?"

Sayer shrugged, swinging his feet to the floor. "I'll live. And it's going to hurt no matter what I do. Hurting on a full stomach sounds better than pain on an empty one."

"Very well." Aramanda took an elaborate silver candelabrum from a table and lit one taper in the fire. She touched the flame to the other five and held the flickering light aloft for a moment, looking around them.

"This is a beautiful house. I had not remembered how lovely the colors and furnishings were. I am sorry," she said then, flushing. "I am certain household decor does not fascinate you."

"You fascinate me." Sayer leaned closer and slid her hair to one side, pressing a lingering kiss to her nape. "Tell me anything. I love the sound of your voice."

"And I, yours," she murmured before she realized it was too late to snatch back the words.

Sayer moved nearer still. Though she said nothing, she basked in the sense of his powerful presence at her side as they walked the long corridors to the rear of the house.

How often had she dreamed of a moment like this?

Alone with him in the darkness, with the promise of a night in his arms . . . Her heart beat hard in her breast, and she quickened her pace to hide her tumultuous emotions from him.

"There, through that door. That is the kitchen."

Shoving the door open with his free hand, Sayer let her pass through first. "What are the chances of getting a fire started in here?"

Aramanda glanced at him, not certain what to make of his words. They were guileless enough, but the husky note in his voice betrayed his innocence. And there was nothing innocent about the eloquent expression in his eyes.

She quickly looked away to where the gigantic black iron stove loomed, an ominous centurion of the kitchen. "It would be best if we did not try to light this. I doubt there is much, if any, coal left with the house empty. I am certain, though, there must be at least a few jars of fruits and vegetables stored in the cabinets—or the cellar, perhaps."

Sayer helped her conduct a thorough investigation of the butler's pantry end the vast kitchen, their efforts rewarded by finding a container of dried nuts, a few jars of fruits, a box of wrapped candies, and two bottles of wine.

"A feast!" Sayer proclaimed when they sat down to dine in the morning room.

"It is, tonight." Aramanda took a seat across from him at the small oaken table, smiling at his pleasure.

The candlelight danced between them, creating soft halos of light and changing shadows. In the abandoned house, their voices, the sound of their movements, and the hiss and snap of the fire were the only things to disturb the hush of the night.

Time suspended in the gentle quiet, giving them both the feeling of being alone in the world with each other, sheltered from the troubles and trials of reality.

Looking into Sayer's eyes, Aramanda saw all the possibilities and promises between them; and in that moment, she felt freed of all expectations and roles, free to trust her heart and take all her chances with him.

Shaken by the realization, she glanced away, reached to take a plump fig from the bowl in front of her.

His hand covered hers, stilling her motion. Aramanda looked up at him, her breath catching when he smiled. "What is wrong?"

"Nothing. Nothing is wrong." Sayer glanced at their clasped hands, then, grimacing at the filth on his own, took out his bandanna and wiped the worst of it off. Taking the fig from her fingers, he held her gaze with his. "Will you let me give you the first taste of the sweetest fruit?"

Aramanda's voice deserted her. *What is he asking?*

She searched his eyes for any hint of teasing, but found warmth and only the slightest suggestion of amusement.

"I am hungry," she murmured, finding his touch and scent as heady as the finest wine.

"Are you?" He touched a finger to her mouth, parting her lips, running his fingertip over the moistness there before offering her the fig.

She couldn't breathe, couldn't move, couldn't think as he placed the fruit on her tongue, his eyes following every motion of her mouth.

"Does it satisfy you?" Sayer asked, his voice a velvet caress.

"It only makes me desire more," Aramanda whispered, the naked passion in his eyes making her feel both bold and needy.

One by one, ignoring his own hunger, Sayer fed her apples, figs, plums, cashews, almonds, and chestnuts. Smiling, he watched her as though her taste were his, the pleasure on his face at her enjoyment of the meal seeming to quell his appetite as much as if she had been the one feeding him.

"Thirsty now?" He stretched out his hand to the wine bottle.

Still relishing the last fruit, tasting only the sweet, wanton savor of temptation, Aramanda nodded.

Slowly, his every movement a concert of grace and strength, creating music where there was none, Sayer took the bottle, pulled out the cork, lifted it, and inhaled the wine's perfume. Aramanda watched, hypnotized by the sensual pleasure he took in performing the simple act.

His hand caressed the body of the bottle, and she imagined those same hands caressing her skin, boldly, surely, leading her to love. He read the label aloud in French, and the lyrical words spoken in his low, rough-edged voice echoed inside her, sending a shiver up her spine. "Excellent."

"How could you know?" she murmured. "And you speak French as if you were born to it. How could you—"

A confident spark in his eye, he poured a silver goblet half full. "Trust me."

Swirling the deep red liquid in the goblet, he noticed that the candles' soft light glinted off the silver like pearls and diamonds swathed in gold. He lifted the wineglass to drink first of its scent, then brought the lip of the goblet to his to sample its nectar.

As she watched the smooth liquid trace a line down his arched throat, her own throat went dry.

He swallowed and looked over to her, his expression intent, his eyes sliding over her face. "The finest ever."

Moving next to her, Sayer rested his arm over the back of her chair, his fingers just brushing her shoulder, and brought the goblet to her lips. "Your turn. If you're ready?"

Aramanda heard the quickening of her own breath, her heart pounding loudly in her ears. "Ye-s." The word caught on her lips.

Yes, I want this. I want to taste everything you can offer me.

Closing her eyes, she parted her lips to his persuasive touch and drank until the cup was dry.

Savoring the sweet intoxication on her lips and the fiery warmth in her belly, she opened her eyes to him, a quickening heat starting deep inside her at his slow, easy smile.

"I'm glad you enjoyed it," he said. "It is delicious."

His arm moved around her shoulders; his fingers stroked her arm. Setting down the goblet, he curved his free hand around her face, bending to brush his mouth against hers, his tongue lightly tasting the trace of wine on her lips.

"Maybe it's you. I don't remember the wine being this sweet."

"Roarke . . ." His name sounded like both a plea and a promise in her soft, breathless voice. "I want . . ." She stopped, her mind whirling, her blood a heated rush.

"Yes?" Grazing another kiss on her lips, his mouth slid against her cheek, the tender line of her jaw, then to her throat, lingering on the place where her pulse throbbed. "What do you want, Aramanda? What can I give you?"

"I do not know. I feel . . . everything. But—I am afraid."

"Of me?"

"Of the way you make me feel. I have never felt this deeply, wanted so much . . ." She touched his face with trembling fingers. "I cannot pretend with you. I am only myself. And it frightens me that I cannot be anything else with you, that I have no defenses. I feel you could hurt me, deeply and irrevocably, and that I could do nothing to stop you."

"I would never hurt you, Aramanda," he vowed, pulling her

fully into his arms and burying his face in her hair. "Never. If you don't believe anything else, believe that."

He held her, and Aramanda listened as the beat of his heart echoed her own, wanting with her mind to trust him, knowing in her heart she already did.

Finally, Sayer moved back, gently putting her from him. "This isn't a good idea."

"But—" Aramanda protested, unwilling to give up the warm pleasure she felt at simply being in his arms.

"Look at me." Sayer gestured up and down his torn, dirtied shirt. "I'm dressed in blood and mud and coal dust."

"I should look at your shoulder again," Aramanda said, struggling to clear her head of the sensual haze his nearness evoked.

"It's fine." Getting to his feet, Sayer swept her up into his arms before she could object. "Let's get you settled by the fire in the sitting room. It's warmer there. You're trembling."

Aramanda nearly told him her trembling had nothing to do with the chill night air and everything to do with him. Instead, she laid her head against his good shoulder, her arm curled around his neck as he started out of the room and down the long hallway with her in his arms. "I do not feel cold at all."

Sayer laughed, a rich resonant sound that filled the house with his presence. "You will. When the wine wears off."

She lifted her head to look into his eyes. "It is not the wine. It is you."

"It's obvious you haven't taken that close a look at me, or you'd want another glass."

"I do not need to see any more clearly to know I want you."

Back in the small sitting room, near the fire, Sayer set her on her feet, his hands lingering on her shoulders. "Aramanda—"

"Stop talking," she blurted out, her need for him suddenly feeling as important as drawing another breath. "There is nothing more to say."

Reaching up, she linked her arms around his neck and leaned into his body, joining her lips to his.

Sayer met her kiss with blind passion. God, how he'd longed to have her again, to fill the empty places inside his soul with the love only Aramanda could give. Now, she was here, in his arms, warm and giving, tasting like wine and temptation, offering him paradise, and he had only to take it.

Except how could he, in these circumstances? She deserved more, only the best of him. And only when she wanted him— body, mind, and soul—with a clear understanding of who he truly was. Only when she loved him as deeply and irrevocably as he loved her.

"Aramanda." He broke off their heated kiss long enough to murmur against her ear. "I want to be with you; I want to love you. But not like this."

"I do not care about mud and coal dust," she said, her eyes glazed with desire. She shivered, her hands tightening around him.

"I care. When we do love each other, I want it to be everything of your dreams, not a night you'll regret a few hours after it ends."

The look she gave him, deep-reaching and disconcertingly direct, nearly made him forget all his good intentions and take her back in his arms to make wild, spine-shattering love to her on the velvet couch.

"I would not regret it. When I am with you, there is no room inside me for regret."

"I'll make sure there never is. Starting tonight." Wrapping his arm around her waist, he led her to the couch and guided her to sit, leaving her long enough to prod the fire back into flaring life.

When he returned, Sayer put his arm around her, holding her close, unable to forsake the touch of her. "I just want to hold you," he said softly, pressing a kiss on her hair. "Just for a little while. While I have the chance."

"You may take your chances anytime you wish," Aramanda said, resting her hand on his chest.

She leaned against him, liking the feel of his body mated to hers, the rumble of his voice in her ear when he talked. "Since you are determined to be noble, perhaps you will now tell me your plans for us. It appears you have no more reason not to."

"My plans for us don't have much to do with the plans you want to hear about," he said, his voice low and husky. "But just to prove to you I'm not always inclined to act on impulse, I'll tell you what I have in mind."

The heat of the fire, the distraction of the wine, and the warmth of Sayer's sheltering arms made Aramanda begin to feel the effects of the long and harrowing day's events. Closing her eyes, she snuggled closer to him and listened, finding herself hearing more the timbre and emotion in his voice than the actual words.

He was speaking most passionately at length about traveling with her from mine to mine and rousing the consciousness of the workers, making them unified, working with her to stop the violence. Though she murmured vague questions and comments in response, her mind was far from his words.

She knew what he was talking about must be terribly important for him to speak with such conviction, but at the moment it was all she could do to suppress a smile.

He sounded hopelessly noble, utterly elegant, and almost divinely inspired; yet all he inspired in her was desire. Not the desire to help anyone or solve any problems this night. Just desire. Plain and raw and simple.

His ardent speech made his chest rumble against her ear. His breathing was deep and fast, the way it would be if he were making love to her, she thought with sleepy satisfaction.

She supposed the thought should have shocked her, but the effects of the wine, exhaustion, and emotional strife left her feeling that it hardly mattered. What mattered was the way only he could make her feel.

Minutes—hours?—later, she felt Sayer shift and made a vague protest as he laid her back on the couch. She felt him unlace and remove her boots, then cover her with something soft and woolly. His lips grazed her cheek, and she felt a curling warmth inside her at his touch.

"Roarke . . ."

"Shhh . . . just sleep," he whispered, lightly kissing her lips, tucking the afghan up around her chin. "I'll be back soon."

Sayer paused a moment longer at her side before easing to his feet. In sleep, the firelight on her face, her long hair unbound and spilling like auburn rain over her shoulders, she was more beautiful than he thought it possible for a woman to be.

"Another night, my love," he told her, touching her cheek. "There will be others. I promise you. Now that I've found you, I won't let you go again."

As he stepped quietly from the room, glancing back at her, his heart twisted with the notion that it might be the first promise he'd ever made but had no power to keep.

Eighteen

Aramanda stood at the edge of the forest clearing, her face turned to the waning rays of the sun. Twilight started to creep in between the trees, purple and misty, silencing the light, and the woods began to fill with small and shallow noises.

A familiar tread sounded behind her, firm and sure, and she stayed looking at the sunset, knowing it was Roarke.

"You've been out here a long time," he said softly, sliding his hands up her arms to her shoulders. His touch was warm through the thin cotton of her blouse. "Come back inside to the fire."

"Not yet. It has been so warm these last evenings, I like to savor it. It grows cold all too soon. Have Scully and Ryan gone on?"

His fingers gently massaged her taut muscles. "Mmmm. They're staying in the town tonight; one of the families there offered to put them up. They'll meet us back here tomorrow afternoon. I thought it would be better if we split up for the night. Word's gotten around we're traveling in a group. I don't want to draw any unwanted attention until it's necessary."

"At least we have the cottage tonight," Aramanda murmured, leaning back against him. "After so many weeks of sleeping on floors and in caves and on the ground, it will feel like a true luxury to spend the night on a real bed."

"What—you don't like camping? All the fresh air and getting back to nature, communing with the earth?"

Aramanda smiled. "All the crawly creatures sharing my bed

and the cold that never goes away and the perpetual dirt in my blankets? No, I do not."

"And here I was looking forward to another night under the stars."

"Be my guest, please. You can continue communing with the earth all you please. I plan to thoroughly indulge myself tonight."

Sayer was silent for several minutes, and Aramanda let her mind drift.

It had been nearly a month since he had fled with her from Tansie's tavern—a month spent eluding the police and Gervase's detectives, traveling from mining camp to mining camp, spreading his message among the workers, rallying them behind his cause. A month also of learning Roarke, and his learning her, forging a bond she could neither explain nor deny. Except—where would it lead?

"Do you regret staying?" he asked suddenly.

"Staying? With you?" She twisted her neck to glance back at him. "If you recall, you did not give me much choice in the matter. Would you let me go now?"

"No."

Aramanda smiled, shaking her head. "Then I have nothing to regret."

"I do," Sayer said quietly. "I should never have brought you along."

"It is too late to consider rational action now. You certainly cannot go back to my uncle and tell him it was all a horrid mistake."

"I could, but I've gotten used to my head being on my shoulders."

"Then I suppose we are stuck with each other."

"It's no sacrifice for me," Sayer murmured against her ear. He stroked his hand over her hair, twining his fingers through its length. "But I know you miss your family, that way of life. You are still a Montclair."

"Am I?" Aramanda considered his words, looking deep into herself. "I have almost forgotten what that means. In these past weeks, we have both left our past lives and created a new one from what remained of the old."

Sayer's hand jerked against her hair, then resumed its slow stroking.

"Yes, I do miss my family. I worry over what they are thinking, how it must hurt them not to know where I am, that I am safe. I wonder whether Penelope has enough jam at tea and if Jessalyn is upsetting herself over Patricia . . ."

"I wonder if Oliver has managed to keep his bear away from the kitchen cat," Sayer said lightly.

"That as well." Aramanda smiled up at him. She sighed. "I worry, too, about what Gervase has done in our absence, if he is closer to pressuring Mama to marry him. And I cannot help but be concerned about the mining families, about Bridget and Liam, and Father Creeghan, and what Jack O'Keefe is attempting without you to keep him in check."

She paused, reaching up to lay her hand on his. "But for all that, I feel . . . changed inside. Despite how I care for my family, I do not miss that life. I always felt as if I were trapped in a role I did not choose. With you, I have freedom—to speak my mind, to have ideas and thoughts in which no proper lady would indulge. It is very heady," she confessed. "I fear I am growing too fond of it."

Sayer turned her in his arms and gave her a look of astonishment. "You mean to tell me you're willing to give up hot baths, morning coffee, and feather beds for a blanket on the ground, cold tea, colder water—and me?"

"Well . . ." Aramanda considered the question with a duly serious expression. "Perhaps not the coffee." Laughing when he rolled his eyes in mock affront, she said, "Do not tell me this is what you prefer. You complain every time you have to drink tea without cream."

"Not every time. And at least I don't sulk when I can't wash my hair."

"I do not sulk. I simply hate dirty hair."

"Somehow you manage to look dignified when you say that." Sayer's expression shifted from teasing to something gentler, more intent. "You always manage that, even when you're tired, and hungry, and cold, in the worst and the best of situations. You might not hold the title, but you truly are a princess at heart," he said softly.

He grazed his fingertips over her face, sliding them under her chin and lifting her face to the first glimmer of silver moonlight. "You've stayed with me, even though you've given up what's surely heaven compared to this. I don't understand it."

Smiling into his eyes, all her heart in the gesture, Aramanda took his hand in hers. "Heaven can wait."

"I hope it will. For us." He looked at her a moment longer, then clasping her hand more firmly in his, started walking away from the cottage, taking her with him. "I want to show you something."

Aramanda didn't question him as Sayer guided her into the center of the forest clearing and stopped, gesturing to the heavens above them.

"Look up," he said. "Tell me what you see."

Tilting her head back, Aramanda stared up at the diamond-and-black infinity. "I see . . . a great winged horse and a serpent and, just there—" She gestured directly above them. "—a phoenix." Darting a glance at him, seeing his wondering expression, she added, "Surely you are familiar with him, the great bird that repeatedly consumed itself by fire and then arose from its own ashes."

"You aren't, by chance, trying to tell me something, are you?"

"Why ever would you believe that?"

"Lucky guess. I get the impression you've done this before."

"Many times, with Oliver and Penelope, and sometimes alone, when I want to be free of all the troubles and pettiness inside the house. I find each constellation, and I remember the myths about them. I think the dreams and imaginations of the people who created them are not so very different from ours. Their tales are much like the bedtime stories I tell Oliver and Penelope, thrown into the sky."

She took her eyes from the vista above and looked at Sayer. "What do you see?"

The moon sketched his features in silver and black as he leaned his head back to take in the universe she described. "I see possibilities. Millions of them, all together, so that sometimes the flying horses and the serpents and the great birds get lost in the grandness of the whole vision. The vastness and the beauty of it is dizzying. It makes everything else seem small and far away."

"Your universe sounds very complex and large. I admire you for challenging it, but I think I prefer my smallness. Seeing the fish drinking the water of Aquarius is much more comforting to me than a grand vision."

"I can't ignore the grand vision," Sayer said, looking down at her with a sudden, easy smile. "But I'd like you to show me that fish."

Smiling back, Aramanda leaned closer to him, pointing upward. "It is there, just a bit to the left of—oh, look! A firefly!"

Indulging in the simple delight, she ran a few paces in its direction, waited until the tiny glow showed again, then gently caught it between her cupped hands.

"Look," she said, spinning about to show it to Sayer. "I thought it was too early for them, but somehow it has defied the impossible and is here."

"There's a lot of that going around lately."

"Is there?" Aramanda watched the small light wink on and off in the dark hollow of her hands. "I would catch them when I was a child and put them in a jar and take them to my room, much to Mama's dismay. I would sit in the darkness and watch them for a little while, then set them free out my window. I always thought of them as magic."

"Fairy lights," Sayer said, then gave her a sheepish, sideways smile when she glanced at him, brows raised. "That's what my mother used to call them."

"You did not believe it, of course."

"Of course not. Well . . . most of the time I didn't."

"I promise not to tarnish your rough-and-hardened image by revealing your secret belief in magic and mystical creatures of the night," Aramanda said, trying to appear serious and failing miserably when Sayer started to laugh.

"My so-called image is so battered and bruised, I don't think even that revelation could do much harm at this point. It might even help."

"Oh, I am certain Jack O'Keefe would be impressed. He could then say you were mad, as well as misguided and led astray by me."

"Mad, misguided, and led astray—at least no one can say I'm boring."

"No, never that."

"I won't ask whether you mean that as a compliment. By the way, where are you leading me?"

Aramanda glanced again at the small light in her hands. "Wherever your dreams take us."

"Not mine," Sayer said softly. He curved his hands around hers, looking into her eyes. "Give me your dreams and let me go with you."

"Then we will go together," she told him, and her words held all the portent of the moment and far beyond.

They continued to look at each other for a long, poignant silence. Then, opening her hands, Aramanda let the firefly wing away, carrying its diminutive glow toward the heavens.

"You see," she said, watching it go from them, "it is one small light, but it still shines among all the others."

"I see," Sayer murmured, yet when she turned to see if he followed the path of the firefly, she found him looking intently at her instead. "I see, very clearly, everything I want to see. Everything there is."

She could think of no reply, could only stare mutely at him, feeling a tenderness that was filled with both laughter and tears.

He seemed to understand and, saying nothing, moved behind her and encircled her in his arms, standing with her under the silent splendor of the heavens, looking for winged horses in the infinity of stars.

* * *

Sayer poked at the fire, sending up a shower of sparks inside the open, stone fireplace as he rearranged the burning logs. Moving a little way from the hearth, he stretched his legs out to the fire, propping himself on his elbows beside Aramanda.

"Not bad, if I say so myself," he said, admiring his effort.

"You do that very well," Aramanda agreed. Sitting on the thick woolen rug, her knees drawn to her chin, she darted him a teasing glance. "It is too bad I cannot say the same of your culinary skills."

Sayer leaned his head back to look up at her. "They're not that bad."

"They are not that good. Galen was right; you are a terrible cook," she said, laughing at his pained grimace. "You have quite mastered the art of getting too near the fire."

"There's never a microwave around when you need it," he muttered.

"A what?"

"Never mind. I just need more practice, that's all."

"Not when I must eat it," Aramanda said, holding up her hand in mock horror. "From now on, I am not letting you near a fire unless it is to start one."

"Dangerous words, my lady," he murmured. Rolling to one side, he reached out and twined a long strand of her hair around his fingers, slowly letting it loose so that the copper color flamed in the flickering glow of the firelight. "I might be tempted to prove to you just how adept I am at that particular skill."

The essence of his touch, fiery and intoxicating, trembled through her blood like the first innocent taste of heady wine.

"Do not make me idle promises, Roarke. I might be tempted to ask you to fulfill them."

"Would you?"

Their gazes caught and clashed, flame and blue night.

"Yes."

Her softly spoken reply, simple and certain, momentarily left Sayer without words.

Inexplicably, for the first time since he'd been thrust into her reality, he felt balanced, sure of what he wanted and why he was here. He was no longer playing a role. He was Roarke to her, for her, because of her; and here, now, in this time and place, there was nothing else he wanted to be.

"Do you believe in destiny?" he asked, catching a look of surprise on her face. "Not just fate, but something that follows you, that compels you to believe things you wouldn't otherwise rationally consider."

Aramanda tipped her head to one side to look at him fully. "It is a strange question to ask. I never suspected you sat about all those evenings at Tansie's tavern contemplating destiny. What is wrong?" she asked, when he rolled back on both elbows, staring into the fire, his expression brooding.

"I am sorry. I did not mean to make light of it. It is simply so unlike you to say such things. I am not quite certain how to answer."

"I'm not quite sure myself," he said. Sitting up, he brushed the back of his hand against her cheek, giving her a small smile. "It doesn't matter. I'm just rambling. I get this way late at night when I've been on the run for too many weeks without cream in my tea."

"It does matter," Aramanda told him softly. "You are speaking of us—"

His eyes snapped to hers.

"Are you not?"

"Is that what you feel?"

"It is what I know." She paused, fighting a brief battle with a hesitancy to speak her true feelings, then said, "If you had asked me a month ago whether I believed in destiny, a lover's destiny, a destiny of souls, I would have told you *no* and believed that to be true. But from the first moment we have been together, even before, I have felt connected to you—"

"—against every odd."

"It is an unlikely alliance."

"The Montclair princess and the black knight of the coal mines? We want the same thing, though."

"Yes . . ."

To love each other, she nearly said, but left the words unspoken. "It seems impossible, and yet . . . my mother told me something once. She said, 'Love is eternal when because of it, you are willing to believe what cannot be believed.' Perhaps that is the meaning of your destiny."

"Maybe it is." Sliding one hand into the hair at her nape and the other around her waist, he drew her unresisting form into his embrace.

His arms held her to him, but it was the intent expression in his eyes that held her prisoner, making her feel he had never and would never again look at another woman but her this way. "Maybe I've been looking ahead for something that's been here with me all the time."

Aramanda lost her breath when he bent and kissed her, slowly, deeply, evoking the feeling of souls meeting. Every other emotion she had ever known was a whisper in the great shout of joy and passion that burst inside her.

She leaned into him, liking the feel of his hardness pressed against her, shocked at the depth and surrender of her own response, then realizing how little convention and all things proper mattered between them. All that did matter was that she wanted this, needed him.

The taste of her abandon, wild and sweet, blinded Sayer to the time, the place they were in. Everything in him remembered the last time he had held her like this and, for an instant, made him forget she was an innocent in this reality and they, only lovers in heart and soul.

Lowering her gently to the rug, he bent over her, teasing the curve of her neck and throat with light kisses, making her silent promises he had every intention of keeping.

"Roarke . . ." she whispered his name like the answer to a prayer, and he pulled back to look at her.

"All these weeks," he murmured, close enough that the words brushed her mouth. "All these weeks you've been an arm's length away, driving me crazy with wanting to touch you, to hold you, to see you like this. It's been too long, more than one lifetime too long, when all I've had is dreams. I don't need dreams anymore. You're more perfect than any dream could ever be. All I need is you, here with me."

He kissed her again, the hunger alive inside him, and Aramanda shuddered as the echo of its power swept through her like thunder.

Part of her reveled in the deep-reaching, intimate emotion, the part that knew him without words and wanted him to take her to the farthest boundary of this feeling and beyond.

But the intensity of it also frightened her. She had never felt passion for a man; and now to have it come all at once, the hunger of desire and all it demanded, without mercy or warning, overwhelmed her and made her feel lost.

The conflict between fear and need made her tremble, hesitate; and after a few moments, Sayer broke off his heated caress to look into her eyes.

"What is it?" he asked gently, concern for her taming the ravening desire in his eyes, his touch. He brushed away an errant strand of auburn clinging to her cheek, a slight tremble in his hand.

"I . . . I am afraid," she whispered, not able to meet his straightforward gaze because she could still see the passion there, waiting to be unleashed again with the merest touch from her. "You make me feel things I don't understand. I want to feel them; I want . . . this, with you, only you. But it is . . . too soon. There are so many things between us still. Roarke . . ."

She looked at him, tears blurring her vision. "I am sorry, I—"

"Don't be sorry. Don't ever be sorry." Pulling upright, bringing her with him, Sayer gathered her into his arms, rocking her against his heart. "I'm the one who should be sorry. I tried to make you feel things you're not ready for, I wanted to make you remember—"

"Remember? How could I?"

"It doesn't matter. None of it matters anymore."

"Roarke . . ." Aramanda wanted to press him, make him explain his strange twist of mood, the odd questions he'd posed to her today. But sensing a turmoil in him, she let it be, offering solace instead.

"We have time," she told him gently. "We have time to be together, time for me to trust what I feel for you in my heart. Please, allow me that."

"I'll allow you anything," Sayer said. Grazing a kiss against her temple, he buried his face in her hair, holding her tightly as if the feelings of the moment were the last they would share together.

"But there isn't any time for us. There's only forever. And sometimes I'm afraid that might not be long enough."

The first streaks of sunlight woke Aramanda the next morning. Burrowing deeper into the warmth of the quilt, she tried in vain to pretend it wasn't real. Though hard and lumpy in places, the bed was still a real bed, and she was loath to leave it.

In the end, though, the smell of fresh-made coffee wafting into the tiny bedroom persuaded her to brave the chilly air and find her way into the main room.

Wrapped in her quilt, she rubbed at her eyes, nearly bumping into Sayer as he started through the doorway between the rooms the same time she did.

"Good morning," he said, smiling and holding out a cup.

"Mmmm. Is that for me?" Not waiting for a reply, she took the cup and tried a tentative sip, sighing as the hot, sweet liquid slid down her throat. "That is nice."

"Come over here and sit by the fire," Sayer encouraged, gently steering her in the right direction. "Who knows? With a few cups of coffee and a little warmth, you might be able to open your eyes enough to see."

"Have I told you I detest clever people in the morning?"

"Yes, indeed, as cheerful as ever. And yes, you've told me twenty-five times, to be exact. That's how many mornings we've been through this routine. Try this chair," he said when she shot him an annoyed glare. "I can vouch for its being the most comfortable of the lot."

"You look as if you'd slept in it," Aramanda muttered, taking in his day-old beard, ruffled hair, and rumpled clothes with a sleepy, half-interested glance. Drawing her legs up under her as she curled into the chair, she laid her cheek against the rough upholstery, and his scent mingled with the blended aroma of coffee and woodsmoke.

"I did. It was either that or the floor."

"Oh, I am sorry. I should have—"

"No. You shouldn't have. Trust me." Walking over to the stove, he poured out another cup of coffee, grimacing after the first drink. "I hate this stuff. I am beginning to give up hope of ever getting a decent cup of tea again."

The cup in one hand, he took another drink and began unbuttoning his shirt with the other.

Wakefulness hit Aramanda hard and fast. "What are you doing?"

Sayer paused with the cup midway to his mouth. He glanced from side to side before looking back at her. "Drinking coffee?"

"No, not that. You cannot—are you planning to undress in here as well?"

"Would you like me to?"

"Of course not. I would prefer you—" The idle motion of his hand freeing another button from its slot arrested her words.

She ran the tip of her tongue over her lips, suddenly finding it difficult to recall exactly what it was she preferred him to do. The continued progress of his hand suggested several things and she flushed, resisting the urge to shift in the chair.

"Yes?" He finished with the last button, and his shirt hung open. "What would you prefer?"

"That you dress elsewhere." Aramanda tried to look anywhere but at him.

He lifted a hand and combed his fingers through his hair, and the supple motion drew her eyes back again. He smiled, and his eyes told her he knew every wicked thought she had about seeing him without a shirt at all.

"See something you like?"

"You are too certain of yourself. And you do not have to do that here. It—it is not . . . it is not—"

"It isn't what?"

"Stop that. And do not ask me what," she warned, seeing the start of a smirk play with the corner of his mouth. "You are doing that deliberately. You know I cannot match wits with you so early in the morning, and you've shamelessly taken advantage of that every day we have been together."

"Sorry," he said with an unrepentant grin. Walking over to where she sat, he took the chair opposite her, stretching his legs out in a comfortable slouch. "You make it too easy for me."

"For someone so clever, I should think you could invent a better excuse for yourself." Aramanda wrapped the quilt more snugly around her, deliberately turning her attention to her coffee mug.

"When is your meeting with the miners?" she asked to divert the conversation and her own wanton musings.

"At one, just after the noon break." Sayer stared at the fire, running the tip of his forefinger around the lip of his mug. "I've been thinking."

"That is dangerous."

He ignored her quip, and Aramanda saw the light humor in his eyes replaced by a familiar, focused intensity. "We'd get a lot further with this if we had someone in government working for us. Even if I succeed in rallying the miners behind the cause of organized labor, we won't get far without the laws to back us up."

"That will be difficult. You could resort to bribery and blackmail; I know it is often done. But there would be considerable risk in it, even if you had the resources to adequately line the right pockets. Money does not always buy loyalty. Otherwise, you would need someone of influence to speak on your behalf, to encourage others to listen to your ideas."

"I know that." Sayer looked at her.

"You cannot think that I have any influence," Aramanda said, startled. "You saw how Gervase thinks of me, and of any woman who attempts to have a hand in business. And Gervase is certainly not going to have even a single good word for your cause."

"I wasn't thinking of either you or your uncle." He hesitated, searching her face, then said, "But your mother does have influence. She owns the controlling share in the Montclair collieries. And the Montclair mines are the largest and most extensive and lucrative in the state. Her voice would get heard. She could convince someone to hear me."

"And you believe I can convince her to speak for you," Aramanda said flatly, not asking a question.

"You might, but I only want the chance to try and convince her myself. If I go back alone, I might as well put that rope around my neck myself. You're the only one who can give me a chance."

Aramanda stared at him, then turned her gaze to the fire.

"I do not know," she said at last. "In helping you, my mother would risk what position she has, and Gervase would surely do his best to see that my family suffered for it."

"Would it be any worse if she married him?"

"I cannot answer that. Neither alternative seems acceptable, and yet . . . I know I cannot stay with you like this forever, running, hiding, pretending."

In a swift motion, Sayer put his cup on the floor and moved out of his chair. Bending on one knee beside her, he laid her cup aside and took her hands in his.

"You don't have to decide now. Just think about it. That's all I ask."

"Roarke . . ." Aramanda drew in a long breath, never more strongly feeling the forces that divided them.

Then she looked into his eyes and saw the hope and the determination and the warmth there and wondered at how Roarke Macnair could make her believe in the impossible.

"I will think about it," she said softly. "I will for you, because if anyone can convince my mother and the coal miners to become the unlikeliest of allies, it is you, Roarke."

"I can't do it without you," he said, his hold on her hands tightening. "You're the reason I've gotten this far. If it's going to work, it'll be because we'll have done it together. Trust me on that one."

"I want to trust you—"

"No. Don't say it." Letting go her hands, Sayer got to his feet, looking down at her, his expression troubled. "I need your trust; but if I can't have it, I will let you go. I don't want you to be hurt. I want to make sure that, this time, you get the chance to have the love and family of your dreams. That's one thing I won't sacrifice, no matter what happens."

Before she could ask him what he meant, Sayer turned and walked into the bedroom, closing the door between them.

Aramanda shivered, though the room was warm, struck by the inexplicable and disturbing sensation that Roarke knew how their adventure would end long before it began.

Nineteen

A thin, persistent cloud cover hid what warmth the afternoon sun might have shed through the blue-and-black shadow of the cavernous mine looming at Aramanda's back.

Damp and chilly, this day was surely the harbinger of a cold, wet night ahead. She sat atop a discarded wheelbarrow turned upside down amid discarded timbers, tools, and piles of lumber as far away from the noise of the massive coal breaker as possible, waiting in the yard at the mine where Roarke had just finished another speech. She watched him as he answered a few more of the miners' questions.

The yard, usually bustling with activity, lay silent. No steam engine whistled; no mine cars climbed the slope; no cages moved in the shaft—the pump house engine stopped. The blacksmith's, machine's and carpenter's shops had closed for the day. The saw-mill engine had ceased its constant wail. She hadn't seen any sign of the manager and clerk inside the colliery office the entire day.

How many hours had she spent like this, watching him? Enough to recognize the admiration and eagerness on the sooty faces gathered around his tall, commanding figure.

With the power of his voice and the strength of his convictions, Roarke gave the miners something they'd long been denied—hope. Many, she knew, would be ready to lay down their lives for him, simply because he had the ability to imbue them with faith in their shared cause.

Hugging her worn shawl to her shoulders, Aramanda let her

thoughts drift. She longed for a hot bath and the luxury of the cozy bed back at the cottage they'd shared the night before. And she wondered what lay ahead.

Sayer had nearly finished his tour of all of the collieries in Schuylkill County, with only one, maybe two left to visit. She marveled at how consistently he'd managed to quell the men's skepticism and, with patience and respect for their concerns, finally win them over to begin to look at their circumstances from a new perspective.

As she looked back at him working his persuasive magic now, it struck her that Roarke Macnair, her Roarke Macnair, was making history.

When the crowd of miners around him began to break up and head back into the mine, she bent to lift the hem of her skirts above the black, muddy earth. As she did, the sound of a horse drew her attention to the front gate.

A tall figure on a gray stallion, a hooded cloak drawn low to hide a face, flew into the front yard straight toward Roarke.

An instinctive terror, born of the constant threat that Gervase might catch up with them any day without warning, lurched ahead of her reason.

She bolted headlong toward him, her boots catching in the thick mud. "Roarke! The rider!"

The horse stomped and reared as the rider pulled him to a sliding halt at Sayer's side.

Aramanda's heart throbbed wildly. Gervase had traced them here, and he would not be merciful.

"No!" She struggled against the heavy mud clinging to her feet and dragging her to a snail's pace.

The rider tossed the hood from his face and turned toward her. His face, dearly familiar, creased with regret at frightening her. "Aramanda—it's all right."

"Liam?" Aramanda stared at him in disbelief, momentarily struck dumb. Then she breathed a sigh and felt suddenly foolish for letting her imagination jump to conclusions.

"Thank heaven it is you," she whispered. Relief washed over

her like summer rain, yet the threat of Gervase lingered, like storm clouds on the horizon.

"Liam!"

Sayer strode forward to greet the other man, the smile of greeting quickly overshadowed with a concerned frown. "You shouldn't have taken the risk of coming here," he said, holding the horse's reins while Liam swung down. The frown became a scowl when he saw the purpling bruise on Liam's cheekbone. "What happened?"

Liam ignored the question. "I had to come."

Reaching them, Aramanda gave Liam a quick embrace which he returned with awkward affection. "I am so pleased it is you. I thought Gervase had discovered us." She, too, saw the mark of a fight on Liam's face and started. "But what—"

"He will soon enough," Liam said, his face hard. "Montclair knows all you've been doing, and he's in a fine rage over it. The only reason he's not come after you himself is the trouble at home. Montclair's had to use nearly every man in the county to keep watch and try to stop the violence."

Liam paused and looked Sayer square in the eyes. "But your devil's luck won't hold forever."

A few of the miners Sayer had been speaking to turned to look at them curiously. Sayer, catching their stares, motioned Liam to step aside out of hearing range.

He laid a hand on Liam's shoulder. "What's been going on at Montclair's mines?"

Liam tensed, but he made no move to break Sayer's hold. "Jack's been a busy lad. There've been more accidents at the mines than ever before, and he's blown two shipments off the track and killed another engineer. Some of your men have left because of O'Keefe's threats. He's never forgiven you for becoming the leader he wanted to be. He'll be bringing trouble to you, and he's not shy about saying it."

"Let him. I have to finish it sometime."

"You'll finish it, all right, brother," Liam said harshly. He pulled away from Sayer, taking a few steps, then turning back. His eyes burned with a fire Aramanda had never seen in her friend before. "Montclair's been blaming you for all O'Keefe's done. And since you aren't there, Montclair is taking his anger out on me and my family."

"Damn him." Sayer raked his fingers through his hair, frustration and fury darkening his face. He held out a hand to Liam. "How?"

"Bridget, the children, are they—" Aramanda left the words unsaid for fear that speaking them would make fearful speculation the truth.

Liam nodded. "They're safe. For now. I've had to leave the boys with neighbors because Montclair sends his ruffians to pound on my doors in the middle of the night. They've broken windows and put the fear of the devil in Bridget. Two nights ago, two of them came into the house and got the better of me." He touched the bruise. "That's when I decided to find you."

Sayer paced. "Bridget, the boys, are they safe with you away?"

"As safe as they can be," Liam told him, "with or without me there."

"You are risking much simply by being here," Aramanda said. "Surely Gervase will know if you are not at work in the mines."

"He knows all right," Liam said with a bitter laugh. "Two days ago, he told me I no longer work for him. And with the Macnair reputation, I doubt I'll find work at any of the other mines within a hundred miles of here."

"Liam . . ." Aramanda gently laid her hand on Liam's arm. She looked at Sayer, tears welling in her eyes. She could see from the hot anger in his that he knew as well as she that Liam and Bridget and their children could not survive if Liam had no work.

"We must do something," she told Sayer. "We must."

"Don't you think I know that?" he shot back.

"We cannot let Gervase do this. It will not end with Liam. Gervase will make all the families suffer until he has his revenge on you."

"If you're trying to convince me, save your breath," Sayer told her, and the expression on his face made Aramanda regret her impulsive words.

She had betrayed him with her implication that she did not

trust him to put his family and the needs of the other mining families above his cause. He looked at her in silence, and she saw the pain and bleak knowledge of her betrayal on his face slowly masked by a chill, hard resolve.

Taking a step toward him, Aramanda lifted her hand to touch him, but Sayer deliberately shifted out of her reach, looking at Liam. "I'll stop it. I'll give Montclair what he wants. I'm going back."

"You—" Aramanda burst out before Liam could reply. "You cannot go back! Gervase will see you hanged, and then there will be no one to stop this madness."

Sayer smiled without warmth, and a brutal fury rose in his eyes. "You've been telling me all along I've caused this madness. You should be pleased I've decided to end it the only way possible."

"It is not the only way." Aramanda cried. His anger did not frighten her, his coldness did. Roarke would not suffer betrayal lightly. "You have shown me it is not the only way."

"Have I?"

"Roarke—"

"Aramanda is right, Roarke," Liam put in. "Montclair only's done what he has because he wants you."

"You've never wanted any part of my fight, though," Sayer said. "You've been forced into the worst of it because we share a name. But no longer."

Sayer paused, then said, "There's a colliery just north of Fountain Springs, a good operation where the foreman needs another experienced man or two and the wages are fair. I put in a word for you while I was there; he'll remember me. It's two days' ride from here. You could take Bridget and the kids in the morning and be a good way there before afternoon."

"It would be best," Aramanda said. She wanted to reach out to Sayer and take his hand, to tell him how much his gesture touched her, but the wall she had put between them stopped her. "I will lend you my cart. If you stay, it will be difficult to make anyone believe you do not support Roarke and his cause."

"Then I'll make it easy for them to believe I do." Liam straightened his stance, looking at his brother with the straightforward resolution Aramanda knew well in Roarke. "I'm staying. I'm with you, in whatever you decide to do."

"You don't owe me anything."

"Maybe not. But I'm staying just the same. It wasn't until I saw my family threatened that I realized what it is you've been trying to do. And how important it is." He held out his hand to Sayer. "It's time we stood together."

The expression on Sayer's face brought tears to Aramanda's eyes. Sayer grasped Liam's outstretched hand in a tight grip and, in that moment, Aramanda felt most strongly that all of them had left their past lives behind and committed irrevocably to whatever future tomorrow would create.

And she now knew what it was she had to do.

"I will go back."

Both Sayer and Liam stared at her in disbelief.

"Are you crazy, woman?" Liam said. "Do you think Gervase is going to forgive and forget just because you're his niece?"

"I do not care what Gervase thinks of me. I will go back and talk to Mama, persuade her to help Roarke. She has powerful friends, far more powerful than my uncle."

Aramanda took her courage in her hands and appealed to Roarke with her eyes. "You wished me to convince her to aid the miners. I will do all I can to do so."

Sayer looked hard at her, locked in a long, silent battle of wills and logic. "Is that what you want?" he asked finally.

Aramanda lifted her chin. "Yes."

"It could work, Roarke," Liam said. "There would be no harm in letting her try. I'm going back with you, so we can both keep a lookout for trouble."

For a moment, Aramanda thought Roarke would refuse, force her to stay. A conflict of emotion crossed his face—anger, doubt, worry—finally giving way to a hard-won concession.

"I won't travel with you, then," Sayer said at last, the words sounding as if he forced them out around his feelings. "My presence would put you at far greater risk. But I'll be close behind. I'll finish my work here today, then take another route back tomorrow. That should help protect the two of you. I'll wait at the estate we stayed in that first night for word from you."

His jaw tightened and tension rippled through him. "But if it isn't quick to come, then I'm coming back, Gervase Montclair be damned."

"Gervase Montclair be damned anyway," Liam said. He gripped Sayer's arm, a promise in his eyes. "I'll keep her safe."

Sayer returned the clasp. "And yourself. I'm counting on it."

"Godspeed to you then, Brother."

"And to you," Sayer said, turning to Aramanda as Liam cast her a quick, knowing glance, then retreated to lead his horse in search of water before the return to Schuylkill.

Aramanda slowly looked up at Sayer, not certain what she would find in his eyes. "I suppose it is settled. I do not need to return to the cottage and—"

As though he hadn't even heard her words, Sayer pulled her into his arms. Bending to her, holding her with a hand twisted in her hair, he kissed her hard and long, passion and desperation and pain all mixed in his touch.

Just as suddenly, he released her. Taking a few strides back, he shoved both hands through his hair, his breathing fast and ragged.

Aramanda stood where he had left her, trembling, pale. Slowly, she reached up and touched her lips, tasting him there.

"Why are you doing this?" Sayer asked finally, his voice harsh.

"Why are *you?*" she countered bravely. "You could flee now, continue to find allies for your cause without ever returning to confront Gervase."

"If I don't go back, I've lost the fight already. But you don't believe that, do you?"

"I believe," Aramanda said softly. "I believe in you."

"I don't need lies," Sayer ground out. Fire flashed in his eyes. "Or is this charity on your part, comfort for a dead man?"

"Do not say that."

"Why? Because it's true?"

"No. This—this is the truth!"

Before he could stop her, Aramanda moved swiftly to him and pulled his mouth to hers.

There were no lies between them then, nothing but a fierce elemental need, and Aramanda willingly sacrificed her heart to its fire. It was truth and eternity, irrevocably binding them together no matter their differences or what forces tried to divide them.

When they at last parted, Sayer kept her in his arms, holding her close to his heart. Aramanda clung to him, feeling desperate and strong, lost and found.

"I did not mean to hurt you with words or what I have done or not done," Aramanda whispered. She lifted her face to his, tears like jewels on her skin. "I would never betray you. I do not want to be divided from you again."

"We won't lose each other again," Sayer said, taking her face between his hands. He kissed her once more, his breath catching on emotions too poignant and intense for words. "I swear it."

"I was wrong to ever believe you did not care," she whispered. "How could I have doubted when there is such tenderness in your strength?"

"I care. For you. Because of you." He looked into her eyes, and Aramanda sensed he wanted to tell her much more, some truth he carried alone. Instead, he gathered her against him, holding her as if they had no tomorrows. "I can't lose you another time."

"Roarke . . ." Aramanda bit her lip to keep from crying, flooded with emotions so deep and true she could only hold tightly to him and let the feelings speak for her heart. "We will not lose each other. I only wish we could return together. I feel . . . uneasy . . . at the thought of being separated from you now."

She shivered, a nameless cold touching her deep inside. Why did this time with him seem too infinitely precious, as if they had few moments left to be together?

"I'll be there soon, my love. Don't worry," Sayer murmured,

holding her as if neither heaven nor hell could ever part them. "Soon it will all be over."

The next morning, after a grueling all-night flight on a borrowed horse, Aramanda convinced Liam to part with her at the foot of the wood behind the Montclair estate.

There she waited, shivering in the dawn chill, until she'd watched Gervase's carriage ponderously wind its way down the long drive leading from the coach house to the main road, taking Gervase for his usual morning tour of the collieries.

As soon as the carriage had safely left the grounds, Aramanda tugged up her damp skirts and made her way through the back gardens to the servants' entrance. Cook—surprised, anxious, overjoyed to see her—let her inside and shooed aside her explanations in favor of getting Aramanda into a hot bath and clean clothing.

An hour later, fortified with tea and fussing, Aramanda went in search of her mother.

She found Cordelia in the sitting room in a chair by the window, staring sightlessly over the front grounds.

The sight of her, sorrow in the slumping of her shoulders and the paleness of her face, flooded Aramanda with guilt.

She had caused her mother's distress. And she would be the one to end it—only to cause it anew when she confessed the reason for her return.

Drawing in a long breath, Aramanda straightened her shoulders and walked to her mother's side, laying a gentle hand on Cordelia's shoulder.

"Mama, I am home," she said quietly.

Cordelia started, her eyes jerking to Aramanda. She stared as if she could not believe the evidence of her senses, then hurried to her feet, throwing her arms around her daughter.

"Oh, Aramanda! Thank God!" Her tears wet Aramanda's shoulder. "I feared the worst. Gervase told us . . . I believed that madman had—" She broke off, trembling.

Aramanda held her mother, soothing her with soft murmurs and reassurances, then gently drew back. "I am fine, Mama. And Roarke Macnair is no madman. He is—"

Cordelia frowned. "Yes? What is he, Aramanda?"

"He is—" Aramanda hesitated, but she knew with an unshakable certainty what was in her heart. She looked back steadily at her mother. "He is the man I love."

"You do not know what you are saying!" Cordelia shook her head in violent denial. "My God, I have dreaded this since the day I was told you were missing from us. This cannot—must not be! He is an uneducated ruffian bent on destroying us. What sort of life could you hope for with a man such as that?"

"A life I have dreamed of," Aramanda said, passion in her voice, "with someone who accepts all I am and loves me because of it, not in spite of it."

"Aramanda, please," Cordelia began.

"It is the truth, Mama," Aramanda broke in, taking Cordelia's hands in hers, determined to convince her, "and nothing you can say will change what is in my heart. Roarke does not mean to destroy us. He only wants peace between us."

Cordelia shook her head. She stepped back from her daughter, her hands clenching and unclenching in front of her. "I find this all quite difficult to believe."

"You must believe me. Roarke wants change, not violence."

Cordelia pulled a kerchief from her skirt pocket and quickly dabbed her eyes. Aramanda saw the familiar stoic facade begin to overcome the outburst of emotion.

"You must tell me one thing, Aramanda, and truthfully. I will know if you are lying." She looked hard at her daughter. "Did Roarke Macnair take advantage of your innocence?"

Aramanda struggled with her conscience. She knew what her mother was asking; and in one sense, she supposed she should admit to their intimacy.

And yet, Roarke had never taken advantage of her. Though he easily could have, and from the way he looked at her, the way he touched her, she knew he wanted her with an undeniable hunger. And she had, on more than one occasion, given him every opportunity to make her his lover.

But he had gently resisted, knowing better than she perhaps, the doubts lingering in her heart.

"No," Aramanda said at last. "He treated me well—gently and with kindness." Her reply fell short of the truth, but Aramanda could not bring herself to give her mother any other response.

She faced Cordelia with unflinching directness. "I chose to stay with him. I could have returned to you, but I chose to stay with Roarke. I love him with all that I am."

And I want the opportunity to tell him that I want us to be together always.

"I see." Cordelia stared at her daughter, and a tiny frown came between her eyes. "It appears your heart has made your decision for you. I always knew one day that you, of all my children, would give your love to someone completely and forever, without thought of suitability or propriety."

"I will never be all you want me to be, Mama," Aramanda said. "And I cannot regret it."

"No, you will never be all I want, Aramanda," Cordelia said. She sighed, her face unhappy, worried. She walked to the window and looked out, unseeing.

"I am sorry I have disappointed you, Mama," Aramanda said quietly. "But I am not sorry for what I am."

"No . . ." Turning back to look at her, Cordelia gave a small smile. "You are so much like your father, Aramanda: Stubborn and passionate and so quick to decide with your heart instead of your reason. Despite all society demands, you are determined to be something opposite. Your father found his happiness that way."

"And I will as well."

Cordelia half raised a hand to her, then shook her head. "Perhaps. I hope for your sake it is true, Aramanda. Of all my children I fear for you the most, that your heart will rush you headlong into disaster."

Aramanda caught her lower lip in her teeth and tried to find words of comfort to offer her mother. "I am not as blind as that."

"That is what your father told me again and again, right up to the winter night he spent helping to rescue two miners from a collapsed tunnel. He caught a fever and died less than a week from that night. His charity cost him his life. Do not make me the usual defense of him," Cordelia said, holding up a hand as Aramanda started to speak. "You were only eleven when he died, too young for him to have shown you all the miseries of the miners' life, to have forced you to know there was such wretchedness in the world."

"Yet I do know it, and I cannot ignore it."

"So I have come to realize," Cordelia said softly. Reaching out, she took Aramanda's hand again. "Come, sit with me and tell me what you have involved yourself in now. And Aramanda," she added with an expression that allowed for no half-truths, "I wish to hear the *whole* story."

Smiling, Aramanda settled on the couch nearest the fire, beside Cordelia, and began to relate her months of adventures and, most importantly, Roarke's plan.

"There are many difficulties with such a plan, Aramanda," Cordelia said at last when Aramanda had finished and was looking at her expectantly with a fearful hope.

"I know," Aramanda admitted. "But I see no other way to end the violence and suffering." She drew a deep breath and asked the question she both dreaded and wanted answered. "Will you help us?"

Cordelia hesitated. Then she lifted her chin. "Your father asked me to do so many times and I refused. It was always between us, to his death. I will not let it come between you and me, my daughter. Besides—" She smiled. "—I see your Mr. Macnair has encouraged you to be stubborn. I fear if I do not say *yes,* you will only disappear again, leaving me to fret over you."

"I confess that would be true. Oh, Mama—" Aramanda impulsively put her arms around her mother and hugged her close. "—I will never be able to tell you how much this means to me. And to Roarke."

"Then do not try." Cordelia straightened. "I will contact the one man I believe can help and arrange a meeting as soon as possible. It would be best if it were here—"

"But if Gervase were to discover it . . . we will have to arrange the meeting when we know he will not interrupt."

Cordelia raised a brow. "That, my darling," she said, touching Aramanda's hand, "is our biggest problem."

Two days later, Aramanda, Cordelia, and Cordelia's guest waited in the drawing room at the Montclair estate, Cordelia sitting in her chair, her hands gripped together in her lap, her mouth a set line.

"Roarke will be here, Mama. Do not fret. Scully assured me he had found him and given him the date and time to meet us."

Aramanda tried to put a confident assurance in her voice, no easy task since she was consumed with a restless anxiety.

She stole a nervous glance at the thin, elegantly-dressed man her mother had convinced to come to listen to Roarke. He'd been waiting nearly a quarter of an hour already, making polite but increasingly strained conversation with them. Now he stood at the fireplace, rapping restless fingers against the cold marble mantle.

Please, Roarke, you must be here. This is our one chance to make a difference together.

"Aramanda, I really cannot impose upon Senator Rawling to wait much longer for Mr. Macnair," Cordelia said finally into the tense silence. "Besides the inconvenience, the longer we draw this out, the more chance we risk of Gervase's discovering this meeting."

She rose from the chair, and Aramanda steeled herself for a battle of wills; but as she did, the butler appeared in the double doorway.

"Madam, Mr. Macnair has arrived."

"Well, Hutchings, for heaven's sake send him in!"

Aramanda's heart began to beat in double time, those few seconds waiting to see him after so many days seeming like endless hours. When his tall, commanding figure appeared in the doorway, she caught her breath.

His eyes immediately found hers, and he held her gaze for an instant, his expression making her feel she and he were the only persons in the room.

"Roarke." Her lips silently formed his name, and he smiled, a warm, intimate gesture that went straight to her heart.

He wore a new suit, tailored to perfection to highlight broad shoulders that tapered to his slim waist and long, muscular legs. His dark hair, even the one stubborn wave that forever fell over his forehead, was combed away from his face, revealing the strong lines of his brow and jaw, as angular and aristocratic as any favored guest to cross the Montclair threshold.

Aramanda felt a rush of pride as she glanced to her mother and found her staring in surprise and even admiration.

When she turned back to him, their eyes locked again. Without a spoken word, she told him of her fears over the past days, her longing for him, her hopes for this meeting, her prayers for their tomorrows.

Sayer's expression softened, his smile easy and assured. The simple gesture soothed her snapping nerves like a magic balm. She felt every fiber of her being imbued with vital confidence.

Trust me.

Though he had not spoken the words, Aramanda heard them with her heart.

A smile still playing with his mouth, Sayer turned to the others. "Good morning." His deep voice filled the room with the dignity of a man to the manor born. Crossing the carpet to Aramanda's mother, he bowed. "My thanks can't be adequate for what you have done—and risked—Mrs. Montclair."

A warm color rushed into Cordelia's cheeks, but she managed to keep her bearing. "Aramanda has made it clear that we—I— have a responsibility to the mining families. I have come to believe her."

She turned to her other guest. "Senator Rawling, may I present Mr. Roarke Macnair."

"Good day, Mr. Macnair. Shall we begin? I'm afraid my schedule is rather full today, and I believe you have much to tell me."

"I do," Sayer answered. "I've been waiting a long time for this."

With a slight nod of approval to Aramanda, Cordelia turned to the waiting butler.

"Close the door, Hutchings. We are not to be disturbed, by anyone."

More than three hours passed before Sayer shoved open the heavy pocket doors. "Then I have your support in organizing the miners to stop work?"

Senator Rawling, a smile in place of the worried frown he'd shown before the meeting, extended a hand. "Indeed, you do. I shall speak with my associates on your behalf, Mr. Macnair. And may I say it has been an honor to meet a man who, in his thinking, is truly ahead of his time."

Sayer's hand jerked, but he recovered quickly. "I offer you gratitude on behalf of the miners. And again to you, Mrs. Montclair," he added, looking to Cordelia.

She smiled, a new softness in her eyes. "Your thanks should be for my daughter, Mr. Macnair."

"I intend to thank her," Sayer said. His eyes slid to Aramanda, and she blushed at the intense warmth there. "Extensively."

Sayer smiled and stepped closer to Aramanda, taking her hand in his and brushing a chaste kiss over the back of it. His mouth lingered against her skin a fraction of a second longer than convention allowed.

"A demain," he whispered, then with a nod to Cordelia, followed Senator Rawling to the front door.

Aramanda's gaze stayed with every graceful motion of his body until the doors to the drawing room blocked him from her view.

"A demain . . . It sounds so lovely."

"Until tomorrow." Cordelia frowned. "I have the impression

he did not mean that in a literal sense, although I cannot tell you why."

"I—I do not know." With a shift of her shoulders, Aramanda tried to throw off the sudden, fearful sense of panic that had no cause. "Perhaps he was speaking of forever."

"Forever?" Cordelia gave a light laugh, brushing a kiss against Aramanda's hair. "You are truly in love, my darling. The only *forever* is in your heart."

The phrase struck Aramanda strangely. It seemed she had heard the words before, an echo in her memory.

Yet they slipped away like elusive spirits, leaving behind only the feeling that their meaning was of vital importance to her and to Roarke.

She turned to ask her mother her impression of the meeting between Roarke and Senator Rawling; but before she could utter the words, the rear door that led to the stables burst open.

Both women started. Aramanda exchanged a frightened glance with Cordelia.

"Gervase!" Cordelia breathed.

"That's right, my dear Aunt Cordelia." A taunt slid down the banister, echoing into the foyer. "And I'm looking forward to telling my father every detail of your intimate *tête à tête* with the man who wishes to destroy him."

"I should have known if anyone would betray us it would be you, Patricia," Aramanda said, refusing to be cowed as her cousin began a slow, predatory descent down the magnificent stairway.

"When did you arrive, Patricia? The house party was to have lasted another week." Cordelia spoke up, although she had paled, and Aramanda saw her hands clench at her side.

Patricia waved a languid hand. "They bored me to distraction. When I heard my dear cousin had returned, I knew things would be much more exciting here, so I had a friend lend me a carriage to bring me back early this morning. And just in time, it seems." Her face hardened. "Had I waited, I would have missed witnessing your conspiracy against my father."

"Conspiracy?" Gervase growled from the doorway. "What conspiracy, Patricia?"

"The conspiracy between Aramanda, Aunt Cordelia, and Roarke Macnair, Father," Patricia said before either Cordelia or Aramanda could stop her.

"Macnair!"

"They have betrayed you, Father," Patricia said, her eyes narrowing as she looked from Cordelia to Aramanda, then back at her father. "Roarke Macnair was here. I saw him come and go. He met with them and Senator Rawling. They spent hours cloistered in the drawing room."

Aramanda watched the fire rise in her uncle's face, staining it an angry red, and she feared for her mother's safety.

"It was my doing," she spoke up, taking a step in front of Cordelia. "I called the meeting and brought Roarke here. I alone am to blame for the deception. And I do not regret it."

"No." A slender hand wrapped firmly about hers, and Cordelia moved to stand by her side. "That is not true, Gervase. Aramanda is only trying to protect me."

Gervase strode to them, his body rigid with fury.

Aramanda braced herself, refusing to leave her mother's side, refusing to back down from him. She felt her mother stiffen beside her.

"You—the pair of you think you can betray me and I will do nothing! I'll see you, Cordelia, and all your brats on the streets for this. And I will see you in hell with your bastard lover."

Before either woman could move, Gervase struck Aramanda full across the face with his palm.

The raging blow flung her back, baring her mother to his second assault. His blow caught Cordelia against the temple, flinging her to the floor in a crumpled heap.

"That is enough, Father!" Patricia rushed to restrain him, her face white. For the first time ever, she looked frightened. "The servants will hear. Aramanda and Cordelia won't dare question your authority again."

Aramanda fell to her knees beside her mother. "Stay away from her!"

His face purple with rage, Gervase stood over them. His breath came harsh and fast.

Aramanda looked away from him to her mother. "Mama!" Very gently, she helped Cordelia to sit up. "Are you all right, Mama?"

"I am quite all right, Aramanda." With Aramanda's help, Cordelia rose shakily to her feet, and Aramanda saw her mother's expression change to a fury and determination she had never before seen. "He will not hurt me or any of my children ever again."

A flicker of suspicion came into Gervase's eyes. "You do not know what you are saying."

Though her silvery hair had come loose, spilling against the angry bruise forming at her temple, Cordelia faced Gervase with dignity.

"I know exactly what I am saying. I want you out of my house within the hour. I own the controlling interest in the Montclair collieries and I am using it to take over our business. With Senator Rawling and others of influence behind me, I will have no difficulty in having you removed as manager."

"You have gone completely mad!" Gervase said, the color leaving his face.

"Father——" Patricia held out an imploring hand. "You cannot let her do this." She looked at Aramanda and Cordelia, her eyes wide. "Aunt Cordelia——"

"There is nothing you can say to me that would make me change my mind about either of you. You disgust me," Cordelia said, looking at the two of them as if they were rats she had discovered in her kitchen.

"I tried to be fair—if not for your sake, for the sake of your brother, my husband. I gave you every opportunity to become even part the man he was." She whisked away the hair falling over her bruise. "But you have proved you are not a man at all. So it is you, Gervase, who will live out your days in the streets."

"Now——" she turned to Patricia "——both of you get out of my house. And if you ever attempt to set foot on this property again, I shall have you arrested for trespassing."

The scowl on Gervase's face turned to vile rage. "You are a fool, just as my brother was . . . a fool who believed charity would win him more than demands. But I won't let you destroy this empire. I will fight you, Cordelia. This business is mine, damn you! Mine!"

"No, Gervase, it is mine." She glanced at Aramanda, and her chin lifted proudly. "Mine and my children's."

"You will regret this day; I will make certain of it."

"The only regret I have is trusting you to do what is fair and right."

"Right! You are a fool Cordelia," Gervase snarled. "It will take you weeks, months to overrule my authority—if you are ever able to do it at all. In that time, I am going to put an end to your meddling once and for all. And I'll put an end to Roarke Macnair as well! He is responsible for this, and I will make certain he pays with his life."

"It is too late for your threats," Aramanda told him. Her eyes hot, fists clenched, she confronted his anger with a bold defiance. "They mean nothing. Roarke is already telling the men to stop work for you, with Senator Rawling's blessing."

"Is he now? Well, then," he sneered, "if I can't have his neck, I'll take his brother's."

Aramanda stared at him, suddenly afraid.

"Ah, Aramanda, so your lover has not told you everything, then." Gervase's face creased in a parody of a smile. "Liam Macnair has been arrested. Lloyd has proved he was responsible for killing one of my engineers."

"Liam did nothing. You know he is innocent."

"He is as guilty as his brother," Gervase said. "And unless you choose to see your friend die at the end of a rope, you had best tell your lover to quit his plans against me."

"Liam is innocent! You know it." Ignoring her mother's restraining hand, she stepped closer to Gervase, trembling with fury. "I will not let you do this. Neither Roarke nor I will."

"Neither of you can stop me." Gervase took Aramanda's chin in a merciless grip. "That bastard you let turn you into a whore is a dead man. But you can tell Roarke Macnair his brother will be waiting in hell for him."

Twenty

A single lamp showed in the window of the church, a dim, diffused glow seeming to hang suspended in the gray evening fog. Aramanda ran the last few feet to the church and up the stone steps. Breathless, her hair falling loose around her face, she shoved open the door and rushed inside.

Father Creeghan waited at the entrance of the sanctuary, looking toward the altar. He turned, his face grave, as the draft of wind Aramanda brought in with her made a swift keening in the narrow space.

"You've come. I knew you would, once you heard—my Lord, child, what's happened to your face?"

Aramanda shook her head at his offer of sympathy. "It does not matter. Roarke—is he here? I have looked at the tavern, his house, everywhere else. I thought—"

"He's here," Father Creeghan said, glancing behind them. " 'Tis a devil's dilemma he's facing, to be sure. The miners need him, and yet with Liam facing the noose . . ." He looked directly at Aramanda. "There's little comfort I can offer him. I think you might do better at helping him."

"Not with comfort. I have none to give. For either of us." Quickly pressing Father Creeghan's hand, Aramanda drew a deep breath and walked down the aisle to where Sayer sat in the front pew, his head in his hands.

Not hesitating, she laid a hand on his shoulder. "Roarke?"

He looked up quickly, and Aramanda caught her breath at the

rage and devastation in his eyes, praying she would never be called upon to witness such a fury of emotion again.

Recognizing her, his face changed and he stared at her like a sinner looking at the open gates of heaven. "You came."

"Of course I did," she chided gently, both humbled and fiercely glad her presence meant so much to him. Sitting down beside him, she curved her hand around his. "Did you think I would not?"

Sayer looked back at the altar. "I don't know. I thought you would have tried to talk to your uncle, told him I was here. At least, I thought you would stay with your family." He paused, and there was pain in his voice when he added, "I didn't think you would come to me."

"It is no use talking to Gervase, even I have learned that much. And I would never betray you to him—"

"Not even to save Liam's life?"

She took her hand from his, his words making a cold place in her heart. "You thought I would? You thought I would compromise with Gervase before I came to you?"

"You'd give your life to your family, to the miners and their families. I didn't know how much you were willing to sacrifice this time." He looked at her again, his face and body tense as if he expected a sudden painful blow. "I—what happened?"

Sayer's eyes narrowed as he took in the bruise coloring her cheekbone. He brushed his fingertips over it with a tenderness completely at odds with the slow-burning anger kindling on his face.

"Montclair." He spat the name out like poison. "He did it. Didn't he?"

"It does not matter—not now. Roarke—"

Sayer slammed a fist down on the hard wood beside him, making her jump. He jerked to his feet, his hands clenching and unclenching at his side.

"It matters. It makes it a hundred times worse. I had convinced myself that killing that bastard wouldn't be worth the cost. Now, I'm ready to pay whatever price there is just to have the chance."

"Roarke, no." Aramanda moved hurriedly to his side, gripping his arm, forcing him to look at her. "That will not help Liam or any of us. There must be another answer."

"Then tell me what it is," he said harshly. "If I don't go through with the work stoppage tomorrow, nothing will ever change for the miners and their families. The injustice and the suffering will go on and likely get worse. But if I don't stop it, Liam is going to hang for my crimes. I can't make a choice without destroying lives, but I have to decide."

"I wish I could make it simple for you. I cannot bear to see you hurting like this," she said softly, her throat tightening as she took his hand, holding on tightly for both him and herself. "But I do not know the answers. It used to be so clear to me. Now . . . I see with different eyes."

"That's the hardest part of all of it," Sayer said, his intent gaze fixed on hers, making her feel he saw through to her soul. "I see with different eyes, too. I look at you, and I see the reason I want to keep fighting, the reason why I care about how it all ends . . . the reason why I want to draw another breath and see another sunrise."

Hesitating, he lifted his free hand and touched her face, drawing his fingertips down her cheek, over her lips, along the line of her chin. "This is the wrong place, the wrong time, the wrong everything to tell you, but I don't care. I might not have the chance again."

The sudden need and longing in his eyes made Aramanda catch her breath. "Roarke—"

"I love you," he said before she could tell him her heart had already heard his words. "I understand now what your mother meant about love answering every question. You did that for me. You made me believe I could be larger than I am, inspired me to accomplish the impossible."

Bending to her, he brushed a kiss against her mouth, lingering and tender. The moment suspended between them, pure and simple, like a first feeling of joy. It eclipsed the tragedy and the danger and the uncertainties, and Aramanda wanted it to last, to lock it away so she could always have it close to her heart.

Then, as quickly as it had come, it vanished when he let her go and stepped away, his face hard with resolve.

"We can accomplish the impossible," she whispered, shaken by the emotion he stirred in her. "Together. You made me believe that. I trust you, and that trust is stronger than any fears I have."

Sayer shook his head. "The way I feel about you has also limited my possibilities. Now and forever. And there's no going back."

Aramanda stared at him, consumed by the wonder of his confession and haunted by the echo of sorrow and rage in his voice. "What do you mean? What are you going to do?"

"I'm going to get Liam out of that jail, even if I have to take his place to do it."

"No, Roarke, you cannot do that. The miners, their families—they need you." She moved close to him again, not touching but near enough to hear the rasp of his breath, to feel his power and heat.

"*I* need you." Laying her hand on his heart, she narrowed the distance between them to a whisper. "I belong with you. I love you with all that I am and all that I can ever be. I came to you tonight because I could not sacrifice my love for you to stop Gervase. I trusted completely that we could find a way together, no matter what the risk. I will not let your cause or my fears divide us anymore. Never again."

"Aramanda . . ." He grasped her hand, holding tightly, staring intently into her eyes; and for a heart-wrenching moment, Aramanda feared he would push her away.

Then, the hesitation gripping him snapped and he pulled her into his arms, kissing her fiercely, passionately, making the blood sing in her ears and rush hotly through her veins, heady and sweet.

"Heaven's going to have to wait a little longer," he murmured against her ear when he finally broke their embrace. Still holding her to him, stroking her hair, he grazed a kiss against her temple. "I've got to go to the jail."

Aramanda lifted her head from his chest to look up at him. "To do what? If you try to free Liam using violence or concede to Gervase and surrender yourself, you will *both* end up at the gallows. Gervase will never keep a promise to release Liam for you."

"I know that. But I have to try."

"Perhaps . . . we can talk to Mr. Lloyd first. It cannot do any harm," she said, interrupting the protest she saw rising to his lips. "You have had your differences with him, but I know Hulsey Lloyd. I cannot believe he will allow Liam to stay imprisoned, knowing he is innocent."

"I can believe it."

"Roarke—"

"But I'll try it your way. I've got nothing to lose."

"And everything to gain."

"For all of us," he said, giving her a small smile. He touched her cheek again, as if committing the feel of her to memory one final time, then took her hand and began leading her down the aisle.

Aramanda took a final glance at the altar. Sayer caught it, looking back with her, his expression a question.

"I was remembering the last time I told Father Creeghan I needed a miracle," she said. "I thought changing the patterns of tragedy for the mining families would be impossible." She turned her gaze back to him. "Then there was you."

"You've made me believe in several dozen impossible things," Sayer said as they walked together out of the church into the growing darkness. "And I don't think you're finished yet."

"Let us hope you still believe that when we are done here," she returned, slowing their pace near the front door to the jail.

Sayer stopped. "What is it?"

"I am afraid."

"I know. I am, too. Let me do this alone."

"No." Aramanda straightened her shoulders, looking into his eyes. "I am not afraid of facing Mr. Lloyd. I am afraid of losing you."

A sudden breath of wind whipped around them and she shivered, inexplicably cold inside. The wind died, leaving behind a strange quiet made more keen by the silver mist that silenced the camp and made it seem as unfamiliar and insubstantial as a dream.

"I feel—I cannot explain it . . ."

"Don't try," Sayer said softly. "Just remember that no matter what happens, we cheated time and found each other. We loved each other again. If we lose everything, we'll never lose that, even if it takes another hundred lifetimes to reclaim it. And don't ask me to explain," he added, starting toward the jail again. "I can't, and I never will."

"That I do believe," she murmured, any trace of lightness vanishing when he put his hand on the jail door and pushed it open.

Lloyd looked up from behind his aged desk as they walked in; the single lamp cast a shadow on his face.

"They said you were back," he said, standing up. "But I didn't believe you'd show here, not even for your brother. You surprise me. Then again—" He glanced at Aramanda "—maybe you've good reason."

"Several of them," Sayer agreed, the tenseness of his stance and the hardness in his eyes belying his easy tone. "Liam is innocent."

"You know that," Aramanda put in quickly, taking a step closer to Lloyd's desk. "You know my uncle accused him only to stop Roarke from calling the stoppage of work tomorrow."

"You've no proof of that."

"And you have no proof Liam has anything to do with the Molly Maguires."

"Only the so-called evidence Gervase Montclair provided you with," Sayer said. "His word and his money in your pocket."

A dark red stained Lloyd's face. "If that's the worst of my sins, then it's even to the least of yours. You've put yourself above all else to win this war you started against Montclair."

"That may be so," Sayer said, stepping forward so only the width of the desk separated him from Lloyd. "But it has nothing to do with my brother. He doesn't like what I do anymore than you. Montclair is using him to break me. You know it as well as I do."

"And if I do?"

"Let Liam go."

"And let you go about your business and leave me to answer for it when there's another *accident* tomorrow at the main mine?"

"There won't be any accident. I'll take Liam's place."

"Roarke, no!" Aramanda flung out an appealing hand, looking from him to Lloyd. "No, you cannot let this happen. You see how my uncle runs his collieries. *I* see it; yet you know I have never supported the violence Roarke has used and I will not now. But I am willing to trust Roarke even though it is my family's livelihood and reputation that is at stake. If you cannot believe him, you must believe me. I have as much to lose by defying Gervase as anyone."

A muscle jerked along Lloyd's jaw. His eyes moved from Aramanda to Sayer, and the two men glared at each other in a silent clash of wills.

Aramanda balled her hands tightly, her nails biting into her palms. The deadly quiet, the unsettling tension cracking in the air made her want to scream or cry out just to relieve the nerve-shattering strain of waiting.

Lloyd finally broke it, looking away from Sayer. Yanking open a desk drawer, he snatched up a ring of keys and, without a word, strode around the desk and out of the room.

Sayer and Aramanda stood together in his cramped office, not speaking, exchanging only a look—his hard, yet with a slight softening when it touched her; hers uncertain, but speaking her determination to stand with him.

The sound of footsteps turned them both. Lloyd came back through the doorway followed by a bedraggled Liam. Aramanda ran to him and hugged him, giving in to sweet relief.

Regarding his brother with a swift, assessing glance, Sayer looked at Lloyd. "Did you leave the door open for me?"

Liam let go of Aramanda, pushing forward to confront Lloyd. "You told me there was no agreement between you and Roarke. I wouldn't have—"

"I know what I told you," Lloyd interrupted, his eyes still fixed on Sayer. "And there is no agreement. I am leaving the door open for you; and tomorrow, if there's even the smell of trouble, I'll be the one to close it behind you."

"I hate to disappoint Montclair after he's gone to so much trouble, but you won't get the chance." Turning to Liam and Aramanda, Sayer reached out and took Aramanda's hand possessively in his. "I'll make sure of it."

Outside Lloyd's office, Aramanda drew in a long breath of clean night air, releasing some of her pent-up tension as she slowly let it go.

"I thought for a moment he meant to take you at your word and give you Liam's place," she told Sayer, curling her fingers more tightly around his to reassure herself he was still with her.

"You would have done it," Liam said, staring at Sayer as if seeing him for the first time. "I never believed you would risk losing your fight with Montclair."

"If I had let him hang you in my place, it would have been lost." Sayer looked down at Aramanda, then back at his brother. "I would have been lost."

Tears started in her eyes as Aramanda felt the power and conviction of Sayer's words affecting her more than any inspiring speech she had ever heard him give. "Now, you have a chance to win," she said softly.

"You're going ahead and asking the miners to stop work then?" Liam asked.

"I have to. I may not get another shot at breaking Montclair. I know you don't trust me to stay out of trouble, but this time I plan to fight with words, not fire."

"I believe you," Liam said slowly, offering his brother his hand. "And this time, I believe you can make a difference."

"We can," Sayer said, returning Liam's grasp and taking Aramanda's hand to include her in their circle. "Together, we can."

After leaving Liam to a boisterous and joyous reunion with Bridget and his sons, Sayer walked with Aramanda back to his house where she had abandoned her pony and cart earlier in the evening in her urgency to find him.

He stopped on the doorstep, facing her, their hands still linked. "You should have stayed with Bridget and Liam. I don't like the idea of your going back to the estate, not while Montclair is there."

"I am a Montclair, too," she told him softly. "I will always be, no matter what has happened or will happen. But I am not going back there tonight. And I am not staying with Bridget and Liam. I am staying with you."

Sayer looked at the face lifted to his, lit by the veiled glow of the stars and moon, all her heart in her eyes, and saw an offer of paradise.

He wanted to take it, to forget he lived between two worlds in a duel with time that could end tomorrow as unexpectedly as it had begun.

But he couldn't shake the uneasiness that had shadowed him ever since they'd come back to the camp and he'd laid plans for the strike at the main mine, couldn't forget the destiny she had lived with him once, in this past. "Aramanda . . ."

"Do not tell me *no*. It will mean nothing. I know you love me, and I love you. Tonight, that is all that matters. We cannot escape who we have been and what we will be, but we can choose to be together."

She curved her hand against his face, a tremble in her touch. "And do not tell me I do not understand all I am offering. I know what I am saying; I know how I feel, and I know what I want when you touch me. I want to be with you."

Covering her hand with his, Sayer turned his mouth into her palm, pressing a kiss into the hollow of her palm. "That's all I'll ever want. And I can't tell you *no*. Whether I have you an hour or forever, I can't tell you *no*."

Pulling her into his arms, he kissed her deeply, forgetting the time, the place, the circumstances, only remembering this was the woman he'd waited an eternity to love.

"You are earning your reputation as a rogue twice over," Aramanda breathed against his ear when he finally released her mouth to nuzzle the tender curve of her throat. "Mrs. Dobson will have enough to gossip over for a month."

Sayer glanced at the house across the street and saw the quick flick of a curtain being hastily drawn back. "You should have chosen a better place to seduce me," he murmured.

"I did no such thing!"

"Mmmm . . . no, of course not." His hand strayed to the small of her back, drawing sinuous patterns along the curve of her spine.

"You only said you loved me . . ." He lightly nibbled her neck, feeling her pulse leap at his teasing caress. "That you wanted me . . ." Gently bringing her body fully against his, he tasted the edge of her mouth. "Wanted to stay with me, be with me . . ."

"I do," she said, breathless with needing him. "But not here on your doorstep with all of the camp as witness. I had thought . . . I am not experienced in these matters, but—perhaps it would be better if we were alone."

"A brazen suggestion, my love. I accept."

Reluctantly letting her out of his arms, Sayer took her hand and started to lead her away from the house.

Aramanda looked back at it, then at him. "But—"

"Not here. We don't belong together here."

"No? Then where?"

"Somewhere that belongs only to us." He looked fully at her, his gaze reaching for her soul. "Let me take you there."

Twenty-one

Aramanda made no other protest as Sayer led her from the camp to the rough path that led away from the cluster of buildings into the shelter of the forest.

The mist hugged the ground and wove around the trees, and the moonlight streamed silver through the branches, making it an enchanted wood guarded from time, a secret haven for lovers.

"You know this so well," Aramanda said, wondering at the surety of his sense of direction even in the midnight darkness. "Have you been here before?"

"Only with you. In my dreams," he added when she cast him an odd look. They came to a small clearing in the trees and he stopped, sliding his arm around her waist.

"Look." He gestured toward the heavens, at the host of stars and the full moon. "This is where we belong . . . where we can see the stars and know there are just as many possibilities for us, just as many promises of happiness."

Aramanda lifted her face to look heavenward. At the same moment, Sayer looked down to her and their gazes met and she saw in his eyes the place where she belonged. "I don't need promises or possibilities. I am here with you. For now . . ."

". . . forever." Gathering her into his arms, he kissed her, slowly, deeply, gently bending her body back.

She held to him, trusting in his strength, moved by the power he had to make each touch, each caress, a feeling of joy and wonder and love.

He lingered over every one, creating a banquet of pleasure for

her to sense and feel, letting her taste his hunger and learn to
crave the wild, sweet flavor of it and discover, with it, her own.

Desire replaced the blood in her veins with fire, and she put
her arms around his neck, wanting him closer. The hardness of
his body matched to hers; his heat, the scent of his skin, and the
night overwhelmed any hesitation.

She took all he offered and gave it back to him in innocent
abandon until he swiftly lifted her into his arms and knelt with
her in the soft spread of leaves and pine straw.

Sayer laid her down and, as he looked at her, he remembered
the vision he had had of her at the curiosity shop when he'd first
touched her—of being with her here as lovers, indulging every
desire. . . .

Then, again, in another time, when he had loved her in this
same forest sanctuary, her love making him whole.

And now . . .

"What is it?" Aramanda whispered, glancing her fingertip
against his face. "You are so far from me."

"No." Sayer bent to her, slipping his hand under her nape and
bringing her against him, losing himself in her eyes. "No. It may
seem that way sometimes, but never doubt that I'm always here
with you. This—" He kissed her, giving her his soul. "This feeling survives everything. It's the only thing powerful enough t
cheat fate and reshape it in the way we want."

The force and passion of his voice trembled through her
blending with the growing ache of longing he roused. He
touched her shamelessly, his hands both tender and bold on her
body, slowly and surely leading her to each new pleasure until
her need for him coiled hotly deep inside her.

When he finally unfastened her dress, slipping it off her shoulders, Aramanda never thought to feel shy. He slid the material
down her arms with languorous ease, his eyes memorizing her
body, his kisses hot against her skin.

The rough firmness of his hands against her softness made
tantalizing *frissons* of pleasure, and she caught her breath at the
sensation of cool night air and his warm caresses on her bare
flesh.

His fingers appreciated every curve and hollow as he slowly drew the billow of cloth down her body, finally flinging it aside.

Clad only in her shift, Aramanda watched Roarke's face as he watched her, aroused as much by the naked passion in his eyes as by his touch. His gaze worshipped her body, making her feel desirable, whole, the center of his world.

She made a small sound of protest when he moved back, kneeling beside her. He smiled, never looking from her, reaching out to run his fingertips down her cheek, and then her throat, to the hollow between her breasts, while with his other hand he began unbuttoning his shirt.

He moved slow and easy; her breath came hard and fast. At last, he finished his task, languidly stripping off his shirt, the moonlight rippling silver on the smooth flux of muscle as he casually tossed it aside.

Unable to stay still any longer, Aramanda slipped her hand up his arm, drawing him back to her side. Her innocent invitation made his need for her race inside him again, mocking Sayer's attempt to ease the pace, shredding his tenuous control.

Their feelings and want of each other had the intensity of a sudden summer storm, elemental and wild, unable to be slowed or contained, determined to be sated.

Pulling free the ribbons of her shift, he slid his hands under the edge of the fragile material, freeing her from it, finding her skin a glide of silk that quivered at his touch.

Bared to his eyes, his hands, and his body, Aramanda felt a primitive yearning when his caresses became intimate, evoking a need so deep and profound she had no words to describe it, no name to give it.

She touched him in return, wondering if her hands could create the same magic for him, the tremor of muscle and the hardening of his body and the urgency of his kiss leaving no room for doubt.

"You're driving me mad," he muttered hotly against her ear, his breathing ragged. "Aramanda—love . . . I want this to be perfect for you. I want it to be forever, but you aren't making it easy to love you slowly."

"It will always be forever," she told him, pressing closer to him, drawing him nearer. "Love me now, and let me love you. Please, Roarke . . ."

Sayer needed no plea from her to answer the call of her heart. Stripping away the remaining barrier of their clothing, he left only the night and the heat of desire between them. She tasted like honey and temptation and felt like paradise, and there was nothing more he wanted than to lose himself in her and make her his own.

Despite their shared hunger and his own desperate longing to have her, he held them to the edge of fulfillment, wanting to give her no reason to regret or fear her first surrender to passion.

He continued making promises with his hands and mouth until Aramanda wanted to beg him to fulfill every one. At last, he moved over her and she willingly, eagerly stepped into the fire with him.

Wrapping her legs around him, she completed the joining he had started, forgetting the sting of pain as she was swept into the kaleidoscope whirl and dizzying height of a feeling beyond pleasure, above ecstasy, a feeling as simple and pure as a first innocent kiss and as complex and breathtaking as falling in love.

Sayer loved her so completely, giving her all of himself and taking back everything she offered so that in the heated, consuming rush and tumult, Aramanda didn't know where she left off and he began . . .

Only that they loved . . . and in that timeless moment, they both truly knew the shape and depth of forever.

When Sayer brought her to the peak of their lovemaking, she cried out his name, clinging to him in joy and wonder while the feeling thundered and burst inside her in a fulgurant shower of flying, falling light the color of love with the voice of angels.

In the echo of the heaven of their making, Sayer gathered Aramanda close, gently stroking her hair, whispering his love to her, not ready to break the link between them.

He knew he would never be ready, and certainly not willing. It had gone too deep for that, marking him forever as hers, and now all he wanted was to find a way to hold onto it anyway he could.

"If I had known it would be like that between us," she murmured, her voice inside him, both laughing and loving, "I would have kidnapped you from Tansie's long before you took the notion to abduct me."

"I could have tried to explain it to you, but I don't think you would have been inclined to listen. You would have accused me of living up to my black reputation as a ruffian and a scoundrel."

"I would have been right. Although . . ." She glanced up at him through her lashes, her smile secret and satisfied. "I confess there is something about the way you stand on a table that puts wicked thoughts into my mind."

"And all this time I thought it was my passionate speeches that you admired."

"I admire the passionate speeches you make—with your hands," she murmured, then blushed.

"Such a wanton," he teased, slipping his fingers under her chin and tipping her face to his. "You're putting wicked thoughts in my mind."

"Only you make me forget myself and say whatever comes into my mind. You are teaching me bad habits."

"I plan on teaching you a lot more." Desire stirring to life in him again, Sayer kissed her soft mouth, making several illicit suggestions with his caresses until her pulse quickened and she leaned into his body.

"Then perhaps you should get started," Aramanda told him, inviting him with the stroke of her hands. "My education has been sorely lacking."

"You don't need to ask twice," he murmured, the motion of his hands on her body starting a now-familiar music in her soul. "Although I'm beginning to think you don't need any lessons. You've taught me more about loving with one touch than I could learn in a dozen lifetimes."

He gave her no time to reply and, in the next heartbeat of time, lost in the sweet wildness of his embrace, Aramanda forgot everything she wanted to tell him.

In the last hours of the night, Sayer built a fire for them under the sheltering canopy of pine and oak. Cradled against his chest, Aramanda had fallen into a light sleep, and he lay beside her, listening to the sibilant sigh of the wind and the snap and hiss of the fire.

The earthy, woody smell of the forest mingled with the wild-roses scent that was hers, a blended attar that seemed strangely familiar, as if he had known it more than a lifetime, longer than his dreams.

Each passing moment in the stillness felt more like a dream to Sayer. It was as if he'd lived this—once, twice—before . . .

"We should not be here," Aramanda murmured sleepily, stretching in a sinuous motion.

"And where should we be?" Sayer asked, hearing the words like an echo. He frowned, trying to shake off his growing uneasiness.

I've said those words before . . . when?

"Back at the camp," she said. Her fingers traced warm patterns on his shoulder. "With your men. You have spent so many weeks fretting over your schemes—and most of the night here . . ." A small, dreamy smile slanted her mouth. "You should rest. You will need all your strength and wits to carry out this plan of yours today."

"I do have plans. I—"

Sayer stopped, suddenly remembering why their conversation sounded like repetition. He'd recalled this night with her the first time he'd seen her at the travel agency, later realizing it was the night before she had betrayed him, sealing his fate.

Putting her from him, he sat up, raking a hand through his hair. But it would be different this time, wouldn't it? This time she had come to him. She hadn't given in to Gervase Montclair.

Instead, they had decided together how to both keep Liam safe and fight Gervase.

She wouldn't betray him again. Not in this lifetime.

"What is wrong?" Her voice, soft and concerned, murmured in his ear. "You look as if you have seen a vision of hell. Roarke . . ."

Aramanda shook his arm, apprehension starting inside her at the glazed, fixed look in his eyes. "Roarke, tell me. What is the matter?"

He turned to her, staring at her as if he hadn't expected to see her there. "I . . . it's nothing."

"Do not treat me as if I were a child. You have told me time and again to speak my mind, to tell you my feelings. Do not expect me to heed you if you do not follow the same standard. I know it is something. Your words are meaningless. I can see it in your face, hear it in your voice."

"It's a bit inconvenient at times, having someone around who knows you too well," Sayer said, giving her a rueful smile.

"It is much too late to lament it now. I refuse to pretend otherwise. You will just have to tell me."

"Persistent, aren't you?"

"Very."

"Then I may as well surrender. It's not important," he said, shrugging off his words. "I'm just worried about a few details of my plan."

Aramanda studied him, her gaze searching. "Why? You have been so certain of it these past days. I find it difficult to believe you are doubting yourself now."

"It's not that, exactly." Sayer drew in a long breath, letting it out slowly. "I've had this . . . vision . . . of you and me . . . about this day and the work stoppage at the mine."

"And?" Aramanda encouraged. She frowned at his hesitation, his pause making her uneasy. "Roarke?"

"In my . . . vision, you betray me to your uncle to protect your family and Liam—and because you don't trust me to carry it through without violence. I . . . die trying to convince you our love is stronger than anything that divides us."

She was quiet for several moments, and Sayer twisted around to face her, inwardly cursing himself for coming even that close to confessing his knowledge of both past and future. It wouldn't do either of them any good, and it created an awkwardness between them he could have avoided.

"Do you believe that is what will happen?" she asked at last, her voice carefully expressionless.

"No. But I won't lie to you. It haunts me because I'm afraid of what we could both lose."

"You say that in your . . . nightmare, I do not trust you." She looked directly into his eyes. "But you do not trust me, either—" She glanced her fingertips against his heart "—or you would know that I have chosen you. I have chosen to stay with you, fight with you, love you. I have learned from you to trust in the power of love. Have you learned it as well or have all your avowals been nothing more than pretty words?"

"All these weeks, I should have been letting you make the speeches," Sayer murmured, his smile rueful. He took her hand and kissed her palm, curling her fingers around his caress. "You're more eloquent with a single look than I am in a month of talking. And more convincing, too."

"Must I convince you, then?"

She tried to keep her voice even, but Sayer easily heard the tremor of underlying hurt and saw the discouragement dim her eyes. That look stabbed at his heart, and all he wanted to do was replace it with the smile he loved.

"No, you don't have to convince me. I've chosen you, too, and I do trust you—with my life and my heart. It all belongs to you. I don't need any convincing to know it, to know I love you. Aramanda . . ."

He took her face between his hands, sure that no matter how many lifetimes he lived, he would never cease to feel the same wonder and tenderness in looking at her.

"I love you. If this is the last place God made, if this is the last hour I have on earth, this is where I want to be, with you. You're my cause now, the only one I'll always fight for in this lifetime, and the next."

He bent and kissed her fiercely, and Aramanda clung to him, certain of their love for each other but disquieted by the desperation she sensed in him.

It was nothing either of them could put into words, but it felt as if a black specter watched them, a faceless apparition that seemed familiar, yet stayed just beyond the edge of recognition.

Determined to banish it, they loved each other again, passionately, with abandon and joy and a ravening need that made Aramanda feel she would never have enough of Roarke, enough of needing him, wanting him, loving him.

Sayer never stopped to reason out his need of her. She filled a place in him no one or thing could, taking away the emptiness and replacing it with all she was and all she could give.

It was the last hour before morning when he finally summoned enough resolve to let her out of his arms and gather up their clothes.

Sayer slanted Aramanda several glances as they dressed; and when he caught her looking at him in return, she started to laugh.

"You are a difficult man to satisfy, Roarke Macnair," she said, her laughter music and color in the chilly predawn stillness.

"Guilty as charged. But if you'd like a few suggestions—"

In the process of drawing her dress up around her shoulders, Aramanda let the material droop, flashing him a provocative smile.

"I do not need any suggestions. You've given me enough of them for many nights . . . and days." She put out a hand when he started toward her, a familiar glint in his eyes. "You, though, have your plan to oversee. I would not think of keeping you from it."

"Wouldn't you? Don't answer that," he said quickly. "You're right. But one more look like that from you, and I'll be ready to say to hell with it all and spend the rest of my life making love to you."

Though tempted, Aramanda held her tongue, silently promising herself she would hold him to his word once he'd won his battle. For now, she knew he needed as few distractions as possible.

Already, the sensual, sleepy haze of their lovemaking was fading from his eyes, replaced by the inward, focused intensity she knew well.

They walked back to the camp in silence. The first edge of the sunrise lined the horizon as they started up the main street, pausing near Liam and Bridget's house.

"Why are we stopping here? Did you tell Liam you would come for him?"

"No." Sayer's hand tightened around hers. "I want you to stay with Bridget until it's over. Don't say *no*. It won't do either of us any good for you to be there, and you'll be putting yourself in unnecessary danger if O'Keefe and his men decide to crash the party. O'Keefe isn't one of your fans, and I wouldn't put it past him to use you to get to me."

"I want to be there—for you. And to show the miners it is only Gervase who refuses to change. I can convince them my mother is willing to use her influence to bring about change." She spoke hurriedly, determined and desperate to convince him. "Most of them trust me. I can help you. Roarke—"

"You've already helped me. Without you, I'd be getting ready to blow something else up instead of fighting with words and ideas. Aramanda, please . . ." He put his hands on her shoulders. "For my sake, stay away."

"I . . ." Aramanda didn't want to refuse him, but some inner feeling, a sensation akin to panicked fear, refused to let her agree. She had to be there, had to be with him. Without knowing why or how, she knew she couldn't stay away.

"I'll be back soon," he murmured, taking her silence as acquiescence. "Don't worry. Nothing can separate us now."

"Roarke—"

Giving her a faint half smile, he kissed her softly, then turned quickly and walked toward the mine, not looking back. Aramanda stared after him, her heart pounding, her hands clenched at her side.

"Nothing will separate us now," she whispered fiercely. "I made you no promises, Roarke Macnair. I will be there, and we will finish this together."

* * *

". . . and there's only one way we can finish this—by making a stand together."

Legs splayed, his blue bandanna clenched in one fist, Sayer stood on a small rise near the main mine, facing the crowd of miners.

"Montclair expects us to either quit or turn on each other. He's waiting—and paying—for it to happen. We can do nothing or keep going the way we started and end up at the end of a rope; and either way, he'll win. Or we can force the changes we want— if you're willing to take the risks, make the sacrifices, and stand united. It's up to you."

A stunned silence greeted his last words. Looking at the trans-fixed and startled expressions, he felt the familiar adrenaline rush that came from knowing he'd succeeded in reaching his audience with only words and the power of his convictions.

He moved back, intending to step down off the rise. His slight movement broke the spell he'd cast, rousing loud cheers and shouts of support from the miners.

Glancing at the faces in the gathering, he caught Liam's eye and his brother flashed him a grin. Standing beside Liam, Tansie tipped him a salute, and Scully nodded in quiet approval. Even Lloyd, flanked by several of his men, looked at him with a new respect.

A few feet behind them, Sayer saw Jack O'Keefe shoot a dark glare in his direction, then turn aside and mutter a comment to one of his companions.

Feeling high on the heady mix of emotions, Sayer started down the rise to join the miners; and as he did, he saw Aramanda.

She stood at the edge of the crowd, looking at him with the direct stare that saw straight to his soul, the same look he re-membered from his first image of her in the auditorium.

She smiled, the gesture both poignant and intimate, and Sayer felt a flash of dizziness. His vision blurred, and for a moment, he saw himself standing alone at the entrance to the mine, the camp a deserted ghost town behind him.

A dark ripple of uneasiness shivered through him.

No, not now. Not when we're this close to being together.

Pushing his way through the crowd, oblivious of the hands that reached out to him, the calls of praise, he strode to her side. "I should have known you wouldn't stay away."

"How could I?" Her eyes bright with tears, she touched his face, smiling up at him. "You were wonderful. You made me believe our dreams can come true."

"They can. I know they can. I just need a little more time—"

Without warning, the thundering crash of an explosion tore out of the mouth of the mine.

Sayer instinctively threw an arm around Aramanda, shielding her against his chest as flying debris and a fiery heat bellowed from the mine.

"My God—" Aramanda held to him, looking wildly around them. "Look!"

She pointed to where Jack stood on the rise, waving a red cloth. Other men wearing the same red bandannas started confronting the miners, shouting, shoving, until numerous scuffles broke out, escalating into out-and-out brawls.

"He must have—"

"Yeah. He must have." Sayer grabbed her shoulders, his face grim. "You stay out of this. Go back to Bridget's. I'll find Liam and make sure he gets out, too."

Bending to her, he kissed her hard, then turned and ran toward the heart of the mayhem.

"Roarke, no—" Aramanda flinched as another explosion roared out of the mine, the force of it knocking down several of the miners.

Through the thickening haze, she saw the chief and his men wading into the worst of it, grappling with Jack's forces, aided by Sayer's supporters. A half-dozen of Gervase's watchmen joined the fray, tackling anyone who seemed inclined to fight.

For several stunned seconds, Aramanda stood frozen in place, unable to do anything but stare at the chaos of bodies and fire.

"I must find him." The sound of her own voice, trembling but determined, startled her out of her numbness. "I must!"

Running into the battle, she skirted the edge of it, stopping when she saw Tansie struggling to drag an injured miner away from the fighting.

Tansie looked little better than the wounded man, his left eye swollen and starting to darken, the corner of his mouth bleeding. "You shouldn't be here, lass," he said as she rushed to help him pull the injured man to safety. "Roarke wouldn't want it."

"It is not his choice."

A man with a red bandanna twisted around his neck landed heavily on his face a few feet from them, felled by a blow from one of Lloyd's constables.

"Damn Jack O'Keefe!" Aramanda cried, drawing a raised brow from Tansie. "Roarke knew he would try to disrupt the strike. I had hoped it would not come to this."

"At least the battle's an uneven one," Tansie said, checking over the injured man with hurried hands. "Most of the miners are behind Roarke; even Lloyd knows now its O'Keefe and his lot that can't get their fill of fighting. Jack thought he could carry on his own battle, but I'll wager there won't be many of those wearing red that'll be left standing or free once it's over. Roarke may just win his war yet."

"I must find him."

"You'll pardon me for saying so, but are you mad, woman?"

"I must find him." Aramanda repeated the words like a magic incantation that could keep the danger from forever parting them. Ignoring Tansie's shouted protest, she strode toward the fighting again, searching faces, seeking only one.

"Aramanda!" Liam caught her arm, spinning her around. An angry red streak marred his cheekbone, and his knuckles were scuffed. "What the hell are you doing here? Roarke said you were with Bridget."

"Where is he?" she asked, ignoring his question.

"I don't know. Scully told him something about O'Keefe's rigging another explosion at the powder shed near the shaft and he went off at a run."

"Does Scully think he can stop it? Surely that's impossible. He must be mad!"

Liam made an angry gesture. "He thinks he's got nothing to lose by trying to prove himself a hero. He wouldn't listen to anything Roarke told him. Roarke went after him to try and keep him from blowing himself up along with the shed. They— Aramanda, wait!"

Wrenching her arm from his grip, Aramanda ran in the direction of the shed.

The fighting ebbed around her, and she blessed Roarke's power of persuasion for convincing so many of the miners to stand behind him. He had turned his back on violence and earned a victory.

If only it weren't too late . . .

Aramanda nearly collapsed under the flood of relief that surged through her when she saw him.

Standing near the entrance of the mine, he held Scully's arm, obviously trying to keep him from going any farther, and made a sharp gesture toward the shed, his expression hard and angry.

She started toward him. As she did, Scully jerked free and bolted in the direction of the shed.

Sayer sprinted after him, catching him in a few strides. He shot out an arm; and at almost the same moment that his hand grasped Scully's shoulder, the shed exploded.

The force of the concussion and the blaze of flame and smoke threw Aramanda to the ground. Breathless, she lay there, her face pressed into the rocky dirt, dazed.

Grit cut into her skin and she tasted a mixture of blood and soot. Pushing herself up on her palms, she struggled to shake off the giddiness, straining to see through the gray haze. "Roarke!"

Agonizing seconds passed as slowly as years. She could just see his shape and Scully's where they'd fallen, both motionless.

"Roarke!" she cried again. She tried to get to her feet, but her legs gave way under the effort. "Roarke, please . . ."

At last, a patch of clearness showed briefly in the smoke and she saw Sayer slowly haul himself to his feet. He staggered as he regained his footing, then dragged Scully up from the ground from where he had fallen on him.

"Thank God," she breathed, briefly closing her eyes, shaken by the profound relief of knowing he was alive.

When she could speak, she called his name again, and Sayer spun around, disbelief and fear transforming his expression.

Leaving Scully standing on his own, Sayer reached her side in less than a heartbeat, dropping to his knees and yanking her into his arms.

"You're supposed to be the practical one of the two of us, woman," he said hoarsely. "You weren't supposed to be here. I thought you were safe. Next time, I'm locking you in a closet."

"I devoutly hope there will be no next time."

"I second that. I've had enough explosions to last me an eternity. Literally."

"How is Scully? Liam said he tried to stop the explosion."

"Scully is crazy. He had a sudden delusion of grandeur. Maybe when he wakes up tomorrow feeling like he was run over by several horses, he'll think twice about rushing in without knowing what he's getting himself into. To hell with Scully," he said, feeling the sick fear of nearly losing her rise up inside again.

"My God—Aramanda . . ." Shaken, trembling with reaction, Sayer urgently ran his hands over her body, reassuring himself she was still whole. "You could have been killed."

"And you are invincible, I suppose," she retorted. Her bravado slipped, and tears welled in her eyes. "I thought I had lost you. I thought you were . . ."

"No. No, I'm not lost. I'm found. By you." He pressed her to his heart, feeling her tremble. "Only you. And it's I that almost lost you, because of this."

"Because of Jack. But it is over. You have won." She ran her fingers over his face, his shoulder, laying her palm against his heart. "And we are still together and we love each other. That is our victory."

"I do love you. I only want the time to show you how much. We are two souls with one breath."

"We have time now," she whispered. "We have all the time there is. Forever."

"I want forever with you, Aramanda. That's all I want now. Forever to love you."

"And I you. Roarke . . ."

Her words sounded distant in the roar of the fire. Sayer closed his eyes, holding her close, rocking her in his arms. The heat of the inferno burned his back, but he felt a coldness creep over him, insidious and familiar.

"Aramanda . . ."

In a flash, he remembered the moment he'd been thrust back in time, the same chilling numbness that had taken over his body. "No! Aramanda—"

He heard his own voice echo loudly inside his head. Her eyes looked into his, filled with love, with needing him, wanting him; but a white mist clouded his vision of her.

Knowing he was losing her, refusing to admit it, Sayer fought with every ounce of will and strength to stay with her, desperation a dark, rising tide inside him.

Disoriented the first time he'd cheated destiny, this time he felt as if his heart were being ripped from his body, a pain so deep and wrenching that only death would have been a relief.

"Aramanda," he tried to call to her. "I want to stay. This can't be happening. Not now. Not again! I won't lose you again. I can't lose you again."

We will always be together. Nothing can separate us now, my love. Nothing. You will always be inside me, always in my heart . . .

He heard the words like a faraway song, a vow from an angel in a heaven he was being cast out of, into a hell he could never escape from because he would leave his soul with her.

Sayer tried to move, to tell her. His body refused to move, surrendering instead to the dull, tingling sensation that spread over him, holding him suspended in time.

The warmth of her faded and she felt as insubstantial as a dream in his arms, her voice a whisper in the wind, calling once more, and again, to his heart.

Darkness crawled in around him, leaving him blind. Aramanda faded completely from his view, becoming nothing but a vision seared in his memory; and at that moment, Sayer knew he was damned.

Her love had saved him. But he no longer had her. Fate had left him nothing but a searing, empty loss where once had been his heart and soul.

The feeling was far worse than grief, than sorrow. It was black and depthless and endless; and it left him alone, imprisoned in himself without strength or will, without hope.

Without her.

Sayer didn't know how long he stayed in the darkness unable to see or hear or feel anything around him. But slowly, he found himself staring into a brilliant tunnel of light that grew dimmer and began to separate the longer he stared into it until finally he recognized it.

The headlights of his Range Rover.

He was sitting inside the mine, near the entrance, his back to hard rock. Alone.

Struggling to his feet, he fought a wave of dizziness. He put out a hand to steady himself against the rock; and as he did, he realized his fingers were clenched around a scrap of cloth.

A blue bandanna.

The emotions rushed back over him in overwhelming intensity. Despair and hope, laughter and tears, the determination to stop injustice and the compassion for the people who lived with it and fought against it.

And most strongly, the profound joy and unrelenting pain of love found and lost again.

"Dr. Macnair!"

Sayer started at the familiar voice, a blending of past and present. He turned, still disorientated, his body responding sluggishly. "Scully?"

A thin figure stepped into the glare of the headlights. The single beam of the light he held wobbled across the stone wall until it rested on Sayer.

"Dr. Macnair, there you are," Malcolm Breyer said. "You've

been gone for almost an hour. We thought you might have run into trouble. Did you get the sample you wanted?"

"Sample?" Sayer stared at Malcolm resurrected, his mind balking at accepting the evidence of his senses.

How can Malcolm be here? How can I be here?

"You . . . I—I can't be here. I . . ." He stopped, putting a hand to his temple, trying to order his thoughts.

I'm back, except it isn't the same; I'm not the same. And why now? Why without her? I can't be here without her. I don't want to be here without her.

"We've got several samples that should do." Malcolm took a step forward, peering at Sayer's face. "Are you all right? You look rather pale."

"No, I'm not all right!" Sayer looked wildly around the small, dim mine room. "Where is she?"

"She?"

"Aramanda. She was here—"

Malcolm raised a brow. "There's no one else here but you and me," he said gently. "Did you fall, hit your head, perhaps? Or maybe the air in here—"

"It's not that, dammit! I was back there—back at the Schuylkill camp with Aramanda. There was an explosion. I was holding her and then . . . then—"

Sayer stopped, slamming his fist against the rock wall, not feeling the pain. The hurt inside him eclipsed any simple physical feeling. He looked down at the crumpled bandanna. "Then she was gone."

"Dr. Macnair, please—" Malcolm laid a hand on Sayer's arm, his expression wavering between concern and alarm. "Your brother is waiting outside. Perhaps if you spoke with him . . ."

"My brother . . ." *Which one?*

Sayer glanced at the bandanna again, then shoved it into his pocket. He took one last look around the room. There was nothing of her left here, no sense of her, no feeling she had ever been here with him at all.

And Sayer sensed no blending of the past and present as he

had before. This was reality, his reality. And here, she was truly lost to him, and he to her.

You will always be inside me, always in my heart.

Except he wanted her in his arms.

"Let's go," he told Malcolm, his throat tight with emotion. "I've been here . . . too long."

Looking relieved, Malcolm gestured toward the mine entrance with the flashlight. "Come outside. I'm sure you could use the fresh air. It's rather close in here, especially if you're unaccustomed to it."

Sayer followed him out of the mine, stumbling as he stepped out into the warmth of the summer twilight.

"Hey, what's wrong? You look like you got the bad end of a good fight." A hand grasped his arm, guiding him a few paces away from the mine. "Are you okay?"

"Will?" Sayer stared at his brother.

"Last time I checked. You shouldn't have been in there so long. Dammit, Sayer, I know you're worried about the possibility of radon, but killing yourself isn't going to do either of us any good. We need you alive and talking if we're going to get this thing taken care of."

"We . . . are you backing me up on this?"

"Did you hit your head in there?" Will asked, his face furrowing with worry. "We've only been talking about this for the last week, planning how to tackle it. Maybe all that microwave lasagna is finally getting to you."

A gurgling sound momentarily pulled his attention from Sayer, and Will looked over his shoulder at the baby secure in the sling on his back. "Hey, sweetie, you're finally awake." He reached behind him and took the infant in his arms. "Maybe you can bring your uncle to his senses."

The baby, her bright red tuft of hair tied with a green ribbon, laughed up at her father, waving her tiny fists at him. Sayer looked at her a long moment, then reached out with a not-quite-steady hand and touched the infant's soft cheek.

"Rose," he whispered, overcome by the flood of sweet feeling that surged inside him at seeing his niece alive and well.

Will shook his head and laughed. "You're the only one who insists on calling Savannah by her middle name. It drives Liz crazy. Look, I've got to get Savannah back. Liz and the boys and I are supposed to go out for pizza tonight. Are you sure you're all right?"

"You go ahead. I'll catch up with you later," Sayer said, not answering Will's question.

He couldn't answer, not without telling the truth. And the truth was, he wouldn't ever be all right again.

"Call when you're finished tonight. We'll wait up. Liz'll throw a fit if you don't."

"I will. When I'm finished."

Hesitating a moment longer, Will shifted Savannah in his arms to put a hand on Sayer's shoulder. "Take it easy, will you? I don't know what's going on, but you look like you just lost your best friend."

Not only a friend. My heart and soul.

Before Sayer could think of a reply, Malcolm walked up, giving them an apologetic smile. "I don't want to interrupt, but we should be going, Dr. Macnair. It's nearly seven."

Seven? I came here in the middle of the night—looking for her. Aramanda . . .

"Am I too late?"

"No. no, of course not," Malcolm said. "But Mrs. Montclair will be waiting for us."

Twenty-two

"The trees—they were just saplings the last time I—" Sayer caught himself when Malcolm flashed him a curious sideways glance.

"Saplings? The Montclairs built this estate nearly a hundred and fifty years ago." A puzzled frown creased between Malcolm's eyes. "Are you certain you're up to this? I suppose I could try to reschedule."

Sayer shifted in the passenger seat of the rover, avoiding Malcolm's probing glance. "I'm fine," he said shortly.

After the incident in the mine, Malcolm must be wondering if he were starting to crack. He was beginning to wonder himself. "It's just that I happened recently to see a sketch of this place shortly after it was built. That was the vision I had in my mind."

A vision of paradise lost.

"I see," Malcolm said, sounding as if he did not.

"Thanks for driving," Sayer said to divert him. "A few minutes with my eyes closed and that headache is just about gone."

"I'm relieved to hear it, because you're going to need all your wits about you tonight."

As they approached the open gates, the guard waved them up the front drive. Sayer glanced out the windows in all directions, a flood of memories and confused emotions washing over him.

Would she be here? How could she be?

His heartbeat pounded in his ears and he found himself gripping the edge of the seat, his heart pulsing with an irrational hope.

No, it was more than that—with a prayer Aramanda would be waiting for him inside, safe, whole, waiting to begin their life together—again.

But if somehow, some way, she were here, what if she didn't remember? Could they discover each other again? Would they ever be given the chance to know forever?

Or had he spent all his chances and bought nothing but an empty existence, damning himself to living eternity divided by time and destiny from the woman he loved.

Sayer didn't even want to consider the all-too-real possibility. As soon as Malcolm hit the brake, he swung out of the rover and took the front steps two at time, urgency dogging him.

Malcolm, slightly breathless, caught up with him as the front door opened. "You certainly are in a peculiar mood tonight, Dr. Macnair."

"Sayer. We're working together, after all." *But I would give everything to hear her call me* Roarke *again.*

"Certainly, if you prefer." Malcolm nodded. He edged sideways a few steps.

The magnificently carved front door opened, and the housekeeper who'd been there the last time he'd come with Aramanda led them into the foyer and down a hallway to a formal living room.

Again, Sayer found himself staring, hungrily, searching for a sign, a sense of Aramanda.

The brief resurrection of hope in his heart waned when, instead, he recognized only one or two pieces of furniture—now with the patina of a century—and none of the faces in the few portraits scattered on the walls. The clothing and hairstyles of the people in the pictures were contemporary, firmly of his reality.

"Mrs. Montclair, Dr. Macnair and Dr. Breyer have arrived," the housekeeper said, ushering the men into the room.

A tall, regal woman in her mid-fifties moved gracefully toward them from the other side of the vast room. As she neared, Sayer found it difficult not to stare.

Except for the distraction of the knee-length tailored dress, discreetly applied makeup, and chic chin-length hair, her striking beauty nearly mirrored that of Cordelia Montclair.

She stood in front of him, then frowned slightly. "Do I have a wart on my nose, Dr. Macnair?" she asked, a flicker of humor in her eyes.

"I'm sorry," Sayer said, grasping for a measure of composure. "It's just—you look very much like one of your ancestors. The resemblance is amazing."

"Ah, you must be speaking of Cordelia Montclair. I've been told since girlhood we're similar in appearance. And indeed, from what I have read of her in the family histories, I believe we're kindred spirits." She extended a hand. "I know your face from the evening news, Dr. Macnair. And you must be Dr. Breyer. I'm Cecelia Montclair."

"Yes. It is indeed a pleasure to meet you, Mrs. Montclair," Malcolm said, his voice betraying a case of nerves.

"Ms. Montclair, if you don't mind. I am a widow. Now, shall we get down to business, gentlemen? I do apologize, but I have an engagement at the opera in an hour, and as you can see, I'm hardly dressed to go."

"I've heard something of your husband and his interest in the mines," Sayer said, trying to reconcile the differences between this new reality and the previous two. He dredged up the name from the last time he'd been here, in this time, this place. "Gerald, was it?"

"Gerald?" Cecelia looked at him in faint astonishment. "Gerald is my brother-in-law, and he has nothing to do with my business, nor would I wish to. John Montclair was my husband, and he was a fine man. I am fortunate that his spirit lives on in my sons and daughters."

"Daughters?"

Cecelia gave Sayer a look that doubted his sanity. "Are you feeling ill, Dr. Macnair? You look rather pale. I have two daughters, one is at college and the other is an attorney. Now that we have that settled, perhaps we can discuss business. I understand you have found evidence of possible radon leakage in one of my mines."

"Yes, we're testing now," Malcolm said.

"Good. You have my full permission to continue until you are satisfied with the results. In the meantime, do you recommend I close the mine?"

"That's the safest measure for the men," Sayer put in quickly, hiding his surprise at her brisk acceptance of the situation, "but I'd imagine many of them would rather take the risks than do without a paycheck."

"How long will the testing take?"

Malcolm shrugged. "If we're able to work uninterrupted, we will have definitive results in a matter of weeks."

"Then I'll have the men relocate temporarily to nearby mines," Cecelia said firmly. "It'll be a juggling act, but I'm confident my staff and I can handle it for that length of time."

"I admire your decisiveness, Ms. Montclair," Sayer said. "And I'm impressed with your knowledge of the situation."

"You seem surprised, Dr. Macnair. I am handling all concerns about the safety of the mines myself. Jim Hatcher was my consultant, but under the circumstances . . ." Cecelia gave a delicate shrug.

Sayer was beginning to feel as lost in this reality as he had after being thrust suddenly into the last. "Circumstances?"

Cecelia arched a brow. "I thought you, of all people, would have known."

"Surely you remember," Malcolm put in hastily, slanting him a disbelieving look. "Jim Hatcher was indicted two days ago for taking bribes from industries to falsify clean bills of health where unsafe conditions existed."

"Yes, it seems my secretary and one of my lawyers had been working behind my back with Mr. Hatcher for years—protecting my interests, they claimed," Ms. Montclair said, a touch of sardonic humor in her expression.

Sayer thrust a hand through his hair. "I see. I'm sorry. I thought I knew Jim better."

Cecelia met his gaze squarely and offered him an understanding smile. "There's no need to apologize, Dr. Macnair. People are seldom what they seem, are they?"

"That's an understatement," Sayer muttered, wondering if she had read his mind. As he looked into her eyes, he decided Ms. Montclair was a woman who knew a great deal more about life than she would ever admit.

"They're all gone now though, and I'm firmly in control," she added. "I'll be happy to hear any concerns either of you have in the future in regard to my mines. The safety of my men is always my priority."

They spent a few more minutes with Cecelia while Malcolm detailed the testing procedures. Feeling on uncertain footing, still lost between times, Sayer managed to force his way through the necessary parting formalities before Ms. Montclair excused herself and the housekeeper led them to the front door.

Once in the foyer, Sayer stopped. Unwilling to leave the one place he'd had hopes of finding Aramanda, he found himself grasping for something, anything of her to take with him.

Except he found nothing of her there. No memories. No images. No sense she'd ever existed at all, not even in the past.

Despair hit him hard and fast as he realized that when he drove up the lane this time, he would leave behind the last vestiges of his hope of ever finding Aramanda forever locked behind the gates of the Montclair estate.

He would not, could not, leave without seizing one final chance for a memory, a clue to where she might be, to what had happened to her.

"Excuse me." Sayer stopped the housekeeper with a quick hand to her arm. "Please, just for a minute."

She looked at him in surprise.

Malcolm hesitated at the doorway. "Is something wrong?"

"Everything," Sayer said. He let go of the housekeeper's arm but appealed to her with his eyes. "I was here once before and you showed me a portrait of—a woman."

"Yes, I remember. The girl with you bore an uncanny resemblance to Aramanda Montclair. She must be related somehow to the family. You two make such a lovely couple."

"May I—could you let me see her, the portrait, once more? We're not—we aren't together anymore."

"Oh, what a shame. I know it's not my place to say, but I can't help but see it must have been a difficult break-up." A sympathetic smile touched her mouth. She leaned closer to Sayer and put her hand on his forearm for a moment. "It's written all over your face."

"We didn't break up," Sayer said, suddenly grateful to have someone, anyone, even a stranger with an empathetic ear, to allow him to vent some of his feelings. "We had to leave each other. We didn't want to separate, it was just . . . something beyond our control."

He heard the despair in his voice, but he couldn't stop. "I'll never understand. I'll never accept it. But she's gone. I've lost her."

He faltered to a stop, the emotions so dark and intense he couldn't put them to words, let alone accept them.

"Why . . . I'm so sorry," the housekeeper said, blinking away sudden tears. "Come on." She glanced up the stairway. "Ms. Montclair's busy upstairs and—oh, what's the harm? If seeing that portrait will help you, then I'm certain Ms. Montclair wouldn't mind. Under all her elegance and pride, there's no one kinder."

"Thank you," Sayer said, following her down the hallway.

"I think I'll wait here, if you don't mind," Malcolm spoke up. Sayer glanced back at him and Malcolm made a small, helpless gesture before quickly backing out the door, shaking his head.

It was useless to even try to explain. "I'll be right back," Sayer said, and turned to follow the housekeeper.

The portrait of Aramanda hung where it had before, the same vision of passionate beauty, the same eyes that had haunted him from the moment he'd seen her in the auditorium . . . a lifetime ago it seemed.

Seeing her image again did nothing to assuage the grief. Instead, it intensified the emptiness to an unbearable ache.

Sayer stared up at her, the cold realization and the torture of being forced to endure his loss threatening to overwhelm him.

The artist had captured her beauty; but her warmth, her caring spirit, her passion—everything that was Aramanda, everything he loved about her—was only an elusive shadow suggested by the curve of her mouth, the lift to her chin, the depth of her amber eyes.

Sayer felt nothing of her here. He could only remember the one time they had stood together here, the first time he had truly started to believe they were destined to love.

I didn't know, Aramanda. I didn't know what it would mean to love anyone so completely—to love you. I needed your faith, your passion to show me. And now you're gone . . .

He looked at the portrait for one last, long moment, drinking in details that would have to last him an eternity in his dreams. "She has the most amazing eyes," he murmured.

In his reverie, Sayer had forgotten the housekeeper. When she spoke, he started, abruptly dragged back into this reality.

"Mmmm, yes, so many people have said. Mrs. Montclair's eldest daughter looks a little like her, lucky girl. Aramanda, the poor child, was such a beauty."

"Why do you say it like that?"

"Didn't I tell you the story? Well, although no one actually ever found any proof, everyone assumes she died in a mining explosion. She loved a rebel leader, and it was because of her devotion to him that she risked her life to be at his side during a riot at one of the Montclair mines." The housekeeper sighed. "So sad, her young life lost and such a romantic love story brought to a tragic end."

"No—" Sayer's heart caught in his throat.

Don't tell me she died. She's out there, somewhere in time, waiting.

"Oh, yes, most of the family believes it's true." She glanced up to him, and her face furrowed in regret. "Oh, dear, I'm sorry. You look even more upset now. I thought seeing the portrait would help. I shouldn't have told you the history."

"No, really, it did help." Sayer looked away from her so she wouldn't see the lie in his face.

Aramanda, love . . .

Raking a hand through his hair, he sucked in a ragged breath, struggling to gather his composure against the insidious, terrible emptiness that had made its place in his heart.

"Thank you for letting me see her again," he said at last, turning back to the housekeeper. "You gave me a chance to say goodbye."

Sayer slid out the back seat of the cab in front of the travel agency and left the door ajar. "Keep the motor running, I have a plane to catch."

"It's your nickel, bud."

The tiny copper bells hanging on the door jingled as Sayer shoved it open and stepped inside the shop. The place still smelled like a Renaissance church and looked like someone's attic. "Hello?"

"Oh, Dr. Macnair!" Lila stepped out from behind a hideous plaster gargoyle, her gray hair wrapped in a kerchief, dust cloth dangling from her fingers. "You're going to miss your plane, dear, but it was awfully kind of you to drop by to say goodbye."

Sayer strode over to her. "Where is she?"

"Now there, young man, I won't have you speaking to my wife in that tone." Weldon, a dusty tricorn hat perched precariously on his head, shuffled up behind Sayer and wagged a crooked finger at him. "I know it's been a hard few weeks, but that's no excuse."

"Tell me where she is," Sayer said through gritted teeth, trying unsuccessfully to bring his temper under control. "I know you can tell me. You're the only ones who can. How do I find her? I have to know!"

"We've already explained our limitations, dear," Lila soothed, patting his arm. "You did have quite an adventure, didn't you?"

Frustration to the point of madness welled up in Sayer. He wanted to shake the truth out of them, but even the thought seemed sinful.

He ran shaking fingers through his hair, then began a restless acing in front of them, knotting and unknotting his fists at his ide.

"You've got to help me! You're my last link to her. I'll do nything. Just tell me where to find her."

Lila and Weldon exchanged a long look. Lila caught her lower ip between her teeth, shaking her head.

With a sigh, Weldon reached into a side pocket of his worn weed jacket. He fumbled in the depths of it, pulling out a ball f twine, a used tea bag, and a wooden flute before finally eizing on the item he wanted.

"Ah, here it is." He handed Sayer a small, leather-bound book. 'This may give you some comfort. It was written by a friend of Aramanda's—and yours, I believe. Father Creeghan."

Sayer took the book, running his fingers over the cracked sur-ace. "Is it a history?"

"Oh, yes, and more. I think it will help you to understand."

"Understand?" Sayer clenched the book so hard it curled gainst his palm. "Is that a comfort, to understand why you rought us together only to tear us apart again? That, I'll never nderstand!"

"Come now, Dr. Macnair, it's no use to get yourself in such a tate. It's bad for your digestion." Lila crooked an arm around ayer's elbow. She guided him firmly toward the front door, pat-ing his forearm as they walked. "Your cab is waiting and, my, hose people do charge a fortune these days."

At the door, Sayer balked. "I'm not leaving until I get some nswers."

"Oh, there aren't many answers, my dear, only truths. You just old fast to your memories and have faith in the strength of your ove." Lila smiled and nodded. "I told Aramanda the same—the nly forever is in your heart."

With a reassuring wink, she practically shoved him out the ront door onto the busy sidewalk.

Sayer spun around, but the door was closed tight and he heard he sound of the lock being bolted.

He hesitated, then climbed back into the cab. Glancing out the ack window at the shop one last time, he found them arm in

arm, waving, sweet white-dentured smiles on their gnome-lik⟨
faces.

He wanted to murder them both.

The mad rush to catch his flight took his mind off Aramand⟨
for a few brief minutes as Sayer dashed through the metal detec⟨
tor and down the "C" corridor to his plane.

"You're late! I've been waiting so long—"

Sayer stopped dead in his tracks at the gate. He knew tha⟨
voice well. "Patricia?"

"So formal, aren't you? I had to say goodbye." Wearing ⟨
short, tailored suit, she walked straight up to him and slid he⟨
arm through his.

"Trisha, that was the last call. It was nice of you to meet m⟨
here, but I have to go. I'll be in touch, okay?"

Trisha touched a kiss to his mouth. "Just make certain this i⟨
only *au revoir* and not goodbye."

"I'll call." Sayer gently pulled away from her.

"No, you won't."

"You're right." He stared at her with nothing to give. And h⟨
didn't have time or words to explain. "I could—"

She stepped back, her eyes fixed on him. "No." Trisha man⟨
aged a weak smile. "You can't. But that's okay. I understand⟨
And don't worry; I won't be waiting by the phone."

"I'm sorry."

Trisha glanced down the tunnel to the plane. "Your loss," sh⟨
said, a half-teasing lift to her chin. Suddenly, the smile left an⟨
something young and vulnerable came into her expression. "Be⟨
sides, since my father's indictment, I've been talking with Adin⟨
The divorce isn't final and maybe . . ."

Shrugging, she left the sentence unfinished.

Sayer touched a hand to her shoulder. "I hope it works out⟨
Really."

"I know you do." She flashed him a brilliant smile. "Now⟨
go!"

* * *

Tossing back his third whiskey—a taste he'd apparently ought forward—Sayer slouched in his first-class seat and anned through every page of Father Creeghan's book.

"After Aramanda's death, Roarke Macnair severed his ties with the violent factions of the Mollies and went on to work in conjunction with the Workingmen's Benevolent Association . . ."

"Damn!" He slammed a fist onto the tray. "It's all about Roarke. What about her? Us?"

A stewardess appeared at his side and bent toward him, her mile forced. "Is there a problem, Dr. Macnair?"

"What?" Sayer asked sharply. She started. "No, I'm sorry, I st . . . Never mind." He held up his glass. "Bring me another, ould you?"

"Certainly, if you want, but that is your fourth. Of course, it's me of my business, but we do like to remind certain of our assengers who drink not to drive when we land. I can call ahead r a cab—"

"I'm fine. Just bring me one more."

Eyeing him warily, the stewardess took his empty glass and oved toward the front of the plane.

As soon as she'd left, Sayer plunged into the last section of e book.

"On a personal note, despite his monumental contributions to the cause of labor reform in the mining industry here in Schuylkill and well beyond, Roarke lived a solitary and, in my opinion, an empty existence. I often counseled him to marry and experience the satisfaction of family life, as did his brother. But his will to love died with the only woman he would ever give his heart to, Aramanda

Montclair. My prayer is that they will find one another again in the hereafter . . ."

"Aramanda . . ." Sayer closed the book and let it drop to h[is] lap. He stared out the tiny window at billowy clusters of clou[d] haloed with sunlight.

"You're there, somewhere where I can't reach you," he whi[s]pered, closing his eyes to the pain. Except he could do nothi[ng] to escape it. "Dear God, I really have lost you . . ."

Though despondence tugged at him like quicksand, inexorab[le] and dark, threatening to drag him down to a lost place he wou[ld] never return from, Lila's gentle voice came to him as clearly [as] if she were sitting beside him.

Hold on to your memories. Have faith in the strength of yo[ur] love.

Sayer turned to the empty seat, her words wrenching his hea[rt] with the harsh reality of how completely alone and barren th[e] rest of his life would be without Aramanda.

He felt Lila's presence more strongly than before and it fe[lt] like a torment.

"How could you say that when you know I'll never touch he[r,] never see her smile again?"

Have faith.

But he had no faith. He'd left it with Aramanda, in a place [he] could not return to. And he was trapped here, in a reality wi[th] no tomorrow.

"Leave me alone." Sayer closed his eyes to the endless vis[ta] of heaven outside the window, to Lila's voice, letting the blac[k]ness steal his vision. "Just leave me alone."

A few weeks later, Sayer sat at his old oak desk in his cramp[ed] office in the biology department at the University of Colora[do,] looking at the mess in front of him. Papers to grade, messag[es] to return, books unread—he'd never catch up.

Good thing he'd canceled that trip to Europe. It was a ba[d]

reer move, but he'd had no choice. Since he'd returned, he
dn't been able to concentrate or organize his thoughts at all.

He flicked the tattered yellow ribbon tied around the neck of
e stuffed koala propped on a corner of his desk. In a lifetime
st, it had been one of her pleasures, and Sayer had been half
rprised to find it in his Philadelphia hotel room when he'd
urned from where he had left Aramanda. He kept it with him,
noring the odd stares and raised eyebrows the bear caused.

It and the blue bandanna were his only links to her, his only
surances they had once loved—past, present, and beyond.
Small comforts—if there were any solace to be found in this
rgatory.

Sayer ran his fingers through his hair and tipped back in his
ather chair. "It's useless," he groaned to himself, letting his
ad lean to the side to stare blankly out the window.

Little flickers of memories plagued him, destroying his con-
ntration so that trying to work, trying to do anything, amounted
nothing more than frustrating exercises in futility.

How was he supposed to go on with life when half of him was
ssing?

It was like walking around without a heart, without a soul. He
uldn't breathe, think, work. Nothing was worth doing without
r, without his heart.

And the memories of their time together, instead of helping,
ly imprisoned him further in a well of emptiness and despair.
I might as well give it up for the day. Again.

Shoving away from his desk, Sayer reached back to the brass
at rack and grabbed his khaki jacket. As he did, the bandanna
l out of the jacket folds into his palm.

He stared down at it, his heart stabbed with the agony of every
ecious memory it held. His vision blurring, he gripped it until
 knuckles went white.

"Dr. Macnair?" a gentle voice that held a trace of an Eastern
cent came from the doorway behind him. "I'm sorry, but your
cretary was out."

*Damn! I'm really not up for some student to come whining to
 today.*

Sayer swiped at his eyes, cleared his throat. "You'll have schedule in a time with me when she comes back. I was ju leaving for the day," he said, hearing the telltale catch of emoti in his voice. He made an exaggerated rustle of noise, tugging his jacket.

"That's too bad. I'm a civil rights lawyer. I've been followi your work on environmental issues for some time. There are couple of projects we've both been involved in, and I thoug perhaps we might be able to help each other. My mother see to think so as well."

Sayer heard the soft, secret smile in her voice. "My name Amanda Montclair, and I've been waiting a very long time see you."

His heart stopped and he whirled around, not daring to believ Then he saw her eyes.